THE HIDDEN RELIC HUNTER

THE LOST PORTAL KEYS

ALEXIS WESTMORE

TDH PUBLISHING

CREDITS

EDITOR: Patrick Lobrutto

EDITOR: Heather Flournoy

COVER ARTIST: Joy Argento

CONTENTS

DEDICATION

To Everyone who has fought their toughest battles
in the quiet places of their own soul.
You are strong, resilient, valued, and needed.

Memoirs of the War

"WITH SUNSET, THE WIND whipped through the uneasy night, ravaging the sparse grass and spiny, evergreen shrubs at the cliff edge. A heavy fog sank low on the mountain and muted the semi-automatic clip of rapid-firing weapons to the east." – from *Memoirs of the 2050 War*

PROLOGUE

S HIRO ESTATE EARTH ALLIANCE YEAR (EAY) 2116
APRIL 12, 2116

"I promise at the end of this consultation, I'll admit something to you that I've never admitted to anyone and show you a relic no one except me has ever seen." Dr. De la Cour turned from the arched stained glass window to face Sylvia, who was already uncomfortable in the straight-back chair across from the doctor's large desk.

Sylvia slid her palms over her black dress pants, physically removing the evidence of her stress while simultaneously forcing her leg to stop bouncing. "What does this have to do with my abnormal MRI?"

"Maybe nothing," De la Cour said, removing a thinly braided leather bracelet as she motioned Sylvia to join her at the window. "Maybe, the first thread to unravel your entire history."

Sylvia stood, legs trembling at the words. She took a deep breath, letting her eyes rove to the high ceiling above the window where De la Cour stood with the tiny, single silver bead held close to her eye as if magnifying the light through the window. The arched stained glass floor-to-ceiling window would seem out of place in any regular doctor's office. Sylvia let her gaze trace down the ancient stone wall. The details carved a pattern toward the window as she took in the straight posture of the stunning woman waiting for her there. It seemed more than out of place; it was surreal. What kind of doctor ran a clinic from a castle? Then again, this woman wasn't an MD but some sort of research doctor. The mix of modern and ancient would have been fodder for her writing mind if Sylvia hadn't been suffering with worsening migraines, synesthesia, and test results no one could explain.

She watched De la Cour rub the silver on the leather band thoughtfully before cupping it and facing the window when Sylvia reached her side. De la Cour spoke, still facing the window. "I have a colleague who can complete some additional testing that will give us answers about your MRI, but it will require some travel."

"Meki said you might recommend travel to the Galactic Core Station." Sylvia instinctively reached for the braided strand. "Is that the relic no one except you has ever seen?" Sylvia's combined writing and archaeological curiosity were piqued by the glyph etched in the silver she had glimpsed.

"I promised answers at the consultation's end, when you return. The others ran out of time."

There's a time limit! Sylvia's mind raced, and her eyes traced the floor in a pacing pattern she wanted her feet to follow, but she felt frozen. Unable to move, she at least forced out the question, "What do you mean, ran out of time?"

"You're human. Your entire life is but a short time compared to mine. If you survive, come see me when you finish your testing."

"Human? Of course I'm human." Sylvia tilted her head sharply. The quick movement caught the penetrating, thoughtful blue eyes staring at her. In light of the discussion, they appeared unique. *What does that make you?*

***

***

SHIRO ESTATE, 66 YEARS EARLIER, EARTH ALLIANCE YEAR (EAY) 2050

Vrishikasana tossed the second body on top of the anesthesiologist, already burning, inside the open glass doors of his seven-by-ten-foot fireplace. The fireplace's heat-tempered glass had the convex shape used by the Orbiters for atmosphere re-entry. The rounded glass created a beautiful 180-degree view of the six-foot-deep fireplace. He traced the chimney inset of reclaimed brick and the mantel of warm mahogany wood. The glass sealed off any lingering smell. *The flames are beautiful without the offensive smell of burning flesh.* He reached for the decanter of wine he'd poured an hour ago to let breathe. He was glad the anesthesiologist and the scrub nurse had asked for beer. He didn't have to contaminate his wine with the poison. *Now, only the doctor remains.* He pulled his pocket-handkerchief from his lapel, laying it flat on the table before tilting the glass of red against the backdrop of its pristine white to judge its color. He smiled at the saturated red that completely blocked his vision of the white beyond it. He swirled the wine, inhaling its aroma, the glass poised at his chest. He had tracked the three of them, and they had communicated with no one. The knock on the door pulled his lips into a tight smile, and he closed his eyes, breathing in the wine. *The doctor is here.*

CHAPTER ONE

APRIL 13, 2116

"Acquisition of immortality is the death of time," Xenos whispered, peering out at the darkness beyond the space-tempered glass of Orbiter C13.

Kinley leaned on the table between them. "No, my friend, simultaneity is the death of time. Immortals simply forget it exists."

Xenos turned from the window. "I may forget time exists..." he said, taking in the features of his old friend. "But not those I've lost to it."

Xenos watched Kinley swallow his words, unwilling to say what they both knew — that Xenos spoke not only of the past but the future. Their future.

Kinley turned the handcrafted tea bowl on the table. "Why do you do it? Why do the Tokoleh Immortals regenerate?"

Xenos waited for Kinley to lift his head, knowing he would see the flash of hope that there was another way. He turned back to let his eyes follow the lines of the large window. The glass reflected his lapis-blue eyes. The landscape of Earth was visible from this banister level of the Orbiter. He let his words form entirely in his mind before he spoke. The rain beat the tempered glass. "I'd like to say it is a selfless reason, a determination to remain and oppose people like Biagio, hunt war criminals like Coriolis, but in honesty..." Xenos lifted his hand from the large white column that stabilized the railing. He used his palm to cover the sliver of moon in the black sky. "Mostly, I don't want to die."

The dark night lit with a bright bolt of silver, catching a figure standing on the cliff overlooking the Orbiter's payload docking wheel that rotated in the cliff as it loaded. The umbrella he held seemed dangerous, but Xenos watched the man adjust the pocket-handkerchief in his suit lapel. *An Immortal,* Xenos thought, watching the man stand carelessly in the storm as he looked out at the night that threatened to burn the dry trees and sparse vegetation dotting the cliff where the Orbiter docked. Xenos imagined the Orbiter's appearance from the man's vantage point. The spacecraft's fuselage hung like a bird cage from the center of a bicycle wheel with spokes that reached out to lock, load, and rotate in a groove cleared deep into the mountain.

Xenos heard the chair scrape. Kinley stood to join him but sat back down when their eyes met in the reflected glass.

"Do you remember any of your life before the last regeneration?"

Xenos closed his eyes and felt the tears threaten. "I can't remember the people. They are erased with the regeneration, but I feel the loss." Xenos took a deep breath to corral his thoughts. *There have been so many wars. Was this last one truly the worst, or just the one I remember fully?* He envisioned the mountain where the Orbiter docked, his eyes still closed. *We built these Orbiter launch sites to save the ones we could during the war. The Tokoleh helped as best as we could.* Xenos pushed back the tears.

Xenos opened his eyes, catching Kinley's in the glass before looking away. "What is it?"

"A darkness beyond night." Xenos met Kinley's eyes in the glass. "When Immortals lose connection with humanity, we're separated from the Source, unable to regenerate. It's a darkness I can't describe — an Immortal's worst fear."

"You think Biagio has done this? Lost his ability to regenerate?"

Xenos pointed toward the threadbare vegetation of the cliff. "Yes," Xenos answered, quiet and firm, his eyes never leaving the window. "The Earth Sectors have not looked this barren in years. The Separatists' proposal for Tokoleh Immortal rule is creating division with the humans' Earth Alliance."

"That isn't new. They created division when they tried to destroy the Portal keys and the Earth Alliance had to hide them. Do you think the Separatists have found the keys?"

"No, I don't sense that, but something is changing, and my gut says Biagio is involved."

Xenos turned in time to see Kinley's shoulders slump as he grasped the tea bowl on the high-top table. He tapped along the rough edge near the rim of the bowl where it was chipped long ago. Xenos watched him place his thumb over the rough edge and his crooked middle finger underneath the handcrafted piece. The

Orbiters were engineered with a sleek beauty, and Xenos knew the sterility was a discomfort Kinley could displace only by bringing a few comforts from home.

Kinley reached for the small map book in his pocket with his free hand.

Xenos smiled. Their discovery of Coriolis's connection to the Separatists had led them to it, and now his book-loving friend had seven days of travel to devour its ancient pages before they had to turn it over to the archives at the Galactic Core Station.

Kinley laid it on the table and spoke with the confidence Xenos was accustomed to hearing in his voice. "You agree if the relic keys remain lost, that will be better."

"Maybe."

"Maybe?" Kinley abandoned his tea bowl to wave his arms as he spoke. "Galactic dice, Xenos! If Biagio and his band of broken Immortals find those relics, they will destroy them."

"Broken Immortals?" Xenos laughed, but the sound was haunted. "As it is," he whispered, then tapped his chin with his steepled fingers. "Perhaps that is it. The Immortals, including us Tokoleh Immortals, are all broken but unwilling to let go."

"Xenoselah," Kinley said, his voice soft, and Xenos watched his own pain and guilt reflect in his friend's features. "Don't," he added when Xenos turned his eyes back to the dark sky. "You, as one of the Tokoleh Governors, have held this galaxy together through the Great Splintering and a recent war that almost annihilated it."

Kinley moved to stand beside him, and Xenos felt the brush of his own sleeve across Kinley's katana, a reminder of Kinley's sworn duty to protect him, a Tokoleh Immortal. The duty was buried deep behind the love of a friend.

"Biagio and that handful of Separatist bullies are not honorable Tokoleh," Kinley said.

Xenos felt his eyes blink rapidly with the remembrance of many lifetimes lived and forgotten as a Tokoleh Immortal. The last war had been at least sixty years ago, but the Splintering had been thousands of years ago — and he had been there. Xenos closed his eyes again, letting his thoughts collide. *Am I any different from Biagio? Ancient, haunted, and broken.* Xenos looked up at the ceiling of the banister room as if he could see through it up to the entry deck of the Orbiter and beyond to the Galactic Core Station twenty-five light-years away, but only the high-ceilinged lights stared back at him. They were dimmed to a whisper of their potential so passengers could enjoy the night sky. Xenos looked again out the window. The man with the fancy handkerchief and umbrella was gone. Maybe he wasn't Immortal, just brave to be out in the storm. Xenos wondered for a moment if the man would be on the Orbiter or staying on Earth. It didn't matter. Earth or the Galactic Core Station, this would be his last trip if he didn't regenerate. And if he did regenerate, the people he knew and loved in this lifetime would be forgotten. It was the price of immortality.

[1.1]

Three floors above the banister room, Sylvia Debair's foot caught on the entry treadway. She stumbled into the Orbiter, her hand still reaching toward the gold hieroglyph markings near the middle of the column on her right.

"Watch where you're going!" A man blasted over his shoulder when she bumped him.

Sylvia blushed, feeling clumsy and angry at the same time. People didn't even bother to look at her when they were angry with her. *I should have stuck with archaeology*, Sylvia thought. Success as a writer amounted to being as invisible as she had been twenty-five feet into a tomb — alone.

"Finger, please," the stewardess said, her eyes covered with goggles that looked to Sylvia as if she was prepared for vascular surgery on a fly.

"Your finger," the lady said again, pushing the tool in her hand back against the wall where it disappeared, enveloped by the white flexible wall. The woman looked up, and Sylvia realized she was holding up the line, her mouth agape at the disappearing tool.

Where is Meki? Sylvia thought, reaching her hand to the woman, uncertain which finger she wanted. She swallowed hard, trying to pretend the tool the woman had been using hadn't just vanished into the wall. "What are you doing?" she asked quietly, ashamed to jerk her hand away like an idiot but not comfortable with the instrument that reappeared when the woman placed her hand on the white wall.

The woman ignored her, and Sylvia's hand trembled as the instrument came closer. She wiped her opposite hand on her dress pants. Sylvia knew this trip was a bad idea, but Meki, her publicist, had convinced the publisher to support a book signing at the Galactic Core Station Hotel during the Earth Week celebration for the first book in her new series. Apparently, Dr. De la Cour's recommendations for a specialist there had tied the knot somehow. Sylvia's hand tremor worsened at the thought, and the woman looked up at her again.

[1.2]

Jezel looked at the passenger. The woman's hand was shaking so much she couldn't see her fingerprint. *This is probably her first trip*, Jezel thought, wanting to be patient, but it had been a long day. She was surprised how many people from Earth had never traveled even to the local space station, much less the Galactic Core Station.

The woman stiffened as if willing her hand steady, and Jezel realized her exhaustion probably had her scowling at the woman. She watched the panic flit across the woman's face, and it made her feel bad. She schooled her face to reassurance just as the woman's eyes began a panicked darting around the space, searching the area in an almost desperate plea for help. *Nice job, Jezel. Just scare the first-time fliers.* "I'm sorry," she said quickly, giving the woman's hand in hers a little squeeze. "The flight isn't bad. Are you flying with someone?" she added when the woman's eyes still widened with fear. The goggles made everything so magnified that facial features could be jarring, and she reached to lift them when the woman spoke.

"Yes," the woman answered and searched more frantically as if the words made the panic surge through her anew. "Meki. He's taking me to see a doctor at the GCS," the woman blurted, then clamped her lips in a tight line as if she'd not meant to say that out loud.

Jezel watched as the woman took a deep breath and then more calmly turned to check again for her friend. The movement shifted her finger in Jezel's hand, and Jezel let her hand go as she stared at the scar that was magnified on the woman's temple. She lifted the goggles and took the woman in for the first time. She was stunned, her mouth hanging open in surprise.

[1.3]

"I'm sorry," Sylvia said, not sure what to make of the woman's expression. "I'm not familiar with space, um...intergalactic travel. Just flying from Pittsburgh to New York and back once a year leaves me sick for weeks."

"I've got to find Tessa," the stewardess said, looking around briefly. "I can't believe it's you. I'm Jezel. I'm so glad to meet you. I just finished your new book!" She leaned to look around the corner. "Michael, bring my book off the staff table." She turned back, and the goggles slipped. She pulled them off. "I'm glad I had these on." She giggled. "I was trying to read your book on the job last week." She pointed inside the podium as if the book were still there. "I forgot I had the goggles on when I pulled it out. The goggles magnified the scar at your temple on your book photo. How did you get it?"

Sylvia touched the scar. *If everyone wore magnifying goggles, they could see me. Or at least my scars.* She mentally chided herself for the thought. "I don't remember," Sylvia said with a tight smile. It was true, but the words were a reminder of things she didn't want to think about right now.

"I'm sorry," Jezel said, pulling the goggles back over her eyes when Sylvia's thoughts creased her brow. "I just can't believe you're on our Orbiter." She wiggled the tool in her hand. "This is a laser marker. It marks the third circle of your fingerprint so the injection device at the Galactic Core Station can inject the chip when you arrive. It reads the laser mark."

Sylvia sensed the stewardess was just chatting, but it was comfortable, and despite the distraction, she still couldn't shake that creeping sixth sense that something was wrong. Meki was nowhere in sight through the narrow opening filling with people behind her. She turned back to Jezel just as a strong hand grasped hers and pulled it from the stewardess.

"You will need to use the auto-marker," Meki said, and Jezel looked relieved.

"Oh, yes, of course," the stewardess said. "Lots of people, especially celebrities and the like, use a covering over their fingers for privacy, to protect their information." She reached inside the podium, toward the back, and pulled from it a silicon fingertip with a generic fingerprint, then slid it on Sylvia's finger. "It was really nice to meet you." The stewardess chattered on as she scanned the laser over Sylvia's finger.

Sylvia tremored at the warmth. Every sensation had seemed heightened since her headaches started. Her doctor called it synesthesia. Meki said it was due to the changes in her brain, and that the doctor at the Galactic Core Station could help her with it. "Thank you," Sylvia said quietly when the stewardess finished. She wanted to get to her room, push everything away for a while, and hopefully rest.

"I don't know where Michael went, but would you sign my book sometime before we reach the GCS? I swear one of the lost places in your book reminds me of the place where I was born."

"Really?" Sylvia said, her interest piqued. It was common for people to find similarities in books to places they knew, and she often researched them later as a matter of curiosity, constantly fascinated by nuances that translated from something in her imagination to something a reader recognized as familiar. "Where is that?" Sylvia continued, thinking it would give her something to occupy her mind on this trip.

"Dursley, England. There's a little manor there, just like in your book."

Sylvia sensed a shiver move along her spine, but she managed to thwart it before it convulsed her body. However, the effort caused her brow to furrow.

Sylvia realized Jezel still had her hand, and she actually could taste the yellow color of her excitement with the woman's touch. The synesthesia was one of the most jarring issues.

"I've not been home for a while. Oh, I'm chatting too much," the stewardess said, smiling warmly.

Sylvia felt the warmth again like sunlight. She appreciated the woman's gregarious nature and smiled as Jezel continued to talk.

"I've been away in a..." She paused. "Training program, but my mum is there."

The next passenger in line made her huffs of impatience slightly louder, and the stewardess dropped her hand to take the hand of the next passenger, still speaking to Sylvia. "I can bring my book by for you to sign once we are past the local space station and into the beltway."

"Certainly," Sylvia said with a tentative smile, then turned and let Meki lead her away. The mention of Dursley and the manor had given her an eerie sense of déjà vu, and why did she feel so embarrassed when people asked her to sign books for them? She was nuts. She wanted recognition for her work but never quite felt she filled the shoes of one who should be autographing books. She just wrote what came to mind in daydreams and nightmares as she watched what happened in a world that spun without her. A flickering memory of the previous night's book signing and the man begging for coordinates to the Lost City in her book sent a new shiver down her spine, and she didn't restrain it. Meki paused, sensing it.

"Are you alright, darling?"

Meki's formality was customary, and she had always enjoyed his English accent. Though they were friends, there was at least twenty years between them. Tonight, the combination of it all made her feel more isolated. "Yes, I'm fine. You know I don't travel well." She gave him a weak smile. She felt a little nauseous, and she didn't know if it was her growing unease about the trip or the slight excitement she had felt at being recognized. Maybe she was better off invisible if she got sick from the energy jolt when someone noticed her outside of a book signing.

Meki guided her through the widening corridor of spotless white. Cold seemed to sweep over her like an ocean wave — heavy, forceful, and dangerous. The sensation was like a prism of conflicting colors in her mind, converging to a crest of billowing white to engulf her. Sylvia paused, tasting salt and brine when she swallowed. Orbiter C13 was more spacious inside than it had appeared from the outside. *More than what it seems,* she thought, touching a column on her left. The emblem on it was like the one she had noticed when she tripped coming in.

"The place appears daft and boring now..." Meki said.

Sylvia sensed he noted both her interest and discomfort. They had been friends for several years now, and recently, the tour had them spending lots of time together.

"...but the entire spacecraft comes to life once we reach the beltway."

[1.4]

Her condition is more fragile than she realizes, Meki thought, watching her small frame move beside him. *She's going to need me.* He needed to get her to her room so he could finish some details before launch. Meki gave the small of her back a little nudge. "Well, it actually flares its colors before the beltway, but the point is, don't judge it by its austerity now." Meki touched the white of yet another column. He didn't want her to experience the spacecraft without his guidance, as it could be overwhelming. But he didn't have time for it now.

[1.5]

Sylvia imagined the white of the ship transforming to a panorama of color as she traced a section of the column on her side wrapped in gold and engraved with hieroglyphs that appeared as stick drawings. Two empty chairs facing a box with the same stick chair and box formation nested inside the first box engraving. The nesting pattern seemed to continue till the center of it just appeared as a dot. She felt a small connection to the pattern. The sensation was not uncomfortable, but her unease still tugged at her gut. "Nothing original in the world, huh?" she said to Meki, knowing he would understand how similar they seemed to the patterns she had pulled from her imagination when she wrote this recent book. She had spent enough time on archaeological digs while in college to not be surprised to find repetition and similarity of hieroglyphs, though the similarity of these were to places she only recalled in her dreams and imagination.

"I guess not, my dear. Let's go to your cabin and check your key, change your shoes, and I will show you around. We have seven days for you to see everything."

"It's hard to believe we can go twenty-five light-years in just seven days," Sylvia said, turning to follow him but unhappy at the sense of foreboding she couldn't shake as they walked.

"Here we are." Meki swiped his ring past the door scanner on the door, and it clicked. He pushed the door open and handed a clear plastic card to Sylvia. She passed her finger over the card along the thin red line and realized she still wore the silicon tip on her left index finger.

Meki watched as she removed it. "The card uses a magnetic strip to open the door. If you had a dimension ring," he said as he twisted the one on his finger, "they could code it to open the door. You can get one at the GCS. They have a jewelry shop that specializes in them."

"Okay," Sylvia said, though the last thing she wanted was something on her hand generating a constant sensation. She had stopped wearing jewelry when the synesthesia worsened. Except for the charm at her neck, she was jewelry barren. Sylvia toyed with the feel of the silicon tip that strangely seemed to have a sound in her head, not just a feeling in her hand. She should take it back, she thought, but she hesitated at the idea of moving back through the crowd of people now meandering about the Orbiter as they found their cabins and settled in for the trip.

Meki must have read her thoughts. "You don't have to take it back. They have plenty of them. It is common for celebrities to cover their fingerprints."

Sylvia's head jerked up, then back at her hand. "I've never done that." She pulled her fingers close to her face as if she could see her fingerprint, then realized she probably looked silly.

"I know," Meki said. "It's not a big deal. They stopped using fingerprint systems on Earth. They use DNA instead, more so after the war, so you would never have had any reason to...be asked about it."

"Oh." Sylvia shuddered at the remembrance of the finger stick when she had gotten her driver's license at sixteen in her hometown in Pittsburgh. Meki knew more about the war than she had ever read about in school. She had always thought he was stretching things when he said they had lost most of their technology during the war's ravaging, but now she was starting to understand why he referred to most things on Earth as 1993-ish. She laughed at herself and gave the silicone a squeeze, realizing she had subconsciously been expecting a fingerstick when the lady took her finger. Her smile faded at the recollection that a chip injection awaited her on arrival at the GCS. She gently rubbed her finger where the silicone had been. She had become so much more sensitive to sound, feeling, taste...everything. She was more than a little concerned about the injection. She tucked the silicone into the pocket of her pants.

"You haven't been as open with me these last few weeks," Meki said, fixing her with a steady eye.

Sylvia felt he was studying her. *Concerned,* she thought, reminding herself to be grateful she wasn't having to do this solo. The headaches alone could be debilitating.

"Are your headaches getting worse? There are ways to reduce the synesthesia. Have you tried the things I mentioned? This trip will be difficult."

"It's not that bad," she lied, looking down at the floor.

She had tried Meki's suggestions — the focus it required just made her head hurt worse. She grimaced when she noticed the mud on her low pumps. The walkway they used to take their luggage to the loading dock, built inside the mountain, was under repair, and a small area had been tracked with heavy mud, the debris accumulated from workers entering and exiting through a maintenance door to the outside gear works. She kicked the functional business heels off to carry them into her room and avoid tracking mud into the place where she would be living for the next week. She noted the medium pink polish on her toes. *At least I have nice feet.* "I'll try the technique again," Sylvia said, realizing Meki waited for more.

Meki smiled and gave her a gentle kiss on the forehead. "I'll return for you in an hour for the grand tour. I need to call the publisher's travel department at the GCS to coordinate our arrival and determine our security options."

"Security options?" Sylvia shuddered, and Meki released her shoulders. She was unaccustomed to feeling uncomfortable with Meki's small gestures. It was this trip, and this...this Orbiter. She would feel better when the travel was over. "I know I'm naïve about the GCS, and all of this intergalactic travel is new to me, but is it dangerous enough to need security there?"

"No, darling," Meki said with a tone that made Sylvia feel both patronized and cared for. She could never decide which to reflect in her face, so she always let it slide. Meki's twenty-odd years' difference from her seemed like a hundred when he spoke. "Great God, dear. Of course not. It's the savages of this world that concern me after that fiasco with the female fan at the Pittsburgh signing, and..."

Sylvia finished his sentence. "And the man last night at the signing, a few hours from here." She couldn't recall the city and worried for a moment that the abnormality growing in her brain was stealing her memory. Maybe it was just stress. This book release had been so unusual, with two readers threatening her sense of sanity with their own reality of her book. "It's been strange."

"Exactly," Meki answered and smiled. Sylvia thought the smile would seem smug on anyone else but looked right against his olive skin as he replaced his glasses and the arms threaded through his dark hair, just gray at the temples. "By the way, the female is a woman named Kita. I'm not sure yet who the man is, but I have people checking on it.

"A little history to distract your mind till I can give you the tour — the Tokoleh almost placed this Orbiter launch in that city where we did the signing instead of here near Pittsburgh."

"Tokoleh?" Sylvia said, taking a tired step into her room and covering her mouth to stifle a yawn with her free hand.

"The Tokoleh are two bodies of 1,729 Immortals that govern the galaxy."

Sylvia's yawn snapped closed. "You can explain all of that when we tour." Meki had prepped her a little before meeting Dr. De la Cour. So, big surprises like a Replica Solar System, which she had up until that point known nothing about, were becoming more frequent but somehow less shocking. Or maybe she was just exhausted.

"Alright. We will be launching soon to the transition space station to enter the beltway. I'll be back before that. Your luggage should arrive shortly." Meki turned and started down the corridor.

"When will I see the doctor there?" The question was out before her mind processed it. She felt panicky, and she clenched her fists, angry with herself.

Meki stopped, and Sylvia sensed he was bracing against his frustration. He turned, and Sylvia could see the concern on his face. She felt terrible. She was being hysterical.

"I'll give you the details once I've coordinated everything with this conference call to the publisher's travel team at the GCS. Will that be alright?"

The question made her feel like a child, and she berated herself. "Yes, thank you." She lifted her chin and relaxed her hands. She was an adult; people dealt with these things every day. "I just don't feel like myself. I know you are making it a priority."

"Indeed, I am."

Sylvia smiled, but it felt weak. She pushed against her unease even as she pushed the door closed. She had a luxury suite for the first time in her life, but it didn't settle her anxiety as she imagined Meki, her last connection to home, disappearing down the hallway.

CHAPTER TWO

J UST ABOVE THE LUXURY floor, the payload gears rotated in the buffer space between the first-class rooms and the spokes reaching out from the fuselage to the luggage loading rim locked into the mountain. Above that rotating wheel was a second buffer region that led to the floor for the two pilots of the Orbiter, each with their own cabin and robot co-pilot, which created a flight crew of four.

"PR742, unlock the toilet paper!" Captain Heath Braxton shouted from his cabin bathroom.

The robot, positioned at the flight console, swiveled its head toward the cabin. "Requesting password for EB72517642 locking mechanism."

Heath pushed on the flush white wall. "There isn't a password for the toilet paper." He swiped the wall again where the toilet paper was housed. "Damn robots!" Heath muttered, watching the blue haze of the password-coded locking system flicker across the white wall with his touch. "God, what I'd give to have human co-pilots again." Then, he realized it had probably been his colleague Tom who reprogrammed this robot to lock down the toilet paper.

Tom, you bastard, Heath thought, running his fingers through his cropped hair and deriding himself for giving his flight partner the command password for his robotic co-pilot. "I'm an idiot!" he shouted, punching the wall.

"Password accepted," the robot said from the console twenty feet away from the cabin door entrance. "Lock released on mechanism EB72517642."

The flexible resin white wall shifted like a wave, revealing the compartment. Heath pulled the toilet paper free.

"No report from the west cockpit, sir," the robot reported.

Heath washed his hands and reached for the clean shirt hanging on the back of the bathroom door. He closed it and engaged the latch for launch. He shouldn't be surprised Tom wasn't back in his cockpit yet. Heath stepped out of his cabin after a quick double-check that everything was secure in his living quarters before starting the launch sequence. He took his seat and nodded at the robot to his right. "Check with west cockpit again," Heath said, adjusting his seat closer to the flight console and then punching a few codes into the computer, which would communicate directly with the robot to his right. He needed to change the robot's command password before he ran into any more of Tom's pranks.

"Yes, sir," the robot said, projecting a screen from its left eye as a hologram, but Heath didn't pay attention as the robot communicated with its counterpart in the west cockpit.

"PR744 has received no report from Major Tom Haddock."

Heath wasn't surprised, but it still pissed him off. His view faced the open sky, darkness and pelting rain on the thick heat-shielded windows his only view. Haddock's cockpit on the west at least faced the mountain, but there was no connection between the two. This prevented breach if one failed. He would have to descend to the buffer rooms, walk over, and go up the stairs to the cockpit on the west side just to watch the luggage-payload rim rotate as it loaded. The cameras would auto-click on when it was done. Power saving kept them off until flight. He folded his hands and watched the rain silently pelt the window. He reached for his phone, then placed it on his leg, determined not to give Tom the benefit of knowing he was anxious.

[2.1]

Kita squeezed between some extra luggage and payload cargo as the buzz of workers exited the last rotating storage room. She would keep the worker uniform on because it was raining outside where she was headed, and Tom had torn her T-shirt when he dislocated her shoulder. She grimaced at the pain in her shoulder when she bumped someone's Emitime School gear as she adjusted in her hiding spot. She realized the gear looked brand new as she stepped free after the door closed. Most kids selected for Emitime took an Orbiter that docked closer to the school.

This Orbiter, the C13, docked on the ritzy casino side of the Galactic Core Station Hotel, not the school. "Well, kiddo, you'll have the best pilot to get you there," Kita said to herself, though she felt almost too exhausted to fly. She touched the bracelet of crystals on her wrist and considered using some of the energy to heal her shoulder. Guilt about how she left things with Jo made her release the bracelet. It took a week to travel to the GCS, and she could use the pilot's cryo for her shoulder and save the energy Jo stored in the bracelet for an emergency. She was certain one would arise.

Kita's dragon-shaped ring vibrated on her finger, and she slid Major Tom Haddock's thin phone from her back pocket. She had connected the signal from her ringphone to notify her when a call came in on his phone. She knew his partner pilot, Captain Braxton, would contact his phone when he couldn't reach him in the opposite cockpit for the launch sequence. There was decreased security with these Orbiters, unlike the Bi209-Orbiters docking at the biosphere.

"Symbol communicate English," she said to her ringphone. A quick blue symbol glowed on her ring and disappeared.

Text on the phone was translated to sound. "Where are you, Tom?"

The fact that the partner pilot didn't use any of the rank-appropriate terminology, though he was a subordinate, told Kita the major and the captain were friends. Kita answered and watched the letters appear on Tom's phone as she spoke, "I'll be there. Start the checklist, and make sure the payload wheel is clear of the mountain this time." Kita used the barb to determine which flight cabin was Tom's.

"That was your fault." The robotic voice on Kita's ring converted Heath's text. "Your cockpit on this damn birdfeeder came in facing the mountain."

So, Tom's cockpit is on this side, Kita thought as she moved to find the maintenance door. The large payload wheel attached to the Orbiter had almost slammed the cliff when they docked. Kita had been watching. Had Tom been in a hurry? She gained a new perspective on Tom's damaged phone. He was either reckless or clumsy, and clumsy didn't make it to pilot. She scrolled through Tom's response preferences — *I didn't know they had a middle finger emoji.* Kita smiled, selected it, and hit send, then turned off the phone. Tom's phone blinked off, and she noted the time. "Stone shit."

Kita found the door she needed. Her hands trembled with fatigue. Only maintenance used the payload-to-wheel-spoke doors on the Orbiter. She pressed hard, forgetting her dislocated shoulder, and the rusted lock resisted. She bit back the pain, breathed, focused, and pushed again. The lock disengaged, and she gasped the night air as she lifted her elbow to stifle the pain in her shoulder. The rush of air from the canyon below clawed at her eyes, and her jaw clenched at the grind of neglected bearings beneath her. The rigger gears rotated the payload wheel, and she calculated the risk as rain added its cold play to the slippery rod that stretched before her like a wheel spoke. Gears linked the wheel spoke to the payload at a nasty angle that stretched a foot. The spoke, however, flared wide beyond it, a streamline of metal reaching across open space to a fuselage suspended at the center of this giant wheel docked to the mountain cliff. Kita jumped, balanced, and raced across the spoke. She had minutes to steal Orbiter C13.

[2.2]

Sylvia held one hand under the muddy shoes, her small clutch wallet dangling from her wrist as she walked across the thick, white carpeted floor toward the bathroom straight ahead. The marble floor of the bathroom caught the light from the overhead fixture. It was dim, in power-save mode, offering just enough light to see. She paused in the semi-darkness, then took a deep breath. The room was beautiful, even in this dim light. Things would be fine. She'd complete her signing, see the doctor, and get back home in time to finish the drawing of the tomb's archaeological finds that Chad — no, not Chad — that life had interrupted. She couldn't blame Chad for everything falling apart after Diana's death. Recalling what she could would enhance her writing, and she wanted it done before her parents visited. Her dad would be interested in the pottery piece she was trying to recreate with her drawing. She planned to put it in her next book. *Mom will be glad I'm trying to move past the pain of it.* She strode toward the bathroom, more momentum in her step. She was exhausted, but she would shower and climb into bed.

The bed to her right was king-size with a headboard of rich linen and a sitting bench at the end against the footboard with yellow pinstripe uphol-stery she couldn't resist. She sat and, with her free hand, stroked the beautiful carved detail on the legs. Color and sound washed through her mind as she touched the leg. She closed her eyes to enjoy this small benefit of what she now called her "complication." She refused to call it a disease, yet.

Her arm, holding the shoes, relaxed. The weight of them caused the shoes to bump her legs. Sylvia's eyes flew open at the intrusion of sensation, and she stood, slightly alarmed at how lost she had been in her own mind. She noticed, now standing with the bathroom to her right, that the wall straight ahead looked dark. The art that incorporated the whole wall seemed to shift and dance depending on the angle she looked at it. It made her a little dizzy, and she turned back toward the bathroom. A small alcove held a desk where the designer created an ingenious use of space where the dancing wall met the wall with the door to the bathroom. The room felt large, yet there was only about four feet of walk space between the sitting bench at the end of the bed and the reading chair poised at an angle on the dancing wall. It formed something of a conversation area between the two. The crystal chandelier set in the tray ceiling in the center drew the eye upward.

Sylvia moved toward the bathroom. She reached for the light inside on the bathroom wall, and someone knocked at the door. Sylvia jumped and dropped her shoes. Hard mud broke across the marble floor, and Sylvia turned to the door, her hand at her chest, pushing at it to try and slow her heart. She was never *this* jumpy when she traveled; she clearly needed some rest. It was probably Meki at the door. "I'm going to pass on the tour tonight," Sylvia said, but the knock came again. She moved back across the carpet. She was going to shower and get a good night's sleep. *That. Is. All. I. Want.* Sylvia grumbled with each step to the door. She turned the knob and opened the door, but it wasn't Meki.

CHAPTER THREE

J EZEL TURNED FROM PUTTING her goggles away when Michael tapped her shoulder and spoke.

"Do you want a break before we have to prep for launch?"

"Yes. Please. Where have you been? And, have you seen Tessa?" Jezel was aggravated he hadn't been there to help her find her book. The line of travelers had been nonstop after the author, and she hadn't had even a minute to look for it.

"Sorry," Michael said but offered no more explanation. He retrieved the goggles when a few stragglers started to file in with the usual frustration of being behind schedule.

"I'll just take five, and I'll be back. I want to find my book. The author is on board, did you know that?"

"What author?" Michael ran the laser tool over the next passenger's finger and let him go when it registered a chip already implanted, no need to be marked for placement.

"Remember the book I showed you on our way into dock here?"

"Oh...yes. I read some of it. Hard to believe it's fiction. The places seem so real."

"I know, right? It makes me want to take more time and explore Earthside instead of spending so much of my free time on Replica Earth and the GCS."

"You grew up on Replica Earth?" Michael asked as Jezel started to bounce off excitedly.

"No, not unless you consider"—she lifted her hands, making air quotes—"'growing up' as awaking from regeneration at age twenty-one and then spending four years training at the Emitime School." Jezel smiled and took the corner to head to the staff room.

[3.1]

Sylvia stared at the stranger in the doorway, holding her luggage and a box of books at his side.

"May I come in?" said the man, swinging the suitcase forward and up to indicate he was there to drop off her luggage.

"I'll take them. Thank you." Sylvia's heart refused to slow down, and she took the first piece of luggage and set it inside against the wall. "I'll get your tip." She let the door close, and he stopped it with his foot. The sound made her jump, but she refused to turn around. He was just here doing his job. She retrieved the small travel clutch she had set on the bench when she caressed the carved leg. Should she use the Tokee currency or her unexchanged cash? She added currency education to her list of things to do on the seven-day trip to the GCS as she carried the cash back to him.

He stood after placing the box of books on top of her second suitcase. "You can swipe your chip or ring." He pointed to a small hologram screen hovering over his hand. "Oh, thank you," he said, accepting the tip and easily reading the look on her face. He tapped the screen once. "You don't have a ring or chip yet. Just sign here with your finger to confirm you received your luggage."

"Thank you," she said, signing the hologram in the space above his hand like she was waving a sparkler. "This is all so new. Who do I contact when I need another box of books brought up?"

"Payload manager," he said, pointing to an extension number on a business card he handed her as he stepped into the hallway.

She lifted the large suitcase onto the suitcase stand near the closet. She refused to put a suitcase on her bed. She shuddered at the sound and color that appeared in her mind, remembering the suitcase's trip across vomit-stained subway floors, trains, roadways, and bathrooms. She forced the thought from her mind and noticed the mud dried on the wheels from the area where they had dropped the luggage for processing. Her eyes darted to the bathroom floor, where her shoes lay in a pile of the same hard mud where she dropped them. She opened the suitcase and began to unpack.

Sylvia pulled open a drawer of a small three-drawer dresser she had overlooked when she came in. The dresser stood against the dancing wall in a similar little alcove that balanced the one on the opposite side of the room. This close, the wall didn't seem to dance, and she realized it was a wall map of the galaxy made with black, white, clear, and gray glass. Lights twinkled in the glass and made it seem to dance. The art design she had originally noticed disappeared at this angle. She stepped forward again and touched the compass art. The wall moved — changed. The metamorphosis mesmerized her, and she dropped her hands to the open drawer when the wall slid back to reveal an additional space.

The stab of fear earlier in the night returned, triggered by the vast darkness that lay beyond the floor-to-ceiling glass in the room that opened up before her. She had relegated her fear to a dislike of travel as their car climbed the mountain, and she had peered through the rain-battered windshield of the car. The Orbiter had glowed briefly in flashes of white light from the storm. Now, it seemed ominous again as she stood inside the Orbiter looking out at the night sky. They had driven up and into the mountain to leave the car for their flight. It was like an airport built inside a mountain, and the only evidence of its existence was what Meki called Orbiter C13, which appeared to hang from a ring that held fast its rim to the side of a cliff. If the Orbiter was gone, she wondered, would one even notice anything but a dark mountain and foreboding cliff?

Sylvia shook her head and released the image of the cliff from her mind. How was she supposed to shake apprehension if her writer's imagination kept racing to dark nights and steep cliffs? She touched the compass on the map, not venturing into the new room with the floor-to-ceiling glass view. Her touch on the compass triggered the two doors to slide closed, forming the wall and restoring the map. She could do without seeing the expanse of Earth from this height.

She unpacked a few more items and decided to find someone or somewhere to get a nice cup of tea to relax, maybe add the willow bark her mom gave her. Then she would shower and finally get what she needed — rest.

[3.2]

Wesley knelt near some excess luggage, one arm braced against a steel rod, the other wrapped tightly around his little brother as the gears whined and the loading bays rotated. They had three steps to make this work. "Alright, one more time," Wesley said as he ruffled the sandy blond hair of his ten-year-old brother, with curls as thick as his. His own hair was lighter, leaning toward the bright blond color of their mother's hair. She was long dead, but Wesley remembered.

"Really?" Cajal huffed in a frustrated whisper. "We've been over it a million times."

Wesley just looked at him using his big-brother-knows-best look.

Cajal surrendered. He lifted his hand, cupping Wesley's ear, and whispered as if he were giving the directives. Wesley smiled as Cajal spoke. "Okay. We mingle and work with the loaders when they board at the next rotation. Then, we hide till the wheel rotates to its next stop." Cajal paused, and his hand fell away. "I keep my head down and stay close to you when we all exit. I take these clothes..." He lifted the clothes in his hands before tucking them in his backpack. "Then I change in the bathroom, which is exactly one hallway over to my right when we exit. You get our papers." Cajal bit his top lip. "Why can't I come with—"

Wesley cut him off with a finger to his lips as the gears started grinding to a halt. Wesley whispered, "Then meet back where we exited, and we will head up to the Orbiter cabins and board." Cajal tried to interrupt, but Wesley tugged his brother's ear and smiled. "Together."

Wesley pointed at the loading doors sliding open. He pulled both their hats low on their heads and turned to push the steel rack where Cajal hid into payload bin four of Orbiter C13. Loud, busy workers pushed in beside him with more to be loaded. Wesley and Cajal hid in the payload till the workers exited. They waited for the buzz of workers at the next rotation to enter before sliding into the frenzy and making their exit. Their hiding during the payload rotation and their exit both went smoothly. However, Wesley knew the second step in his plan would be the most difficult, but nothing worth having was ever easy, and having a life of freedom for him and his brother was worth using every criminal skill he had ever developed.

Cajal headed toward the next hallway, and Wesley gave him a nod. He would return looking like every other kid headed to the GCS for Earth Week celebration. Now Wesley just had to work his skills to make sure that when Cajal returned, he had the tickets and paperwork he had promised him. Paperwork that said Cajal was registered at the Emitime School for gifted children, and tickets that said Wesley, though actually only twenty-six, was thirty-four and Cajal's father, rather than his brother. Their tickets to freedom.

Wesley leaned against the wall, out of the way of travelers loading luggage at this section, and unclipped the carabiner from his belt loop, pulling the tip of it and the dimension ring it held from his front pocket. He had not shown it to Cajal. He planned to show him how to use it on the trip. He wanted to keep Cajal as naïve as possible about how he used it to craft his trade, and somehow, waiting till this job was over seemed to create a separation between the past and the future.

He held the ring in his closed hand for a moment. He didn't want this beautiful tool tainted — this would be the last time he used it for this type of work. He would give this ring to Cajal once they arrived or buy him a new one. *Cajal will be a properly trained Intuit,* Wesley thought. He let the small ache in his chest at his own missed opportunities for the Emitime School remain for a moment before pushing it away. Wesley rubbed the ring again and remembered Cajal would be back soon. He smiled. *You will be qualified for any job, little brother, even with the elite Alliance teams.* Wesley remembered his one run-in with the elite team, which consisted of Tokoleh and Earth Alliance members. He should have taken their offer, but Cajal had been very small then, and he had promised him they would never be split up. He slipped the ring on his hand and turned so the hologram displayed from his ring was in shadow as he typed a code on it with a few clicks and a new determination. This was the best choice. *Cajal will be trained by the best, not a self-taught Intuit-turned-thief like me.* Wesley moved along the wall toward the closed information desk. The squared-off area was paneled floor to ceiling with steel while not in use but would slide back to reveal glass once the work was complete and the information desk reopened. It was the glass area that was protected. It held a computer connected to the main server. He only needed brief access.

Wesley slid his hand into his pocket and touched the second object he would be giving Cajal. He slipped in behind some scaffold and plastic, making his way around to the access panel on the far side where the fire exit door for the cubed room would be. It was the only section not covered by steel. Wesley pulled close to the wall to avoid shuffling the plastic that provided his cover. He reached the glass door and pulled once on it — a smart thief tried the easy way first — but the door didn't budge. Wesley knelt and pulled the lighter from his pocket. With a flash of memory, he passed the lighter to his left hand. Only a handful of people would recognize the engraving now scratched almost completely off. He took a deep breath — not to steady himself, as he could do this in his sleep. No, he had to do this slowly, thoughtfully, so he could explain it to Cajal later. Not the crime, but the technique. Wesley touched the ringphone on his right ring finger with his right thumb. The ring began to hum with an almost imperceptible vibration. He then flicked the lighter in his left hand and watched the small flame come to life. He looked up at the small black glass two-by-two-inch panel inset within the clear glass beside the door. He closed his eyes. With his left hand, he stabilized the lighter with his palm and fingers, then lifted his thumb to within a half inch of the flame, and with his right hand, he placed his thumb on the black glass inset. The entire process usually took less than four seconds, but today, he watched the Oscult in the back of his mind. This is how he would describe it to Cajal, piece by piece. The heat warmed his left thumb, sending signals to both his Human and Intuit networks. Wesley watched the heat, as a color, lace along his Intuit network, his first network. He weighed the energy in an instant in network two, sending reserves to the silver Oscult of his mind via network three. He made a mental note to discuss with Cajal the close connection of the Intuit network with the Human network when using the Oscult. He passed the required amount of energy through to the fourth network before watching it flash quick and bright orange into the fifth network. The converted energy exited the fifth network down his spine, hissing with an electric ripple as the black glass cracked beneath his right thumb and blue silver sparked behind it.

Wesley released the lighter, letting the flame go. He pulled his shirt free and pressed the lighter into the false skin he had paid to have grafted at his side for smuggling. He didn't want to have the lighter taken at the last minute as they boarded the Orbiter. He pulled on the emergency door, and it opened. Wesley tapped the ring, and a hologram screen appeared above his hand. With a few quick steps to open the computer connected to the server, he would be in the system.

The hologram screen blinked PASSAGE PAID and confirmed their tickets. They were already registered as travelers, but he had needed to steal a password once they arrived because they changed daily at all the Orbiter systems. His manual override of the system with the stolen password would result in records that showed them already checked in, since they had actually crawled in through a breach to the worker's tunnel at the loading section under construction repair. The construction work was why he selected Orbiter C13 as their best choice when he made his original plan. Wesley had been unwilling to risk evaluation of their fake identification at the exterior gates where security was tighter. Wesley removed the ringphone and slid it back into his pocket, attached by the carabiner to his belt.

Once they arrived at the Galactic Core Station, he could access the funds transferred from this last job, exchange it for Tokee currency, and begin a new job, a new life. He had already put all his savings in an account linked to the school for Cajal just in case there were any snags. No one would care about a man who worked at the biohabitat maintenance plant while his son went to school. It was common practice for those who wanted to stay near their children during their training at the boarding school to find work at the Galactic Core Station. He would have peace, and his brother would get a real education and learn to use his Intuit skills to be more than a thief.

[3.3]

Vrishikasana tapped the camera icon on the hologram screen above his ring-phone. He didn't need a picture of the hieroglyph on the column, but he needed this angle to watch the Marshal. He finished with a passenger and replaced the laser tool back in the wall. V-Kasana touched the column's marking as if studying it. There were three other people similarly posed at columns. Their fascination seemed genuine, and he let his thoughts drift as he walked through his mental checklist while he waited. He checked his ringphone. Just above the time was a notification. He tapped it and read the message.

TANNER: Recruit has the book and the first two numbers.

V-KASANA: MST

Meet, Secure, and Terminate, V-Kasana thought, pleased at the small, unexpected opportunity he had found. He glanced casually around the space. This area opened up wide, supported by several columns that formed an opulent opening for a formal staircase to his left. The elevators on this floor were behind him and forward beyond the podium at the entryway. He had heard the exchange as the stewardess left to find her book. He traced the symbol on the column anew. He could barely see through the narrowed walkway leading back to the Orbiter entrance from this angle. However, it was this angle that kept him from the Marshal's line of sight and still gave him some visibility. His visibility had been good enough to read the self-recrimination in the man's face when the stewardess practically announced she had just returned from regeneration. She had to be a new Immortal. He rubbed his lapel flat. He felt naked without his handkerchief, but it drew too much attention when he was working. It was sad so few people appreciated the way simple things like handkerchiefs carried history the way Immortals carried lifetimes. The thought reminded him of the stewardess. *Young Immortals have no essence. No sense of the past,* he thought. It was disturbing. He closed his ringphone camera after checking the time. *Perfect.* Time to walk back that way so he could be close enough to hear any conversation regarding the Marshal's report. This Marshal had a history that had been hard to access prior to the trip, so he was gleaning what he could prior to defining his own plans. He had a preference for preparation and sensed this Marshal was similar if the look on his face at the stewardess's declaration was an indicator. The Marshal had missed that she was Immortal and was not pleased with himself. V-Kasana smiled and moved toward the corridor. His frustration would make him slightly careless. *Jia would not have overlooked it.* Jia Liu was a Marshal he was more familiar with. He consciously relaxed his tightened jaw. Jia had never seen his face, and he planned to keep it that way.

[3.4]

Michael checked his watch when he saw Jezel approaching. He had fifteen minutes to get the Marshal report before he was needed to help the staff transition the Orbiter to flight status. His duty as staff was to cover for his work as floor Marshal, but he tried to be considerate, and the staff knew his role. Michael tapped his ringphone. The number to the Marshal security office on the bottom floor went through.

Jia answered immediately. "Hello, Michael. Are you ready for report?"

"Yes, I've got fifteen minutes before the staff will need me to help prep the Orbiter for atmosphere flight."

"That's good, because I'll need the extra five minutes to detail you on a new development."

"Okay, I'll meet you at the banister room since you are closer to the first floor. It's fairly quiet till everyone figures out it's there."

"No, meet me at the Marshal's security room."

"Will do. I'll be right down." He tapped the ring off. He knew she wouldn't say more. He paced to the elevator in three long strides. "Oh, sorry, Jezel," Michael said, bumping her in his haste to the elevator.

"Michael, have you seen my book? I thought I left it on the table in the staff room, but I can't find it."

"I think I saw it next to the coffeepot in the day room," Michael said as he watched the numbers of the elevator scroll up from their last delivery. "That's where I read a few pages while I waited for my coffee."

"Great," she said, exasperated, and leaned on the podium. "That's on the second floor. How did it get there?"

The elevator dinged, and Michael stepped in. He shrugged at Jezel. "Not sure, but I'll help you look for it once we are in the beltway." He smiled. *She is solid at her job, but I need more details if she is Immortal.* "I'll need more coffee."

"You're the only one who uses that antiquated coffeepot," Jezel said, seemingly aggravated that she wouldn't be able to get to the second floor till after launch.

Michael laughed as the elevator door closed. It wasn't true, but he probably used the coffeepot more than most of the staff. Mainly because it was one of the few things that reminded him of growing up here on Earth. He swiped his ring and then tapped the code for the secure floor. Why did Jia want to do a report in the Marshal's security office? There were four Marshals on any given Orbiter, two to provide security for each twelve-hour shift. One served as staff while the other manned the security office, and the two off-duty rested.

The elevator slid open, and Michael's boots struck the rubber floor, never making a sound in the wide expanse. He scanned his firing sector out of habit and noticed the lights were off in the hallway to his left, just beyond the desk. That led to the Marshal's cabins, and he was reminded of the benefit of the rubber floor.

"I'm in here." Jia's soft, solid voice carried just enough to be heard as she rolled a chair back to a doorway in a side office to his right.

Michael turned and walked around the enormous main desk toward the briefing room.

"I thought it would be quicker to go over these things down here because we've received several notices from the GCS that have a security code that would take forever to open on one of the floors."

Michael took a seat, and his shoulders relaxed. "It's practicality, not a problem, gotcha," he said as he leaned the chair back comfortably. "I'm listening."

Jia dexterously pulled up a few screens. "The Universal Bureau of Negotiations sent somesing unusual with its update from the GCS."

"Somesing?" Michael teased. Jia was tough as hell, and a friend forged from close, difficult work both related and unrelated to either of them being Marshals.

She punched his shoulder. She was a Griffon, so it actually hurt, but he deserved it. So, he rubbed his shoulder and listened.

"The UBN sent..." she began again.

Michael leaned forward, giving her his full attention.

"...an update from the GCS, but there was an addendum about upgraded security protocols that requires a ring scan signature from each of us to acknowledge we have reviewed it." She pushed away from the screen and stood so he could slide over and read it. "I've already signed it. Lanky and Long can sign it when we switch shifts."

Michael nodded. Lanky was only two inches taller than Michael, who was six foot four, but he didn't have Michael's thick build, and he seemed to be all arms and legs when he got you in a grappling hold. Long was the only Marshal that Michael had ever known who was brave enough to keep long hair through their basic training. He had seen him get thrown in hand-to-hand by the braids, and Long broke the man's arm in a mid-air twist he'd never seen done before. It was common for Marshals who graduated together to be paired and placed with an established Orbiter team. Michael's prior experience had taught him how that fostered support and interdependence in a team, and Michael was proud to be part of this one.

Jia picked up her tea and leaned against the counter. "There is only one other issue that requires the secure system, and I'll show you that when you're finished reading."

Michael scanned the security addendum and then slid his hand into the scanner to his right. He felt the warmth of the laser as it scanned his hand from fingertips to palm, then vibrated slightly around his ring and shut off. He removed his massive hand and spun to face Jia. She reached across him, slid her hand into the scanner, and then tapped the screen to open a new box. Michael leaned back to give her some room, then rapidly shifted his weight forward again, causing the chair to clack when a picture filled the screen.

Jia jumped at the noise. "What is it?" she asked, pulling back to stare at him.

"Nothing, I just think I've seen this."

Jia sat down hard on the table. "You've seen this?" Her hand touched the notched area of the relic and rotated the image on the screen around its engraved marks near its smooth edge with her finger.

"No, it's not the same," he said, looking closely at the screen. "What is it?"

Jia visibly relaxed. "It is an artist's rendition of an ancient artifact that has supposedly been hidden for decades, if not more."

"And why is it important to us?"

"There is a rumor that it has been found, and the UBN is very interested in its whereabouts."

"Is it the security, diplomacy, or negotiation department of the UBN that is interested in it, and why?" Michael checked the lower right-hand corner of the screen, remembering that Jia had scanned her ring hand to access it. Sure enough, there it was. He picked at the red five in the corner of the screen as if it were a sticker he could remove. "What makes it level five security?"

"I don't know, but you gave me a heart attack when you said you had seen it."

Michael touched the screen, enlarging it to look at the engravings. "No, it wasn't this. The engravings are different. It was just a drawing in a book Jezel is reading. It's not the same."

"Was the book about ancient artifacts?"

"I don't think so. It's fiction. Artifact designs like this are probably all over the Rompnet from artists if authors want to use them."

"Yes, but few people on Earth have access to the Rompnet other than those with intragalactic access codes associated with the Earth Alliance infrastructure. Earth only has the mainframe system since the war."

Michael slid his chair back. He had forgotten about the limited technology of Earth since becoming a Marshal and spending most of his time on an Orbiter. "I'll look at it again when I go upstairs." Michael started clicking the pen he'd removed from his uniform pocket and opened a small notebook. "What's the report on it?"

Jia silenced the clicking with her hand over his. "Nothing. That's why I don't like it. And, in answer to your earlier question about which department — security — the UBN notice is simply to be aware of it and to contact Rosalind Mathing directly if it shows up on one of the Orbiters."

"Hmm..." Michael closed his notebook and let out a long whistle.

Jia's narrowed eyes reminded Michael she knew the name had registered. Michael was team commander of the Dark Squad before joining Long in Marshal training. Rosalind had pulled the strings to get him in, and the transition had been unusual enough that Jia knew not to ask questions. He respected her for that — they both had their secrets. Rosalind Mathing, as UBN director of security, was the grand keeper of secrets. *She certainly knows too many of mine.*

Michael rubbed the edges of the closed notebook with his thumb. He wouldn't be writing any of this down. If call response was to Rosalind Mathing, he had better just keep this in his head for now. He looked at his watch. Jia checked the clock on the computer, and they both headed for the elevator as Jia gave him the rest of report. They would be locking down to launch soon. Michael stepped into the elevator, his gut sensing something he could not see. He crossed his arms at the familiar unease that had told him more than once before that there would be trouble.

[3.5]

Several floors above, Wesley and Cajal crossed the Orbiter threshold with an artifact strikingly similar to the one Michael had just seen.

CHAPTER FOUR

J EZEL FINISHED WITH THE last few fatigued boarding groups and placed the roster sheet in her locker. She kept a printout version because she inevitably misplaced her hologram pad. She smiled when Tessa's fingers laced around her middle. She spun in her arms. "I met the author," Jezel squealed, planting a quick kiss on Tessa's lips, then wrapped her index finger in the twist-out curl near Tessa's ear.

"Sylvia Debair?" Tessa asked, smiling and dropping her arms to squeeze Jezel's hips. "It feels so good to be traveling together again."

Jezel stroked her thumb across the furrow in Tessa's forehead. "It is good. Why are you worried?"

Tessa pulled Jezel's hand to her cheek and kissed the palm. "I don't think you rested enough during the training that followed your regeneration."

"I'm fine. I plan to make sure I get some rest this trip." Jezel wiggled her hips. "I've got a good book to snuggle up with."

"Did she sign your book?"

Jezel sighed. "No, it's on the second floor." Noise beyond the locker alcove pulled their attention. "Stragglers."

"I'll get them. You go get your book."

"Thank you!" Jezel hugged Tessa. "There are only two passengers left on the roster, a father and son, it's probably them." She gave Tessa's ear a nip with her teeth and smiled.

Tessa closed her eyes and took a deep breath.

Jezel knew what she was thinking. She now understood the fear of losing someone you love. Jezel waited for those golden-brown eyes to open.

"I'm so glad I didn't lose you," Tessa said, squeezing her fingers cupped around Jezel's.

Jezel tapped Tessa's wrist in a now familiar gesture between them. "Me too."

[4.1]

Wesley tried to look calm, but the excitement of being this close to freedom from his old life and a new life for him and Cajal was difficult, even for a con artist like himself. He watched Cajal's eyes as the laser scanned his finger. His chest squeezed. *I'm so proud of you, little man.* Cajal gave no hesitation when the stewardess pulled his finger to the tool, gave them a nod, and headed away. Wesley didn't care to have been dismissed so quickly, but he smiled at Cajal's look of disappointment. "Don't worry, son," Wesley said, as a reminder to his brother of their new identities as father and son. "There will be other pretty girls who notice you."

Cajal elbowed his side. "Where do we stay?"

"I printed a map," he said, lowering the map so Cajal could see. "Here." He pointed to the floor third from the bottom of the Orbiter.

Cajal took the map as Wesley oriented to find the stairs. He preferred them to elevators, and they were going down, so it wasn't too much to ask of Cajal with his backpack.

"What's the K-hold floor?" Cajal asked, checking the map as they walked.

"It's the cheapest way to travel on these Orbiters, being more like open bay areas." Wesley saw the stairs and headed to them as the first information came over the intercom.

"Five minutes till launch lockdown."

"But we're not staying in K-hold, right? It looks bare compared to the other floors on the map."

Wesley nudged Cajal's shoulder to increase his speed as the boy looked up. The door to the stairs was straight ahead.

"There's a steward headed in our direction, and I don't want to be redirected to the elevator."

"Okay."

Wesley closed his eyes at Cajal's immediate compliance. He never fought him when he knew it was important. *No kid should live with this kind of risk.* "No," Wesley answered Cajal's earlier question sharper than he intended, his anger at himself bleeding through. He paused, taking a reflective breath once he had pressed through the door to the steps. "The K-hold usually houses the Dalen."

Cajal folded the map as they took the stairs and looked up at him. "Isn't that the group you said you wouldn't work for because they were slave traders?"

Wesley paused on the landing, now comfortable that the steward would let him find his way. "I probably shouldn't have called them that, so don't repeat it. The people are housed, and the government of the sectors provides food and all their care, but they have no freedom and have to do the jobs assigned to them. They give up their freedom to be Dalen." Wesley started down the next flight of stairs.

"Why would they do that?"

"I don't know." Wesley increased his speed again. *How do you explain the Dalen?* Wesley thought, gently nudging Cajal down the stairs with his hand on his shoulder. He had scanned all the data available on the Rompnet for these Orbiters, and some of them had alarms if people were in the stairwells during a transition. He didn't want to draw attention. "I think when you are born into or have to adapt to a social system of constant survival, there are too many barriers to overcome that you can never seem to get out." It was true for him. The life he'd started as a petty thief to get food for him and Cajal seemed like millions of choices ago. The cost to get out had seemed too high a price, but now he was going to make it happen. "Let's pick up the pace. We only have a few minutes till they start the procedure for launch."

[4.2]

Asher locked the last sculpture into its display on the wall in the common area. The Tokoleh had added the special glass to both display and safely transport the sculptures for the Earth Week ceremony. He could feel the weight of this trip. He closed his eyes and spoke quietly to himself. "Infinite beginning and end, you are in all things, but I see you here." He opened his eyes and let them follow the lines of his sculpted work. *Can one relic bring hope to the Scholar's Council?* He squeezed the leather pouch that hung inside his robe. "Did I do the right thing to remove it from its hiding place?" His question was a quiet one. A question he wanted to ask his wife. She was gone, but he still spoke to her often. It served to soothe the pain of missing her. He still felt the tether to her. The Elderwise agreed to attend this Council upon his request, and he would need them. His mind wondered again. "Will bringing the relic out of hiding be enough to generate support for the changes scheduled for discussion Earth Week?"

"Did you say something, sir?" the steward asked as he moved skillfully behind Asher, who was still staring at the encased sculptures.

"Just to myself," Asher said with a smile. "Did you catch those two passengers headed toward the stairs?"

"No. I'll make an announcement requesting passengers use the elevators now that we are close to launch."

Asher waited, sensing the man wanted to say more. He seemed to study Asher's sun-darkened skin.

"Would you be so kind as to find the bench outside your cabin? Your section staff will be coming by to check each passenger is safely strapped in for launch lockdown."

"Certainly," Asher said.

The steward stopped and stepped back toward the statues like one of the soft waves that nudges a child's toy back to shore. "You sculpted these, yes?"

Asher didn't speak but watched the steward move to stand in front of the white wall with an up-light that made the statues come to life in light and shadow. The glass covered the front but left the top open. He reached over the top to touch the horse. An alarm buzzed, and he pulled his hand back.

"Invisible laser alarm across the top. The alarm cuts off on its own unless the piece is lifted. Then, it needs to be reset. I wanted people to be able to touch them, and this is the best the Tokoleh could do and keep security. The lasers run perpendicular to the wall, and you can reach between them."

"Why a horse, a fish..." The steward now stood close to the glass, his hand poised over each one as he spoke. "...a dog, a cat..."

Asher smiled as the steward's tongue moved back and forth across his upper lip as if it guided his hand when he tried to speak and concentrate.

"...and a very large bird — wait, it's a Griffon?" The alarm sounded again, but this time, the steward just shifted his hand, and it stopped as he touched the flared wing of the Griffon.

Asher smiled at the unreserved joy on the man's face. He felt his own joy find the lines in his face. "They are sculpted for the Scholar's Council ceremony. They represent the Five Original Sectors of Earth. Each will be taken back by the representatives of those sectors and kept in their respective Halls of Justice. They are reminders of the Earth Week celebration, which is often forgotten once the fanfare has passed."

"Is it true that many people in the Earth Sectors don't know about the GCS and Replica Solar System?" the steward asked, pulling his hand carefully from the sculpture to avoid the alarm.

"It is true," Asher said. "But, more are aware now, since the UBN's efforts after the war. *Even more will know if the vote goes as I hope at the Council.* With his arms folded inside his robes, he again squeezed the relic's leather bag. *The vote to renounce the secrecy the Tokoleh has fostered for years will be violently debated,* he thought and wondered again at the small part he might be able to play in the process.

"I sometimes visit my dad at the Griffon grounds near the GCS Hotel when I'm not working." The steward faced Asher now, a new lightness in his features. "He said not a day goes by that one of the riders he carries admits they never even knew Griffons existed. It's so hard to believe — they are amazing creatures — I grew up helping my father train them."

"It's unusual to hear anyone appreciate a Griffon," Asher said.

The steward shrugged. "My father always said, 'You just have to remember, they are not pets.'"

He looked back fondly at the Griffon. "They are powerful beasts with the mindset of a bird of prey. You can't trust them."

Even as the steward said the words, Asher noted the distance in the man's voice as if he spoke his father's words, not his own. He sensed the man's loss. "You're human but grew up on Replica Earth training Griffons. Who did your family lose to the Griffon transformation?"

The steward looked up, surprised.

"My father's best friend, Sam." The steward turned back to the sculpture and placed his hand against the glass. "He was like an uncle to me. He helped my mum and me when Dad was away on Griffon transports." He used his sleeve to wipe the smudge his fingers made on the glass. "My father is a human Griffon who trains the young, feral Griffons brought to the GCS from Griffern. Even with his training and skill, they wouldn't let Sam stay with us. He was shipped to Griffern when I was twelve."

"Have you visited the planet Griffern?"

The man shook his head.

So, he's never seen again this man who was like a second father to him. "I'm sorry for your loss," Asher said, feeling the weight of the man's grief in his own and wanting to alleviate it. "I hear there are researchers at the GCS looking at ways to reverse the Griffon transformation."

"I've heard that, too," the steward said, smiling weakly. "It's something to hope for, at least. I need to get to my station for launch lockdown. Do you know how to use the transition seat bench outside your cabin?"

"Yes. And, thank you for your time — it is a precious gift," Asher said, his hands folded in his robes as the steward departed with a wave. "Don't give up hope," he whispered as his hand squeezed around the heirloom the robe hid, and he wondered if he had the strength to win his own fight. The fight against transformation had taken him close to sixty years of his own Griffon life to master and now seemed to threaten daily.

[4.3]

Kinley watched Xenos watch people. He could tell he was worried about more than his hard personal decisions. It was as if the man were weighing each of the lives before him and finding it worth the cost as the banister room filled with passengers. Many of them gazed from the windows, despite the intercom call to start returning to the seats outside their cabins for launch lockdown. "Why are you smiling?" he asked, wondering if he would be as a good a man if he had watched humanity for thousands of years.

"I just enjoy the energy when people gather this time of year."

Kinley nodded, stepping down from his stool to head back to their cabin. "When did Earth Day celebrations at the GCS start?"

Xenos looked thoughtful as he approached Kinley to make their way back. "About sixty years ago."

Kinley watched Xenos's face darken, so he let the silence remain.

"It was the atrocities to humanity of every species by men like Coriolis during the last Earthside war that finally pushed the beginnings of change. The Tokoleh and the Scholar's Council agreed to the Earth Week celebration at the GCS to expand Earthside exposure to the Replica Solar System."

That explains the connection between the shutdown of many of the regeneration chambers Earthside with...wait, maybe not. Kinley paused his thoughts for clarification. "Was part of that agreement forcing Immortals to return to the GCS for regeneration?"

Their conversation was interrupted by the vibrating hum of the ring Xenos wore. Xenos tapped the band once, and a blue holographic light traced around his right ear. "Hello."

Kinley paused, listening to the one side of the conversation. It was probably Wynter calling about the few loose ends of their investigation. Her strength and speed as an Escape velocity Puller created unimaginable opportunities for her photography skills. He hoped she finally had a picture of Coriolis. A face that could be charged and arrested with the mounds of evidence they secured against the war criminal.

Xenos began walking as he spoke. "Yes, that is a law that governs at the Scholar's Council, but it can be overruled if we have evidence...hold on." He stepped into a nook out of the way, and Kinley instinctively took up a subtle position of protection as people began moving back toward their cabins. Xenos switched to a hologram screen that appeared over his hand, and Kinley watched with his peripheral vision as Wynter came into view.

She was shaking her head. "Just more documents," she said as she shared the screen from her camera. "It's as if the man is a ghost, only existing in the documents."

"Perhaps he is," Kinley said, his eyes still focused on the passengers flowing past them as if they stood on the riverbank as the water moved by. "Maybe he's dead."

"Maybe," Xenos said, then spoke to Wynter. "I will submit my report regarding the so-called treatment centers and the evidence for their criminal purpose to the Scholar's Council." Xenos held his chin and then tilted his head toward Kinley. "Did you bring the 'UBN Articles of Prosecution' I laid out in the office before we left?"

"Yes." Kinley furrowed his brow. "I packed it with the other books. They're in the room."

Xenos stepped from the nook, and Kinley sensed the new purpose in his friend's stride as Xenos switched from hologram to earpiece and spoke to the air, making the turn to the elevators. "I'll research the convergence of law on the prosecution of a deceased versus disappearing criminal. Threatening assets can't bring the dead to life, but you would be surprised how close it gets." Xenos reached to tap the band of the ring and disconnect, then paused, his head twisted, listening. Kinley suspected he heard something as Wynter moved around on the other end of the line. Xenos smiled. "And don't touch the new Murano glass in the library."

Kinley actually heard the silence on the other end, followed by, "Ummm." Kinley shook his head. The woman was incredibly versatile with photography and skilled almost as well as Xenos in understanding the law between the two solar systems. Just don't let her touch anything glass if you want it to remain in one piece. And galactic dice, if she wasn't drawn to it like a moth to a flame.

"We're headed into the elevator," Xenos said, the smile still broad on his face. "Mark the logbook at the office as an extended investigation and forward the data files." He hung up without further comment.

The elevator pinged, and the doors slid open.

A man bumped Kinley's shoulder without apology. "I'm getting off the lift, so signal should improve."

Xenos and Kinley stepped inside the elevator.

Curious for answers from their earlier conversation, Kinley asked, "Why did you choose the GCS for your regeneration instead of one of the sites still operational in the Earth Sectors since we were already here?"

Xenos pressed the icon on the panel inside the door, but Kinley noticed his friend's eyes following the man moving away from them toward the banister room windows. Xenos spoke, still watching him. "Most of the ones Earthside are cryo-regen healing now, not full regeneration, though there are some."

Xenos let the doors close, and Kinley imagined what Xenos's thoughts might be as the image of his cancer-ravaged body reflected in the doors. It aged him, but Kinley felt the Immortal was still the more handsome of them and carried with him a strength that was beyond physical.

"There is a doctor at the GCS who does specialty research for the Tokoleh. He may have an answer for restoring my memory after regeneration."

The weight of those words held Kinley fixed in place as the elevator pinged on the next floor and a couple stepped on with their five-year-old.

"Kinley — the door!" Xenos shouted.

Kinley responded with instincts generated from years of investigating and protecting a man who seldom missed a detail and commanded only in times of emergency. The couple had separated Kinley and Xenos, with Xenos stepping to the rear to avoid the woman's large bag.

Kinley shoved his fingers into the few inches of space, his palms pressing against the closing doors. The doors pressed closer together, and Kinley pulled against them just as the child fell to his knees, pulling at the scarf that wrapped around his neck and down into the dark crack to the shaft between the elevator and the floor between Kinley's feet. His mother tugged at the scarf near his neck as his father pressed against Kinley's leg. As he pulled uselessly at the material winding down in the shaft, the elevator alarmed and tried to move. Kinley pulled against the doors. He could feel his twisted finger leveraging for purchase against the cold steel. Kinley's lean, muscular arms started to bulge against the fabric of his shirt. His chest burned, and he closed his eyes against the pain as the doors began to budge open and the elevator stopped, but the boy remained pulled tight at the floor between his feet. His face was red and frightened, twisted at an awkward angle as he strained against the floor, his small hands pressing hard to either side.

Kinley sensed Xenos knelt behind him as he focused on his breathing to slow his heart rate and create human thought, which helped forestall a complete shift to Griffon. *He's helping the parents,* Kinley thought as his heightened Griffon hearing registered the snip of scissors against fabric. *Where did he get scissors?* The elevator door slipped a quarter of an inch. Kinley grunted, pushing back at the door and clearing his mind of all thoughts. The task needed a beast.

[4.4]

Xenos squeezed the scissor handles hard. A few snips and the scarf began to unravel as the mother pulled it free of her son's neck. She stood, pulling her son up into her arms as his father patted his back and spoke softly to quiet his tears.

Xenos watched with concern as Kinley moved to the back corner with his hands covering his eyes, allowing the doors to close now that the boy was free. His breathing was heavy. Xenos knew he would need to be left alone for a while. He had pushed close to Griffon transformation — and his beast form — to wedge those doors open. As if understanding, the woman turned instead to thank Xenos. Xenos faced her even as he handed her purse to her husband. "I apologize for going through your things," he said, and the woman registered for the first time the hair shears had been hers.

"Why didn't I remember I had them?" she said, tears forming as she pressed the child's head nestled at her neck. "How did you know they were in there?"

Xenos patted the child's back. "I noticed the large makeup bag sticking up from your purse when you came into the elevator. I thought you might be a makeup artist or stylist. It's a profession that utilizes sharp objects, so I checked."

"Thank you," she whispered. Then, she waited as they all listened while someone on the outside gave instructions to her husband regarding the elevator panel. "Please tell your friend thank you as well," she added once her husband was busy with the task. "Will he be okay?"

"He can push his strength very close to the line of transformation. He will be fine. I will pass on your appreciation."

The woman nodded and shifted her son to her opposite hip as she stepped to where her husband pressed icons on the panel.

Xenos moved toward Kinley and placed a hand on his friend's shoulder. *Why do some of the best people only have one lifetime?* he thought, knowing he had to find some answers before his own death or regeneration, whichever he finally chose. "You are the bravest person I know."

Kinley shuddered once but looked up, blinking against the light. "You say the nicest things when you want something."

Xenos shook his head. Though he had seen Kinley risk himself often, putting his own mortality in the balance gave everything a new perspective. "You would have transformed before you let that child die," Xenos said as the steel elevator doors creaked open.

"Yes, I would," Kinley said.

"You have only one lifetime, and much of it is spent avoiding a DNA transformation that will leave you a feral beast with no return to your humanity," Xenos said, thinking about how many times Kinley had risked that to protect him.

"I decided a long time ago that threat would not prevent me from using my strength to protect. I failed at that once. Never again."

Xenos saw the unspoken pain of that failure in his friend's eyes.

Kinley squeezed Xenos's shoulder as they stepped out of the elevator. "I know the cost to live the life I love." Kinley motioned toward another elevator with the hand that reminded Xenos his protector would ask his body to pay any price to protect him — or those in danger nearby.

Xenos pushed the stairwell door open. "The stairs give us more time before the destination."

Kinley stopped, and Xenos knew he was running the words through his mind, still in transition from beast to human. He waited. Regeneration, though new life for the Immortal, was the same as death to those who loved them because they would be forgotten in the regeneration. One way or another, this best friend, like so many others, would be gone soon. Disease and illness could kill Tokoleh Immortals just as anyone else if left unchecked without regeneration. That was the curse of mixing Immortal DNA with humans. Death or regeneration — regardless, both meant loss.

Kinley moved toward the stairs, and his somber look told Xenos he understood, but he said the words anyway. "Time is about how you spend it, not how much you have."

CHAPTER FIVE

K ITA STARTLED WHEN THE launch alarm blared. The luggage-payload
wheel attached to the mountain mobilized, locking for travel, and Kita's
foot slipped. She elongated the next step with her other foot and shifted her
weight to gain her balance, fighting her first instinct to roll. Bad idea on a
two-foot-wide spoke a mile above the earth.

Rain pelted her exposed skin, and she pushed her exhausted legs against the
wind. Forty-eight hours without sleep tracking the traitor here. She had to make
it. The wind crescendoed against the alarm of the Orbiter in its launch lockdown.
Stiff fingers wiped rain from her eyes and then poked the entry panel with a
sequence of numbers. Sleep deprivation made the wind and launch alarm wrestle
in her mind like instruments in a song. The urgency built in her chest like a guitar
fighting percussion in a crescendo to crush the words of a song to a stream of tears.
I have to get in. Kita tilted her face into the rain, her ear near the entry panel lock,
hoping for that quiet click amid the chaos. The final alarm blasted, and lightning
cracked the sky, its brief light exposing her. *This is my fault.* She closed her eyes
against the tears. *No one can see you cry in the rain,* she thought. "I'll fix it," she said,
letting the tears fall for just that moment, then she turned her face from the rain to
the door and yanked the handle. The heavy door swung open with Kita's forceful
jerk, and she rolled inside immediately, standing to check her surroundings before
resetting the door lock.

The corridor was quiet, and she slumped for a moment against the door. The
full weight of a lifetime of running sat heavily on her like the water that pulled
the natural wave out of her black hair. Several wet strands traced along her cheek.
"Why is Sylvia helping the Separatists?" Kita muttered to herself as she pushed

away from the door and reached for the rail to climb the stairs to the flight deck on Tom's side of the Orbiter.

The excitement she first felt when she picked up Sylvia's book and realized what she had found was turning into the pattern of endless searching she had vowed not to do again, but here she was stealing an Orbiter — and this time, it wasn't on orders.

The robots used as co-captains were easier to manipulate than people realized. For all their interaction and security capabilities, they were still a digital system without intuition, and all you needed were the correct codes. The hard part would be staying clear of conversations with Captain Braxton. She pulled a plastic tube from her pocket and swiped her gloved thumb with the blood before pressing it to the plate near the door. There was no hesitation as the plate read the DNA as Tom Haddock and the door slid open.

[5.1]

Asher rubbed the knots at the joints of his hands. They seemed to ache more when not busy forming something new. He scanned the Orbiter from his launch safety seat outside his cabin. He didn't move as fast as everyone else and had taken his seat after leaving the steward to avoid having to rush. He scanned the people still passing in the open corridors, pushing the limits of time. Something had happened with one of the elevators, and the delay had made people get up and move about again. *My last trip to Earth,* Asher thought and remembered the clay he had stored in the payload of the Orbiter. He had been permitted to bring back Earth clay to the GCS, and he was pleased. He gritted his teeth when the recurrent pain in his chest tightened like a vise.

"Are you okay, sir?" asked a stewardess with gentle brown eyes.

"Yes," Asher said, lifting his head and releasing his chest. "I just need to get my medication."

"Let me get it for you."

"Thank you." Asher twisted slightly in his seat to scan his ring but didn't have the flexibility to reach it strapped to the seat. He pulled at his ring, feeling the tightness grip his chest with new strength, but he could not slip the ring past the large knuckle.

The stewardess gripped his shoulder as Asher tilted forward, pulled by the heaviness in his chest. "I'll use my override," she said swiping a master keycard by the scanner. "Where is your medicine?"

"A brown leather bag on the sink in the bathroom."

The stewardess darted inside. "Nitroglycerin," she said, and Asher barely heard her over the sound of her movements through the propped-open door. Asher imagined her pulling the light-protected bottle from the case.

"My dad takes this," she shouted as she made her way back through the room. "It will help." She opened the bottle, dropped a tablet in his hand, and stood by. She appeared determined not to leave.

[5.2]

Kita stepped through the inner door to the hallowed world of the flight cabin. Her hand cast a shadow across the last steel barrier from the panel lights glowing on the right. The door would open with a passcode that Tom had listed on his phone. She had memorized three from the list. The exterior door, this one, and the one she would need to verify herself to the robot co-pilot. She checked Tom's phone one last time to make sure she had read the robot's name right. *Motorcycle*? She typed in the passcode, and the solid door slid back. An almost human-looking robot with one highly polished, chrome-embellished index finger turned in the seat and faced her.

"Hello, Motorcycle."

The robot blinked, mimicking some of the natural body language of the thespian robots. Kita smiled. Tom must have monkeyed with this one's programming. The military didn't bother with those accessory features, and the Orbiters built by the Immortals during the war were still under the UBN military umbrella.

"Good evening, Tom. Your voice frequency and structural outline are altered."

"I had a sex change," Kita said, strolling to the seat beside the robot.

Motorcycle turned back to the control panel in his seat. "Change is good sometimes."

Kita smiled and sat down, noticing the sticker precisely placed on the side of the robot's shaved head. She couldn't read it because the robot turned toward her.

Surely, he wasn't sent out from the factory with it. "Did you shave your head?" Kita asked, curiosity getting the better of her.

"We reset the programming for hair growth, remember?" The robot tilted its head in suspicion and Kita shivered at the realness. The machine learning in some of these AI systems was unreal. Combined with the humanness of their appearance, it was no wonder the Tokoleh required their right index finger to always be manufactured as pure chrome.

"The code, Tom," the robot said. A red light flashed at the transparent tip of the robot's chrome finger, indicating this flight would go nowhere without it.

Kita gave a sigh of relief at the reminders of his very mechanical nature. "672G541. Now turn that stop light off and get the precheck finished, then call flight cabin two and check the status with PR742."

Kita read the sticker on his head when he turned back to the panel. "Most motorcycle problems are caused by the nut that connects the handlebars to the saddle." Had to be Tom's doing. Kita grinned and, for a moment, felt bad that she had punched him so hard. Then she remembered he had dislocated her shoulder and was glad she had made his nose bleed.

"When did I put these directions on your head? I can't remember," Kita said, pressing one of the corners of the sticker.

"Last week, April fourth, Earth Alliance Year 2116, at 10:45 a.m. Galactic Core Station time when I arrived on the Orbiter, and you upgraded my system for the trip to Earth indicated by my new, top-clearance security name, Motorcycle."

Kita turned her laugh into a cough. "Ah yes, I remember," Kita said, glad to know the robot was new. It would have the glitches that would allow some tweaking if she needed it. "I may switch your voice to something a little more British."

"But my Kentucky accent has a great slow vibe for my singing."

"You sing?"

"I playlisted our whole trip. Do you remember nothing?"

Kita pressed her fingers into her forehead. "Okay, we don't change the voice, but I want to see the playlist before you break out into song."

"Absolutely! I'm glad you now see the importance of my archival resources beyond maps."

Kita paused the kneading of her forehead. *This robot had been specifically selected by Tom for maps? Pilots don't select their AI co-pilots,* Kita thought, then asked, "How far back does your archival data resources reach?" She let her thoughts continue while she waited for Motorcycle's answer. *Maps?*

"My music archive goes back to the fourteenth century BC."

What other archives might this AI have access to besides maps and thousands of years' worth of music?

[5.3]

Sylvia reached the elevators and headed to the dining room for some tea, but the elevator wouldn't work, so she took the stairs. She ran into two men coming up the stairs who told her the dining room would be closed till tomorrow morning. She followed at a distance as they all returned to her floor. She couldn't help overhearing them discussing a book the shorter man carried as they made their way back. She shamelessly eavesdropped when the one wearing a sword spoke of the book's unique Earth Sector maps and hieroglyphs, but she could make little sense of what he said. Maybe she would get a chance to ask him the book's title. For now, they seemed to forget she was there, and she didn't mind for once.

The discussion reminded her of her love for all things ancient. *They're exiting on my floor*, Sylvia thought. *I can't just follow them down the hallway to their room and ask to see their book.* She almost laughed out loud at herself because she considered it. Instead, she turned back on the landing and moved back down the stairs to the Orbiter entry level, which was just below the luxury suites. Her heart was pounding. *I should be in my seat.* Her palm slipped on the bar of the stairwell door as she pushed into the corridor that would take her to the column with the hieroglyphs she had noticed coming on the Orbiter. She slid her hands up and down on her pants as she breathed deeply to slow her heart. The effort almost quieted the darting ribbons of color behind her eyes. Something about the columns seemed to tug at the colors when she thought about the glyphs.

Halfway down the corridor, orange color flashed in her mind, and she squeezed her eyes closed against the pain it ribboned behind her eyes. She could feel the pattern on the column as if she touched it now. It was vivid, and she hesitated, remembering the taste of the color. She had learned in the few months of dealing with the synesthesia that orange was often associated with pain or danger. She had seen it when she touched the photo the reader had given to her at the signing the night her world started falling apart. It was her first synesthesia experience — the migraine had put her in bed for two days. She shuddered at the memory. The color orange had lingered like a filter and was so overwhelming she had turned off every source of light in the house, even her small digital alarm clock, but the color remained.

"Ma'am, are you okay?"

Sylvia looked up at the stewardess and realized she had sunk halfway down the wall she was leaning against. She released her arms wrapped tight at her waist. "I'm fine. It's just the travel."

"Your first intergalactic flight?"

"Yes," Sylvia answered, glad for an excuse for how the stewardess had found her.

"It's common to feel a little nauseous when we reach the beltway for injection, but the atmosphere launch isn't so bad. I do need you to go to your launch seat, though. What's your cabin number?" The stewardess tapped a screen she held in her hand.

Sylvia gave her the number.

The stewardess smiled. "I'll come by and check on you before launch. Medical has standard medication packs available for first-time fliers."

[5.4]

Cajal checked the map as they entered their floor. "Our room is on the other side, closer to the elevators." Cajal pointed to the map and then pressed his face to the glass wall of the rec center in front of them. *Maybe I can see our room on the other side.*

"Don't put your face on the glass," Wesley said, laughing.

Cajal pulled his face from the glass at his brother's tug and smiled. The launch delay announcement had made Wesley relax, but the look on his face said he was thinking about a job. "Come on," he said, racing ahead. He didn't want him thinking about work, which always took his brother away from him. He checked the map as he ran. Wesley had given him the number for their room.

"Here's your keycard," Wesley said when he caught up to him at the room. "Go on inside and wait for our luggage."

Cajal took the card and turned his back on his brother. *I won't cry. It's stupid.*

"Hey," Wesley said.

Cajal could feel his brother's hand near his shoulder before it fell away.

"I've let you down too many times. I know..."

Cajal squeezed his eyes closed, pushing away the anger and hurt before turning. Wesley had to work. "You will always find me because we're one heart," he said, using the phrase his brother had used when he was little. As a child, he had feared Wesley would not be able to find him when he was left with nomad Auntie Adina, who wasn't his aunt at all.

"Auntie Adina will be the first to come visit." Wesley smiled, and Cajal felt that happy place in his heart. His brother knew him, loved him, and they were going to make a new life. A normal life.

"This is it, for real. I deliver this tool, and I'm done." He touched Cajal's shoulder. "One last delivery, and I'm your new-work-a-nine-to-five, no-travel-job, stay-at-home brother — Dad, I mean."

Cajal looked up at him; he knew it was true. His brother had never lied to him, but a normal life felt impossible. He looked down at the puzzle box before shoving it in his pocket.

[5.5]

Wesley knew it was hard for Cajal to believe, but it was true this time. They were as good as free. His savings were safely in an account for Cajal separate from him, set up through a depository for his schooling. All he had to do was put the tool in some weird-ass sculpture that would be at the ceremony, and he'd get his last big paycheck that would start their new life.

"Look at me." Wesley knelt and lifted Cajal's chin to see his face. "Can I have the puzzle box?"

Cajal pulled the box from his pocket and handed it over. Wesley quickly altered the numbers on its face, and the box slid open.

"I'm going to show you some magic."

Cajal smiled. Wesley knew he didn't believe it was magic, but it made the learning fun, and his little brother couldn't resist when he did these things with him. Cajal dropped his backpack and sat on it, his narrowed eyes focused on every step.

Wesley watched Cajal's eyes track his movement as he lifted the decorative antique from inside the puzzle box.

"What is it?"

"It's a tool of some type," Wesley said. "And it's very, very old," he added when he thought about the price it had brought. "Put your hand out."

Cajal obeyed, and Wesley placed the relic in the boy's cupped hands. "What's the color?"

"The colors are mixed together," Cajal answered, his brow furrowed with frustration.

"Okay. Close your eyes. Can you see the network in your mind?"

Cajal squeezed his eyes tightly closed with focus. "I do." He then continued, not bothering to mask the monotone in his voice, when Wesley tapped his duffel, indicating he wanted something from the new school books they'd been reading together. "The cerebellum connects the Oscult of Intuits to their network. It is the place of human voluntary motion regulation and forms part of the Rainbane hindbrain in Sahaja Intuits."

"Good. What does it look like?"

"It's silver and looks like a knot of tangles in the back of my brain."

Wesley smiled. "Can you open your eyes and still see them?"

Cajal squinted one eye open, and Wesley laughed.

"It's not funny," Cajal said, closing his eye tight again. Wesley knew this part was always the hardest.

"It's okay. Open your eyes."

Cajal pushed the relic at his brother and jammed his hands into his pockets.

"Let's look at the puzzle box and go over it. Then you can practice while I run this errand." The pilot had announced a delay, and Wesley wanted to be rid of this last connection to his past. He placed the relic back in the puzzle box and closed it. He shook the puzzle box and got the effect he desired. Cajal looked up and stopped tracing the floor with his foot. Wesley ran his fingers over the numbers. His father had first shown him the Sudoku game. Wesley found this puzzle box during a job in Egystan. It used Sudoku in its locking mechanism, so he used it to teach Cajal. Their mother had been really good at the game. The memory of their parents flooded his mind and wrapped the last string of determination around his heart. They would have the normal life that had been stolen from them when their parents died.

"You miss them, too, don't you?" Cajal said, and Wesley recognized the familiar pain in his brother's face.

"Yeah," Wesley said, taking Cajal's hand and putting it on the code line with the numbers missing. Every line of numbers on the box had just enough numbers missing that it was nearly impossible to complete the puzzle unless you knew the code line. Once you had the code line, you could finish the squares and open the box.

"Do you remember the code line?"

Cajal bit his lip. "I still have to write out the hints."

"That's fine," Wesley said. He had learned much faster, but functioning under duress created a different type of memory. Cajal was going to have the time to learn the right way.

Cajal pulled his little notebook from his pocket and slid the mechanical pencil from the strap that held it snug to the notebook's side. Cajal clicked the eraser end to get the lead to pop out at the tip. "I would remember the code if you didn't make me erase it every time I wrote it down."

Wesley didn't speak.

Cajal began to scribble, speaking in a quiet voice like he was just letting his thoughts outside. "Five energy forms."

Wesley watched as he wrote them down with the names given by his school-book.

1. Heat, 2. Liquid, 3. Particle/Wave, 4. Gas, 5. Thought.

Wesley had made three the first number in the code line. *Everything is both particle and wave,* Wesley thought, just as Cajal mimicked the same words as he worked and scribbled the number three down.

"I liked them better when we called them fire, water..." Cajal cut off his muttering when Wesley tapped his duffel again.

"You have to learn the school terms to understand the science behind your networks."

"I don't need the science," Cajal said, taking the puzzle box from Wesley's hands and closing his eyes. Wesley knew each of the numbers for the puzzle box code was a color Cajal could see with his network. He also knew Cajal figured if he could do that without the science, he could learn how to turn fire into sparks without it.

"Can you see them all?" Wesley asked. "The numbers as colors in your network?" he added, knowing it was hard to focus on the academics of the network when Cajal so intuitively used his network. But energy exchange was a different level of skill, and he wanted Cajal to learn the right way, not the hard way. Not the painful way he had.

"I can. The five crisp colors of the five networks that reach to the Oscult become hundreds of hues, and I can see every number as a color." He was running the eraser along his lip. "The orange now is the only one that doesn't disappear."

Cajal opened his eyes and noticed his brother's hand was wrapped around his own as he held the puzzle box.

"The orange is brighter in your mind because you connected your energy to me when I touched your hand. Orange is the EvP network and is the network used to push energy to the physical world."

"Why did the other colors disappear?"

"The colors are always there, but you see the color of the network you are using," Wesley said, pulling his ring from his pocket. "What you see is about your perspective."

"What's perspective? And what's the perspective when I can see hundreds of hues of color?"

The prism stone set in the ring caught the white light from the hallway, and a rainbow of colors refracted through its clear-cut stone as Wesley set the ring in Cajal's hand. "Perspective is just a viewpoint, a way of seeing things. Those hundreds of hues can only be seen when you are open to every solution. Think of it this way — when you are trying to see the right number for the code, you have to be open to all possibilities. That is when you need every hue of color. However, once you know the color and the number that goes with it, you have a single answer, and you need a direct line to communicate that with the outside world. The crisp color of the orange line of the EvP network is all you will see when you are giving an answer to the world." Wesley's eyes looked past Cajal at some distant place. "The conversion of energy through the five species networks you hold which allow you to, for example, take in light, turn it to fire, and expel it back into the world, can be incredibly dangerous and needs to be governed by someone who has first learned how to see every possibility, consider every perspective." Wesley closed Cajal's hand around the ring. "It can be painful if you release it on yourself or others without control. Hold this — it helped me when I was learning."

Cajal blinked slowly as if the ring made a connection in his mind, then looked up at him.

Wesley watched the determination in his brother's eyes become confidence. He could do this with his eyes open now that he had his brother's ring. He had felt the same way when his dad had given it to him.

[5.6]

Cajal smiled. His vision was blurred as he allowed his eyes to relax and not focus on any one thing around him as he looked into his own mind. "I'm doing it," he whispered, almost to himself. *I'm going to learn so much when I get to my new school. Wesley will be the proudest big brother ever.*

Wesley spoke quietly. "Talk me through it."

"I can see the Oscult body like a tangle of silver in my mind, and the network color of each species. Red for the Intuit line." Cajal breathed, squeezing the ring as if it were a cue to jump to the next network. "Blue for the Immortal line." He quickly pumped his hand on the ring, his mind using it as a trigger to leap to the next network line. The blue line made him feel...something uncomfortable. "Green for the human line," Cajal said, feeling a release in his shoulders. He could sense the room around him with all five of his senses. There was even a taste in the air. He tilted his head. "Why are you not breathing?"

Wesley released his breath with a puff. "I was thinking about teaching you how our minds can connect at the Oscult. It would let me see what you are doing with your network."

Cajal shivered. He didn't like the idea of anyone else in his head, not even his brother. He kept his eyes closed so Wesley wouldn't see his discomfort, but Wesley could always read him. "Don't worry, little brother. I looked into how the school teaches it, and it is less invasive. I'll leave it to them. Now, finish up."

"Yellow for the Griffon line." Cajal squeezed the ring again, and orange flashed in his mind and disappeared. "The orange for the EvP," Cajal said with a sigh of failure. "I lost it." Cajal frowned, and his focus on his surroundings returned as his network went black.

"That's still great," Wesley said.

Cajal couldn't help his smile. "Was it?" He had felt so close to his brother at the end, almost as if he were helping him, but the sensation had been distracting.

"Yes. Practice in the room while I'm gone, and you can show me when I return."

Cajal was disappointed at the reminder his brother had to leave, but the small success felt good. "Wait!" he said, dropping the pencil he held in the same hand as the ring and nudging the notebook away with his foot. "I can *see* the code for the puzzle box."

"Okay — what is it?"

Cajal knew Wesley was anxious to get the antique back out of the box and to its final drop. He focused on the puzzle box in his hand, then squeezed the ring in his opposite hand, his thoughts open to every possibility. The hues of color fanned out from the five networks. He closed his eyes, fatigue made it harder now, but he had his brother's ring. He could do it.

Cajal startled when Wesley took the ring from his hand and pushed it onto his right thumb as he held the box with the relic in his left hand. *I get to keep it*, he thought with excitement and felt his back straighten.

Wesley smiled. "Just follow the energy in and out."

Cajal pulled the residual energy from each empty box where Wesley had selected and hidden a code number. Cajal's mind rolled through hundreds of colors, searching for a match to the energy wave he pulled in from the empty square. Cajal could see each number and store the energy in his Oscult. This was a transfer of energy to thought, or he could pass the energy back to the puzzle box and expose the numbers just as Wesley had marked them.

Cajal wanted to experience that moment of touching the world with a spark of his energy. That conversion of energy was cool.

"Use thought energy to pass the energy between your networks and touch my hand," Wesley said. "It is easier to keep energy the same. It is harder to convert it to something different."

Cajal grinned. His brother was going to show him how to convert energy, not just see solutions.

Wesley stretched his palm out to Cajal.

Cajal never opened his eyes but sensed where his brother's hand was and touched it. A small current of electricity passed from his finger to his brother's palm. Cajal jumped. His eyes flew open, and he stared at his brother.

"You did it!"

"I did!" Cajal shouted, then pursed his lips with a wave of doubt. "That just felt like the shock I get when I take my socks out of the dryer."

"It is similar. The only difference is you created it from the air, watched it channel through your networks, and controlled its release."

Cajal stared at his free hand. The ring was still a little too big, even for his thumb.

"You really did do it. Let's get this box open." Wesley tapped the box with its contrasting wooden structure and its technological face. "Open it."

Cajal grinned and punched in the numbers he had stored as thought in his tangle when he decided to convert the residual energy to electrical current. He paused, realizing he didn't know in which network he had made the choice to do so. He wondered if that was significant. He bit his lip and looked at the numbers that were revealed in the code line on the glowing top of the puzzle box.

The puzzle box top lit as the rest of the empty nine boxes filled with numbers and the box drawer slid open.

"You are going to be an impressive Intuit," Wesley said with a fist bump to Cajal's ring hand.

Cajal grinned with pride, watching Wesley take the antique carefully in his hand and make it disappear when he wrapped it with a masking net he pulled from his pocket.

"We just have to get you into that school," Wesley said.

"I don't need school," Cajal said, wanting to ask him how he'd made the masking netting work. "You can teach me better than they can. Let me go with you."

But Wesley took the card and swiped the door panel again, handing it to Cajal when the door clicked. "Practice," he said, pointing Cajal inside before turning to head toward the stairs.

Cajal stood for a while in the open doorway. The familiar wave of emotion hit him. It sometimes took a while, but Wesley always came back. Cajal wiped hard at the tear on his cheek. Wesley would be back soon this time, and they were going to hang out the whole trip.

He twisted the puzzle box, its lit hologram squares on top now blank and ready to be used to hide something new. He kicked his backpack to nudge it into the room, then sat down hard on the bed and raised his arm to throw the puzzle box. He didn't have anything special to put in it.

He wiped his face again. "Stop being such a baby," he said out loud to himself and swiped his finger across the box he cradled in his left hand. The blank squares rolled through number sequences.

Wesley had shown him how to set the puzzle box the day he gave it to him. They had spent the whole day together that day trying to find something really cool to hide in it. He closed his eyes and focused on the network of silver in the back of his brain. It was that day that he first learned to see it. Cajal opened his eyes and looked around the room. The two twin beds made Cajal feel grown-up because his bed was identical to Wesley's with its own night table and lamp, but he couldn't practice in here. He needed an adventure. He would surprise Wes with something really cool in his box. He jumped from the bed and raced to the door.

[5.7]

V-Kasana watched as the stewardess interacted with the headmaster of the Emitime School, pleased again that so many people he considered a threat to his work didn't know his face. He was headed to reconnoiter the sculpture area and paused when the alarm went off in that direction. *Max is scheduled to send one of the Dalenborn for the relic pickup at the sculptures tomorrow,* he thought. Now he was concerned too many people were getting involved. He'd evaluate the area and make a final decision. *Doing the pickup myself reduces the risk of problems.*

"Thank you," Asher said to the stewardess and removed his hand from his chest.

"Did it help?" she asked, her hand rubbing his back. By the look on her face, she, too, noticed the alarm from the sculpture area had stopped. It had blared just before she had raced into the headmaster's room, then two more times while she waited for his medicine to work. *She appears as thankful as me to hear it go silent,* V-Kasana thought.

"Someone touching the sculptures, I suspect," Asher said with a smile.

She nodded. "I won't have to check it out since the alarm stopped."

"Thank you. The medicine helped very much. Please go ahead with your duties, I will be fine."

"Okay." She patted his shoulder and then pointed to the button on the side of his chair. "Push this." She demonstrated, and a hologram screen appeared in thin air in front of him with a list of items displayed as icons. She pointed to the one in the middle. "This one calls one of us, but this one"—she pointed to the corner—"calls medical staff, and this one calls the Marshals."

V-Kasana shifted around to view the column on this floor from an alternate angle, placing his back to them. The call system had been updated if it could be used to call the Marshals now.

"Thank you very much. I will be fine. I feel much better already."

V-Kasana rotated once more just in time to see the stewardess smile and hand Asher the bottle of medicine. "Good. I better get started on my sector walk-through."

V-Kasana cradled Asher's correct bottle of medicine in his pocket as the stewardess turned and seemed to notice a young boy exiting from the stairs. Her furrowed brow and glance at her watch said she wasn't pleased to see a child roaming alone this close to launch. She started toward the boy, and V-Kasana moved off toward the sculptures, which would take him by the headmaster. He planned to return the bottle he'd stolen, and now he could do it without re-entry to Asher's room. "You dropped your bottle of medicine," he said, tucking the bottle in the outside low pocket near the floor and removing the one Asher had placed there. No evidence. He liked the end of his plans to be clean.

He tapped his ringphone, preparing a message to move the dropoff day beyond tomorrow. *What day gives time for the traffic around the sculptures to die down?* he thought as he approached the sculptures.

[5.8]

Cajal spotted the stewardess. Her brisk walk said she was determined to see him back to his room. He took off at a run, but not away from her — that would make things worse. Wesley had taught him that. Rather, he ran right at her, waving at an old man seated outside his cabin. "Grandpa," he said just loud enough for the stewardess to hear as he passed her. He watched with his peripheral vision as she smiled and moved away.

[5.9]

Asher watched the boy running his way, his aura glowing orange — *Trouble,* he thought. Asher smiled as the boy waved at him when he passed the stewardess. He was trying to avoid capture. Asher chuckled, remembering his own thirst for adventure as a child. His seventy-ninth birthday approached, and he was glad for the moment of childhood memory. The memories of those dark years of war plagued him too often these days.

"Hi," the boy said, a little breathless.

"Hello, young man."

"My name is Cajal. Can you tell me how to get to the..." Cajal unfolded the map to find the name of the display. "Earth Day Sculptures?"

Asher watched as the boy's aura shifted from orange to yellow, so controlled he was certain he would have missed it had he not just had an episode that triggered a portion of his Griffon genes that heightened his vision. The G125 tablets he kept in the nitroglycerin bottle manufactured on earth weren't as effective as Nathan's original injectable form, but his injectable wasn't on the market. He considered penning a letter to the man.

He had not felt the chest pain associated with the beast since the war, the war that nearly brought his Griffon through full transformation to destroy what human was left in him. *We managed to save the children,* he thought. The only solace in a dark time. It was the children saved during the war that led him to the school where he had been now for more than forty years.

The boy's aura appears yellow now, Asher thought as he watched him cock his head to one side, waiting for an answer. Sahaja Intuits could often flare glimpses of the other species from their human network. A child with that kind of Intuit network control over their human network had to be from the school, but he didn't recognize him. A quick thought about the possibility of his mind failing pushed him to ask. "Do you attend the Emitime School?"

"No, but my bro — um, dad is signing me up for next year."

Asher smiled, feeling a renewed strength. The flashes of color across the boy's aura reminded Asher of the deep loss the world had experienced with the extinction of the Rainbane Reborn, the only descendants of the Rainbanes who had all five networks fully intact, not just flashes of what once existed. The school was a well of talent, and he enjoyed training the students, though as headmaster, he did little of that now. "Well, then," he said, unlatching the straps of the seat. "Let's go see those sculptures."

"Wow," Cajal said as they approached, and he reached out to touch the glass. "The sculptures look so real. Can I touch one?" Cajal's eyes never left the glass as he stood before it with his head leaned to the side to match that of the dog staring back at him.

"I'm Asher. Cajal you said, correct?" Cajal nodded and Asher looked for a box or something. The boy was too small to reach the top of the glass, but his aura glowed violet with such happiness and contentment that Asher felt stronger just standing next to him.

"I shouldn't take them out this close to launch, but here." He lifted Cajal. The violet aura cascaded around him, and he felt fifty years old again. A Griffon's strength was the last thing to go, but he knew it was the boy's sharing of energy that gave him strength to lift him with such little discomfort.

The alarm buzzed when Cajal reached through the laser. He jerked his hand back, his body weight shifting them both back a step, but Asher noted the boy had pulled the sound of the alarm to silence through his network even before he had pulled his hand away. *Instinct*, Asher thought and was impressed with the child's natural adaptation to his environment.

"Make your hand flat and slide it sideways into the cylinder," Asher said, then watched as the boy's small hand wrapped the floppy ear of the Labrador whose head appeared to look up at him. Asher closed his eyes to look at his own single network. There were Sahaja of every species, but Sahaja Intuits had the strongest connection to the human network. All species had a link to the race of Rainbanes that were now extinct. If trained, Sahaja could track movement through their network with their eyes open. It took great effort to see the network in your mind's eye, even with eyes closed and focused. His own network glowed with a new strength, something that felt more like purpose. He and the Elderwise had to convince the Scholar's Council to push for transparency about the Tokoleh-Earth Alliance existence so children like this would not miss the opportunity to train their skills at the Emitime School. That transparency would also push the investigation of the disturbances near the exoplanet beyond the Milky Way. Something in his Griffon instincts told him their failure or success impacted the future for this child and others. He set the boy down, disconnecting their energies.

"Can I pet him again?" Cajal asked, then bit his top lip as if he regretted the request now.

Asher moved to turn off the alarm at the panel with his code. He lifted the dog from its shelf and placed him in Cajal's arms.

"Why is there a hole in the back?" Cajal asked as he admired the statue.

"The opening holds a candle to burn for an hour each day, to commemorate Earth Week," Asher replied, adding to himself, *a reminder of the Tokoleh-Earth Alliance, if they agree to reveal it.*

The Orbiter's intercom crackled followed by the pilot's voice. "All passengers. This is the final call to return to your cabin seats before launch check."

Cajal stared at the dog for a very long moment, then stroked the tiny emblem near his tail. "My br — um, dad..." Cajal bit his lip. "This symbol is for the Earth Alliance, right?"

"Yes. Does your dad work for the Earth Alliance?"

Cajal stroked the dog's floppy ear, then lifted it to Asher, avoiding the question. "If I work hard at school, he said I may be able to join a special team from the Earth Alliance."

Asher took it and turned to place it back on the display shelf. "The Earth Alliance has—"

"Excuse me, sir," Cajal said, and Asher turned from the display case to see the boy speaking to the steward.

Asher sensed the boy was creating a distraction while he put the statue back, realizing the boy might think they would get in trouble.

"Can you help us get into our seats?" Cajal pointed at the map he pulled from his pocket, drawing the man's attention down to him and away from Asher.

"Sure," the steward said, looking briefly at his watch and then the map where Cajal pointed.

The steward was quick to get them into their seats. Then, he pulled up his cabin roster to check them off his list. "Headmaster Sharma?"

Asher nodded, and Cajal looked uncomfortable. Asher smiled. The boy didn't know about them checking the roster. He was probably planning to sneak back down when the steward left.

"My room is downstairs with my father." He began unbuckling his strap. "I'll just head down there."

"No," the steward said firmly. "Stay with the headmaster till after launch, then I'll make sure you get back down to your cabin. What's your father's name? I'll tell the staff to let him know where you are when they do the cabin launch check."

"Wesley Sco — Hamilton," Cajal said.

Asher noted the steward didn't notice the boy's stumble but tapped a note onto the side of his screen. "Your name, and what floor?"

Cajal gave him his name and the floor and sat back in his seat. He pulled a puzzle box from his pocket. "Will you tell him I found Mrs. Jones?" He waved the puzzle box as if he had been sent to get it from her.

"Sure, kid."

Asher leaned back in his chair. Cajal's aura was orange as fire. Asher's ability to see auras was rare, and he was grateful for it now.

The steward checked their straps, a few other details, and headed to the next cabin.

"Mrs. Jones?" Asher said, realizing the boy was nervously fidgeting with the box. "Did she give you the box?"

Cajal shifted the box from hand to hand.

Asher let the silence sit. The boy didn't want to lie to him but was being careful.

"Jones is the key word to indicate I'm safe, and Smith means I'm in trouble. My..." Cajal hesitated, then waved the box. "It was a gift."

He hadn't answered the question, but Asher let it slide as he seemed to calm while he worked the puzzle box. *Cajal,* Asher thought about the name the boy had given. His focus on the puzzle reminded him of his precious Alana. *Would our child have been this precocious if you and he had survived?* Asher released the memory of his wife and gripped his chest as the pain took his breath.

CHAPTER SIX

WESLEY DARTED FROM THE room. Cajal was gone, and they had given the final call for launch. He never should have left him. He should have taken him with him. The dropoff had been too easy; maybe it was a trap. Someone had taken him, but he'd been so careful. He ran both hands through his hair and tried to take deep breaths. *No one knows about Cajal.* The thought was a comfort, and his breathing began to slow. He had gone looking for something to put in that box — Wesley was sure of it — but where did he go? He headed down the corridor, determined to take the elevator to the top floor, then check the stairs and every floor all the way down.

"Watch where you're going," said the man stepping from the elevator when he bumped Wesley's shoulder while pushing his ponytail to his back.

Wesley continued checking the map as he entered the elevator.

"Damn the Source."

Wesley heard the man's shoes halt in the hallway with the curse, then pick up pace as if he turned back. Ponytail caught the elevator door and stepped back inside. Wesley returned to reviewing the map but kept his peripheral vision aware. The man stood in the corner, his arms folded, watching the numbers on the panel. He appeared frustrated that they were headed to the top floor, but he didn't bother to push another button, which meant he had been headed down, not up. K-hold was the only thing below their floor.

Wesley looked up briefly. He was getting careless. *You're not free yet.* He nodded at the man and looked back at the map, but he felt the man's eyes remain on him. The elevator opened and he stepped off, quickly stepping to the left in case the man followed. He watched the elevator doors close in the reflective glass designed to make the space feel larger. The man's eyes met his.

[6.1]

Kita flipped open the final checklist of the flight manual and ran her finger across the first sentence backward from period to capital letter. She was grateful for the little tricks she had learned to keep the mundane from becoming errors.

Motorcycle, now fully convinced she was the appropriate human by virtue of a few correct passcodes, awaited command from his pilot.

"Your precheck finished?" Kita asked, not looking up.

"Yes, all systems satisfactory for low atmosphere flight. Recheck for intergalactic beltway travel set for one hour."

"Excellent." She pulled Tom's phone from her pocket and typed to Heath: *I started final precheck, don't call me on the overhead. After precheck and launch, I'm headed to bed. She's yours till we get through the beltway.*

Kita set the phone to her left in a cubby that was packed with a magazine that must have been Tom's and the book she had brought — Sylvia Debair's book. If Heath handled the transition from Earth launch to the space station, followed by the injection for the beltway, she would have a little over an hour to check the interior Orbiter cameras and find Sylvia's launch seat.

The phone vibrated in the cubby. She lifted the book to reach the phone and read Heath's text.

HEATH: Sounds like you got laid by the liquor, not the ladies.

Kita smiled. She would probably like Heath. *Tom got laid, all right,* she thought. *Laid on his ass.* She hit the middle finger emoji again and hit send. Kita dropped the phone in the cubby and opened the book to the map page she had marked. *What maps does Motorcycle have access to in his archives?* she thought. "You know, Motorcycle, picking music is like picking your nose — it's a private thing. How did you select the music for your archive?"

"I didn't select it, and I didn't get to pick my nose," Motorcycle said, touching the protrusion on his face. "Although I do have a feature that lets you change my eye color."

Kita laughed, but she had her answer. Motorcycle held an archive specifically for Tom, and she would bet the music was a cover for the ample data space required for the archived data. *I need access to it.* Her ring vibrated. It was Jo. She tapped the band for the text screen, not the hologram for video.

JO: Where are you?

Kita typed a reply on the keyboard displayed on her hand. *Getting ready to launch. Can I call you later?* It wasn't a lie, but Jo wouldn't understand how stealing an Orbiter related to helping the Earth Alliance.

JO: Yes.

Kita knew Jo wanted to talk. They were friends, but Kita wanted more, though she wouldn't say it. Jo was an Intuit, therefore, there couldn't be more. So, Kita had requested a transfer. Now this. All her past shoved back at her, and no one would understand the danger until it was too late. She had to do this. Sylvia could not help the Separatists. She felt glad for the purpose it gave her. The distraction.

[6.2]

Cray tightened his ponytail as he stood next to the steel doors, eager for the elevator panels to open. The whole ride had been a struggle for his mind to recall why the man on the elevator looked familiar. Finally, he had remembered. The doors slid open, and he burst out, "Max, remember that thief who got the best of you in Tiran?"

Max looked up with a scowl. "There's an argument starting up between one of the 'new recruits' and one of the bred slaves on monitor three."

"I'm not kidding, Max," Cray said, raising his voice for emphasis. "I just saw him on the elevator."

Max turned his back on the handful of monitors and faced Cray, his arms folded as he leaned on the Formica top that made a square in the center of the room. "Who is he with?"

"No one, I think he's a stowaway. He had a map like he was looking for a place to hide."

Max grinned. "Why don't you help him find a place?"

[6.3]

Wesley raced for the stairs. He could just scan each floor briefly and then hit the stairway. He'd report him missing and stop the launch if it came to that. He had made the dropoff. He would worry about the man in the elevator later. Cajal had probably already been returned to the cabin by a staff member. Wesley hit the stairwell door hard and pushed through to the stairs. He reached the second floor and glanced through the glass. *The cabins on this floor must be on the far side,* he thought, noting the dining tables were cleared. The marble bar reflected the moonlight from the 3-D wall display of the near midnight sky.

Wesley checked his watch at almost ten p.m. He made a mental note to bring Cajal here for breakfast and the sunrise on the 3-D display. A smuggler friend had mentioned it, saying, "It's the only way to keep your days and nights straight when traveling in space." Wesley hoped that was the worst of his problems this trip. A red light above his head flashed, and he bolted down the stairs two at a time. They were ready for launch, and he had only a few minutes. They would turn the stairway cameras on to check the stairwell soon. The third floor received a cursory glance through the glass. The clip-clop of feet on the stairs below forced Wesley to bypass the banister room on the fourth floor. Someone was coming to clear the stairwell before the launch. He didn't need any more attention.

Wesley reached the fifth-floor landing and realized the sound below had stopped.

The silence made his movement to face the door seem loud. Through the glass, he saw the floor where he and Cajal had entered to reach their cabin earlier. He checked his watch — 9:54. He could cut through the open recreation area and get to their cabin on the other side near the elevators. Maybe Cajal was back, finished with his adventure. Through the glass window, the free weights and recreation gear were now under chrome-fitted shields to prevent movement during launch. His hand froze half-twisted on the door handle; the shield covering the rack of basketballs had eyes. He registered that it was the reflection of eyes behind him in the glass of the door one second too late.

Pain lanced through the back of his head, the floor swayed, and then there was nothing.

[6.4]

Sylvia flipped through the pages to ignore the grip of the straps in the launch seat, but the relaxation effort failed. The straps down over her shoulders and across her chest tightened with every breath. She closed the book and reached down to press the button below the seat for the hologram screen. She tapped the icon to adjust the air vent flow high above her. She pressed again, then again. "It's really hot in here," she said to no one. The air seemed stagnant, and the straps pinched her shoulders with the movement. She leaned her head on the headrest to force her lungs to take in air. Orange glowed in her mind even with her eyes opened.

Sylvia closed her eyes, hoping the pain starting behind her eye would go away. A silver thread of light flashed from a dark tangle in the back of her mind. The orange disappeared, and air seemed to move deep into her lungs. *Relax.* She watched the silver run from the tangle to a sheath of color that stretched down her neck and out to her hand. She traced the raised letters on the cover of her newest book with her eyes closed. *The Recollectors* embossed on the weathered leather gave the book an aged feel she loved. It felt very...familiar, like the column she touched coming in. Sylvia's eyes flashed open. Her heart flipped to a stop, then raced as she gouged at the button below her seat as if it were a help button. Orange flashed bright in her mind, and the latch she pulled at burned her hand. A vision flashed in her mind: a pool of blood, a body. She had awakened from dreams this vivid before but never had them while she was wide awake. She had to get off the Orbiter. She had to stay on Earth. Something was wrong here.

"Ma'am, are you okay?" The stewardess tapped the icon to close the hologram screen on display but Sylvia ignored her. "Ma'am," the stewardess said again, but Sylvia continued to tug at the latch. She knew her eyes were wide with fear because they were letting in too much light.

"I need to get up."

"You're okay. This is common for first-time travelers."

"No, I need to get off. I can't go."

"I have the medicine I told you I would bring from the medical staff." The woman took Sylvia's hand from over the latch. "Galactic dice!" she shouted, jumping back and dropping the packet of medication. She stepped away from Sylvia and scowled, rubbing her arm from shoulder to hand. "That was unnecessary."

"I'm sorry," Sylvia said, feeling relieved that a sliver of her fear was gone but uncertain what she had done. She could at least think now, the color in her mind more an afterglow — still burning, but a dying ember.

The woman's face relaxed. "I shouldn't be so thin-skinned." She smiled and bent to get the medicine from the floor. She used her left hand, shaking her right as if it was tingling. "My sister used to do that. I learned to keep my guard up against accidental encounters till she came back from Emitime."

Is that the hospital? Sylvia thought. "Your sister did what?" she asked, but the woman had already started speaking.

"This is really difficult for some people the first time." She handed Sylvia the packet of medicine. "It dissolves. You won't need anything to drink."

Sylvia nodded and let the packet fall into her hand. "Um…" *She's talking about first-time travelers, not your condition,* Sylvia chided herself.

"Yes?"

"Never mind," Sylvia said, twisting the necklace at her throat. Meki had said he would join her for launch, and she considered asking the stewardess about it but changed her mind. *Courage isn't courage if you're never afraid.* "I was just reminding myself it's okay to be afraid sometimes and just keep going."

"That sounds like good advice."

Sylvia touched the book again as the stewardess walked away.

I think my biological father told me that, Sylvia thought, remembering the phrase about courage just before a tinge of that vision flashed and made her nauseous. Sylvia pushed away the thought. The only parents she had were the two people who had raised her with more love and devotion than she could describe. She wouldn't reach for memories of the ones who had abandoned her.

[6.5]

In the elevator, Cray slipped the interference chain around the thief's ankle. He relaxed just a little. Intuits were very dangerous when they wanted to be, and he wasn't taking any chances with this one. However, if he managed to get him to the lockout room on the K-hold floor, Max would have him either broken or dead within a half hour of launch. Either way, he would move up a notch in Max's estimation, and that was the path to success.

CHAPTER SEVEN

MEKI SLID INTO THE launch seat next to Sylvia, clipped the straps, straightened his tie, and brushed a hair from his coat sleeve before Sylvia could speak. "Sorry, love. I received several calls that created more work, and there was a queue at the stairs when I tried to come up."

"Not a problem." Sylvia smiled. She had been prepared to do this alone. Now, she didn't have to. Meki was here.

"*The Recollectors* is a work of art," Meki said, pointing to the book in her lap. "It was brilliant to have some of the pages fold out."

A little feeling of success bubbled in her thoughts. "Is that your favorite thing? The maps?" Sylvia asked as she opened the book to one of the fold-out maps and thought about her personal copy of the book. It was in her suitcase. She'd had it specially bound and enjoyed the special touches she had added for herself.

"Actually—"

The speaker above them interrupted his words with a blast: "This is your pilot, Captain Braxton. The launch cameras are on. Staff will be placing your launch seats on automatic lockdown. Please make sure you are in your seats and ready for launch."

"You better place it in the panel at the side of your chair before launch."

Sylvia did, then cupped her hands to fight the urge to pull at the strap across her chest. "How did your calls go?"

"I received a call back from the security team at the GCS. The Earth Week security seems to have increased, and I need to deal with a few more details before we arrive. I'd like to make those calls before we reach the beltway." Meki grimaced. "I noticed you're wearing your trainers. The calls shouldn't take long, and we can do a quick tour before tomorrow. They should have the broken lift functioning by then."

Sylvia tried to look down at her sneakers, but the straps were too tight. She thought about telling him she'd rather go to bed, but he seemed quite excited to show her around. She felt a tremor in the Orbiter, and she gripped the seat arm. "Can you tell me about the different floors on the Orbiter?" Sylvia asked, trying to distract herself.

"Absolutely," Meki said. "Well, the lowest level of cabin features is the K-hold."

"K-hold?" Sylvia asked, her curiosity piqued.

"The K-hold on this trip is housing a Dalen work group," Meki began.

Sylvia smiled. Meki's face said he realized the conversation was distracting her from her discomfort. "Thank you," she said just as he spoke.

"The Dalen serve..." Meki paused when the stewardess arrived.

The stewardess rubbed her arm unconsciously before reaching over Sylvia's head to key the automatic lockdown. "Your sector steward told me you were coming over, so I saved this seat for last check." She said to Meki, "Thank you for getting here quickly."

Meki gave a nod, and the stewardess left. "The Dalen serve a purpose."

Sylvia appreciated his efforts to keep her mind occupied.

"They often complete jobs no one else will even attempt. Some of them are dangerous, so they have handlers."

Sylvia's stomach tightened, and for several minutes, she focused on breathing. Meki's voice seemed to go distant just before she felt a slight pop in the Orbiter, like it had unsnapped from the mountain. Meki was talking, but she couldn't hear his words. Her arms and legs were heavy when she tried to lift them, and her abdomen and chest were smashed with the weight of the straps.

The Orbiter exploded into the air.

Sylvia screamed. They had to be flying straight up. She managed to grip her shoulder straps just as her stomach dropped to the floor.

"Don't hold your breath," Meki said when Sylvia's yelp of surprise turned to silence.

Sylvia took a breath. Her stomach seemed to find center again, and she released the straps.

"They've dropped the boosters. We're past the Karman line, which..." Meki paused and squeezed Sylvia's wrist in support. "...is about sixty-two miles above Earth's sea level. The International Federation of Aeronautics and the UBN consider it to be the line between Earth's atmosphere and the rest of the galaxy."

"Oh." Sylvia swallowed the bile in her throat and tugged at the strap across her chest. "Why do we have rooms if we have to stay strapped to a seat?"

"They will be by to release the auto-lock since we may transition right to the beltway. The Orbiter's news channel is reporting solar flares, so we may not dock at the local space station. Regardless, the worst part is over." Meki twisted the ring on his hand. "Once the auto-lock is released, you can go to your room and rest till I come back. Then we'll crack on with the tour."

"Thank God," Sylvia said, her hands relaxing to her lap. "Rest is the one thing I've wanted since I got on this flight."

[7.1]

In a small, isolated room in K-hold that created its own gravity, Wesley pushed at the smooth wall with his good hand, trying to reorient and stand. Two of these rooms existed on every floor to allow emergency work that might need to be done during launches and didn't require lockdown like the rest of the Orbiter. He tried to focus to remember what they were called, but his head throbbed. *Lockout rooms*, Wesley thought, trying to look around. His left eye was almost completely swollen closed, his right eye was matted shut with blood, and he was certain his left arm was broken. He cradled his arm and misshapen hand as he slid back to the floor. Bile rose in the back of his throat as he touched the bone protruding from his index finger just below the middle knuckle. Despite his efforts to pull energy from the particles that formed the wall, his efforts failed. The brace they had on his leg caused too much interference for him to move energy between his Intuit networks. The arm fracture was still aligned and hadn't broken the skin, but he couldn't heal the arm or his hand with that damned brace at his ankle, even if he could stomach realigning the small bone. His head lulled back against the wall. *I'm going to pass out again.* He forced himself to try to make a fist, asking the pain to keep him alert. *Cajal. They can't find out about Cajal.* It was the only thought that kept his mind focused. In that focus, he heard the heavy breathing of his assailant.

"Your freakish games of energy exchange can't help you now, Intuit," his captor said, holding something reflective.

Wesley recalled the stainless steel retractor he could no longer identify through his blurred vision.

"I regret I let my anger push me to be so destructive so fast. You can call me Max, though you may not have known that was my name on Tiran."

His movements indicated he was wiping something from the tool. *My congealed blood,* Wesley thought. He struggled, through the unrelenting pain, to recall any face from the Tiran job that matched Max's blurry outline.

"We're past launch, and I've checked — you don't show up on the rosters. For once, your con-artist tricks have backfired." Max moved to the front of the table, clearly unable to keep the smile from his face. "No one will even know you're missing."

Wesley vaguely remembered a stewardess dismissing him and Cajal at the fuselage entry door checkpoint. She probably never checked them off the roster. He smiled despite the pain. These men thought he was here alone. A tear streamed from his closed, swollen eye. *They don't know about Cajal. He will be safe.*

Max strode forward and slapped him hard.

The pain shuddered him back to his reality.

"Before I'm finished, you will beg me to let you die, but it will not come till I rip out that Sahaja Intuit network braided around your spine. Yes, that's right. I know you're a Sahaja Intuit. No standard Intuit could have done what you did on Tiran."

Wesley wished he felt like smiling at Max's ignorance. If Max knew the truth, he'd be in even more danger than death. The Separatists still hunted Rainbane Reborn like himself for worse things than death. His parents had instilled in him the importance of hiding that truth with their death.

Max squatted within Wesley's blurred sight, and Wesley held his breath to avoid the gasp when Max gripped his chin, turning his face up.

"You made a fool of me once."

Wesley felt the cold metal of the retractor at the skin near his finger's exposed bone.

"It won't happen again. Where is the nesson you stole when our paths crossed the first time?"

They're not looking for the relic I placed at the drop. Wesley took another breath, trying to keep his hand from moving. *They want the Curganesson ring.* The weight of the retractor shifted near the exposed nerve and sent pain shooting up his hand, then released, allowing him to think again. He groaned. *Are they connected?* The thought made him recall the graft the woman had crafted to hide the Curganesson ring around her wrist. His one mission for the Earth Alliance. *The one good thing I've ever done.*

The door burst open, and Wesley thought he recognized the voice of the man who had brought him here, the one with the ponytail. "We've had a fight in a side corridor of K-hold, and two men are dead."

"Well, get it cleaned up and get the bodies in the crematorium before—"

Ponytail interrupted. "I tried. The staff came down for after-launch floor checks already and..." Ponytail paused. "I don't know if they were dead before launch, but it's a mess. We had one body moved before the Orbiter staff arrived, and I told them he was in the K-hold infirmary. I plan to tell them he died there when the Marshals ask why we moved the body."

Through his blurred vision, Wesley watched Max stand and walk back to the table near the door where Ponytail stood.

Ponytail took an involuntary step backward, but Max stared at the table where he laid the retractor. "Get the body you moved into the crematorium. The body will be cremated and dumped with the trash."

"But the Marshals will request the roster and know another man is missing."

Max turned his back to Ponytail and stared at Wesley.

Wesley slumped against the wall, hoping to convey a sense of helplessness that wasn't far from real. The position allowed him to use his peripheral vision, which was less blurry in this eye. Max lifted the retractor again, and Wesley gritted his teeth. The pain was already so intense he could barely form thoughts.

"I have just the man for your infirmary," Max said, squatting again.

He was so close Wesley could smell the sweat of his exertion when he pressed the retractor edge against the exposed nerve. Wesley screamed.

Max released it. "You almost look too good to have survived a launch unharnessed."

Wesley panted and swallowed back the sigh of relief for the moment of focused thought. *Why does nerve pain hurt so damn bad?* He closed his good eye, already feeling the angst to do what Max wanted to not feel the pain again.

"I want you to concentrate. Tell me where you hid the nesson, and when you wake up from your coma in the infirmary, I may let you live."

Wesley knew he would only suffer worse. "I can show you," Wesley croaked, his throat raw from being choked earlier by Ponytail, who now stood at the door.

"Take him to the infirmary and have medical put him in a coma."

Ponytail grunted. "You want a desensitization chamber tagged for him later?"

Wesley flinched, and he saw Max smile.

"I see you've had an exposure to the chambers?"

Wesley's mind was racing. He had no idea where the Curganesson ring was now, but he had to convince them to keep him awake. He had heard of the rehabilitation coma treatments used on Dalenborn who caused too much trouble, but he had actually experienced the desensitization chamber, and it had almost broken his mind. He had to survive and see Cajal to the safety of the school. It was the only thought that stayed his mind against collapse. "You can keep your training wheels on me." Wesley jiggled his ankles with the braces. "I'll take you to the Curgan—"

The blow was fast and hard. Wesley felt his head strike the wall with a thud, and then darkness claimed him as he felt his body go limp.

[7.2]

Sylvia smiled, though her body chaffed at the launch straps. Comfort in that luxurious bed beckoned. "Tell me more," Sylvia said, feeling chatty now that a shower and slumber were only minutes away. A verbal tour till the stewardess arrived to set them free from this roller-coaster ride would suffice. The thought made her think that next time, she would tell them her five-foot-four frame was too short for this ride.

"Well, sometimes the Dalen Overseers bring in new recruits if the ones born as Dalen can't do the work required. Many people who aren't born into the Dalen join for various reasons, but there are rumors that if a particular job requires a skill they don't have or is too dangerous, the Dalen are not opposed to securing less savory characters. Humanity is not fit to rule itself sometimes."

Sylvia realized Meki had thought she was asking for more about the Dalen instead of the Orbiter, but now she was too interested to tell him. "You mean taking people against their will?"

"Yes and no, they—"

Sylvia interrupted him. "They can't do that. There are international anti-slave laws."

"You're correct. The problem lies in the structure of the Dalen. They contract many new recruits by offering them what they want and delivering it."

"Then I don't understand."

"Many of the new recruits are those that have chemical dependencies. The Dalen house them, feed them, and provide the chemicals they have become so dependent on. In return, the recruits do many risky jobs no one else would do."

"Doesn't that get out of hand?"

"Usually, by the time the chemicals become their only happiness, they are doing jobs that are likely to kill them anyway. My understanding is they either get to a point where the chemicals themselves are in such a high dose that it kills them, or they die on the job."

"That's horrible and dangerous, not just for them. Have you seen it? I mean, do you know if that is really true?"

"I've seen it," a female voice behind Sylvia said, causing Sylvia to jump against the launchstrap. "And it is," the woman continued as Sylvia twisted to see the stewardess near her cabin door.

The stewardess lowered the tablet and stepped to their launch seats, braced on the wall. "I once noticed a crew extracting material from a mine that was collapsing, and I spoke to the foreman." The stewardess held the auto-lock till a beep signaled the release. "Each worker kept going back in even when sometimes the one who had gone in before didn't return. Every worker was alert, but there was a hunger in their eyes." The stewardess knelt and helped Sylvia free her latch while Meki worked on his own. "I asked the foreman, and he said the ones that live get their choice of relaxation when they get home. I didn't find out till later what that was, but I think I knew it when I saw their eyes." The stewardess stood. "There was nothing that mattered to them but that next hit."

Sylvia looked from the stewardess to Meki. "How can the Universal Bureau of Negotiations you were telling me about let people continue to be born into that kind of environment?"

Meki cleaned his glasses with a small cloth he had pulled from an inner pocket. "I'm a publicist, not a politician, but those people are considered bred Dalen — the Dalenborn — not recruits. Some of them end up in these guaranteed death jobs, too, but most of them just provide a workforce for normal services all over the intergalactic region."

"*Slavery* is the term I prefer," the stewardess added in complete agreement with Sylvia's disdain.

"It is not slavery," Meki said, standing. "The Dalen structure provides housing, food, work, and a stable environment for them. In return, the Dalen provide a workforce. They have a choice to leave, but many of them come from generations that have never taken care of themselves."

Sylvia stood, then sat back down when the floor started to sway. The conversation between Meki and the stewardess was escalating, but Sylvia was wondering whose shoes would be the hardest to replace if she vomited while the two of them argued practically toe-to-toe.

"How can they take care of themselves when their education is restricted, and the Dalen promote an ignorance that creates either dependence and obedience, or rebellion and addiction?"

Meki's jaw tightened. "Many of them live long, happy lives, breed more workers, work in their designated field, and die never choosing to leave."

"Yeah, and some of them die in a fight like the ones in the K-hold, and no one even cares. Their bodies will be dumped with the trash when we pass the IFA space station."

Sylvia's nausea vanished. "Someone died? On the Orbiter?"

The stewardess stepped back from Meki, and Sylvia looked up in time to see the woman recognize the very quiet despair Sylvia heard in her own voice. "When you came to bring my medicine, I..." Sylvia looked at Meki and then at the stewardess. *It sounds ridiculous to say I felt the death.* Sylvia took a deep breath. It had been her own fear that drove her to want to escape, not the impending death of strangers. She was being ridiculous.

The stewardess knelt again. "I'm sorry. I wasn't supposed to say anything till the Marshals came through. Did you see something?"

"No," Sylvia said, rubbing the notch in her neck under her gold chain.

"Forgive me." The stewardess reached toward her, then paused, pulling back as if thinking better of it. Sylvia tried not to feel hurt as the woman continued to speak. "I shouldn't have blurted it out like that. I just get so angry."

Meki twisted his ring. "I apologize, too. I just happen to know some very good people who are Dalen, and they are not slaves. They work very hard and enjoy their work." He nodded at the stewardess, then said to Sylvia, "I need to finish those calls. Will you be okay?"

"Yes, I'm going to shower and rest." *Unlikely,* she thought, then realized when she stood that she felt so tired she didn't know if even death would keep her up. Her finger brushed the embroidered emblem on the headrest of her seat. She shuddered with the vision she'd seen earlier. *I need to look at my copy of* The Recollectors, she thought with a restless energy.

CHAPTER EIGHT

T WENTY-FIVE LIGHT-YEARS AWAY AT the Galactic Core Station laboratories, Nathan lifted his lab coat from the hook on the back of the door. The empty hook beside it tugged at his thoughts, but he couldn't go there. He should take it down or at least use it. Elizabeth had been gone for years, but he had never used the hook for anything once he finally removed her lab coat. Elizabeth hadn't been wearing it at the time of the murder, so the police gave it only a cursory investigation. It was evident a Griffon killed the man, and with Elizabeth permanently stuck in her beast form, it wasn't difficult for them to make their case and have her shipped to Griffern.

He gripped the hook with his index finger and leaned his forehead on the door. Every lab experiment he tried pushed the evidence of her permanent separation from him. He had not found a way to reverse the DNA conversion once a human with Griffon DNA turned on those genes. He turned and faced the expanded lab. After his discovery of the Tokoleh energy channel modulation, the funding allowed him to add three thousand square feet to the space. Still, it had not brought him any closer to Elizabeth. He opened the vaccine refrigerator, pulled out the vial of G125, and walked back to his office. He needed to make some new. The sunlight from the large windows in his office were a contrast to the window-free walls in the lab. *One of my big successes.* Nathan scoffed, rocking the vial and recalling the roadblocks that had kept it from helping the Griffon population at large the way he had planned. He was not in the mood to make more as he paced back to the lab. The cold air blasted him as he buried the vial deep in the back of the refrigerator. His ring vibrated, and he tapped the speaker, recognizing the number. "Hey, Rosalind."

Rosalind's voice held command but was light as air. "I noticed the storage of G125 you keep here is getting low. Bring some when you come by the building. I may need your medical opinion on a few issues as we address security upgrades."

Nathan closed the refrigerator. "I may not make anymore," he said, knowing he had been putting it off. "I've got a..." Nathan paused, rethinking his words. He was still unsure what the video conference with Dr. Tucker would reveal. "A consult today. I can't come by."

"Nathan. We've talked about this. If you stop taking the medicine, you are at increased risk to convert your Griffon DNA. You were lucky to have only switched on the promoter expression of the gene when Elizabeth..." Rosalind cleared her throat.

Nathan didn't speak. He knew he was among the few people who could make her slip from her usual commanding sense of getting things done. He waited.

"You can't help Elizabeth if you're a feral animal with no recollection of your human mind. Bring the G125! If the consult is in your lab and not the hospital, Jenny can manage it without you. That's why you have an assistant. I'll see you when you come by."

The line went dead.

"Yeah, Casanova, that's why you have an assistant." Jenny's voice rang out from the far side of the lab, still unseen from where Nathan stood.

Nathan smiled and felt his shoulders relax a little. "Casanova? You're such a spy." He headed toward the hoods lining the far wall where he knew he would find her working on the DNA samples from the client on the Orbiter. The blood the client was scheduled to give while on the Orbiter was technically to test the new quantum transporter installed in Doc Turner's medical bay. The "consult" for the client was a piece he couldn't tell Rosalind about, not yet. Nathan ran his hand through his hair as he watched Jenny add a reagent to test if the samples remained consistent despite their quantum transport from the Orbiter to his lab here at the GCS.

"I don't have to spy." Jenny remained at the hood, not turning to look at him as she worked. "When you come in, hang out in your office staring at the hook on the back of the door, and talk about giving up on your research, I know you've been with a woman and you're feeling guilty."

Nathan didn't speak but turned to walk back toward his office. There were drawbacks to people knowing you so well.

Jenny dropped a pipette in the trash and turned on her round rolling stool. Nathan's lab experience told his ears what his eyes couldn't see. "Did the quantum transport from the Orbiter damage the samples?"

The wheels squeaked, and Nathan paused, feeling her eyes on his back. "She's been gone for years, Nathan. She wouldn't blame you for finding someone new."

Nathan closed his eyes and thought about last night. He had already decided not to see the woman again.

"Sex gives you connection at a physical level, but you won't let anyone in beyond that. Let someone in."

Nathan tapped his ring and continued toward his office as the hologram screen appeared over his hand. Jenny knew his question about the quantum transport was his effort to circumvent the conversation. She would have notified him immediately if the samples were damaged by the new transport system connecting his lab with the fleet of Orbiters. "Let me know when the samples are cleared of bloodborne pathogens and we can work with it outside the hood. It's our best lead. I'll get Elizabeth back."

"Then stop letting the beast in you make decisions," Jenny said, turning back to the hood.

Nathan pushed his office door closed. He was honest about his walls with the women he went out with. Why was it his fault no one could breach them? He lifted the few syringes of G125 that still lay on the desk and tucked them in a box. He stepped toward the window, the syringe still in his hand. From his fourth-floor view, he watched a Griffon descend near the Galactic Core Station Hotel. Its broad wings stabilized the massive beast as it settled to land with two riders secure on its back. *Maybe I'm trying to save me as much as you, Elizabeth,* Nathan thought, flicking the liquid in the syringe to knock out the air bubbles and wondering how close he had come to flipping on the genetic code that would strip him of his human mind and have him ostracized as a beast.

"Nathan?" Jenny knocked on the door before slowly pushing the office door open. "Listen, I'm sorry. I just worry about you."

Nathan didn't turn from the window, able to see her in his peripheral sight.

"I cared about her, too, and now I worry that even if we figured out a way to fix the genetic expression, we would never find her. How would we even get to Griffern, where they took her?"

Nathan turned from the window. "There is a group of Dalen who travel there to wrangle young Griffons born from the feral ones and bring them here to be trained for the hotel." He pointed with the syringe at the window.

Jenny smiled with visible effort. "Then what are we waiting for? Tell me about the new energy channel you found in the first sample."

Nathan gave himself the injection in his exposed deltoid muscle and dropped the syringe and needle in the sharps box. He slipped his button-down over his T-shirt. "I have to validate the discovery first." He sat at the desk, Jenny leaning over his shoulder as he scribbled a protocol. "Once you clear the blood, I can compare it against our old samples using mass spec for the DNA sequence I think is different."

The phone rang out in the lab.

"Grab that," Nathan said. "We can discuss the details of the technique from De la Cour's publication after I do this video conference. By the way, Rosalind knows you're a post-doc. She likes giving people a hard time."

"She calls me your assistant because you forget I'm a post-doc. It reminds you." Jenny winked. "Some of De la Cour's work also might augment ours with the upcoming appointment for the Immortal deciding between cancer treatment assisted cryo-regen and full regeneration."

Jenny moved toward the phone as she spoke. "You want me to take the G125 to Rosalind's office while you conference?"

Nathan checked the time on his ring. "I've got an hour unless Maggie's calling to juggle my clinic schedule." He lifted the box of syringes. "I'll take the G125 to Rosalind at the security building. You manage the conference call with Dr. Tucker, I'll get the phone."

Jenny squeezed his arm as he passed, and Nathan recognized her appreciation of opportunity. *I need to give her more responsibility. It's just so hard to let go.* He reached for the phone. Then, he let it ring when he read the number. He recognized it only because he'd signed so many death certificates for the Dalen working there. He didn't need to hear the prerecorded message. He knew where to go.

[8.1]

Sylvia let her hand linger under the hot water before twisting the knob for the shower. *Rest.* She was going to shower and rest. She put her back to the shower's heat as she faced the mirror, and her hair fell in chaotic sprigs from the once tight bun. *Who had strawberry, and who had blond?* She remembered the confused question she had asked in her childhood when science taught her why she didn't have the dark hair and brown eyes of the people who loved her, who she called family. *I want dark eyes, not blue, so I can look like you,* she had said, crying in her mother's arms.

The mirror fogged with the room's humidity and stole her features even as she watched her crystal-blue eyes disappear. A loud thud knocked the door, and Sylvia jumped. This flight was going to kill her. She relaxed, her hand pressed against her bare chest, and took a deep breath, turning toward the door. It was probably Meki. She closed the bathroom door. It could wait till tomorrow; her shower and rest could not.

In the steaming shower, Sylvia stood in the stream of water. The silver tangle she could see now more visibly at the back of her mind seemed the root of her synesthesia. Colors fell through her mind with each individual blast of the shower spray. The minutes were hours as she tried to find the warmth, not the color, of the water cascading against her as her senses combined. *Maybe I should take a bath instead of shower,* she thought, bracing against the violent shudder she always felt at the thought. Even as a child, she had not liked standing water. She closed her eyes, trying to balance her senses. The color shifted to sound with her effort, but it was loud and crushed her ears. She covered them to mute the unnatural echo that made the water resonate like crashing water to a swimmer trapped by an ocean wave. She was almost in tears. *The tangle of silver shimmers like the veil map.* Sylvia squeezed her head in her hands. The vision again, the pool of blood, was now red eyes. The tangle in her mind glowed. Her fingers gripped the grooves in the tile, and she leaned into the wall away from the water, exhausted by the effort to manage whatever this was. *Rest,* her mind begged. *The veil.* Sylvia pushed from the wall. *It's different in my copy of the book.* She stumbled out of the shower and rushed back to the bedroom, falling to her knees at her suitcase. Her phone pinged, and she turned toward the makeup bag in the bathroom where she had tossed it. She lifted her book and moved to the bathroom, flipping to the page with the transparent water map she had named "The Veil." She marked the page with her finger and lifted her phone to read the text.

MEKI: Little late for the tour. You rest. I'll take you to breakfast to watch the sunrise.

"How do you watch a sunrise in orbit?" she typed without hitting send. It was almost eleven. He probably thought she was sleeping. She rubbed at the circles under her eyes, recalling the last few weeks. The slow onset of the synesthesia after the migraine, the reader who had given her the photo that troubled her so much, and the fanatic who threatened that his life was forfeit without the coordinates to the Lost City in her book. She deleted the text. She was sleeping in tomorrow. Tonight, she was reviewing this page. She pulled on the terrycloth robe and felt the deep carpet of the bedroom envelop her feet as she walked toward the turned-down bed.

A rapid knock at the door stole the small comfort she felt, and fatigue cascaded like darkness through her mind. She grasped the foot of the bed. Meki must have changed his mind, but she would rest tonight.

The pounding persisted, and Sylvia trudged to the door, more than a little anger taking root at Meki's persistence.

Sylvia opened the door. The last tendrils of her nerves were ripped bare at the sight, but her scream was lost in the gasp of air when the bleeding woman collapsed against her chest, knocking the wind from her as they hit the ground. Sylvia scrambled from underneath the woman as the door swung shut, and the book in the woman's hand dragged blood down the front of her robe.

The door had closed automatically, and Sylvia shuddered, the silence reminding her that her scream had been silent as well. The woman was sitting upright now on her knees.

"Don't tell them where it is," the woman whispered, but Sylvia wasn't concerned about the book.

Sylvia helped prop the stewardess, whom she now recognized as Jezel, against the bed in the angle where the bench and the footboard met.

"You're going to be okay. I'll call for help." Sylvia stepped on the corner of her robe in her haste to stand and almost fell on the woman before catching herself on the bench.

Jezel touched her arm. "I'm okay," she said. "It's not as bad as it looks." She reached to wipe the blood from her lip. "The book just busted my lip."

Sylvia knelt back down, afraid to pull against the woman's grip. "What happened?"

The woman smiled, and blood touched her teeth. "I found my book." She waggled the book in her hands, and Sylvia saw the blood from the woman's lip that had so freely coated the book's edge and her robe.

Sylvia started to stand again.

"No," Jezel said, and the fear in her eyes stopped Sylvia cold. "Listen first."

"Alright," Sylvia said. "But are you sure you're okay?"

"Yes, it's just a busted lip," Jezel said. "You can't tell them where it is."

Sylvia noted she didn't see any active bleeding at her lip now. "Go on," Sylvia nudged, watching the woman's face.

"I found a short, stocky man reading a book waiting near the elevator. He hid it and walked toward the stairs when he saw me."

Jezel coughed, and Sylvia suspected the force must have caused the split in her lip to reopen with fresh blood.

"It seemed suspicious, and I thought maybe he had stolen my book, so I followed him after giving him a head start on the stairs." Jezel rubbed her sleeve across her mouth, and Sylvia sat back a little, relieved to see that seemed to be where all the blood had come from. "He entered a side hallway that led to K-hold, and I found him arguing with another man. The other man was bald and older. He was trying to give the bald man the book, I think to hide it, but the bald man threw it, not even looking. It happened so fast. The book hit me before I realized it." Jezel touched her lip again.

It was swollen, but Sylvia couldn't see the split causing the bleeding. It was probably on the inside of her lip. "Let me get a cold rag for your lip," Sylvia said. The woman looked pale.

"Let me finish," Jezel said, halting Sylvia's movement. "When they realized I was there, the stocky man ran at me. He tackled me before the bald man wrestled him off me. It was almost lockdown, so I ran to one of the lockout rooms on that floor."

Sylvia watched the woman, feeling her face might look as pale. "Did you tell the Marshals?" Sylvia remembered the rumor of the fight in K-hold. That could not be it. No one would be fighting over her book.

Jezel gripped her stomach with a look of surprise. "Don't tell them where..."

"I know. Don't tell them where the book is. I won't. It's your book." *Readers are insane.* Sylvia thought, then twisted her lips at the reminder that every writer was a reader, which made it all make sense. Then Sylvia's attention was drawn to the new stillness of Jezel with her head lulled awkwardly to her shoulder. The force of the last several minutes flooded in on her with accumulated thoughts connecting in a pattern that shifted everything as Sylvia lifted Jezel's chin. Sylvia felt nauseous; Jezel's face was ashen. "Don't tell them where it is," Sylvia whispered, realizing Jezel hadn't told her everything because she thought she had more time than she did. Panic struck through her, and she reached to the woman's lip without thought. It was swollen, but there was no laceration. The blood had been coming when she coughed.

Jezel winced at Sylvia's touch, reaching to stop her, then her head lulled to the side again, and her arm went limp.

Sylvia pressed her fingers at the woman's neck — the pulse was thready. Sylvia leapt to her feet and scrambled to the bathroom to find the empty medicine packet from the stewardess. There had been a number on it. She dumped over the makeup bag as she lifted it in a rush, pulling the foil packet free from underneath. She repeated the number as she moved to the phone.

She glanced at Jezel but couldn't tell if she was still breathing. Tears burned her eyes as she pressed the numbers on the digital phone screen built into the nightstand. She breathed herself when someone answered on the first ring. "A woman is dying in my room," she blurted, then gave her name and room number and hit speakerphone to race back to Jezel.

CHAPTER NINE

"ONE DEAD. ONE MOSTLY dead, and that's my official report," Marshal Pierre said, kicking his feet up on the main desk's corner edge.

Michael picked up his coffee cup near Pierre's feet, giving the size fourteen boots a shove off the desk to move past him to the opposite chair. "Is the medical team down there already?"

"Yes," Jia said, coming in to brief them. "I called them when Lanky confirmed the scene."

Pierre nodded and raised his *La Planete Des Singes* mug in salute at Jia's use of his nickname. "The Dalenborn is dead, and the new recruit." Pierre paused to check his notes. "Dalen number 14214, is in a coma per Max Fisher, the man in charge of the Dalen workforce staying in K-hold. Old Doc Turner gave the man's care over to the Dalen medical provider." Pierre leaned forward in his chair. "Doc said they carry their own specialized medical teams due to the hazardous work they do and are better equipped than we are to care for him since..." He nodded his head toward the door, representing the one team member still not with them. "Long missed the chance to get the man off at the space station when we didn't dock."

"What happened there?" Michael asked Jia.

Jia stepped closer to the two men, braced her hip against the desktop, and crossed her legs. "Long went directly to Major Haddock's flight deck to report the incident in person since, at the time, we were uncertain about details, security compromise, etc. But there was no response except a display message on the outside door hologram from the robot co-pilot indicating he was not authorized to open the cabin while Major Haddock was resting, and that any flight questions should be directed to Captain Braxton, who is flying the first leg of the trip. At that point, Long—"

The door swished open, interrupting Jia.

Booker Naidoo strode through the door. He met the Marshals with penetrating green eyes set brilliant against his dark skin. Michael smiled, seeing his niece's eyes in the ones staring at him now. Naidoo's intricately designed braid held his long hair in place, forcing it to fall down his broad back. It was his hair length that spurred his Marshal nickname, Long.

"Does my sister wait this long for you?" Michael asked, taking a sip of coffee.

"Your sister is better looking than you, so I make her a priority," Naidoo said, grinning.

Michael laughed. He knew she kept them both in line. He missed her and his niece. *I need to see them soon,* he thought, then pulled his attention back to Long.

"Captain Braxton is flying the first leg of the trip and, as you'll soon find out, making good time of it." Naidoo picked a piece of lint from the embroidered patch of his Marshal uniform. "The space station is bottlenecked with flights from other Earth Sectors due to solar superstorms, so there was no mandatory dock at the space station." He tapped his ring to bring up a hologram and smiled.

Michael knew that smile. He had seen it many times when Long had covered his back. It was a smile at the rush of energy that vibrated through his EvP connections from the red sandstone at the center of his ring. Long was an EvP by galactic category, but his family was one of the few who could trace their human ancestry back through Earth genealogies, his heritage tracking back to a Scottish immigrant who married a Jamaican beauty and held a family so tight even the war couldn't bury their history. He admired Naidoo's commitment to family and was grateful his niece would have her father's EvP strength.

"You have the new beltway maps in your ring programming?" Pierre asked, standing to get closer to the hologram displayed above Naidoo's ring.

"Aye." Naidoo pointed to a coordinate on the screen. "And Captain Braxton has us now already to the beltway injection point, and we've started our first orbit for injection."

Michael caught Jia's eyes. They were usually on the same page, but his time in command of his own team meant he respected the chain of command. He stood at Jia's nod of agreement, then spoke. "Rosalind sent a secure message regarding a relic that's been recovered and may be on its way to the GCS via one of the Orbiters. We're considering this a connected incident until proven otherwise. Rosalind will want no stone unturned and still want us to arrive at the GCS on time." Michael watched as the Marshals all nodded, acknowledging the UBN director's expectations to make the impossible doable. "We could pull out of the injection, but it would be difficult, expensive, and leave us for possible days at the space station."

"In a jurisdictional pissing contest about whether the death occurred before the Karman line," Pierre mumbled, crossing back to his seat and taking a gentle sip from his oversized mug.

Michael walked to the whiteboard and tapped its edge. The hologram screen overlay disappeared, and he picked up a marker to write by hand.

He pointed at Pierre. "I'll need the notes from your inquiries. Start typing up a report for Rosalind." Michael began writing down the information they had so far. "It might not be any more than a fight that left two men unconscious to suffer the trauma of an unharnessed launch, but the Overseer has some explaining to do. I'll find out who gave the green light on the K-hold prelaunch check." He wrote that up on the board under points to investigate.

"Naidoo, check with Captain Braxton and get Major Haddock involved. Confirm the point of no return with injection."

"I finished the security checks, Long," Jia interjected, looking at Naidoo. "There are no breaches, so you can use the secure system from the computer now."

Naidoo nodded and typed on his enhanced hologram screen that laser displayed on the back of his ring hand.

"Pierre, you check with the Dalen medical team to confirm they are capable of managing the man till we arrive at the GCS. You know how Doc Turner hates touching people..."

"Especially sick ones," Naidoo chimed in with a grin as he typed.

Michael shook his head, but it was true. "And find the protocol options for discarding the body of the deceased man. I'll be down to help with investigation interviews when I answer a few questions from the staff."

"Jia's already running a cross-reference on the staff to see if any connections link them with the Dalen." A thought flickered in Michael's mind about his missing that Jezel was a regenerated Tokoleh. Jia hadn't missed it. *Focus,* he thought. His personal vengeance for a death in his previous squad would have to wait. It was creating a distraction.

The main security phone rang on the desk, and Jia shifted to reach behind her to pick it up, still leaning against the massive central desk. Her face clouded as she listened.

[9.1]

Water gurgled with the hiss of air, moving oxygen through the humidified ventilator. The thief's chest rose and fell with it.

Max watched just beyond the door, his hand in his pocket fingering the lighter the Dalen surgeon had removed from a graft of skin in the man's side. It had been found on X-ray, the last identifiable item for the man, and Max had stripped him of it. *You won't need it, thief. You won't remember yourself when I am done.* Max smiled at the convenience of this opportunity. *Once I have access to the desensitization chambers in Piano Cave, you will tell me anything I want to know.*

Boots smacked the hallway behind him, pulling Max from his thoughts. He turned. "The thief is now only a number?"

Cray nodded confirmation, touched the send feature on his ring, and then walked away.

Max tapped his own ring to pull up the file Cray had sent. He typed *Dalen 14214 DNA* on the hologram screen. The report popped up on the hologram, and a cascade of DNA sequences filled the screen. Max's shoulders relaxed when he saw the thief's species code in the sequence. He didn't know how to read it but recognized it was different from the real Dalen 14214. Max smiled. *It's the thief's DNA that now matches the files for Dalen 14214.* "Only Cray and I know of the switch," he said aloud. Max dropped his arms with the quiet admission. The thief's DNA was now in the system if the Marshals checked. The real Dalen 14214 body was ash that had been dumped with the trash on fly-by and dispersed near the space station. The thief now replaced him as Dalen 14214, subject to the contract that gave Max the power to do whatever he needed with him. Soon, the other dead man from the altercation would be sent to the crematorium. The Marshals were unhappy that the only people they had for investigation were either soon to be ash, or comatose and unrecognizable to anyone. With that thought, Max stepped inside the thief's room. "How is he?"

The nurse, who was focused on the tubing system, looked up at the question. "Dr. Sarron said he is stable now, but we almost lost him."

"Please thank the team," Max said with sincerity. He did not want the thief to die before he got what he needed from him.

[9.2]

Michael headed for the elevator as soon as Jia briefed them on the call. He knew there would be trouble with the newly regenerated Tokoleh Jezel. He mentally kicked himself again for overlooking that in her bio. Now, he was headed to a passenger's room where the Tokoleh woman was just short of death per the dispatcher's alarm. The dispatcher had called Jia after patching through the medical alert to Dr. Turner. Why had Jezel gone there? What had happened? Questions were accumulating faster than he could find answers, and he was angry with himself.

Michael knocked before entering the room, though the door was ajar. The supplies outside the room were indication enough that Dr. Turner was here. At least fifty small hand-braided Celtic knots of forgiveness hung on the gurney in the hall. Each one was hand-woven by Blondan, the assistant who performed all the physical exams for Dr. Turner.

"Page one twenty-six, paragraph three is positive, but negative for sentence one seventy-three of the same," Blondan said as Dr. Turner scribbled in a handheld notebook, and Michael stayed against the wall waiting as Blondan palpated the ashen Jezel's abdomen. Michael had never gotten used to the fact that Dr. Turner didn't like people and refused to touch patients.

"Check paragraph six, page one again," Dr. Turner said.

"I did that while you were writing. It remains, but it is only a two-by-table one."

"She'll have to go to surgery." Dr. Turner turned for the door, noticing Michael. "Come see me in the clinic if you have questions. She has internal bleeding. She's going to surgery now. She is too unstable for cryo, and I'm not losing a newly regenerated Immortal on my watch!"

Michael nodded and held the door as Blondan, one of the few men he'd ever met taller and wider than himself, lifted the woman with gentle but expedited care. Her Tokoleh rebreather and monitor were in place. Blondan twisted and ducked his head to carry the woman through the doorway.

A woman sat on the bench at the foot of the bed, her face buried in her hands.

"Ms. Debair," Doc Turner said.

Michael watched the woman look toward them. Her eyes were blue and haunted.

"Yes, Doctor."

"Please have Michael bring you with him when he comes. I have a few more questions, and I don't want him to detain you."

"I'm a Marshal on the Orbiter, Ms. Debair. I'll see you down to the clinic," Michael said, with a nod to the doctor.

"Thank you," she said, fatigue in her voice. She reached absently for the clothes that hung on the open bathroom door as if they were waiting there for the tomorrow that was fast approaching. She stepped into the bathroom to change. "I'll be right out."

Michael nodded and turned to step out into the hallway to wait. He noticed a familiar face near the library access on this floor. The man had passed very close to him while he was preparing to take report from Jia earlier in the flight. The man calmly moved into the library, with no evidence of dis-ease, but he added the man to his mental checklist and decided to remain in the room, with the door ajar, where he could watch the hallway unseen and wait.

[9.3]

Once the bathroom door closed, Sylvia leaned against it and squeezed her eyes shut against tears. She took a slow, deep breath and pushed back at the ribbon of orange that swirled in her mind. Its movement seemed to spin and pulse with her headache. Gently, she pushed away from the door and removed the robe, only now realizing how practically bare she had been, shifting around the room with a group of people as they tried to save a life. The bathroom was cold without her robe, and she shivered recalling the doctor's words in her mind. *Regenerated Immortal.* The words were new and unfamiliar, yet they tapped at her thoughts like a finger tapping against thin ice covering a calm spot on a dangerous frozen river. Sylvia dressed quickly and stepped from the bathroom to find Michael sitting in the chair across from the striped bench at the foot of the bed. He was writing in a small notebook. Sylvia scanned the room before speaking, and she wondered if she would be able to sleep here after tonight. Her eyes met Michael's, and he stood.

"I'm sure this has been difficult, Ms. Debair, but I need to ask you a few questions as we make our way down to the clinic." Michael gestured toward the door, and Sylvia felt a flash of anger.

She had managed to keep her wits about her as a woman collapsed and almost died in her bedroom, and this man thought he was sweeping in as a hero to see her safely down to the clinic. She could find the clinic on her own. Part of her said she shouldn't be so angry, but it was the angry part of her that spoke. "I can make it to the clinic on my own, and I will answer your questions once I have assisted the doctor." She felt better once the words were out, and she didn't stop to see if he followed as she walked out the open door and made a left. She knew the doctor had turned that way.

Sylvia rubbed her eyes against the bright light of the hallway as she tried to read the placards that gave directions along the hallway. The stark walls had shifted from white to a panorama of colors and designs as beautiful as any estate back home. She rubbed her eyes again. The walls had been white, she was certain.

"It's visual imagery. The wall decor, that is." Michael reached her in only a few strides. "They display an image only. It's too much trouble to lock down pictures, drapes, etc. The staff turns them on once we are in the beltway."

She figured he had done something to her door to keep him behind her for those few moments. *Did he search the room? No, he hadn't taken that much time.* Sylvia barely had time to process the thought before the memory of her book gripped in Jezel's hands made her stumble. The image shifted to a manor with an ivy-hidden glyph that mimicked the one on the Orbiter's columns. Michael reached for her, but she pulled away, righting herself. Jezel's book was still in her room, and she was probably wrong for thinking it, but she intended to look at it before letting this man know it existed.

"What time did the woman appear at your door?" Michael asked, putting his notebook away.

Sylvia figured he thought that had caused her to stumble, and he was trying to put her at ease. So, why did it make her more angry? "I said I would answer your questions when I finish—"

Michael's ring chirped, and they both jerked at the interruption. He didn't pull up a hologram screen to read the message, so Sylvia figured it was private. She did see a flashing red five display on his hand before he tapped the ring off. "Damn it. I have to leave."

Sylvia felt relief that it appeared something would force him away for now, yet a part of her sensed that same impending doom she had felt with her first view of the Orbiter.

"Forgive me for interrupting your evening." His eyes locked with Sylvia's as he took a step between her and the portion of the wall where she tried to find directions.

She gave no response, but stepped around him to continue to read.

"I would like to say go on to bed and we will chat in the morning, but I'm afraid that would be misleading. I plan to return tonight." He glanced at something on his ringphone. "Or rather, I plan to return shortly since it is already hovering midnight."

Sylvia said nothing, letting her thoughts trace through a hundred ways to get back to her room and the book before he returned and still check on Jezel. *Jezel. What had the woman meant with the broken messages she gave me?* Sylvia thought, ignoring the barrel of a man before her. Finally, he pointed at a sign near the elevator, and she saw the arrow for the clinic. "Thank you," Sylvia said, pacing to the elevators, her mind still on the book shoved underneath the bed by one of the seizures Jezel had just before the doctor arrived. The doctor had told the man named Blondan that Jezel's Life Companion had been contacted and was meeting them at the operating suite waiting area. Maybe Dr. Turner would introduce her, and she could get some answers. The elevator dinged and the doors slid open, but Sylvia turned and ran back toward her room. *I need to get the book now.*

Sylvia's chest heaved as the elevator doors began to close. She had picked up her parka and wrapped it around her arms to hide the book. She was too afraid to glance at it till she was alone in the elevator. She hadn't seen anyone, and she was glad the elevator doors had closed. Someone had just started to push open the door from the library.

[9.4]

Asher held his left arm. It throbbed with a pain as familiar as the one that informed of pending Griffon transformation. Only this pain was the pain of a human heart taxed by years of Griffon restraint. Dr. Renner had explained the damage the process of Griffon transformation caused the human heart. Griffon hearts were twice the size of their human counterparts. The pain confirmed his foreboding that he might not survive this trip. He and Cajal had walked back to the sculptures once the steward had released the auto-lock on their seats. Now back at his cabin, Asher watched as the young man pushed on the door of the stairs. "Cajal."

Cajal spun. His eyes held the eagerness for adventure. "Yes?"

"I have something for your puzzle box." *Source of the Universe, forgive me for burdening this child,* Asher thought as the boy moved to come back. He had to hide the relic somewhere in case he didn't make it, and this child was special. Somehow, he knew it was the right thing to do.

"Really?" Cajal raced back, almost tripping as he tugged at his pocket, pulling the puzzle box free.

Asher reached inside his robe to the leather pouch hiding the relic. "You are the keeper of the key now." His Intuit wife's deathbed words to him, he would pass to this young Intuit. His episode Earthside convinced him his heart wouldn't survive a transformation. Better to put the relic back in the protection of an Intuit than give it to the Council. *At least till I know if they are going to reveal the truth to Earth. Cajal would be a student, and he could bring the key to the Council later. I'll write that letter to Dr. Renner. The injections might give me more time.*

Cajal hit some numbers on the face of the box, which filled the sudoku numbers and slid open.

Asher watched as Cajal looked up, eyes wide, then snapped his mouth closed as if to keep words from tumbling out. Asher pulled the key from the bag and placed it in the puzzle box. Asher wondered at that moment what Cajal was thinking as one of his hands traced his pocket, which appeared to hold something important to him.

[9.5]

It looks just like the one Wesley had, Cajal thought, forcing his hands not to shake with excitement. For a moment, he felt guilty for the hologram-mesh-covered piece he held in his pocket. He had meant to put it back in the open back of the dog but had wanted to see what it was before he did so. He was sure Asher had put it there after he sculpted the dog. Now the man was giving him a gift. He relaxed. He would have time tomorrow to put it back, whatever it was, and it would give him a chance to figure out how the hiding mesh worked. Wesley said a lot of people used it, but he had never had some of his own.

Asher paused, and Cajal thought for a moment he might change his mind, then realized he was just thinking. He watched him pull the relic back out from the box, then place the aged relic in Cajal's small hand. Cajal stared at it for a very long time, then blinked to pull his thoughts from the colors and sounds that raced through his mind. He looked up at Asher. It was different from Wesley's. He could taste the colors, and he almost said so before catching himself. A lot of people didn't understand that colors had a taste. Wesley did. "Are you sure I can keep it?"

"You must keep it," Asher said, then grimaced and gripped the robe at his chest.

[9.6]

The screen in the briefing room was dark, and Michael took his seat next to Pierre. A level five security meeting with the UBN director herself meant something very important weighed in the balance for the Tokoleh or Earth Alliance. The UBN was the united front of both.

Michael pulled out his pocket-sized notebook and nodded at the screen where Rosalind would soon appear. "She can identify meaning in the smallest detail, and you don't realize it till later when she has all the answers and you're still scratching your head."

Jia and Naidoo laughed while Pierre smiled. Michael didn't mind that the others teased him about his "affection" for Rosalind. It was his secret that she had helped his dark squad team when they lost their team member in a betrayal that went higher than his pay grade. That was his past, and it needed to stay hidden.

The screen flashed on, and the Marshals leaned forward. Rosalind Mathing's voice seldom rose, and she spoke sparingly. "I have additional details before you enter the beltway."

Rosalind's small frame moved gracefully from behind her desk, and she appeared taller in front of the wall-sized screen that displayed her to the Marshals. The robotics that stabilized her legs hummed with her movement.

Damn, she is beautiful, Michael thought when she pushed her red shoulder-length ringlets behind her ear and tapped the small device there to enhance her communication with them.

"First, the relic I advised earlier to be on watch for has been confirmed stolen. There is no evidence at this time that the thief or the relic is on any of the Orbiters. However, if it is, isolation of the item and the criminal before arrival at the GCS is understandably preferred. The large influx of people this time of year puts a strain on the security system. Your assistance in screening what arrives is appreciated. Second, tell me the details of the tragedy that occurred in the last hour aboard the Orbiter?"

The Marshals all looked at one another, finally landing on Jia, who nodded vigorously.

"No, Jia did not tell me anything when we spoke," Rosalind said. "It isn't complicated. You four are all here. I did not indicate I needed to speak with everyone, which means you were all already up. Pierre isn't cupping his ape mug with two hands as if the warmth could transport him to the South of France. So, it's cold. Therefore, he has been up long enough for it to get cold but too busy for it to be gone."

Pierre glanced at the mug stabilized with his one hand on the handle, propped on the knee of his crossed legs.

"Go ahead, Michael. I can tell Jia gave you the lead on it by the way she looked at you when I asked about it."

How does she watch so many faces and movements at once? Michael thought. He prided himself on observation, but she was a machine.

"Michael, let me hear the events that have my Marshals out of their warm beds."

Michael detailed the information they had so far, as well as the plans to conduct additional interviews with the Dalen and Sylvia.

[9.7]

Rosalind didn't wait for the gaping mouths to close when she pointed out several obvious points. People accustomed to mobility were often shocked at the observational ability one develops from a childhood of recess spent with your wheelchair parked under a tree.

Rosalind steepled her fingers and tapped them at her chin. *Nathan has another dead Dalen at the Piano Cave,* she thought before speaking. "The Dalen workforce is small. Find out their project at the GCS and contact me your first day out of the beltway." *Maybe these Dalen are replacements.* The thought reminded her she was still waiting on access approval to what was going on in Piano Cave. The work presently fell under the purview of the Tokoleh Governors. Rosalind dropped her hands abruptly at a thought. "Michael, there is an Immortal on the Orbiter named Xenos. Ask him to assist you with the investigation."

"Yes, ma'am."

Rosalind disconnected and smiled. The investigation was a UBN reason to connect with Xenos. He was on sabbatical from his time as a Tokoleh Governor, but he would know what was going on at Piano Cave. She just had to convince him her concern warranted a breach of Tokoleh protocol. Telling him a key to one of the Tokoleh-Earth Alliance Portals had been found, then stolen, would be of interest to him on its own. That would bring him to her for a discussion. Then she could offer her new find of evidence in the Archive that might identify the war criminal he was chasing. And that would be worth a trade of information about Piano Cave.

[9.8]

Asher breathed deep through his nose as the pain eased in his chest. *How long do I have?* he thought and reached for the pills he'd left in the pocket by his launch chair. *The medicine usually helps.*

"Are you okay?" Cajal asked, touching Asher's arm.

Asher patted his hand, touched by the boy's concern. "I just need to remember to take my medicine," he said, glad the pain had eased without a second dose. *Hopefully, the medicine will work long enough to see this through.* He lifted the relic from the boy's hand and placed it in the box. How could he explain the importance of the key's transfer and the purpose Cajal now held? "You must keep it safe. It is very special." He tapped the numbers on the screen to set the lock.

"What's the code?" Cajal asked, realizing Asher had locked it.

"It's easy as pie, but..." He paused when a pain tightened his chest. "You'll need these two hints. The second one is a seven..." Asher continued with a blow of air through pursed lips when the tightness released. "And the last five is an eight. It sounds like nonsense, but remember everything I said and you'll figure it out," Asher said. The lock would keep Cajal busy trying to figure out the code till he could explain everything. He rubbed his left arm. Maybe he'd forgo the formal letter to Dr. Renner about the injection and send a message instead.

"Are you sure you're okay? I can bring my dad back. He's really smart."

"I'm good. Bring your dad to breakfast tomorrow at the 3-D display dining room around nine if you like. I'll be there then."

Cajal squeezed the box tight between his two hands. His right foot was pointed toward the stairs, but he gave Asher a quick one-armed hug. "Thank you." Cajal tucked the puzzle box away and ran for the stairs.

CHAPTER TEN

K ITA STEPPED FROM THE cabin toward the flight console. "Motorcycle, pull up a map of Earth."

"Which one?" the robot asked as he scrolled through the maps flashing across the projected screen from his left eye.

"The most recent," she said, toweling off her hair.

"Very well," Motorcycle said, blinking twice to enlarge the map so she could see it from behind him.

"Stones end, Motorcycle! That's a map from before the Splintering. I said recent map."

"You mean most recent cartography, not most recently viewed. You humans have poor communication skills."

"Most recently viewed?" she said, moving toward the map. *Only the Archive and the Elderwise have this map.* The thought reminded her the Elderwise were bringing it to this year's Scholar's Council. *Why would Tom have a copy and be reviewing it?* "Leave it up," she said just as it winked away and a new map appeared.

Motorcycle mumbled, and Kita smiled. These robots were supposed to be the step before symbiosis and were said to have capabilities for mimicking human behaviors through a machine-learning mechanism. If Motorcycle had learned how to grumble under his breath, he was halfway to human. "Put the maps side by side," she said, flattening the veil map page in Sylvia's book on the small island between her and Motorcycle as he faced the flight console hologram screen.

"Present map of Earth and...pre-Splintering map of Earth," Motorcycle announced when the first map appeared again.

Kita studied the pre-Splintering map on the hologram and then placed Sylvia's veil map over it. She traced the faint silver-blue haze illustrated without the land mass in Sylvia's book. *The veil.* "It fits perfectly," she whispered. It had to be the Separatists who had given Sylvia a map of pre-Splintering Earth for her to create this veil. Maybe the map was Sylvia's payment for helping the Separatists. *A map for her book that had not been seen in centuries — that would certainly help book sales.* She lifted the book, holding the veil unfolded up to the light. And there it was, the pre-Splintering map hidden within the veil. "What else have you hidden here, Sylvia?"

A memory twisted in her with hope, then sorrow. Kita pointed at each map when Motorcycle joined her. "This one is Earth as we know it. This..." She pointed at the map with the single solid land mass. "This is the Earth pre-Splintering." She unfolded the veil map fully from Sylvia's book. "And this one—"

Motorcycle traced the map, interrupting her. "This one has no land mass."

"Correct, because the Waterworld predated visible land mass." Kita didn't point out what she had seen hidden in the veil.

Kita pushed away from the island. *Waterworld and Central Plain history were all but completely lost after the Splintering. What are you doing, Sylvia?* she thought as she reached back to touch the map.

"My machine learning indicates your slow, gentle touch of the map represents a human emotion unfamiliar to my learning log." Motorcycle moved his hand from the veil map to the pre-Splintering Earth map. "You remember this time when the land was whole?"

"No. I don't remember the Earth before the Great Splintering. Many super-continents formed and changed between the time of the Waterworld and the Great Splintering, which is what makes this map so unique. Unlike Pangea's break, some two hundred million years ago, the Great Splintering occurred during the history of the Immortals some forty to fifty thousand years ago," Kita answered.

"Yes. I have access to that general information in my database but have never interacted with an Immortal regarding its history."

"Well, you're out of luck here. I was a child during the war of 2050, just sixty-some years ago, and kept in cryo most of that time. I'm certainly not old enough to remember the Splintering thousands of years ago." Kita took her seat and sat back, thinking about how old she would be had her mentor not demanded she be kept in cryo. She unconsciously touched her face that still held the youth of her twenty-odd years. Twenty-eight? Thirty? She'd stopped trying to track the years. She'd been in and out of cryo too many times to remember in her childhood. "Technically, I'm probably almost a hundred when judged by years of time passed." Kita shrugged. "But in years lived, I'm in my late twenties by best guesses."

"You are Tokoleh?" Motorcycle asked, managing some frustration in his tone.

"Not Tokoleh." Kita looked down at the armrest. "Many children orphaned during the war were kept in cryo, not just Tokoleh Immortals. The Tokoleh expended much effort during the war. Their resources saved many lives." It was one of the reasons she had joined the Alliance and became a pilot. The other reason was more personal. She wouldn't share that with anyone, not even a robot with a memory she could erase. "What do you know about the Splintering? Do they build you with stock memories of events in Earth's troubled history?"

"Built. How rude," Motorcycle said.

"I'm sorry," she said, unwilling to point out that the symbiosis with a human he so desired required someone to agree to symbiosis with it. "So, tell me what you know of the Splintering."

"First, explain the emotion associated with the gentle, slow touch you gave the map. I need to log it for my learning."

"No," Kita said too quickly.

Motorcycle pulled back at the word.

His gesture made him seem almost human momentarily, and Kita grimaced. "Damn it, Motorcycle, you're a robot."

"I'm not a robot," Motorcycle said firmly. "I am a symbiotic companion selected by you, the pilot of this vessel, to facilitate a partnership for long-term deep space travel."

Kita startled. This was not a robot designed as a co-pilot for this trip. Tom selected this robot for a mission separate from common space transportation. She had to find out if that mission involved Sylvia and the Separatists, and why Tom?

She had to be careful. Motorcycle seemed to be new in his learning. The computerization that allowed her to be accepted by him by simply knowing the codes could be offset by his machine learning if she gave too much away. Hesitantly, she spoke. "Do you recall the plans we made before we landed? I got in a fight while visiting the local pub, and I'm having trouble with my memory." *Stay close to truth,* Kita reminded herself. Tom had got in a fight — with her. And the knot she had left on his head might very well impact his memory. She was sure the sedative she injected would. She didn't know how much machine learning Motorcycle had accomplished with Tom in the brief week it would have taken them to get to Earth. She wanted to get as much information as possible before she cleared and reset Motorcycle's computer memory later. She wanted as little evidence as possible of her being here.

"Perfect," Motorcycle said. "A negotiating tool. I will share that data information when you share the emotional data for my machine learning. What marks such gentle, slow evaluation of data that you gave to the map?"

Kita sighed. "No deal," she said, standing to take her hair towel back to the cabin.

"What?" Motorcycle blinked, then realized it raised the maps from the island to a hologram of maps now displayed between them. "What is wrong with you people?" He blinked again to make the duplicate screen go away. "It is a logical trade."

Kita smiled though her back was to him. "We're not logical. That's what makes us human." The sting of the words made her smile fail. She was unwilling to share it because it hurt too much to remember. She couldn't think about that. She now knew Tom had been part of something bigger than transport between Earth and the Galactic Core Station.

She couldn't do anything about Sylva till she confirmed her identity and if she was working for the Separatists. So, for now, she could figure out Tom and Motorocycle's mission. The Alliance would need to know if the Separatists were using Orbiters. This personal mission was revealing more information than half the directed exploits she had been given in two years.

"Come on," Motorcycle said.

Kita turned at the very human sound of it. Maybe the symbiosis of these robots was more like raising a child. It was as if Motorcycle had picked up the mannerisms of someone human but not yet able to understand the reasons for his patterns. Kita sat down on the edge of the bed in the cabin facing back out to the console where Motorcycle stared at her through the open door. She looked down at her hands. She remembered something her mother had said when training her and her best friend when they were young, before the war, before the cryo, before her failure. She had wanted her mom to demonstrate how powerful she was to her friend. She had thought it would make her friend as eager to develop her skills as Kita had been eager to develop her own.

"That would teach her that I value power," her mother had said.

"But you can tell her different. Explain you are just showing her," Kita had argued.

"Children will do what you do, not what you say to do," her mother had said, lifting Kita onto her lap as her friend called for her to come join her in the woods for hide-and-seek. Kita could still see her friend racing into the woods, eager to play rather than train.

Her mother's words did not seem a good answer at the time as she eased the determined furrow from Kita's brow with a gentle touch of her hand and a release of soft energy that bloomed in Kita like sunshine. She now realized they had been her mother's guiding rule in all that she trained them to do before she died. There had been so much death. *That's why they call it war,* Kita thought, then shook her head, wondering how she had failed when she had such a marvelous teacher. She wouldn't fail again.

Kita looked up and waited for Motorcycle to notice the eye contact. "Loss..." Kita whispered. "Or maybe reverence for something lost." She moved toward Motorcycle. "That's the feeling." Kita touched the silver-blue haze of the pre-Splintering map and then the veil map that sat perfectly over it. "The map reminds me of my mother. She used to tell me stories of the silver veil and the history of our species before the Great Splintering. They were just fables to teach me, but they were from a time with her." Kita looked up at Motorcycle and was surprised to see concern in his expression.

"I'm sorry," Motorcycle said. "And thank you." He rubbed at the sticker on his head as if it was a nervous habit. "That is an important human emotion to log."

Logging human emotion was the path to his symbiosis, and for the first time, she considered what it was to be this robot that wanted to be human.

"The only data you have not accessed is the second mission data for this trip. However, you created a separate password for it. If you hit your head and do not remember the password, I can give you the hint you left as a backup for your human forgetfulness."

"The second mission data, right," she said, trying to keep the keen interest out of her tone. *The Separatist Mission?* Kita thought. "Give me the hint, Motorcycle."

CHAPTER ELEVEN

SYLVIA FLIPPED THE PAGES of the book as she sat, waiting for Blondan to return. He had left her there in a waiting area while he collected the first readings since Jezel's placement in cryo. "She is stable enough for surgery," she heard him tell Dr. Turner just beyond the waiting room. She read the penciled notes Jezel had made about the place the book reminded her of. *She even drew an emblem next to the glyph I imagined connected with the manor,* Sylvia thought, reaching to run her fingers along the design of each, then felt her stomach tighten at the streak of blood thick across the page just beneath. She almost closed the book, but the angle of the light made her turn it instead. *There is something written under the blood.* Sylvia felt nauseous.

"So, page seventy-five, paragraph six is fine?" Dr. Turner's voice questioned as he walked through the doorway across from where Sylvia sat.

Sylvia jumped, the words finding a weird association since she was reading when he spoke and was still unaccustomed to their weird team approach to medicine. Blondan had explained his savant-like skill at visual memorization that made him a walking medical reference and the literal hands for the idiosyncratic Doc Turner, as everyone called him.

"Yes," Blondan answered, ducking to get through the doorway. "Actually, improved the last half hour in cryo-regen."

"Good. Put her down."

"Put her down?" Sylvia jumped to her feet, fumbling with the book. "You've just spent the last..." She glanced down to check the time on her phone, glad she had picked it up when she retrieved the book. "...hour or so trying to save her."

It was almost 1:30 a.m. Sylvia wondered if her fear for Jezel was mingling with exhaustion and making her feel dizzy and sick.

Doc Turner turned from the cryobay to face her. "Put down to full cryo," he said, "Not euthanize. You need some rest." He looked at her fully for the first time over his glasses that hung precariously at the end of his nose.

Sylvia relaxed. "Oh, sorry. I probably spend too much time at the vet office with the shelter team. And not enough rest recently," she conceded. "So, she'll be okay?"

He rubbed his index finger and thumb down his mustache. "Difficult to say, but her vitals are stable enough from cryo-regen now for her to go into full cryo."

"Is that full regeneration?" Sylvia asked, looking to Blondan since Doc Turner had headed toward the reception desk.

"No," Blondan said, waving a hand for her to follow him into the corridor. He popped back into the cryobay, where he manipulated some features she could not see from where she stood. "Regeneration returns an Immortal to their youth," Blondan said, stepping back to her in the corridor. "Cryo-regeneration allows Immortals to use their DNA to heal injury while full cryo is more stasis. It keeps injury from worsening." He hit some patterns on a panel, closing the cryobay door. "She needed to do some healing in cryo-regen before we could take her to surgery. Doc was afraid we would lose her otherwise. Her bleeding was severe. Now she'll wait in full cryo-stasis till the operating room is prepped."

"Why not regenerate then?"

"Regeneration has a high cost and..." Blondan looked at Doc Turner, who had met them in the corridor.

"And is a process that requires the Source," Doc finished.

"The Source?" Yeah, that was going to have to wait till she had some rest. Sylvia pulled the book to her chest. "Can I stop by and check on her tomorrow?"

"I think disintermediation is best done now, Turner," a firm, beautiful voice said from a room down the hall. "Jezel asked to speak with her before surgery."

Doc Turner stared over his glasses, then nodded at Blondan.

"Disintermediation?" Sylvia rolled the word around.

"Her economics vocabulary is like a separate language," Blondan whispered. "She was the Depository Symbias. Now runs an investment consulting firm. She's Jezel's Life Companion, so she is allowed to travel with her."

Life Companion? Sylvia thought, recalling Jezel had mentioned introducing them.

"Unless the Marshals make you part of the investigation team, her LC is the only one who can give permission to pull her from Doc's cryo care."

It appeared she would have this LC's permission, but Blondan's words sparked an idea. She would press Michael to be part of the investigation. After all, it was her book at the center of the altercation. The thought reminded her she was withholding evidence, and she grimaced, squeezing the book at her chest.

[11.1]

The room was silent when Blondan left her at the open door. A beautiful woman in a stunning suit and blouse turned toward her. Only the furrowed lines of worry marred her perfect skin. Sylvia watched as the lines relaxed at the touch of the pale hand inside what she assumed was a cryo system. Sylvia made her way slowly to the cryobed, unsure of what she would see inside.

"It's mine," a weak voice said.

Sylvia looked down at the book and then up. The beautiful suit followed her movement with sharp eyes, pursing her lips when Sylvia spoke. "The book? Yes. I know."

"No, the blood."

"Wait, love," the suit said, covering Jezel's hand on her arm with her opposite hand before turning her focus back to Sylvia.

"I'm Tessa Danquah. I know how important it is to Jezel that she speak with you before going into surgery, but she is far beyond where she should be doing so."

"I understand," Sylvia said. "I don't want to jeopardize her health."

The words seemed to relax Tessa, Sylvia noted, so she pressed on. "This is her book, and she asked me not to tell them where it was, so I didn't." She first met Jezel's pale blue eyes inside the cryobed. It looked like a tanning bed on steroids took an Indiana Jones Disney tour. She couldn't help but notice the glyphs that marked its top, now partially open.

"Thank you," Jezel said, her voice weak but determined. "The blood. It's mine. I tried to cover the numbers someone had written there."

Numbers? Sylvia's mouth went dry as she recalled the many requests for coordinates. "Do you mind if I record our conversation with my phone?" She paused, feeling the weight of embarrassment at not knowing what was actually wrong with her and how much to admit. "I'm having some trouble with my..." *Head? Mind? How do I explain?* No explanation seemed necessary when Tessa spoke up.

"You can record the conversation if you leave the book with us."

Sylvia thought about it. She had hundreds of books just like it. She had her original unique copy, and she had scanned this one while in the waiting room. She needed Jezel's information about the blood, the emblem, and the numbers. "Okay," she finally said to Tessa, then reached toward Jezel, halting before touching her. "I can't promise Michael or one of the Marshals won't come by looking for it." She handed the book to Tessa. "But I won't volunteer any information."

The red recording light glowed as she held the phone close to the cryo system, awaiting Tessa's guidance on where to place it. The woman was fiercely protective, and Sylvia's chest felt a little hollow as she watched the connection between them. Jezel's thumb circled a pattern on Tessa's palm where the two women's fingers loosely entwined. *Chad used to do that when we had movie night,* she thought, closing her eyes. Her life six months ago seemed too far away. "Will you tell me about the emblem you drew beside my glyph design?"

"It's a design we found on a wall inside the manor on Jezel's estate," Tessa said, a little guarded. She looked at Jezel, who smiled so widely at her that Sylvia felt she was intruding. Tessa pulled her eyes back to Sylvia. "Jezel thinks the man who stole the book recognized..." She paused, pursing her lips. "The emblem from that wall."

"Is that unusual? Do not many people know about the manor?"

"Why did you draw the glyph you drew associated with the manor in your book?" Tessa asked rather than answering the question.

Sylvia shrugged. "I combine things from my mind, my experience in archaeology during college. This particular glyph is commonly seen in tombs and on artifacts Earthside. It isn't rare." She traced a visual symbol of the Ankh in her mind.

The silence from the two women pulled her back, and she caught them staring at each other as if communicating without words about something she had just said. She almost missed Jezel's slight nod before Tessa turned to her. "Then why did you draw the one that is distinctly used by the Tokoleh rather than the one that is used Earthside?"

"What?" Sylvia said, reaching for the book before realizing how rude that appeared. *Artistic license,* she thought, her brain a blur as she waited for Tessa to find the page. Her mind flipped through a thousand images, then she gasped at the vision that haunted her dreams. The red eyes disappeared as quickly as they had appeared, and she put her hand at her mouth to stave off the wave of nausea.

Tessa watched her but held the book out. Sylvia took a deep breath, examining the Ankh on the manor's crest she had created. It was different from the one she recalled from the tomb. *How did I do that, and what does it have to do with the Tokoleh?*

Jezel coughed, pulling both their attention. Tessa quickly closed the book, laying it out of Sylvia's reach as she leaned in to adjust Jezel so her head raised slightly. "It's enough, my love. I know your heart. Rest."

Sylvia watched as Tessa pressed a kiss to the woman's forehead before tapping a glyph that began to close the top. Sylvia didn't dare speak till Tessa touched the lid gently and turned toward her. "I've been through this before."

Sylvia did not miss the determination now in the woman's eyes. "That sounds ominous," she said, hoping to convey that she recognized the weight of the situation.

"I almost lost her. She is my focus. I tell you that because you may be in danger, but I cannot be available to help you anymore."

Sylvia nodded, feeling something twist in her gut.

[11.2]

Sylvia pressed the playback button as she laid her phone on the nightstand so she could change. She straightened her suitcase on the luggage stand, refolding the items she'd dislodged earlier. She pulled her archaeology field jacket out. She often wore it when she was writing, as if that would keep her connected to the dream she had let go. She blew out a breath as she listened to Tessa's voice describe the fact that she had created a glyph on the crest of her fictional manor that she never recalled seeing before. "How did I depict a glyph that is located on a hidden wall buried inside their manor?" Sylvia asked the empty room. "Maybe it's just an error?" She tried to make sense of the fact that the Ankh she created was specifically different in a single way that made it a representation of the Tokoleh, a governing body of the galaxy she had not even known existed. *No wonder the woman is wary of me*, Sylvia thought. *It sounds unbelievable that I didn't do it on purpose, but I've never seen those Ankh designs before except in my dreams.* Sylvia's eyes went wide, and she paused in the half fold of her field jacket. She jumped up, racing to stop the playback on her phone. She slipped the field jacket on, the feel of it causing her to shiver with anticipation. She had to go back to the columns she'd seen coming onto the Orbiter.

[11.3]

Kita read the message from the Marshals on the screen again regarding the death in K-hold. She hadn't had time to consider Motorcycle's riddle of a hint regarding the passcode for the second mission data. She'd been bombarded with questions from Heath about the standard protocol recommendation for the beltway injection modification. They had accepted her recommendation to bypass the space station, which meant she had not yet had time to confront Sylvia. Now that she had found the pre-Splintering map in Motorcycle's possession, the recent chaos made the hair on her neck stand up. She would need to lie low for the next three days in stage one of the beltway. Focusing on what Tom and Motorcycle had been up to would keep her occupied and possibly prove valuable information for the Earth Alliance.

She looked at Motorcycle sitting to her right. "Mind if I call you M? Motorcycle is a long name."

"Acknowledged. I will add it to my list of alias names. However, Motorcycle is still required to access any sensitive data under passcode."

"I'm not interested in any sensitive data right now, just show me the recording of the transit out from the GCS last week. Did you...um...we have any delays due to the Orbiter's operating systems?"

"Don't you remember?" Motorcycle said, reminding Kita that M recognized her as Tom. M shook his head as he tapped the controls on the panel in front of him. "No wonder they use AI. It's a wonder humans remember their names."

Kita would've laughed if she wasn't concerned about what problems they might have with the modified injection or their three-day exit on the other side if Tom had compromised the Orbiter. "Is this the recording of the transit out?" Kita asked as the video rolled. Pirating of the Orbiters was a reality that had to be considered. Two had been attacked within the last three years with significant losses. "Pause it right there," Kita said, leaning across the console between them to zoom up the frame on the replay video from one of the external cameras. "Okay, M, it takes almost a day — at the least twelve hours — to get everyone loaded and the Orbiter checked for the return flight. Then three days in stage one of the beltway where we are now — moving away from the space station — three days in stage seven on the other side near the GCS, and literally nanoseconds in stages two through six of the beltway."

"Correct. Will there be a quiz at the end?" Motorcycled grinned. "I have an excellent memory."

Tom definitely mucked with this robot, Kita thought, *or maybe it was his machine learning.* Either way, she was grateful not to have to make the trip with a no-personality bag of bolts. "Yes, I'm counting on your memory," Kita replied, then touched the console. "Here, where I paused the video. Use this external camera as a reference point on the Orbiter and give me the computer's probability calculations for the Orbiter's return flight coordinates at each beltway based on the present conditions of the Orbiter. Once you have that running, remind me about the trip we took from GCS to Earth. Include our map discussion to give it narrative. It makes it more human." She felt a little ashamed and weird at the same time because she knew somehow that would matter to him, and it might get her info until she could figure out the second mission passcode. "I'm looking for NEs," she said. The coordinates would help her locate the nebulous-envelopes should she need to use one if there was trouble. The thought yanked Kita's mind. *NE Sim-transport via the Orbiter columns would be a key benefit of Tom to the Separatists.*

Motorcycle leaned back in the flight chair once the numbers were running. "The data regarding the map is in the second mission data and will require the passcode, but we forged our relationship when the UBN assigned me as a replacement for your previous dismantled AI, and we began our journey to Earth."

"You can leave out all the touchy-feely stuff, M, just give me the operational data," Kita snapped, now that there would be no map data.

"Big data's got your number." Motorcycle's soundtrack from his archive collection kicked on. "Someone wants to use the NE to dis...app...ear, but big data's got your number," he sang.

She was certain he added his own words. No Earth song included nebulous-envelopes. Ninety percent knew nothing beyond the space station.

"Sing with me," M said.

"No, and don't do that. You'll get your wires crossed." It freaked her out for him to sing when his face and design so closely resembled a human.

"Well, I think you can't sing. I think you're a robot. Real humans care about these touchy-feely things. Just on our way to Earth, you talked about how nice it would be when the Earth was once again whole like the map, not splintered and broken apart like it is now." Motorcycle gestured at the two maps that were still displayed.

Tom wanted Earth whole again? Kita stared at the map. Was Tom helping someone else? The Separatists wanted rule under the Immortals to be absolute. Why would they bother to restore Earth to a single land mass, and how would they?

"Wow, you're really good," Motorcycle said, causing the map to flicker when he tried to mimic her stare. "You seem human when you stare at the map like that."

"Well, I am human," Kita said, pulled from her thoughts of the map back to identifying NE escape routes. Tom had definitely been working with or for someone other than the Galactic Core Station. She would have to think about that later. She tagged several of the probability numbers and copied them into a command line of code she was running on an alternate screen.

"I knew it. You're an AI like me with a program modification for human."

"I work for the Earth Alliance. I'm an Escape velocity Puller who can't afford to get too close to anyone." She paused at how true those last few words were. "That doesn't make me a robot," Kita said, trying to wriggle any info she could from him about Tom by sharing a small piece of herself. She could erase anything she wanted from his memory.

M looked disappointed, and Kita watched his external visual screen pop up in front of him from a laser at his eye that beamed the information from his internal data system to the external screen. He searched for Escape velocity Puller. "I didn't know you worked for the Earth Alliance," Motorcycle said as *A, B, C, D, E...* scrolled on the screen. "I should learn more about EvPs."

Yes, Kita thought at the small success. Whatever Tom was doing, it was unlikely to be for the Earth Alliance. "Don't bother looking it up in your system. EvPs are as human as the rest of the population. Thousands of years have left no one as only human. Most only have a trace of their EvP, Griffon, or Intuit DNA, and we all have a touch of the Immortals in the human DNA we carry, but some of us have more. I'll explain it once I get these numbers down."

"Fine, I'll describe the trip to Earth with no touchy-feely." Motorcycle's holograph screen disappeared. "And I'll keep my playlist selection to songs from the last two hundred years in celebration of Earth's reset to that time period after the war," M said with what Kita had to admit was an impressive DJ voice.

Kita nodded. "Data, please."

"The Orbiter transitioned from the GCS to Earth with no significant operational defects."

"Now, that's brevity," Kita said, clicking through some of the internal Orbiter cameras to find an internal camera reference. She froze, then zoomed in on one of the camera systems. Sylvia stood on tiptoe, braced against one of the columns in the main corridor as she reached up over her head. "I gotta go. She's trying to use a nebulous-envelope." Kita jumped up, spinning the chair as she did so. *Where is she trying to transport and why?* Kita's mind was racing. *Does it have something to do with Tom's betrayal of the Orbiter?* Kita stopped as if she hit a wall with her final thought. *Can I do what has to be done to stop her?*

"What?"

Kita moved so fast that she stood with her hand on the door before M looked up. Motorcycle whistled low at the speed she had displayed to get there. "I take it EvPs are fast."

"And strong, but we pay a price. Run a standard probability norm on the vector I concatenated from the coordinates from each beltway stage. I marked it random variable X."

"How original." Motorcycle leaned toward her screen, then stood to move into Kita's chair.

"Bite me."

Motorcycle raised an eyebrow.

"Never mind. It's just a saying."

Motorcycle tapped his head at the sticker as if storing the information. "What fixed variable do you want me to use?"

Kita turned back to him with new insight as the door slid open. "Use two. I want a narrow window of probabilities between the coordinate of that internal camera on my screen and the external camera on yours. Call the cell number in your system when you have them." Kita checked her back pocket to be sure Tom's phone was still there as she stepped through the door to the stairs.

Motorcycle enlarged the camera screen and tilted his head at the lady in the picture, reaching well over her head to the top of a column. Motorcycle looked back at Kita, trying to gauge something.

Kita gave him the OK sign, yet she felt anything but. She would not transport with an Intuit again, but as the door closed, she realized Earth couldn't afford for her not to if Sylvia was the Sahaja Kita thought she was. Kita pushed away her frustration, and the dark corridor enveloped her as her thoughts propelled her.

[11.4]

Kita watched as Sylvia stood on tiptoe. She imagined there was a haze of purple circling Sylvia's thoughts with every touch of the symbols. Sylvia's hand trembled as she transferred the hieroglyphic emblems to a piece of paper by pencil-shading with the paper over the emblems. Kita paused at a column behind Sylvia and listened. She was muttering to herself as she traced the emblems. Kita couldn't make out all the words, but she caught the word *Ankh*.

Maybe she is talking herself through the jump. Kita looked up and saw the three pencil-traced ankhs on Sylvia's paper. The Tokoleh Ankh was the one used for transport.

Kita closed her eyes. She searched her own mind and closed her EvP connections. Her jeans held the phone tight in her pocket, and she struggled a little to remove it and check that it was on vibrate.

She sent a text to the line Tom had marked as Motorcycle on his phone.

TOM'S PHONE: Anything?

MOTORCYCLE: Yes. All numbers for the first beltway stage listed below.

Kita checked the numbers and then typed

TOM'S PHONE: Any have a confidence level of greater than 95% in 120 seconds?

She already had the timer set to countdown on the phone.

MOTORCYCLE: Yes, one of the nebulous-envelopes within reach in next 90 seconds.

Kita looked up at Sylvia, tracing her finger over the Tokoleh Ankh with its extended bar to one side. Situated on the top ring of the column it was difficult to see, but she was certain Sylvia could feel it. She appeared to be focused on it.

TOM'S PHONE: Shut off the internal cameras and encrypt our conversations. Put it under passcode Motorcycle.

Kita tucked the phone away.

She would need her strength to hold Sylvia through the transition. She couldn't let her die — Kita needed answers. The whole process would have to be quick. There was a thirty-second window by which they could use the column to transport, she just had to get the coordinates from Sylvia to know where she was going. Would she give them? Not doing so, she risked death. The nebulous-envelopes provided simultaneity travel. However, it was like two asteroids dancing when the two dimensions came this close to one another — dangerous — but it was only in these envelopes that the column Portals could be used for transport. She should have twenty-five seconds left.

[11.5]

Sylvia's heels tapped the floor, and she wrapped her arms around the column, though she could only reach halfway around. "Ahhh..." She sighed heavily. "I feel better," she said to the column. "Will still be glad to be done with travel, but..."

The force behind her knocked Sylvia's breath from her, pushed her body tight to the column, and the voice behind her spoke fast. "Give me the coordinates. I'll keep you safe."

"Okay. Yes," Sylvia said without thought, her mind on her own plans, not considering what the statement meant.

The woman reached above her head, not needing to be on tiptoe due to her height. Sylvia sensed something different in the space around her, like that dip you feel in your gut when an elevator first drops, as if someone pulled part of the floor from beneath you. The hieroglyph glowed beneath the woman's hand. Sylvia shook her head. It had to be the synesthesia.

The column shimmered but maintained its mass.

"The coordinates?"

Sylvia smiled at the color that flooded her mind. She knew they were numbers, but they each had a color. Sylvia felt euphoric for a moment, then cringed at a vision of a man collapsed in a pool of blood. She shuddered and heard her own voice whimper with the pain in her chest. She tossed her head, but the vision didn't disappear. His eyes were red as if the blood from the gash on his forehead filled them. The dead man stood and spoke. "You've done nothing, you've been nothing, and soon you will be dead — and the next day, no one will remember you were here. What are you willing to sacrifice to change that?"

Sylvia bit her lip, trying to control her thoughts, but the nightmare vision squeezed truth from her as if each tendril of thought was steam to be condensed, at his whim, to the weight of water.

"Sylvia. The coordinates, or you'll kill us both," the voice behind her said.

The hideous vision in Sylvia's mind continued tapping his skull. "What will you sacrifice? Who will you sacrifice? You've already sacrificed one friend — buried in a tomb, not for her."

"Diana," Sylvia whispered her friend's name.

"Yes, she's already gone — no sacrifice there." The hideous vision tapped his skull again. "Think. Your family? They're not really your family after all." The vision appeared closer now. "Hmm, friends? Do you have any of them? Awww!" The vision mocked then leapt at her, and Sylvia reflexively jerked. His hands grabbed her vest, and with dreamlike fantasy, the sticky feel of blood grazed her neck. "Oh, this is wonderful," the vision mocked. "It's already done. You sold your soul for a role, the chance to be what everyone else wanted!"

The smell of decay barraged Sylvia's senses with every word he spoke, though his teeth were perfect and white against his bloodied face. "Now you are going to die, and the sacrifice of yourself doesn't matter." The vision grinned and laughed a hollow, distant laugh of a kindred spirit. "There isn't enough time for you to find yourself!"

Sylvia pulled away from the vision and pushed back at the force that held her pinned to the column. She couldn't breathe.

[11.6]

Kita sensed Sylvia's shift and hesitated. She pulled back the energy and almost staggered. Had Sylvia decided not to transport? Something wasn't right.

"No, Sylvia!" A voice echoed in the open space just as a large man leapt at Sylvia's shoulder, pushing her and Kita backward. Kita already held the momentum of the pulled-back energy when she sensed Sylvia's hesitance. They all collided to the floor. The three toppled, the man landing almost on top of Sylvia, while Kita somersaulted with a roll, feet tucked overhead with the momentum carrying her center of gravity over that bad shoulder. She stood, accustomed to moving fast from a roll, and recognized the man's face. A Marshal.

Kita stepped into a side corridor and headed back toward the cabin. If the Marshal started asking about her, he would soon find she wasn't on the roster. Sylvia had hesitated. *Why? She had the coordinates — she said as much.* Kita shuddered, remembering it, and her pace slowed. The woman had to have the other coordinates, and the only reason to hesitate was to not take Kita with her. The idea supported her theory that she was helping the Separatists.

[11.7]

Michael pushed up from his plank position over Sylvia. "What were you doing?" He reached out a hand to Sylvia, who stared blankly up at the column behind him. "You can't transport through the columns just anywhere. Lucky for you, this lady..." He looked up to acknowledge the woman who had been at her back, but she was gone. "She was slowing the mass shift of the column, or else you would have quantized," Michael continued as he looked around, then noticed Sylvia stir.

She grabbed his outstretched hand this time and stood to her feet.

Sylvia brushed the strands of hair from her face. The vision was gone, but the memory of it remained. *Michael thinks I was trying to transport using the column?* Sylvia turned her hands palm up and then down. "I'll help with the investigation," she said flatly, remembering Doc's words. She needed answers. "Will you tell me more about this Orbiter?"

Michael started walking back along the corridor toward Sylvia's room. "Thank you, and yes, but I need to go to the K-hold first and help Pierre question the Dalen. Answer my questions as we walk back to your room, and I'll come back when I finish and answer questions about the column and the Orbiter after you've rested."

"I'll come with you."

"I don't think so. The questions I have I can ask right here."

"What about the questions I have?"

Michael continued to walk. "I can't take you into an investigation."

"Then perhaps you can figure out by yourself why they were fighting over my book."

"What?" Michael wheeled on her. His eyes appeared angry with fatigue and frustration.

Sylvia realized it was probably three a.m. by now, but she placed her hands on her hips. He had kept her up this long, he could put up with her till the sun rose in that blasted 3-D sunrise! "Listen, nobody knows that book better than me. If someone lets something slip about the book, you may not realize it. Someone wanted Jezel's book, and I intend to find out why." She looked down at the floor and briefly lost her bravado, afraid her vision would reappear. She twisted the chain at her neck and looked up to find Michael's eyes. "Meki says my writing seems real, though it is fiction. I don't want anyone else to die."

"Meki? Was that who tried to help at the column?"

"Help me? No. I don't know who that was. I couldn't see a face. The person came from behind." Sylvia paused. "She asked for coordinates?"

Sylvia said, only now really hearing the words. *Maybe she wasn't trying to help me,* she thought, recalling Tessa's warning as she tried to remember where else she might have seen the Ankh with the long left arm she had just copied from the column and was so clearly depicted in her book. The vision flashed again, only the red eyes, and she blinked fast to clear it.

Michael tapped his small notebook with a pen. "You have to have coordinates to travel by Sim-transport. So, you gave her the coordinates so she could help you transport? Where?"

"No. I didn't even know there was such a thing. I...I don't have any coordinates." She felt Michael's stare intensify with her stumbling.

"So, an EvP who could help you Sim-transport via the columns just stopped by to give you a hand when you almost pulled yourself into the Simultaneity without a clue?"

Sylvia could hear the sarcasm in his tone.

"I'll recognize her when I see her again," Michael said.

Sylvia felt a flash of anger at his stare. *Does he think I'm lying?* Sylvia thought before saying out loud. "Please find her and ask her. I'd love to know." Sylvia uncrossed her arms and began to walk. She didn't want to think about if someone had just tried to kill her in a way she did not even understand.

"So, tell me about this book. When did you start writing it?"

Sylvia smiled, glad for the more mundane question about the book. "It's always hard to say. A book is a conglomeration of many ideas, experiences, and imagination." That last word brought a flash of the dead man from her vision, and she shuddered.

"What is it?" Michael asked.

"Nothing." Sylvia twisted the gold chain at her neck. "I just..." *See a vision that terrifies me when I consciously reach to the past.* "The book is a mix of imaginings that often repeat in my dreams."

"Is it possible they are your memories?"

Sylvia halted at the cutting clarity of the simple question. She dropped the necklace and stroked the notch at the base of her throat. *Could this change in my brain be messing with my memory?* She looked up at Michael, who had his broad shoulders facing her. "No, they are just daydreams...and nightmares. My turn," Sylvia said, moving again. "What happened at that column?"

"I don't know. You tell me."

Sylvia gave him a side glance to watch his features when she spoke. "I don't know. I was just tracing the symbols." He didn't smirk or laugh, so she continued. "Can you explain what the column does, and maybe I will understand?"

"Let's take the stairs," Michael said, touching her elbow when she moved toward the elevator.

They descended the first flight of stairs in silence, but Michael broke it when they touched the first landing. "The columns can transport you via a nebulous-envelope." He paused, rubbing the back of his neck. "It's dangerous, and no one has used them since the war. Why are you headed to the GCS? I thought writers were stay-at-home kind of people."

"Stereotype much?" Sylvia answered but smiled. He was just doing his job, and she was tired and cranky. "Actually, I've been on the road more this last year than any in the past." She wrapped her hand around the handrail where it touched the wall. Blue rolled through her thoughts like a faint wisp of fog, and she released it with a sigh. "The book's success led my publisher to push for three extra venues, and Meki, my publicist, recommended the GCS."

"So, this trip to the GCS was your publicist's idea?"

Sylvia touched her necklace and started down the next flight of stairs, letting her free hand trace the rail. The blue wisp of the rail danced again through her thoughts, just background noise as she became more accustomed to the synesthesia. "Yes. He says it is a great platform to promote the book to the most diverse group and..." Sylvia paused, wondering if she should tell him of the doctor Meki scheduled her to see at De la Cour's recommendation.

"And...?" Michael nudged, slowing on the steps.

They reached the next landing before Sylvia answered. "I had an abnormal MRI test last year, and Meki recommended a doctor at the GCS to get a second opinion. I started getting migraines toward the end of my tour." She took the next step ahead of Michael and stepped toward the cement wall of the staircase, forcing Michael to her right where the rail ran. The wall of the stairwell was warmer where the light hit it. She closed her eyes at the yellow that colored her thoughts and tasted of citrus.

"Any other problems other than the migraines?"

Sylvia watched as his lips tightened in a straight line. Sylvia pulled her hand from the wall and stroked the skin at her neck. The synesthesia was too hard to explain. "No, not really."

Michael touched Sylvia's elbow, pausing them on the landing before the last flight of stairs. "Maybe the migraines got worse because your mind is trying to remember something you don't want to remember." He faced her square. "I need to know this before we go through that door down there. Did you want to transport when you were at the column? Were you trying to escape?"

"No!" Sylvia's head shot up to meet his eyes, and for a moment, they were the eyes from her vision, red and penetrating. She shook her head, and the vision disappeared.

"It just seems unusual for someone to be that close to transporting and not mean to?" Michael pressed. Then, he must have seen her fear because he gave her a bit of space.

The remembrance of the string of numbers that jumbled and rearranged in her mind just before the colors became the vision. Sylvia's mouth felt dry. "It isn't a place, it's fiction!" Sylvia crossed her arms, rubbing her shoulder with her opposite hand, trying to find the warmth she had felt earlier when she touched the wall, but the warmth seemed sequestered within that silver tangle in her mind. She looked at the doorway looming at the foot of the stairs and had a sudden urge to run in the opposite direction.

"Maybe it's not a place," Michael said, leaning against the wall. "Maybe someone gave you the coordinates, and you forgot."

Sylvia's vision from the column earlier flashed before her in the doorway with a white-toothed grin. Sylvia bolted. She was halfway up the stairs they had just descended. She gripped the rail, forcing the blue cold of it through her mind, pushing the vision away. She had been reaching for the warmth at that silver tangle, reaching for a memory.

The vision flickered again, its red eyes ablaze. *Don't do that,* it warned.

One of the colored threads in her mind seemed to suck the vision into a thought, and it vanished. She grabbed her throat to stifle a wave of nausea. She stopped. Her chest heaved with exertion, and her heart raced. The color in her mind was gone, and so was the vision, but she had crossed some invisible line like water racing down a cliff toward the edge, fast, unforgiving, and immutable. She stood motionless, letting her mind hear her heart. She turned back toward Michael. She was standing on the third step from the next landing. He still stood where she left him. His mouth was agape. Sylvia closed her eyes. The vision returned as she knew it would. She had to face it here in her mind first because something told her all her imaginings were more real than she had realized. The vision disappeared. Sylvia started back down the stairs and spoke when she reached Michael, though she didn't stop.

"Maybe someone did give me coordinates," Sylvia said, pulling the door open. She looked over her shoulder, trying on a confidence she didn't feel. "Maybe it's all more real than I realize. Let's find out."

Michael held her blue eyes with his brown, and she was certain he would see her vulnerability. He glanced up at her hair, and she imagined how wild the strawberry blond curls looked in a knot held up by a failing clasp. His eyes blinked several times, and Sylvia felt heat in her limbs.

CHAPTER TWELVE

T WENTY-FIVE LIGHT-YEARS AWAY, DARKNESS swallowed a small transport spacecraft in low orbit around the biosphere of the Galactic Core Station at Replica Earth. "It's as beautiful as Earth," Seldon told his co-pilot.

"Better, I say, with the atmosphere wash every two weeks." Hawk looked through the heat shield glass and saw worry reflected on his middle-aged face. The darkness of space engulfed the thriving biosphere as if to imprint its presence on the environment that made such a contrast to itself. "The dark seems so...invasive," Hawk said. "I feel like if I turn my head when I look back, the vibrant greens and blues of Replica Earth will be gone."

Seldon adjusted the instruments as their trajectory path shifted slightly. Replica Earth's Orbiter-Docking-Ring allowed the Galactic Core Station to reach out from it like a soap bubble. "Orbiter coming in from the beltway," he commented, seeing a ping on the radar. Hawk had his head down, checking their communication system. They were expecting a call.

Hawk looked up as a flash of neon barely dotted the darkened sky. The beltway was too far away for them to identify the color, but the tiny flash of light registered its quantum dot signature on the controls. "Quantum dot registry says Orbiter 7."

"Have you seen one of the Orbiters dock?" Seldon asked.

"No. You?"

"Yes. Once. And I've been on an Orbiter twice. The Orbiter itself docks to ports positioned all around the Galactic Core Station. The ports are all connected by that structure there that looks like a ribbon wrapped around an ornament.

Travelers exit the Orbiters and process through the Galactic Core Station before Sim-beaming to Replica Earth."

"What was it like watching it dock?" Hawk asked with interest.

Seldon snorted. "I don't remember much about it. I was piloting a transport like this one, and the Orbiter was docking when we arrived. We had a brood of Griffons from Griffern for training at the GCS Hotel. Even just after hatching, they are aggressive, primal predators. One escaped and almost destroyed the ship before it was put down."

"Are they as large as everyone describes? The only Griffon I've ever known is human. I've never seen one in its beast form."

"Large doesn't describe them," Seldon said, and a shudder gave away his fear. "It's a predator two times larger than any lion you've seen on earth with a wingspan that can lift them and support them to fight or hunt with the sight and intelligence of the great birds of prey."

The Rompnet-connected video rang instead of the phone. Its eerie echo in the transporter felt ominous. Hawk looked to Seldon.

Seldon nodded. "That should be V."

Hawk diverted the call to the secure system. The voice came through the line before the video appeared. "Our launch on Orbiter C13 was delayed. What is the status on the fuel-cell ship arrival meeting your transport?"

V. placed his monocle over his left eye when Hawk answered. He moved away from a group of people who had crowded him at the banister. Hawk knew the monocle projected a sound shield, amplified the signal, and enhanced vision for hologram weaving, but the amplification must not have been enough for the secretive man to make the call from his cabin.

"It is still on schedule, sir," Hawk repeated when V. did not respond.

V. tapped his ring. A blue haze wrapped his ear, but he kept his monocle in place to amplify the signal. "Excellent. Is the energy system stable enough to handle the influx during the Earth Week celebration?"

"Yes, sir, we've been watching the energy-generator rooms through a patch we made to the GCS security system," Seldon began. "Nothing to report. All parameters are normal, including energy flow from the Replica planetary systems into the room's energy-generator hold cell and energy out to Earth through the Umbilical Portal."

"Which planet is feeding the GCS energy-generator rooms today?"

"It's Griffern's turn. I mean, Replica Saturn's rotation, sir," Hawk answered, unsure which title for the planet V. preferred. "We have limited readings in our transporter, so our numbers can be off by two percent, but Seldon says that is acceptable to identify any problems."

"Very well. I'm uncertain how well our communication will continue in the beltway. Keep a log. I may want you to send readings for my review. What are your coordinates?" V. tapped his ring as he listened, and a hologram appeared above his hand with an image of the Replica Solar System where Hawk and Seldon orbited the Replica Earth and its Galactic Core Station.

Hawk checked and responded with the coordinates, watching the video screen as V. zoomed the hologram screen to focus on Replica Earth. He typed the coordinates on the laser keyboard displayed from the hologram on the back of his hand. The precise position of Seldon's spacecraft appeared. "Maintain your position," V. said as he copied the coordinates into a line of code Hawk couldn't read.

V. continued. "The fuel-cell ship should be with you by then, and I will have the relic secured from the dropoff. Let the fuel-cell ship captain know about my delayed launch on Orbiter C13."

"Yes, sir." Seldon flipped a switch to open an alternate line, spoke briefly, and closed the line. "Fuel ship notified, sir."

"Excellent," V. said before he disconnected.

[12.1]

Three minutes, V-Kasana thought, changing the time on the self-destruct command line titled: Detonate.

[12.2]

"What do you think the V stands for?" Hawk asked.

"Victor? Maybe not. You never have a pronounceable name when you're thousands of years old. Regardless his name, I don't like knowing his business."

"Some of the recently born Immortals have modern names," Hawk said, ignoring the implication of Seldon's words. "But, then there are only a handful of the new Immortals, right?"

Seldon turned thoughtful. "Doesn't immortality make most of them sterile?"

"I don't know. Just glad V. is Sim-beaming to the fuel ship and not ours." Hawk set the parameters to maintain their orbit.

"Hawk! There's heat signal at the o-ring. Ejec—"

The detonation of the spacecraft was silent in the vacuum of space.

[12.3]

Kita scribbled the translation over the words in Sylvia's book. *Isvara Tamas Sat Tula Adharma*. The blatant restructure combining two conflicting philosophies had intrigued her. The Tokoleh first law stated light and darkness existed unbalanced. It was why they forbid Intuits and EvPs from being Life Companions. *I should have called Jo*, Kita thought. Instead, she had opted to access their shared work panel at the Earth Alliance, knowing Jo wanted to discuss why Kita transferred from their unit. It was getting harder to work with Jo and not want more. *Jo is an Intuit, which means off-limits for anything long term.* Intuits touched the Source, and that was dangerous for EvPs connected to the Simultaneity. Kita touched the video screen, remembering her run-in with Sylvia and the Marshal. Kita closed her eyes, recalling the energy she sensed the woman held.

"Do you believe the Tokoleh first law?" Kita asked when Motorcycle returned with a cup of coffee for both of them, though only she could drink hers.

"Isvara Tamas Sat Adharma — light and darkness exist unbalanced," M said but didn't answer the question as he raised the coffee to his lips, watching the steam cause his one chrome finger to fog. "Why do humans watch steam over their coffee?"

Did he just deflect? Kita thought, letting the conflicted enlightenment of him trying to be human with a behavior acquired from machine learning wrestle with the fact that he didn't have a belief system, only programming. "Are you aware that you cannot answer the question?"

"I can answer," M said, looking firmly at her. "Yes, I believe light and darkness exist unbalanced."

"Very well. You agree a belief is the acceptance that a statement is true."

M nodded slowly, as if checking a definition within his database.

"Then why do you accept that light and darkness are unbalanced rather than the translation in this book that light and darkness are balanced and unbalanced?" she asked, turning Sylvia's book for him to see. "Or this one..." she said, pulling a tiny book of her mother's from her pocket, "...that says light and darkness are balanced."

M stared at her blinking, then walked to the service area and dumped his coffee out.

"Really, Kita," she said under her breath. "Do you have to hurt the robot's feelings?" She laughed at the absurdity and truth she felt of it. *You have to stay in here now that you've been seen by a Marshal, so you better stay on M's good side. I'll need his help if Sylvia tries Sim-transport again. Re-engage him,* Kita thought as the console screen pinged.

"Hey, M, there are more details of the two Dalen in K-hold." Kita indicated scrolling data when he moved her way. "They didn't make it to launch lockdown, and at present, one death has been confirmed, and the other suffered a severe injury at launch and is in a coma." Kita sighed and stood, walking to her cabin. Complications were mounting. "Will you make a report for me, Motorcycle, following the Marshal's investigation?"

"Sure."

Kita rotated her shoulder. It was about ten percent better. The cryo system in her cabin improved healing, though not as significant for her as Immortals who could use their DNA.

She considered watching Sylvia, herself, and the Marshal on the video feed with Motorcycle to get his objective opinion about what Sylvia had tried to do. Something just didn't fit.

She had to keep an eye on her. She was just so tired of chasing problems.

"Hey, Motorcycle. Do you think that passenger will try Sim-transport again?"

"I am unable to calculate those probabilities with the limited data at this time."

"Keep an eye on her, then. We can't afford any more injuries on this flight."

"Simultaneity transport is certainly a creative way to get hurt," M said. He paused his work and turned to her. "You didn't answer my question either. Why do humans watch steam over their coffee?"

Kita held his eyes, knowing his machine learning told him that mattered. "It reminds us of things that are warm," Kita whispered, stepping through the doorway to the quiet of her cabin. She closed the door. *Jo, I do want to be home.* Kita pressed the wall of the sleeping cabin, letting her weight test her bad shoulder and feeling more than her own weight as her head sagged, bearing the pain. *How many fights, how many flights, and none of them as important as this one right now. Nowhere can be home till Earth is safe for all of us.* People were counting on her, and she didn't want to fail this time.

[12.4]

Kinley watched the argument at the table to their left. He and Xenos had picked a table near the center wall so they could enjoy the 3-D sunrise from multiple views on the floor-to-ceiling surround display while they enjoyed breakfast. They arrived early and watched as other passengers trickled in. Only this couple appeared to have been here overnight. The woman's blond hair was loose and falling from a bun at the back of her head, and the man's five o'clock shadow was well past a second five o'clock.

"We're in the beltway — no turning back now," Kinley said, lifting the tea to enjoy the heat of it as he watched the arc of the sun begin over the mountain scene. He checked the watch he had begun wearing to ensure he didn't miss dispensing a dose of the new medication Xenos started last month. "Six-oh-two EST on the money. Sunrise on schedule."

Xenos closed his eyes, clasped his long fingers together at his crossed knees, and let out a quiet breath. "I can feel its heat. It seems so real."

"Your health would benefit better by real sunlight," Kinley muttered. The thought pulled a deep frown to his lips, and he sat his tea back on the table, careful to avoid the frayed leather of his most recent book find, *The Ancient Law of the Tokoleh*.

"And your health would benefit by avoiding the allergens that plague those old books you hoard."

"You know I'm looking for a way to keep you from losing your memory when you regenerate. There has to be a way, Xenos."

Xenos uncrossed his legs and turned toward the table. He looked stronger today. Perhaps the new medicine was helping, but it wouldn't be enough. The sunlight seemed so real as its light spilled against the side of his friend's face and cast a shadow on the round table between them.

"What have you found? I know it must be something," Xenos said, reaching his long fingers to tap the book. "This blanketed your chest, and it was three a.m. You are a stickler about your sleep routine, and this kept you up."

Kinley smiled. "I did find something, but it raises questions about Immortal biology. I'm hoping to get permission to use the UBN archives when we arrive. They're bound to have a copy of the book I need. Their resources date back—"

Kinley was interrupted by the shadow of a tall man just before the man spoke. "Excuse me, I'm Michael, one of the Marshals on the Orbiter. May I take a minute to ask you gentlemen a few questions?"

"Certainly," Xenos said, standing to give his chair to the blond with her to-go cup of coffee.

Kinley smiled when Xenos reached to link a pinky with the woman in a traditional Immortal greeting. The facial expression was priceless.

"It's like a handshake back home," Michael said, helping her out as he himself linked pinky to pinky with Xenos in a brief greeting of acquaintance.

"Oh, okay. I'm Sylvia," she said, releasing the double clutch on the coffee and extending her hand pinky bent to offer the greeting. She sat as Xenos pulled a chair from the next table.

"Are you a Marshal as well?" Kinley asked, closing his book and marking the page with a parchment bookmark of Tokoleh hieroglyphs Xenos had given him.

"No. I'm just helping with the investigation."

"Investigation?" Xenos leaned forward.

"Yes," Michael said, setting his notebook on the table. "I know you were a Tokoleh Guardian in the past, Xenos. I could use your help."

Kinley slid his book onto his lap, where he gripped it so no one would see his hand tremble. *How did a perfect stranger know something about Xenos that he had not known?*

Xenos reached to Kinley's cup of tea and turned it so the small chipped section faced Kinley. It was the position that made it easiest for Kinley to lift it with his injured finger. To others, it would appear as if he was moving it as he leaned in toward them at the table.

Kinley knew Xenos's kind gesture was answering his concern not only for the realization of something he had not known about his friend, but also for his greater fear that he himself would soon be part of another forgotten life. He had been assigned as a Governor Protector for Xenos. The fact Xenos once served as a Guardian explained a lot about his ability to investigate but equally reminded him how many lives and people the Immortal had forgotten.

"That was another life, Marshal. I have had many, and I have forgotten much about each of them. How did you come across this information you share so freely?"

"Rosalind, the director of UBN security, said you were on the flight with Kinley here, and if she could pick anyone to be her eyes here, it would be you."

Xenos leaned back in his chair, his eyes closed and his hands steepled, his elbows resting on the arms of the chair. Kinley knew Rosalind would not have divulged Xenos's role as a Guardian, so the man still had not answered the question. Xenos appeared to decide to let it pass for now.

[12.5]

Michael noticed the similarity of mannerisms to Rosalind in this man. She had been sitting just like Xenos sat now the first time he met her. He looked at Sylvia. Her blue eyes were the only thing visible as she stared over the large cup gripped in her two hands and perched at her lips. *Stop looking at her lips,* he told himself. She had switched from tea to coffee around three a.m. when they finished questioning the Dalen and visited the man in the coma. He needed her help with the book and couldn't afford to miss something related by keeping her out of the loop, but her proximity was distracting.

Xenos interrupted his thoughts. "What is the problem, and what do you know so far?"

Michael visibly relaxed. "I'll start at the beginning."

Sylvia sat her coffee on the table and pulled Michael's copy of her book from the oversized pocket inside her field jacket. Kinley leaned in to see the book cover, drawn by the detail of the leather spine that faced him with the book face down.

Xenos's eyes never opened, and Michael continued. "One of the relic Portal keys of the Five Sectors was found."

"That doesn't sound like bad news," Xenos replied, his steepled hands now on his lips. "Many of the Tokoleh and other species have sought to find and restore them to their proper place now that the war is over."

Kinley's chair creaked as he slowly sat back in it as if he was afraid he might give away some detail that Xenos was so carefully keeping hidden. Michael figured he knew what that was. "I know the Tokoleh are divided on the issue about whether to reveal the existence of the Tokoleh and Replica Earth to Earth. Whoever finds those keys can control that choice."

Michael laid his elbows and broad forearms on the table, his eyes focused to watch for any reaction to the information Rosalind asked him to relay. "There were two relic Portal keys scheduled to be presented at the Scholar's Council. It was one of them, and it has been stolen."

Xenos's eyes opened with a control that reminded Michael that this Immortal had lived many lives. "Are you certain?"

"Yes. Rosalind confirmed it yesterday, just before we started our injection to the beltway. I thought it best not to disturb you last night till I gathered more details, and we had another issue."

"Humph," Sylvia muttered. "It didn't stop you from bothering me."

Xenos smiled. "You authored the book that lays on the table," he said, lowering his hands to his lap. "You long for an archaeological path you abandoned, and you're key to his investigation. I'm not certain which point is most important."

Sylvia's eyes went wide, and she reached for the book, Michael assumed to confirm that her name on the cover was not visible as it lay face down, accidentally knocking her coffee. "How did you know?" She grabbed the coffee before it fell. "That I wrote the book?"

"So, you're the one who taught Rosalind how to do that," Michael interrupted, intrigued again by the similarity between Xenos and Rosalind.

Xenos laughed, and Michael watched Sylvia physically calm with its openness. She relaxed her hands on her lap.

"No," Xenos said, reaching for the book. "She taught me. She is the most gifted investigator I have known through many lifetimes." His hand hovered over the book. "May I?"

Sylvia hesitated, and Xenos added, "The initials on your field vest are S.D. You introduced yourself as Sylvia, and the name engraved in the leather spine is Debair. Therefore, you are most likely the author of the book."

Sylvia touched the charm on her necklace, an action Michael had determined was a nervous habit she performed frequently. She nodded for Xenos to take the book. "Actually, the S.D. initials on my field jacket are for Sarah Daniels, my real name. Sylvia Debair is my pen name."

"Thank you," Xenos said, taking the book and tilting his head with interest. "Perhaps you will tell me why you are so important to this investigation."

She looked at Michael, her hesitancy clear when she bit her lower lip. Michael nodded and swallowed the pull he felt when she did that.

[12.6]

Sylvia was impressed with Xenos's insight. It made her curious. Maybe he had some of the answers she needed. She wanted to ask, but not with Michael here. She didn't want him to know how completely ignorant she was of this new world around her. Perhaps she would glean more information from their reaction to her story.

"Well, I guess I have to start in the middle to give you the details in the most organized manner," Sylvia said, taking in the three men seated around her.

"Please do." Xenos sat back in his chair and crossed his legs as Sylvia began to speak.

"About two months ago, a reader showed up at a signing and asked me for the coordinates to the Lost City in my book. I thought little of it at first because people often build reality into the books an author creates, but this reader was adamant that the place existed. There was something important hidden there, she said, and she needed the coordinates or the Earth as we know it would be destroyed. Meki, my publicist — who happened to be with me because it was the last leg of the tour before our flight out to the GCS — contacted security to have her removed, but she left." Sylvia didn't mention that the reader had given her a photo that haunted her. She hadn't even shown Meki. She pushed the thought of the photo away, took a sip of coffee, and continued her narrative. "I put it off as just the ramblings of a reader too involved in the book. Then, right before this flight, at our last signing, a man showed up and asked for the same coordinates, telling me his life was forfeit if he did not get them. Meki had him removed, but I'll never forget the look of panic on his face as they dragged him away."

Sylvia paused and looked around the table at her listeners as she took another sip of coffee. She was definitely feeling the weight of exhaustion. Xenos sat with his legs crossed and her open book balanced on his knee. His lapis-blue eyes focused through narrow slits created by heavy lids. His furrowed white eyebrows were the only hair on his face or head. His face, though touched by age, still held the handsome features of a strong man. His friend Kinley was wiry, and his eyes were kind but alert, as if a great worry pulled all of his features from their natural state of peace. He appeared fit, and Sylvia decided that misjudging his meekness for weakness would be a mistake. Michael, to her right, with his bulk, seemed to overtake the table. His elbows and arms covered the table where he sat, and she wondered for a moment what his handwriting looked like in the small notebook that lay beneath them. "Can I see your notebook, Michael, when I get to the parts regarding the investigation downstairs in the K-hold?"

"No," he answered, turning to a page even as he answered. "I can fill in anything you forget when you get there. So, did you put coordinates in the man's book before they carted him away, since you failed to mention this to me earlier?"

"No, I..." Sylvia pulled at her necklace, remembering the face of the stranger and the flash of orange that she had tasted as much as seen when they took him away. That was when her migraines had worsened. "I didn't even sign it," she finished, staring now at her hands in her lap.

"Go on," Xenos nudged with kindness, and the intensity in his voice caused Sylvia to look up.

"Then, here..." Sylvia continued, "... on Orbiter C13, a fight broke out in K-hold. One man died, and the other is in a coma. One of the staff said the man had stolen her copy of my book, and she followed him down to the K-hold to get it back. She ended up at my door bleeding and asking me not to tell them where her book was. I think she may have suffered a blow to the head. She is with Doc Turner now. The interviews indicate it was a fight that developed because the book is banned by the Dalen, and the new recruit that stole it was trying to get one of the Dalenborn, known for smuggling contraband, to give him money for it." Sylvia touched her index finger to her thumb in her lap to avoid reaching for her necklace, then turned at the noise of two small groups entering the area and seating themselves for breakfast. *Xenos seems to be taking in every detail about them*, Sylvia thought, watching his keen eyes and following their line of focus. "That man with the hard jaw and deep-set eyes runs the K-hold. He was with the man in the coma when we were there."

"Who is with him?" Xenos asked.

"I don't recognize two of them, but the one to the left of him he introduced as Cray and seems to be with him most of the time."

"No, I mean, are they Griffon, Escape velocity Pullers, Intuits, or Humans?" Xenos clarified.

"What is an Escape velocity Puller?" Sylvia looked around the table, but everyone stared as if she were joking. *There is something really wrong with me,* she thought. *I must be hearing things or misunderstanding words.* "Can you excuse me? I need to use the restroom."

"Wait, Sylvia," Michael said, touching her arm as she stood. "It's okay. A lot of people on Earth are unaware of HIFs...Human Interplanetary Forms. Something that will hopefully be remedied soon." Sylvia noted his deliberate focus on Xenos. "It's not like they teach it in the schools. It's just that most of the people who travel to the GCS *are* aware of it."

"So, Meki would know?" Sylvia asked, a tinge of frustration in her voice.

"Maybe not. You said he was your publicist."

Sylvia relaxed and touched the back of the bistro-style chair. Her legs felt weak. "Forgive my ignorance, I'm...learning." She looked at Xenos, who she expected would be frowning at her, but his eyes had such deep compassion she could not look away.

"The Scholar's Council is scheduled to meet during the Earth Week celebration. They are the advisory unit for the Tokoleh-Earth Alliance. As Michael said, the issue of divulging the Tokoleh's existence completely to Earth is on the agenda for continued discussion and voting. So, you are not alone in your..." Xenos paused and appeared to study her. "Lack of knowledge," he finally said with a smile that was gentle and eyes that were curious.

Kinley spoke up, asking to see her book. Xenos passed it to him, and Sylvia noted concern in Kinley's winter-gray eyes. She took her seat again. The seat was solid, but Sylvia felt she was falling, off-balance at the waves of new information. "And this key Michael said was stolen is important to that?" she asked, struggling with why Michael thought this meeting might be related to the man stealing Jezel's book.

Kinley looked up, his finger marking the page Xenos had flagged. "The headmaster of the Emitime School is scheduled to present one of the hidden keys as a good-faith gesture to promote support for revealing the Tokoleh to Earth." Sylvia watched Kinley's focus as he watched Xenos, who now appeared to be staring at the mountain range displayed on the 3-D screen behind her. "He is the representative for the Elderwise." Kinley paused, and Xenos looked from the mountains to Sylvia, his eyes holding a deep sorrow.

"He is on this Orbiter, so the stolen relic must be the second one. We should schedule time to see him before we arrive. I think he would be interested in your book," Xenos said.

Sylvia gripped her hands in her lap. *Why would this headmaster be interested in my book?* Sylvia thought, then recalled her book's reference to a school. She lifted her gaze to meet the pained look in Xenos's eyes.

"If your book is a reference for finding the lost Portal keys," Michael said, his eyes hard, "we have to consider the events in K-hold are connected until proven otherwise."

Sylvia's mouth went dry. He thought her book had somehow been more important than just contraband? She swallowed and closed her eyes, reaching gingerly for the tangle in her mind. *What does this missing key do?* The vision flashed red in her mind, blood seeming to form the red eyes. She blinked her eyes open. "I'm so sorry about what happened to those men," she said, feeling the tears. "I promise I don't know anything about the keys or where they have been hidden. This," she said, touching her book still in Kinley's hand, "is a work of fiction."

"I believe you," Xenos said and gave a barely noticeable nod to Kinley.

"I have a book you may be interested in," Kinley said, tapping his pocket.

"I overheard the two of you speaking about a book that discussed hieroglyphs related to places on Earth on the stairs before launch. Is that the one you mean?" Sylvia asked.

"Yes," Kinley said with a smile Sylvia could feel mirrored on her own face. They both liked old things. "I'll even explain HIFs using the maps in it if you will bring me one of these," he said softly, touching the leather cover of her book.

"Sure," Sylvia said excitedly. "I have a box of them in my room I was going to pre-sign. Not that you'll want it signed. Just that I have one. I mean, I have one you can have." She stopped talking and shoved the coffee to her lips. Why was she suddenly so nervous? She felt completely lost. "Where do you want to meet?" Sylvia asked, trying to change the subject.

Just focus, learn what you can, get to the signing, see the doctor, fix whatever is going haywire in your brain, and get back home to your normal life, she thought.

"Let's meet at the library," Xenos offered. "The ex-Depository Symbias may agree to join us that close to the medical bay, and I need to speak with her."

"Tessa?" Sylvia blurted, the bizarre title of Symbias causing her mouth to work without her brain.

"You know Tessa Danquah?" Michael asked, and Sylvia didn't miss the deep furrow in his brow as he scribbled in his notebook.

"She's Jezel's..." She paused, trying to recall the words.

"Life Companion," Kinley offered.

"Yes, Life Companion. I met her when I went down to check on Jezel. Sorry, I just don't travel well, and this trip has me anxious." With that, she decided to shut up.

"Maybe I can put your mind at ease," Kinley said, still leafing through her book. "We have you at a disadvantage. Humans are the DNA scaffolding for all species — including Griffons, like myself." He lifted his hand from the book to touch his chest. "Escape velocity Pullers, usually called EvPs for short, Intuits, and even Tokoleh, who are the Immortal, all have human DNA. However, many years have bred out exclusive traits of any single group. The Guardians, a group established by the Tokoleh, constantly monitor for those who show evidence of the skills and strengths of the individual species. When they find them, they are encouraged to attend the Emitime School and train to hone their skills and discipline their strengths."

"You're a Griffon? You look as human as me." Sylvia sat her coffee down but kept her hands wrapped tightly to the cup.

Michael twisted and waved his hand for a waitress. "This could take a while," he said.

Sylvia rolled her eyes, then smiled when the exhausted brunette seemed to look right past him and walked toward a couple at a table near the 3-D display of the sunrise to his back.

"I am human, but my accessory DNA is Griffon," Kinley answered, smiling at her interest.

Sylvia smiled back and leaned in toward the table. This man, with his dark black hair tied with a leather strap, his ancient books, and his sword at his side, was fascinating. "That is really cool. What is it like? Do you have a superpo—" Sylvia bit her lip, cutting off the word. She leaned back in her chair, chastising herself for being silly. *Superpower...really, Sylvia?*

"Actually, I have extreme physical strength and keen senses. As a matter of fact, despite your friend's bulging muscles, I could overtake him physically with little effort."

"There is a trade-off, though," Michael said, twisting in his seat, seemingly determined to catch a server.

"Indeed," Kinley said, fingering a page in the book. "Using our Griffon strength can trigger the genetics of our Griffon form. If transformed, one cannot return from it. The GCS has a few Griffons in their animal form, used for flight and travel."

"That's terrible," Sylvia said, tracing the rim of her coffee cup and giving new thoughts to the synesthesia and migraines. *Am I possibly a Griffon?*

Michael bumped her arm, turning back in his seat, and her fear of the unknown, combined with her exhaustion, came out at him in a rush. "Why don't you get up and go order something at the kitchen instead of expecting someone to immediately come wait on you?"

Michael pushed his chair away from the table and stood. "You can't order at the kitchen, but it appears another waitress just came on shift, and I know her. Would anyone else like something while we educate Ms. Debair?"

Xenos and Kinley both nodded that they did not.

Sylvia didn't answer at all. She knew the remark was a snark at her, but she didn't care. She blamed him partially for her night turning into madness, and she intended to stay mad at him for a while. When Michael waited, expecting a response from her, she spoke to Kinley. "It seems so unfair. Your human existence jeopardized, and you not even understanding what is going on."

"The Guardians try to identify Griffons early and get them to Emitime since they suffer the worst from not knowing," Xenos offered.

"Or our parents know and send us to the school to manage it," Kinley said.

"Is it possible I could be a Griffon?" Sylvia asked, looking at Xenos.

"It is unlikely, dear," Xenos answered. "Griffons usually have a very primitive, aggressive temper that gets them in trouble at an early age, and we usually find them before the age of ten."

Sylvia winced, knowing Xenos's small smile was to confirm for her that her recent outburst did not qualify as evidence of the aggressive Griffon temperament. "That doesn't sound like Kinley," Sylvia said, looking across the table at the quiet man now absorbed in her book.

Xenos's smile widened, but Kinley looked up from the book and spoke. "When you see the Griffons at the GCS, you will understand. They are magnificent beasts, built with the body and strength of a lion as tall as a horse with a wingspan to lift them to any height. In them, you will see both the strength and primitive nature of the species and understand what it is I govern every day."

Sylvia didn't know what to say, and she could see Michael coming back toward the table. The picture in her head of an animal that large was probably going to give her nightmares. She decided to change the subject. "Who are the Tokoleh, and why do they have the Guardians? Why not do it themselves?"

Xenos laughed, and Michael, just arriving at the table, looked down at himself. "What did I miss?"

Sylvia answered, not wanting Xenos or Kinley to start on about her Griffon concerns. "I just asked about the Tokoleh. Is that all you got for your effort?"

"Samara had to clock in at the back but gave me a cup of coffee and said she would be over." As if on cue, his stomach growled.

"Michael is what we call true human," Kinley said as Sylvia started to speak. "He carries the DNA of all species, but in small amounts that makes him more human than anything else. His stomach gives him away."

Xenos laughed at this, but Kinley continued with a smile. "Humans are hungry all the time."

"This is true," Michael said, rubbing his solid abdomen good-naturedly. "So, what is your question about the Tokoleh?"

Sylvia was going to repeat her question but realized Michael was looking again toward the kitchen. She crossed her arms till he looked back at her. "Why do the Tokoleh use the Guardians? Why don't they look for the individuals showing these special skills?"

"Guardians are Tokoleh," Michael said.

"What?" Sylvia asked, her brow furrowing.

Xenos leaned forward. "There are three branches of the Ancient Tokoleh: the Source Protectors, the Governors, and the Guardians. All Tokoleh are Immortals, but not all Immortals are Tokoleh."

Sylvia's brow didn't unfurrow, but she leaned back in her chair, repeating the words to herself, waiting for Xenos to finish when the waitress arrived at their table.

"Thank you, Samara," Michael said as the waitress moved her finger across a hologram screen above her ring finger and touched a menu button. "Can I get the sausage and—"

A loud crash drew everyone's attention.

Sylvia watched Samara race to the scene near the booths. Her co-worker was trembling, and Michael scanned the scene, standing when he noted the exhausted brunette surrounded by shattered glass.

"That's why I didn't recognize her," Michael said, as if speaking to himself. "The other waitress is new and probably space-sick." His stomach growled. "I'll go see if I can help. Xenos can tell you all about Immortals. He is one." Michael stood and moved toward the chaos.

"Are you Tokoleh?" Sylvia asked, her own stomach twisting a little with hunger.

"Not active," Xenos answered. "Tokoleh Immortals are allowed a hundred years between our time of active service as Tokoleh."

"Do Immortals get to choose?"

"Well, it's not that simple, but the easiest explanation is the Tokoleh forms two protectorates of the Source. The Governors provide the ruling body of the galaxy, while the Guardians provide the protection. The Immortals not serving in one of those capacities live their lives and may apply to sit at the Scholar's Council each year along with representatives from each species. The agreement between the Earth Alliance and the Tokoleh is balanced by this."

"That helps. But I meant, do the Immortals get to choose if they want to be Tokoleh?"

Xenos looked at Kinley, then into the sunlight, and closed his eyes.

Sylvia bit her lip, realizing this answer was not just for her.

"Yes. We have a choice. However, there are fewer and fewer of us, and there is a lot of pressure for us to contribute because our extended lifespans create continuity. Each term as a Guardian or a Governor is a thousand years, with time between service broken up by the hundred-year sabbatical." He opened those penetrating eyes. "I have served approximately forty terms."

Sylvia swallowed. She had been thinking it all seemed like fairy tales and folklore with mystics hundreds of years old. The Immortal sitting at this table admitted to being 40,000 years old. She almost laughed at the fact that her love of archaeology made her more interested than frightened by a lifeform with a true, timeless existence. "That reaches back to a time of the Neanderthal."

"We are the reason humans won out over the Neanderthal. We were but an energy form needing residence."

Sylvia's eyes bulged. "Homo neanderthalensis and homo sapiens," Sylvia muttered, her mind reeling. Many didn't realize they were two distinct species, one still here today, and one extinct. Sylvia swallowed. "You're saying the Immortal energy selected homo sapiens for residence, giving us the advantage that led to our progress while the Neanderthal declined."

"The Rainbanes were the first offspring of homo sapiens touched by the Source. Their connection to and separation from this galaxy is a history all its own. However, their reborn bloodline was hunted and mostly obliterated during the last war," Xenos said, and Sylvia saw sadness in Kinley's eyes, as if Xenos had never revealed the extent of his lifespan and the revelation had brought him great pain.

Kinley smiled when he spoke to Sylvia, but it looked like it took effort. "I'll show you the hieroglyphs that represent the Earth Sectors from the mapbook. You have one here in your book." Kinley looked away from Sylvia's still shocked face to Xenos. "It will give us both some structure to hang our new discoveries on."

"Earth Sectors?" Sylvia asked, grateful to move to a topic that wasn't giving answer to one of the great anthropological questions in a way that conflicted everything in her world.

"Yes. I'll explain Earth Sectors, and you can explain this altered glyph." He tapped her book and glanced at Xenos, who had his eyes closed again, his face unreadable.

[12.7]

Xenos let the sun warm his face as Kinley's hurt look appeared in his mind. He was tired of losing people, tired of seeing the sadness when they felt their love insignificant displayed against the extending canvas of his immortality. He would not regenerate. He would help Rosalind with this investigation and get her help with Coriolis. *I'll hold on to this lifetime, even if the cost is my immortality.* Xenos opened his eyes with resolution and saw Sylvia looking past Kinley as he flipped a page.

[12.8]

The smell of sausage and gravy reached Sylvia before Michael arrived at the table, and she was pleased to find no associated sensations of color or sound claimed her thoughts. *Maybe the synesthesia is resolving.*

"Are we back to the investigation?" Michael asked as he sat down. "I'll be through with these biscuits in a few minutes," he added when he noticed Sylvia eyeballing his plate.

Kinley tapped Sylvia's book and pushed it closer to her. "Is this the book from the altercation?"

"It is the same book, but not the one from the altercation. That one has not been located yet. I'll know more when Jezel can be questioned." Michael answered. "Why do you ask?"

Kinley shrugged. "I would just like to see the one that is the focus of the investigation."

"Tell me the rest of your story," Xenos said to Sylvia.

"There really isn't anything else. I wrote the book as a work of fiction, and on more than one occasion, someone has thought it was real — asking for coordinates to the Lost City I describe in the story."

Xenos rubbed his chin. "And this Lost City doesn't exist."

"No, I pulled it from my imagination," she said, fighting to stay angry with Michael despite the fact he had turned the plate toward her with one biscuit left as if an offering of peace. Yep, she was going to be persuaded by biscuits and gravy.

Xenos stood gracefully. "Meet us in the library near the medical bay tomorrow." He pressed his index finger to his lip, his thumb under his chin. "Make that the next day. That will be our last day in Beltway One, and we will see what we can have for you." He reached out a hand to Michael, and Sylvia watched as their hands slid together this time — their fingers interlocking, then pressing knuckle to knuckle. Sylvia replicated the pattern when Xenos turned to her and realized the equality the gesture seemed to have. Her face must have given away her curiosity. Xenos gently pulled his hand free and repeated the earlier gesture.

"This," he said, curling his pinky with hers, "is the common gesture among Immortals for a new acquaintance or formal greeting." He pulled his pinky free, demonstrating how easy it was to disconnect from the gesture.

"This," he said, placing their fingertips tip to tip like their two hands formed a fence, then offsetting the alignment so their fingers slid together till their knuckles bumped and steepled their thumbs together.

"That is a handshake among friends," Kinley interjected as Sylvia examined the feel of their hands together.

"No one can squeeze my hand so hard the bones ache," Sylvia said, repeating the gesture. "I like this handshake." Sylvia paused and looked at Xenos, who was watching her as if she were a child unwrapping a birthday gift. "It feels more connected than the first, but not controlling."

"It is a handshake among friends, colleagues, equals."

"Thank you," Sylvia said, sensing there was great meaning to those gestures for Xenos. The thought made her recall how ancient he was.

"You look as though you want to rest," Kinley said to Sylvia. "I will be in the smaller library on the other side of this floor tomorrow classifying some of the hieroglyphs in the book, if you are interested."

Michael moved to dump his plate.

"Absolutely," Sylvia answered, pushing a stray strand of hair back behind her ear. "And I'll bring your book."

Kinley and Xenos moved away, speaking between themselves.

"So, we are in Beltway One for three days?" Sylvia asked when Michael returned.

"Yes."

"Then how do we get there in just a week?"

"It takes three days in Beltway One to reach the speed or wave frequency or whatever it is for the Orbiter to travel as quantum. Beltway Two through Six is traveled in quantum, then it takes about three days in Beltway Seven to slow, shift, and travel the rest of the distance."

"How—"

"Don't ask me," Michael cut in. "You'll have to speak to one of the pilots about how it all works. I can't even explain how you can walk around in an airplane when it is traveling five hundred miles an hour."

"I was going to ask, how was your breakfast?" Her tone was hard and angry. People did that to her all the time, just interrupted or spoke over top of her. "You do that a lot, and it's rude!" She usually just stayed quiet, but she was tired, confused, and hungry since she hadn't managed to get a bite of that biscuit. She was going to bed and planned to sleep all day.

"Think about where Jezel's book might be," Michael said, something a little hard in his tone.

Sylvia blew out a breath, causing a strand of hair to flutter.

Does he know I know where it is? Why does Xenos want to speak to Tessa? Does he suspect she has the book? I may never sleep again at this rate, she thought. "I'll think about it for sure," she said.

CHAPTER THIRTEEN

V-KASANA TOSSED THE HOLOGRAM webbing over the camera before crossing to the statues. *I'm not trusting my anonymity to a pilot,* he thought. He checked for backup cameras. The corridor was bright with the extra lights that lit the statue's display. The artist had done an excellent job, and many people had set the alarm off reaching in to touch them. However, he needed to reach deep into the open space in the back to retrieve the stolen relic the thief should have left there. The GCS Separatist cell had acquired access to the passcodes for the alarm by one of the pilots in addition to the blind eye the pilot would turn, literally, by shutting off the cameras now and when he used the columns to Sim-transport in Beltway Seven. V-Kasana didn't know which pilot, and it didn't matter. The Separatist strength was built on limiting access to who represented the group within different organizations. He punched in the codes. The dropoff should have occurred at six a.m. this morning. It was the best time on one of these trips, with most people too exhausted to be up. It was almost five p.m. now, and the day had been quiet. He punched in the codes and reached into the large hole in the back of the sculpture.

"There's nothing there." He spoke out loud with the shock of it. He leaned his head over to look, though he did not anticipate seeing anything. It would have been covered with hologram masking to avoid anyone seeing it if they looked inside. He pulled the dog from the shelf, glad the alarm was shut off, and turned it upside down. *Nothing.* He quickly moved down the line, checking each sculpture. They were all empty. He removed his glasses, placed the monocle over his eye, and checked them all again for hologram weaving. There, in the hole where it should have been, was hologram residue. "It was here."

[13.1]

Cajal opened his eyes. He was facing the wall, and he rubbed his eyes, pausing before rolling over. A part of him didn't want to do so, afraid Wesley would still not be there. It wasn't uncommon for him to be gone for weeks at a time, but he had said he would be right back. He turned reluctantly, and his chest tightened at the empty bed across from him. He checked the clock on the nightstand between the two beds. It was six o'clock. The gripping pain in his chest relaxed. It was still early. Then, swinging his legs around, he noticed the clock said p.m., not a.m. He jumped up. "Six p.m!" He and Wesley were supposed to meet Asher this morning. Colors flashed in his mind, and he stopped pacing, trying to get them to calm. He and Wesley would have the rest of their lives together once they made it to the GCS. He was able to take care of himself till then. "How did I sleep so long?" he said, pulling clothes from his backpack. He had spent most of the night after he returned comparing, in his mind, the two antique pieces that looked so similar to his eyes yet were so different to his Ensight, as Wesley called it when he used the tangle in his mind to see them. The only thing that seemed different between the antiques was the colors he could see when he held them. He had tried to get the puzzle box open so he could hold one in each hand but had settled for recalling the colors of Asher's gift in his mind when the box would not open.

He lifted the twisted sheets, looking for the one he stole from the statue. *I fell asleep with it in my hand,* he thought, recalling his heavy eyelids trying to use his Ensight last night to see its colors. "There," he said, finding the relic. The hologram masking was in the bathroom. He laughed, remembering his thought to use the masking as toilet paper to see if his poop would disappear. He had changed his mind since it wasn't his, but he had left it in there. He placed the masking over the antique and moved back to the bedroom. Wesley would tell him to take a bath, but it was already six o'clock. He could just wait till tomorrow morning to bathe. He laid the antique and its masking on the nightstand while he dressed. It was definitely Wesley's. He would put it back tonight and find Asher. It worked out that he had overslept — it would save him explaining why his dad hadn't come with him to breakfast.

[13.2]

The dining area was packed as Meki and Sylvia approached the table behind the hostess. Meki had moved their reservation back to seven, and she wondered if they would have a spot. Surprisingly, she saw Michael sitting near the back to her right with a man who had long braids and gorgeous dark skin like her dad. The thought reminded her she needed to talk to her family soon and catch them up on things. Michael noticed her smile and gave her a wave, causing the man across from him to turn and grin. Sylvia blushed.

"Who are they?" Meki asked. His tone was strained, and she sensed he was trying a little too hard to be polite tonight. Something in the conversations with the GCS had pissed him off. Sylvia was reminded that they had decided to have dinner to discuss the events of the last twenty-four hours and outline plans for the GCS based on what Meki had discovered from his phone calls. "The large one is a Marshal. I'm not sure about the other one. Michael said the Marshals on the floor are plainclothes and only wear uniforms when working in the security room. So, the other one could be a Marshal as well. I only met Pierre and Michael last night." *This morning, rather*, she thought.

They reached the table, and Meki pulled out her chair then took his seat, removing his glasses and placing the tip in his mouth, his jaw tight. He placed them back on and lifted the menu. "There are a few things still not finalized. They may move the signing. Oh, and your mum reached out to me before we reached the beltway." He waved his ring. "Your phone will not work on the Orbiter. She wanted me to remind you to use the willow bark she sent in your tea if your headaches continue."

"What? Why? I mean, thank you. I will." Sylvia said, answering to everything.

"The books and items for the signing would go through customs and into Sim-transport quickly any other time, but security is enhanced for Earth Week."

Sim-transport? Sylvia thought, lifting her water at the sudden dryness in her throat. She didn't want to tell him about her experience at the column.

Sylvia relaxed. "So, they use the Sim-transport just for material transport?"

"People transport that way as well." He laid his menu down. "I realize all of this is new. There are other transport methods. Sim-transport is the quickest and is used there as easily as elevators at home." Meki's jaw relaxed. "Matter of fact, it is like taking an elevator without the drop in between. You step in a pod at the GCS in low orbit and walk out of a pod into the local airport on Replica Earth."

A pod? Sylvia glanced at Michael's table. *Had Michael overreacted about the danger at the column? Or are the pods just safer?*

"I'm glad you have a way to spend your day tomorrow, because I'll be cracking on a new schedule if the signing is moved."

"No problem," she said. "I'm eager to learn about the Earth Sectors from Kinley."

"Forgive me for not telling you about that. It is something those of us who know seldom think about. Also, your mum said your father wants a picture of you at the Archive once we arrive. Don't let me forget to take you there."

"I understand," Sylvia said. "I think the Marshals will have more investigation before they close the case with Jezel. That will tie me up some, too. So far, the working theory is the man who stole the book was a recruit who joined to get access to a drug called Cazemal. He was hoping to sell the book as contraband to get cash for more than his allotment. How does Dad know about the Archive?" she asked.

"I told him about it. He's an archaeologist with a daughter who has the same love of all things old. I thought he would want to know we would have access to a facility that housed many of the archaeological finds removed from Earth during the war to protect them." Meki smiled.

Sylvia shook her head.

"By the way, I heard a subordinate..." Meki started.

The waitress appeared.

"I'll have the chef's signature dish," Sylvia said, eager to order and find out what Meki knew.

"And you, sir?"

"I'll have the salmon and a Sancerre."

The waitress fumbled at her apron, realizing she hadn't brought the wine list.

"It's fine," Sylvia said. "I'll just have my water."

Meki tapped the vintage book menus. "It's a nice touch, old-school class," he said, handing them to the waitress.

Sylvia, undeterred by the classy ambiance, leaned forward, both elbows on the table. "The subordinate did what?"

Meki's smile faded. "The Dalenborn Overseer told me a subordinate gave the K-hold prelaunch go-signal to the staff before everyone was secure."

"Why were you at K-hold?" Sylvia remembered the argument with the stewardess.

"I went to offer to take the dead Dalen's ashes back to Earth." Meki pursed his lips. "He was Dalenborn, not a recruit. I couldn't let him be dumped like space trash. Humans create the cycle of wars. I support the Dalenborn because they are the best example of a humanity that can continue without destroying themselves and everyone else."

"Michael told me a little about the Earth Alliance. It sounds as if they, too, try to keep some peace and stability between the Tokoleh and Earth."

"The Earth Alliance gives humanity the ammunition to continue destroying itself," Meki said with such disgust that Sylvia decided she would steer clear of the topic for now. She'd get Kinley's opinion on it tomorrow. *It's inevitable that people will disagree, and I'm already in over my head,* she thought, reaching tentatively to see if any small memory about the group was tangible. The vision immediately appeared, so real his bloody hands gripped her blouse, and Sylvia gasped as if she'd just been pulled from underwater and was about to be pushed under again.

Meki reached to her. His hand covered hers, and for a moment, the vision dissolved. Sylvia saw a woman's legs removing a uniform. It was tattered, but the insignia on the pocket was similar to one she had seen recently. The memory vanished, and Sylvia took a sobering breath. "I'm fine," Sylvia said, and Meki patted her hand before removing his. *Where did I see that insignia?* Sylvia thought, then blinked rapidly with recognition. She'd seen the insignia on the Marshal uniform. She needed to talk to Michael.

[13.3]

The small library felt cramped to Xenos, accustomed to their library at home and to even larger resources such as the UBN archives, but Kinley didn't seem bothered by it. Kinley sat at the rectangular table with books and papers spread to cover the desk. Xenos relaxed in his chair, letting his head recline on the soft leather. "So, you think the man over the K-hold is lying about the fight?"

"I'm not sure who is lying," Kinley said, looking up from the table, carefully placing his pencil over the hieroglyph he was copying so as to not lose his place. "I do think it was about the book."

A door creaked, and Kinley turned as a man entered with a tray. "Would you gentlemen care for anything from the dining room?"

Xenos steepled his fingers thoughtfully. "An 1863 of the Aye Tister Di," he said.

"How is he supposed to know which wine is from the Aye Tister Di?" Kinley asked. "No one even speaks that language anymore."

"Ah," Xenos said, his eyes bright. "I think that is one of the reasons Immortals enjoy wine so much. It holds on to its history even when it changes."

The man cleared his throat. "I know which one it is, sir." He nodded at Xenos, then spoke again to Kinley. "There is only one."

"How in the world do you know they have a bottle of the very rare wine you have preference for tonight?

"He is an Immortal Wine Master, are you not, sir?" the server said with an awed expression. "There are probably only three hundred of you in the world."

Xenos nodded. "I am. When you have lived as long as I have, sometimes only the wine can express the year, and that in itself is a clue to where you will find it."

Kinley shook his head and smiled. "I'm learning lots of new things about you this trip." His smile faded as he turned back to his work.

Xenos sensed his friend's mood and spoke to refocus their discussion from him to their work. "What do you think of Sylvia's book?"

Kinley shrugged, his eyes never leaving the page as he recreated the hieroglyph from the Tokoleh book in his journal. "You saw the book she wrote. It's as if she is on the brink of telling the reader what she knows, yet is hesitant, unwilling — I don't know. I'll go over the Earth Sectors with her tomorrow and tell you what I think."

Xenos nodded as Kinley made another notation. "You know they will take your journal when we arrive at customs," Xenos said. "Every reference to that book you hold will be confiscated."

"They won't look through my journal," Kinley said, then frowned. "They will."

Xenos raised an eyebrow. "They will probably have an escort for us at customs assigned to take it from you and deliver it to the archives."

Kinley squeezed the bridge of his nose.

Xenos had made this argument before, but Kinley had seemed determined to get the information down.

"Why can't you get us permission to make a copy? You will serve as Tokoleh again and will have access to it then. Why not have a copy now?"

"Most of the Tokoleh do not care if it is copied. However, it is one of the issues agreed upon in the Alliance. If we openly disregard it, then it gives the Separatists more leverage to call the Alliance a failure. Those things may change if the Scholar's Council votes for more transparency with Earth about the Tokoleh."

The door opened, and both men fell silent.

"Your wine, sir."

"Thank you. Would you like a glass? Kinley doesn't drink in the library."

The man's eyes bulged, but Xenos noted that Kinley wasn't surprised. He was accustomed to Xenos's love of sharing fine wine.

"Sit over there," Kinley said. "Drinking wine around ancient manuscripts — it's just ridiculous!"

"My break is not for ten more minutes, so I can't sit, but I'll take a glass," he said, holding out the extra glass, having already poured one for Xenos, and handed him the bottle.

"You have to sit to enjoy wine," Xenos said, spreading his white napkin out and tilting his glass against its backdrop to evaluate the color. "Otherwise, you're just drinking, and that's a foolish habit. Come back on your break."

The man stood straighter, placing the glass back on the tray. "I will. Thank you, sir."

Xenos nodded and set the bottle on the table between the two chairs when the door clicked closed. "Wynter has a photo lead on Coriolis. I printed it," he said, lifting the folded paper from the book Kinley had loaned him, *Memoirs of the War*.

"Can you see his face?" Kinley said, standing so quickly he bumped the table.

[13.4]

Kita crawled into bed. It was midnight, technically the end of day two, and she hadn't slept much. She had identified the additional nebulous-envelopes expected through each of the beltways, which had led to a conversation this evening that had kept her up four more hours watching the cameras with Motorcycle. She rubbed her forehead as she stared at the ceiling, recalling the conversation.

"How am I supposed to know?" Motorcycle had whined. *Really,* she thought, recalling it. He had actually whined, and it was uncanny how annoyingly human some of his machine-learning features were. He had continued reluctantly, "You said you would tell me when you wanted the cameras turned off, but you didn't know when at the time we spoke." He had then crossed his arms and not spoken another word. Kita felt some remorse as she closed her eyes and let her head rest in the soft give of the pillow. *He wants to be human,* she thought, feeling a little ashamed of manipulating his robot mind with passwords and codes that made him think she was Tom, completely undermining his efforts to be human with the blatant evidence that he was a computer.

I did apologize, Kita thought, placing her hands under the pillow behind her head. She had assured Motorcycle that it was her fault for not remembering the conversation. He seemed pacified, but it didn't help her to know when Tom had planned to turn the cameras off or why. So, she had spent the last four hours checking all the cameras and trying to decide whether there was any detail that would give it away. She was exhausted beyond words now, and any further effort would be worthless in her condition. The only thing unusual she had noted was a kid that kept wandering near the statues. The area had been busy since the time they had focused their search on the cameras around 8:30. She couldn't check anything prior to then because she had asked Motorcycle to turn off the internal cameras when she had gone down to meet Sylvia at the column.

Kita bolted upright. That was it. Tom was going to shut off the cameras so Sylvia could use the column for Sim-transport, and she had almost helped her. She had to stop working with half information. Kita lay back down. There was nothing she could do now. She would keep the cameras on in case Sylvia tried again. "Send a message to the Marshal's office that there has been increased activity around the statues today and might warrant a once-over to check it out."

"Roger."

Kita wondered if Motorcycle knew where the term came from or learned it as a human response from Tom. In the quiet, she considered Motorcycle's riddle for the second mission data.

"The password hint: when I become the nut," Motorcycle had said, tapping the sticker on his head.

Kita had been too busy to think about it until now, as she recalled the sticker's words: *Most motorcycle problems are caused by the nut that connects the handlebars to the saddle.* Kita rolled to her side, thinking. *The nut was the operator, whoever sat between the handlebars and the saddle of the Motorcycle. The operator for Motorcycle was...*

Kita sat up. "Is Tom the password?"

"No."

Kita's head dropped to the pillow. She needed that information. She lifted Sylvia's book. The veil map page pulled free as she twisted. She folded it inside and almost cried at the childhood memory of old books, torn pages, and treasure hunts. *I miss you, Mom. I'm so tired.*

CHAPTER FOURTEEN

I T WAS DAY THREE, and Naidoo checked the statue alarm system. "Everything is on and operational," he said, speaking as a blue haze glowed around his ear.

"Alright," Jia said. "I'll request the camera feed from the pilots, and Pierre can review it here."

"Sounds good. I'll finish my circuit on this floor," Naidoo said, catching the eye of a young boy who looked away.

[14.1]

Cajal dropped his eyes from the man near the statues. He stood near Asher's cabin. He had tried several times to take the antique back, but someone was always around. Now, one of the men Asher had pointed out as a Marshal was checking the area. He was starting to panic. He recognized the colors of the antique as the same as Wesley's. What if it got Wesley in trouble when someone found it was gone? *Maybe the Marshal is looking for it now,* he thought, squeezing his hands into fists to steady himself.

He closed his eyes and calmed his thoughts. Wesley knew how to take care of himself and had always taught him panic was the enemy. He had time. He took a deep breath and knocked on Asher's door. Asher had offered to introduce him to Captain Braxton. The pilot went off duty tomorrow and would be coming down to meet Asher to talk about adding flight training to the Emitime program. Cajal was excited and only felt a small pang that Wesley wasn't back yet, but he would have tons to tell him when he did. The thought reminded him of the antique his brother had taken to drop off. *What if Wesley isn't back because he's looking for who had stolen the antique?* He ran from Asher's door. He had to get back to his room and leave him a message in case Wesley returned while he was trying to put the antique back.

[14.2]

Sylvia tilted the light to get a better view of the hieroglyph in the lawbook. She drew each symbol on the sectors of the map she had traced from the mapbook. "I see now. The sectors are assigned broadly, whole continents incorporating several countries as I know them." Sylvia smiled as she stroked the page of the book. It was so ancient. She didn't care what anyone else did, she planned to sit right here and help Kinley copy these two books. "What?" she asked, looking up to see Kinley watching her from the seat Xenos usually occupied. "Sorry, I was so focused I didn't hear what you asked."

"Are you sure you have never been to Tag-Baran?" he asked, his finger poised over a section in her book.

"I'm sure," she said, then paused. "Does it have a different name?"

"It has several names: Replica Saturn, Griffern, but Tag-Baran is the Earth Alliance name for the Griffon planet."

"I certainly haven't been there," Sylvia said. "It's a great idea to copy this into one of my books. When we finish, I'll put it back in the box with the pre-signed books, and no one will bother it." She looked up, a catch in her throat. "Thank you for including me in this."

Kinley closed Sylvia's book, his finger marking his spot, and smiled. "I think your archaeological knowledge is just what I need."

Sylvia smiled. "I hope we find a way to help Xenos." She felt better spending time with Kinley. She was going to see the specialist at the GCS, find out what treatments she needed, and use her new connection with Kinley to foster her archaeological passion in more than her writing. She had a purpose now for this thing she loved. "I think we will have to work on this literally till the last day to get it all done."

"I agree," Kinley said.

Sylvia smiled, wondering again why he had been so open with her about his fears for Xenos. Kinley's search to find a way for Xenos to keep his memories with regeneration made Syvia's struggle feel both supported and fragile. Memories were important. She needed to fight for hers.

"I know you have plans this evening, so I will start on it when you are done."

Sylvia sighed. She would rather stay here in the library. Meki had changed their tour plans again. However, she had agreed to dinner at 7:00 p.m. with Michael to go over some details of the investigation. Sylvia bit her lip. They both knew dinner wasn't necessary for that. "Three days in space," she said, realizing too late she'd said it out loud. Kinley looked up and smiled but didn't ask any questions. She was glad. How could she explain that three days in space made her feel disconnected in a way that had her body twitching for intimacy. She looked down at her hands. The left held the page down while her right rested comfortably atop the book, nib pen in hand. When was the last time these hands touched someone? She had to think about it: six months, eight? Regardless, no one serious since she and Chad broke up. He blamed Diane's death for their drifting apart. Had there really been years since that tragedy? It seemed like yesterday. She'd buried herself in work, just like now. Working with the nib pen and the glyphs felt like art, and she was lost. She looked up from her hands to see Kinley reading. She'd lost track of time in this work, and she liked it. This trip was going to be okay. She actually felt like she had made a friend with Kinley, and that was something she didn't do easily.

The door opened, and Sylvia looked up to see Xenos and Tessa enter.

Kinley stood, and Sylvia registered the concern on Kinley's face even before he spoke. "What is it?"

Xenos sat down, his legs crossed, his index finger on his lip, and his thumb under his chin in that thoughtful manner. It was only then that Sylvia realized Tessa was standing at the table with Jezel's book and fury in her eyes.

"Where did you get your information?" Tessa said through gritted teeth, opening the book and turning it for Sylvia to see. Sylvia sensed the woman's trembling hand was her effort to rein in her rage, not fear.

"I...I made it up. It's all just my imagination. It's not real."

"It is real!" Tessa exclaimed, then tempered her voice. "It is real, and people have died to keep hidden what you have revealed with a carelessness I can't begin to fathom."

Sylvia shot a look at Kinley, but he was focused on Xenos as if he could read the man's thoughts as he sat stone-still. Sylvia swallowed and looked down at the page of her book, Tessa's hands held open. She blinked to focus her blurred vision at the sight of the blood. Sylvia pulled the book to her. *Oh no, did Jezel die?* Sylvia shot up from her chair. "Jezel? What happened? I thought she was going to be okay."

Tessa turned from the pacing she had started and stared at Sylvia. "You thought she would be okay, so you revealed Jezel's home as the location of a hidden timepiece in a book that you knew would be distributed not only on Earth but promoted at the GCS, where the Separatist will take notice of it as well."

Sylvia ran her hands through her hair. *What is she talking about?* Sylvia squeezed her head at the temples, her hands buried in her hair as she gripped it and pushed back at the pain in her head. She tilted her head up and focused through the ache behind her eye, forcing herself to hold the gaze of a woman who loved someone so fiercely she didn't think she would ever see its match. It was then that Sylvia realized Jezel wasn't the one who died. This woman held part of Jezel with her. Sylvia could literally feel it. Tessa's emotions touched the energy of the room and became a color in her mind. It receded to a network of ribbons she could see in her mind as she began to understand, began to somehow connect with Tessa's pain. The pain behind her eye was still there, but it seemed as if it followed the pain she had pulled from Tessa, and she could focus around it now. "I promise I don't know about your timepiece, and I'll do anything I can to help Jezel, but she's not the one who died protecting that secret, is she?"

"No," Tessa said with a weight that rolled her shoulders forward with what seemed an equal measure of relief and pain. "Jezel is okay right now," she said, moving back to the desk. "But this book puts her and her entire family at risk."

Sylvia wrapped her arms around her waist and sat down, unfolding her arms only to touch the pages of the book. "What are the numbers she hid with her blood?"

"The numbers underneath Jezel's blood are the longitude coordinates for her family's manor," Tessa said. "Jezel thought someone had randomly figured it out from recognizing the description you give of the manor."

So, she covered them with her blood and asked me not to tell them where *it* was?" Sylvia sat back in the chair. "When Jezel asked me not to tell them where it was...*It* wasn't the book. *It* was the hidden timepiece."

"I'm having trouble with this, Xenos, but you may be right," Tessa said.

Sylvia glanced at the man who now stared directly at Kinley, who Sylvia hadn't realized had stood and moved toward her. She closed her eyes and almost cried anew at the evidence he had been ready to come to her defense and yet trusted something in his friend that had stayed his hand.

Tessa leaned across the desk and unfolded the map on the opposite page. "Jezel doesn't care much about numbers, but I do." She tapped a small emblem in the corner. "Those are not random glyphs."

Sylvia touched the emblem and fought back the wave of nausea as the vision of the dead man appeared, reaching for her. She pulled her hand away and swallowed hard.

"They are ancient Tokoleh numbers, a system that hasn't been used in a very long time. When I looked at the page, I realized they hadn't known the coordinates and wrote them down." Tessa paused, waiting till Sylvia looked up from the page.

Sylvia did and felt the penetrating stare cut as deep as the words when Tessa tapped the book as she spoke.

"They translated them."

Sylvia's head dropped into her hands. "What have I created?" she whispered.

"It looks like a road map to the hidden Portal keys, if you know how to read it," Xenos said, tapping his steepled fingers on his chin.

Sylvia lifted her head, dropping her hands to the table. "But I don't know anything about Portal keys. I didn't even know the Tokoleh existed till this trip."

"I believe you," Xenos said, standing.

Tessa made a harumph, and Xenos modified his statement. "I believe you believe that."

It's only fiction if you don't believe. Isn't that what that reader had said when she gave her the photo, or had that been Meki? She was struggling to recall under Tessa's intelligent glare. "What do you think?" Sylvia asked Tessa.

"I think there is something else in there that Jezel wants you to see."

Sylvia felt her neck jerk back with surprise. It was the involuntary response of surprise that allowed her to see the flash of something hidden in Tessa's eyes. There was something important left unsaid.

"Jezel has a sixth sense about people, and she trusts you. By extension, that means I will trust you. For now."

There it was. If Jezel were awake, she would tell her more than Tessa was willing to give. Sylvia felt terrible, but she needed to play that card. "Let me speak to Jezel."

[14.3]

"Need to move dinner to tomorrow," Sylvia said as she texted the words to Michael. Sylvia felt a tinge of hypocrisy at the thought of what she was about to do but nodded as Tessa entered the waiting room. The woman had sent her a message only moments ago confirming she would allow her to speak with Jezel. Sylvia understood. It was a lot to ask, and she was grateful Tessa hadn't exploded at the request. She was beginning to see what Jezel must love in this fierce, beautiful woman.

"Thank you for agreeing," Sylvia said. "I do know this is difficult, and if it matters at all, I want her recovery to be as smooth and comfortable as possible."

"If I did not think that was true, you would not be here," Tessa said as they walked back toward Jezel's room. "Jezel would kill me if she knew you had asked to see her and I didn't let you. She came through surgery well, but Doc Turner recommends she rest in cryo because of the..." Tessa paused. "There are some pre-existing issues."

The words made Sylvia rake at herself inside. She was reasonably certain whatever that pre-existing issue was, it had something to do with the hidden timepiece, and to some degree, she was using this opportunity to get something she needed. They both knew it and had at least apparently come to the conclusion it was necessary. "I would like to know why she came to me with her book. I mean. She asked me to do something..." *Or rather, not to do something,* Sylvia thought, recalling the woman's words: *Don't tell them where it is.* "I want to do what she asked, but I'm not sure I understood all of what she wanted."

Tessa's brow furrowed deeper, and her hand pulled from the doorknob, leaving the door ajar. "As I said, *she* trusted you, though she confessed to me she didn't know what you were," Tessa said with a demeanor that was both businesslike and thoughtful while ultimately conveying she was still weighing the evidence.

Sylvia tasted her fear as real as when she climbed on the Orbiter. "I'm..." She swallowed. Her mind released the silver thread to the manor memory she had tried to recall, and the vision of the dead man with the red eyes disappeared. "I'm trying to figure that out."

"Are you Tokoleh?"

"No," Sylvia said quickly. "No, I'm not even Immortal," she added, surprised at the understanding she had gained in her few days with Kinley. She felt something soften in her mind as the tangle glowed along with a blue ribbon of thought. *Focus on helping Jezel. Let everything else find its place.* She took Tessa's hand. "I care about Jezel. She won my heart a little with her chatterbox greeting when I came on the Orbiter."

Tessa gave a knowing smile that Sylvia knew was due to a memory of Jezel and not her acceptance of Sylvia.

The joy of that smile pushed at that blue network, and Sylvia reconsidered. *Maybe I should wait till she is healed more. What if this sets her back in her recovery?* "If you don't think it is a good idea to talk with her, I will wait and ask when she has had more time to heal."

"Shouldn't I be allowed to make that decision?" a voice croaked from inside the room.

Tessa and Sylvia froze, then stepped through the wide door together. Jezel's smile was big and found Tessa first. Tessa moved to her with fluid grace. Sylvia watched as the woman lifted her arm just at the elbow to touch Tessa's face as she bent to cradle her head against the pale hand, strong despite the injuries and determined in its movement.

"She knows where the key is located, Tessie."

Tessa's back went rigid.

Sylvia watched as Jezel's thumb stroked Tessa's face, and as if it physically pulled the tension from Tessa, she saw the woman's shoulders and back relax.

"Come sit down," Jezel said, and Sylvia made her way to the chair. She was glad she had brought her original copy of her book since she did not see the one she left with Tessa anywhere. "I tried to recall some of the memories I now associate with my description of the manor." Sylvia cleared her throat. *How do I explain this irrational fear of red eyes concocted by my imagination?* "I experience nasty side effects when I try to recall some of my memories."

"Hmm, like what?" Jezel asked.

Tessa shifted, one-handedly pulling a chair to the cryo bed, never releasing the interlaced hold she had with Jezel's fingers on the frame.

Sylvia licked her lips. She wasn't prepared to express something she still couldn't understand. "I don't know how to explain it, but I thought if you could give me some information about the manor, I don't seem to have the same problem with newer memories." Sylvia shrugged. "It may not help, but I can't express how shocked I am at the possibilities you and Tessa have described."

"Will you try it here with us?" Tessa asked.

Sylvia realized it was the first time Tessa's voice had released the edge it held when she spoke to her. That was something, at least.

"I...I...it's embarrassing." *Why am I telling them this?* Sylvia stroked her book. She had to admit there was something calming about being with the two of them. "I'll try."

Sylvia closed her eyes. She could see the tangle in the back of her mind. With a thought, she wrapped the idea of the manor from her book with a single glyph from the page and tugged at the tangle. Her stomach lurched, and she gripped the book in her hands. A ribbon of color unfurled with red eyes in its wake. She felt the sweat bead, and the hair at the base of her neck stood up. *Why am I so damn afraid? It's my imagination, not even real.* But she could hear her breathing shallow and rapid as he reached for her.

Sylvia's eyes flew open. "I can't"

Jezel pulled her hand free of Tessa's loose hold and reached for Sylvia. "Sit with it. A little each day. I'm too young as an Immortal to have any deep answers for you, but I see the flare of that Immortal strand humans carry when you reach for it."

"I can do that." Sylvia gently squeezed Jezel's hand.

"Good. Tessa and I will keep looking at the book you left us till the Marshals confiscate it. Then we will buy a new one at your signing." Jezel smiled, and Sylvia was amazed at the beauty the woman radiated even as she healed. "We'll handwrite some details about the manor for you."

"And we will let you know if we notice anything else in your book that might help."

It was the first time Tessa had offered her help without a nudge from Jezel. The idea of that seemed to lift some of the lingering gray of her mood. She failed again to face this warden of her mind, but she had some direction. "This is my cabin," Sylvia said, standing to point at the Orbiter diagram, which was in every room for emergencies. "If it is easier than finding me, you can place your manor notes in the locked drop box at my door."

Tessa nodded, but Jezel spoke. "I forgot they installed those when they added the business suites. That will work."

"I'm going to head back to my room. Thank you." She squeezed the book tight to her chest and stood.

"There's a page hanging out," Tessa said, reaching with her free hand.

Sylvia turned the book so she could view the pages, not the spine. It was the veil page. It folded out differently in her hand-bound copy than in the ones they had printed, and she hadn't folded it properly. "I'll fix it later. It will have to be refolded." It was then that she decided she would take a detour. *Maybe if I relax, I can sit with this demon.*

[14.4]

Kita pulled at the biosuit she'd secured from the emergency response desk outside the boiler room. "Galactic dice, these things are tight as wetsuits," she mumbled. She'd left the cockpit exactly half an hour before the Marshal was scheduled to arrive for what he had told Motorcycle was standard protocol questions in an ongoing investigation regarding the deaths in K-hold. She tapped the microphone in the biosuit. "Testing." *Hmm, the sound's too clear.*

She moved toward the boiler that fed the steam room as she checked time in the right corner of the helmet. "Shield," she muttered after seeing her face reflected in the stainless steel of the boiler. The face shield on the helmet went black. "Better." She couldn't afford to be in the cockpit when the Marshal arrived, but if she didn't speak to him, he would just come back. So, she would talk to him from here. "He can watch me..." She grunted, pulling on a hose clamp cover. "...fix this hose." She staggered back as the clamp tip broke when the cover popped off. *Oops, now I do have to fix it.* She shut off the boiler and then disconnected the hose that fed steam to the steam room from this boiler. She let some of the residual steam push out into the room before she moved over to the manual intercom on the wall and removed the hologram webbing she'd placed over the camera earlier. The camera viewed the intercom and this side of the boiler room. She wanted them to see her here now, at least part of her. She stood on tiptoe to shift the camera view slightly.

"Speech conversion broadcaster," she said, hearing the click of the mechanism in the helmet that converted your voice by an AI system to broadcast your voice if the helmet mic wasn't functional. "Testing."

The robotic sound of the word made her grin. "Perrr-fect." She moved back to the intercom a few feet away and pressed the button for her cockpit.

"Hello, you've connected with Major Haddock's cockpit. Identify the problem."

Kita felt a little guilt at exploiting how dependable AI was when protocol was involved. "Hi, Motorcycle, it's me." She rattled off Tom's password.

"Tom? I thought you were going down to the steam room to relax before our meeting with the Marshal."

"I did, but something was wrong, so I stepped down to the boiler room to check it out. Is the Marshal there? I don't want to hold him up."

"Yes, he arrived just minutes before your call patched through."

"Marshal, I apologize. I need to get this boiler system checked so I can send a work order to the engineers, or the steam room will be down, and you know how travelers like their luxury."

"Not a problem," an unfamiliar voice said.

Kita was glad it wasn't the Marshal from the column. Not that he could identify her in the suit, but his keen eyes had told her he didn't miss many details and she would have to be careful not to lie in front of Motorcycle if questions came up about Sylvia.

"I only have a few questions."

"Shoot," she said, pressing the intercom on the wall to keep the line open as she moved back to the boiler to fix the hose. *Hope no one decides to use the steam room for a while.*

[14.5]

Cajal climbed the stairs, knowing Wesley preferred them. He had checked the 3-D room for Asher, but Asher wasn't there. After using his Ensight again on the antique, he confirmed the antique was Wesley's. *Asher can help me give it back and find Wesley.* He pulled on the heavy door to enter Asher's floor again. Maybe Asher had been resting. Cajal paused at the commotion of people near Asher's door. He started to back away, wondering if they had found the antique missing from the statues and were here to blame Asher. He'd wanted to put it back before they found out. He didn't want Asher to be upset with him. His back was against the bar on the door when they wheeled the gurney out. They had him covered completely.

Cajal rushed toward the gurney. "You've got his head covered," he shouted, but a lady turned and held him back.

"He can't breathe," Cajal protested.

The gurney hit an uneven spot, and a limb fell free from the sheet to bang against the gurney. Cajal's eyes widened, and he couldn't hear anything else as he backed toward the door and rushed down the stairs.

[14.6]

Sylvia turned in a circle, taking in the space. *There's not a lot of steam.* Sylvia dropped her head. It was par for the course. She'd felt motivated to find a relaxing place to do what Jezel recommended and just sit with the vision, one little piece at a time. But, despite the luxury of the room, the dissipating steam made her feel more exposed than relaxed. She collapsed on the wooden bench and opened her book. "At least I can be comfortable while I refold the veil map," she said, unfolding the page and pressing out a crease that had formed.

Sylvia jumped when the door pulled open and an astronaut walked into the space. She rubbed at her eyes. *Did my vision shift from a red-eyed warden to an alien?*

"Sorry, I didn't realize anyone was in here. I was just down in the boiler room fixing the steam line. The steam should be flowing again soon."

"Oh, that's great!"

"Not exactly the best place to come to read." Astronaut pointed at the book and tilted its head.

Sylvia laughed, and it felt nice. Maybe it was the robotic voice or the easy sense of humor, but this "alien" made her feel strangely comfortable. "I'm not reading, I'm just refolding this map."

"And you came here to do that?"

"Actually, I came here to try and relax and sit with my thoughts."

"May I join you?"

"Sure." Sylvia patted the bench.

Astronaut took the seat and pointed to the map. "What is that?" it asked, pointing at the map.

"It's just a veil map I designed. You can lay it over the maps in my book and see little hidden details."

"You mean like that hieroglyph."

Sylvia looked down, startled to see a single eye. She'd designed the veil page to lay over the maps, not over the regular pages. *I didn't put any special designs on the standard pages.* She lifted the veil, and the glyph disappeared. She turned the page, placing the veil over the next one. Nothing. She flipped back, her heartbeat thudding in her ears as she laid the veil across the page, and the eye reappeared. Sylvia swallowed hard and folded the veil page back up. There it was, a glyph she never recalled designing on the page. *Exactly — one you can't recall.* Sylvia blew out a breath and let her head fall back against the wooden plaits that formed the back of the bench seats. She gripped the veil page in her hand and tried to relax to keep from damaging it. She purposely kept her veil page unbound from the book because she used its folded form as a bookmark. The mass copies had the veil page bound into the book's map section. She rubbed at her eyes with her free hand.

"Am I intruding?"

Sylvia lifted her head. "No. I just…" She paused, wondering why she wanted to tell this stranger about the vision. "I'm just finding it hard to be with some of my own thoughts."

"I can relate to that."

"Really?"

"Sure." Astronaut shifted, and its knee bumped Sylvia as it removed the glove covering its right hand — a woman's hand. She laid her hand out open, palm up. "We're two humans who understand painful pasts that connect us. Place your hand on my palm, close your eyes, and find one of those hard thoughts."

Sylvia reached her hand out but hesitated. She couldn't sit with this terrible fear with a stranger. Her hand hovered, and she noted the scar on the woman's wrist where the skin looked scratched and irritated. She wanted to take the woman's hand, but she couldn't trust herself. She needed to sit with these things alone, not embarrass herself in front of strangers. And now there was this new strangeness of a glyph miraculously appearing on a text page where there had never been one before. It was too much for herself, much less a stranger. Sylvia pulled her hand back toward her chest, rubbing at the charm that lay beneath her shirt. "I better go, but thank you."

"I didn't do anything."

"Apparently, you fixed the steam room," Sylvia said, casting her eye around and finding it difficult to see beyond the rising steam in the room. "And you made me feel comfortable even though you look and sound like an alien." Sylvia laughed, and it felt good. She felt good, or at least better. "I should go."

"Tell me this. Does your veil map use steam to reveal the hidden things?"

"Not steam so much as heat. It's a chemical compound containing carbon applied to the maps to make the hidden things only visible when the light designed in the veil map creates heat that breaks down the compound, releasing the carbon." She pulled her lips tight to keep from saying more. She didn't want to reveal that the glyph was a surprise to her. She'd never laid the veil over pages in her book, only the maps. Suddenly, she needed to get back to her room and see if the glyph was on the pages of the mass books or just her original copy.

CHAPTER FIFTEEN

V-KASANA SLIPPED DOWN THE corridor. They would be approaching a nebulous-envelope in Beltway Seven. It was day six, and he would use the column to Sim-beam to the fuel-cell ship. He needed more of the Arnica Montana. He reached into his pocket as he neared the camera that faced the column, adjusting the packets of willow bark he would treat with the Arnica. He would need the chemical safe-space and freedom to work that the Separatist fuel ship afforded him. Chemistry was precise work, and he liked it, though he seldom had time to do it anymore. He tilted his head down as he approached and tossed the hologram mesh up over the camera. He would not take any chances. *Too much uncertainty surrounds this entire project.* He had selected this column because it was away from public view and only had one camera. It was possible the cameras had not been shut off. There had been enough mistakes already. He checked the time on his ring. *Ten seconds.* The Intuit on the other spacecraft would be prepared to balance for the Sim-transport in five seconds. He reached up and pressed the hieroglyph. The column shimmered, and V-Kasana could feel the vibration even as he held the mass to balance — four heartbeats — then he disappeared.

V-Kasana shivered as the glow around him and the column shifted from blue to violet, then black. Sudden, deep, final — then darkness was gone.

"Vrishi, it's good to see you." The woman's voice was melodic. V-Kasana turned to face her even as the Intuit released her hand from the glyph inlaid on the table before her that matched the column glyph. He hated that she knew his name, much worse that she abbreviated it, making him sound like a pet, but she was the only Intuit on the fuel ship.

"Zierda. Where is Biagio?" he asked, unwilling to let her know how it grated on him.

"He is preparing for the Scholar's Council. He is not pleased you failed to retrieve the relic."

"I cannot retrieve what is not there!"

"He understands that and has new information for you. The man, contracted to deliver the relic, designated the money for the Emitime School. He hid it pretty well, and our resources have not yet been able to isolate for which student, but once we know, you are to find them."

"I already have a project for my time at the GCS," V-Kasana said calmly, not taking a seat, instead moving out of the large room toward the hallway and his rooms where he could locate the Arnica. The coating of the willow bark had to be precise to have the effect he wanted. He would need this batch once they arrived at the GCS.

He tapped his ring. The second nebulous-envelope approached in just under thirty minutes. That was plenty of time to coat the willow bark and be ready for transport back to Orbiter C13.

Once he had coated the willow bark, V-Kasana stood at the column with Zierda again at the table. They didn't speak. The nebulous-envelope approach ticked down on his ringphone and he reached to the glyph. V-Kasana felt the release from the Simultaneity as he reappeared in the barren corridor of Orbiter C13. He walked in front of the camera, reaching up to pull the hologram masking free once he was past. He squeezed the treated willow bark in his opposite hand.

[15.1]

"You dropped this," Sylvia said, lifting the picture from the floor.

Kinley shifted his book to point at the table. "Just lay it there," he said, reaching for his tea and stirring it. "Thank you, for the willow bark. You say your mom collects it for you?"

Sylvia nodded.

"You should try it," he said, waving his spoon at Xenos to his right and Michael, who sat across the table.

Sylvia laid Kinley's picture on the table, pressing out the wrinkles. "Yes, she gave it to me for my headaches. I've been using it for years." *But it doesn't help the headaches I get now much,* Sylvia thought.

"Well, tell her thank you. It helps my arthritis." He rubbed his hand before lifting his tea.

"Wait," Xenos said, staying his hand. "How long have you been drinking this in your tea?"

"Couple days," Kinley said, lifting an eyebrow.

Sylvia tilted her head in question as Xenos took the cup and smelled it. "Do you smell that woodsy smell?"

"Yes. I can smell better than you. I presume it's the smell of the willow bark."

"No," Xenos said, his lips in a hard line. "Willow bark has a more wintergreen smell."

Sylvia pulled her own tea close and breathed in the aroma. "It's always had that smell," she said. "But it smells stronger than before, now that you've said something. Has it gone bad? I've had this batch for a while."

"Perhaps," Xenos said, but something was off in the way he closed his eyes, tilted his head, and furrowed his brow as if reaching for a memory he didn't want to find. Meki had a last-minute public relations issue to address and couldn't make it. Now, she wished he was here. He was so much more gifted at reading people. Most passengers were last-minute packing, but Sylvia had asked to spend some time with these new friends, and they had agreed. Tonight, they had each selected a book to read a passage from at dinner.

"Go ahead and read," Xenos said, opening his eyes. "Just hold on the tea for a moment."

Both Sylvia and Kinley pushed their tea away at the same time.

"Alright, from *Memoirs of the War*," Kinley said, skimming to the back of the book to find the passage. "This section has some incredible imagery and will give you a firsthand account of the war through a sniper's scope.

"With sunset, the wind whipped through the uneasy night ravaging the sparse grass and spiny, evergreen shrubs at the cliff edge where a heavy fog sank low on the mountain that muted the semi-automatic clip of rapid-firing weapons to the east.

"The minutes crept by, and hours of silence begged the moon to hide its bright light in the fog and bring with it the cover of darkness. The drag and crash of the river rapids below pulled at the wind; the wind eased and eddied the fog, stirring it as mischief but not dispersing its thick coat. Something shifted from the fissure cut into the mountain, upright in the black stillness like an evergreen set taut to its full height, and a deep voice spoke, just above a whisper, 'Now — make haste but be silent. Hold to the shoulder near the mountain and carry the children; the rockfall will give us away.'

"Crumbled stone shifted beneath the traveling feet as the wind lifted and swayed the trees, casting shadows of the refugees huddled and moving as one along the

treacherous steep of the mountain. Their desperate vigilance availed them little as the 'River of Falling Banks' held true to its name. Stones and earth broke free, rolled, and splashed into the raging water, creating an ominous sound of loss. A small child gasped, then buried her head in a blanket, her cries muted and her hands as tight to the neck of the one who carried her as the hands of the carrier held fast the mountain to regain his footing. Behind them, a sound of snapping twigs sheared the night when someone's boot lace caught in the low-growing briars of a dead bush.

"When at last the rage of the river engulfed their ears, every nerve set raw, plucked to shreds. The refugees seemed to brace themselves to be broken by the hate that blasted its way behind them or the river that stood before them and dared them to try for a different shore. The river flowed north to Pittsburgh from the mountains in the south, and they need only follow it there.

"The riverboat buried in fog yielded to the merciless throws of the river while tethered to a great tree at its bank. Its master stood wet on the rocks that caught the creaming white of the great river's spray. His face was grim, and water dripped from his long beard as his head tilted to listen in the distance. 'Be quick, the lot of you, or I'll leave you for the dogs that follow.' He turned his face back toward a man as wet as he was in the boat. 'We'll have to shoot the rapids at the portage and exit further up the river.'

"A child cried as he was passed into the boat, and the wet fisherman pinched the child's nose and mouth till the child's eyes bulged with a primal fear that resolved to submission. Two more children passed into the boat, the last holding fast to her blanket as her carrier followed her and shuffled quickly to the far side, shielding her from the splashing current as the fisherman lifted a struggling small man fighting every blast of the river to gain the boat. The shivering woman behind him pressed upon him bodily to move quicker. Bullets ripped the air and, wet to their core from the river spray, the last of the group slipped deep in the water, holding fast to the vessel when it rocked away as the fisherman on the rocks released the tether and jumped to the boat. The bright tracing rounds blasted the area, and the broad man who had steered the group down the mountain reached with the fisherman to rake in those who still clawed at the sides of the craft as the river beat against them and nearly swallowed the boat, dragging it fast away.

"A single figure raced across the crumbled stone at the river's edge, screaming unheard to not be left behind. She slipped madly across the wet, mossy rocks and into the deep, struggling to reach the boat only to be pulled back and down by the current. Struggling to the surface, she pulled and clung to the root of the great tree as

the rapids pounded the area; her screams for the boat's return were buried in gasps for air."

Xenos reached for the book but halted.

The pain in his face forced Kinley to stop reading. Sylvia had noticed it too.

Xenos's hand fell back to his lap as if he had lost all energy, and his words were distant. "Her boot laces had been trapped by the dead bush, and the branches refused to release them even as her fingers bled to get them free," Xenos said quietly, adding to the story what seemed like a picture from his mind reaching back in time. "Amazing the detail you can see through a sniper's scope."

"It's not exactly dinnertime cheerfulness," Kinley said, reading Xenos's face. He closed the book.

Xenos gave a grief-stricken look to Kinley. "I'm glad you read it, though. I put the book down myself after the first chapter because the sniper who wrote it spoke so candidly of the devastation of a war I've wanted to forget."

"I'm so sorry," Sylvia said. "This is my fault."

"Do not feel bad," Xenos said reaching to touch her hand that traced aimlessly on the picture she'd lifted from the floor. "Please use the Coriolis comrade photo to mark your place, Kinley. Perhaps I will read it in its entirety later."

Kinley nodded but didn't move to lift the photo. "It was a lead in our hunt for the war criminal Coriolis, but it looks like a dead end."

Sylvia paused, glancing down at Xenos's hand.

"Thank you for recommending we do this," he said to Sylvia, then settled back in his chair.

Sylvia's eyes lifted to his.

"She was delayed in her descent to the river," Xenos said, his words a whisper. "I've looked for that woman for years. I didn't realize till we reached the shore that she was not with us. I know now she is gone."

"You were there?" Sylvia said, her eyes widening and her whispered words sounding loud in the silence of the table.

"Yes," he answered. "I carried the child. The woman handed her to me as we descended the cliff and she paused to free her bootlaces from the brush. Once in the boat, I had shifted the child to the floor and covered her. I had seen the glint of sniper glass. Many children during that time were targets because of their gifts. My immediate concern was that the child might be a target."

Sylvia closed her eyes at his pain but also sensed release from the man. Maybe Xenos wanted to forget this life even as she and Kinley tried to keep him in it. Her heart ached. She wanted this evening to be a happy memory. "I'm sorry the tea is bad," Sylvia said, wanting to shift the focus from Xenos, who seemed uncomfortable sitting with the haunted memory.

She lifted the picture from the table when his face twisted with some remembered pain. She'd noticed a detail when she smoothed its edges, one that might be good news and lighten the mood. "Well, I have some brighter news. The painting behind this man looks like the missing Rembrandt. Maybe you've found 'The Storm of Galilee' painting and can collect the reward." She smiled.

Kinley's eyes shot to Xenos.

The man's ancient face was stone, carved with some new decision. He blinked slowly as if returning from a dream. "The tea isn't bad," he said, holding Sylvia's eyes with his deep lapis-blue ones before he lifted the picture from the table. "It's poisoned."

Michael reached abruptly for Sylvia's cup. "Poison?" he asked, smelling the liquid.

She'd forgotten he was beside her. It was strange for him to have been so quiet. "Has anyone had access to your willow bark?"

"No," she said. "Wait. I brought two pouches of it with me. I couldn't find this one," she said, pulling a leather pouch free from her purse, holding the straps with the tips of her fingers. "Then a steward delivered a box of books from the payload bay I had requested for signing, and it was inside."

"Do you remember putting it in there?"

Sylvia let her head fall back as she tried to remember. "No, but I also don't remember not putting it in there. My suitcase is packed to the hilt, and there was a lot of stress and rushing around before the flight." Sylvia recalled the fear that had gripped her only a week ago. Her mind poked at the fear, then layered over it Xenos's words. *Poison. Is someone trying to kill me?*

Xenos seemed to read her thoughts and said, "It's wolfsbane. In low doses, it can cause nausea. If you only recovered this batch recently, then what you shared with Kinley previously was from the batch in your suitcase?"

Sylvia noticed Kinley rubbing his stomach, and hers twisted.

Michael and Xenos appeared to take in Kinley's motion as well.

"Yes," Xenos said. "It is probably the culprit for your episode of nausea."

Sylvia searched the table, wanting somewhere for her eyes to land that didn't make her panic escalate. "Why hasn't it made me nauseous?"

Michael answered. Apparently, his stint of silence was over. "It impacts each species differently, but it can cause heart trouble, hallucinations, and death if the dose is high enough."

Species? What does it do to humans with strange visions lurking around their memories? Sylvia thought. Maybe the vision was a hallucination.

"Is there anything else you may have forgotten to tell me?" Michael said with a frustration Sylvia had already seen once.

She tried not to flush at the recollection of how they had made up after the flash of conflict when she told him she had Jezel's book. The kiss had led to more heat than either of them had expected, but they'd managed to reestablish some lines after the one-night fling. It was funny — she felt like they were friends now, as if they'd just needed to get over that, but the night had scratched the itch she had only recently allowed into her awareness. It was clear it had been a non-repeatable moment of lust and built-up tension when he was gone before she awoke, and she was glad. "No, I'm an open book," she said with a smirk.

"Well, you might want to be a little more careful since it appears someone is trying to make you sick, if not kill you."

The words bounced around Sylvia's mind like a ringing gong. Was it possible this was what was wrong? That she was just sick from something in the willow bark she'd been putting in her tea? "You're right," she said, distracted by her thoughts as she replayed the weeks leading up to her flight.

Michael turned his focus to Xenos and Kinley. "The evidence we have so far indicates the Overseer for the Dalen has lied about a few key issues. However, my efforts at a repeat interview have been blocked. I'm going to need Rosalind's clout and push to make that happen, but I intend to bring all of these pieces together, and I will appreciate any input you have."

Xenos steepled his fingers. "I recognize the wolfsbane because the Separatists used it a lot during the war to mask the gifts of the species so Guardians could not locate them. I think your investigation is but a thread in a bigger tapestry."

CHAPTER SIXTEEN

C AJAL SAT ON HIS bed. It was the final day in Beltway Seven, and the sculptures along the hallway had flowers, hand-drawn pictures, and other trinkets almost overflowing the glass features that held them. Cajal had been one of the first to place something inside once the news of Asher was made known. He had not left his room since. Instead, he had spent every day working the puzzle box, trying to figure out the code from the hints Asher had given him during the time they had spent touring the Orbiter. He felt bad that he hadn't missed Wesley as much then and hoped Wesley would come back soon. Asher never would. He nearly threw the puzzle box in frustration and grief, but then he clutched it to his chest, lay back on his bed, and cried. The doctor had refused to let him in, saying these things shouldn't be seen by a child. He wiped at his tears, anger replacing loss. Tonight, he would sneak down to where they were keeping Asher's body until they reached the GCS. He had seen the death-cryos used to keep bodies preserved for burial. *They put Father in one,* Cajal thought. He would say goodbye to Asher.

[16.1]

Kita scrolled through the parameters for the docking system. She rubbed her eyes, feeling every moment of the seven days the trip had taken. She had taken over the flight three days ago. She had worked all the details out for docking, knowing she would have to dock manually to avoid the security system. She could then exit without being noticed. "Four more hours, and we will be docking at the GCS," Kita said, pulling up the screen for a 360-degree view around the craft.

"Four hours, two minutes, and fifteen seconds," Motorcycle responded.

"Show-off," she said, grinning at his precision and reminding herself to make sure she erased any information that might be problematic for her once she was free of him.

"What's our next adventure, friend?" Motorcycle said, lifting his cup of coffee in a manner Kita realized was almost identical to her own. "We have 525,600 minutes..." he sang, queueing yet another soundtrack from his archive.

"Who knew having thousands of years of music at your fingertips could be so fun?" Kita said. "Symbiosis." She smiled, watching again how he cradled the cup in two hands, a mimicry of her. *Motorcycle so wants to be human*, Kita thought, marveling at the fact that she would kind of miss him. "Wait," she said to no one. *When you become the nut connecting the handlebars to the saddle, you become the human.* "Symbiosis is the password," Kita shouted.

"You remembered!"

Kita grinned. She could now get the passcode-protected data then erase his memory. The grin faded. It would be easy to wipe the memory of this trip from his system, but with that, he would lose all his machine learning, and she couldn't shake how horrible that made her feel.

CHAPTER SEVENTEEN

N ATHAN FELT GOOD ABOUT today. All the Orbiters had landed yesterday. The patients, both expected and unexpected, were safely transferred from the Orbiters, and his research funders were present. The race
would be a great way to relieve the residual tension. He could beat Rosalind
if he remained focused. Ultimately, the whole day was to start off the Earth
Week celebration, and Rosalind supported his lab's fundraising race just for
a chance at bragging rights.

He noticed Rosalind in his peripheral vision and wondered how she would
take the news if the imaging identified an untrained, adult Sahaja Intuit. His
heart ached for her loss, but she would be angry with sympathy. He watched
her stroke the metal of her robotic legs. They were functional — more than
functional, when you added the connection to her brain that could see things
in one five-thousandth of a second. He was amazed at what she could design.

[17.1]

Rosalind smiled and fingered the latch on her engineered leg.

The cold of the latch was blue in her mind, and she pushed the color
through her network as far as it would go, watching its energy shift form. The
injury to her spine inhibited her ability to transfer the energy of her Intuit
network outside her body, but she still had this. "Are you ready?" she said,
registering Nathan's grin as a sign his mood had shifted. He was thinking.
She could see it in his bright green eyes.

Intelligence was the strength of his human form. Speed, power, and instinct
represented the strength of his Griffon form. She would have better luck against
him in this race if he were thinking, not instincting, as the Griffons did. She

worried about the dangerous line he walked near his primitive Griffon form. It had strength, speed, and power but no return if it went too far.

"I'm instincting," Nathan said as if reading the look on her face as they took start positions.

Rosalind laughed, knowing her often-used quip to him — *think, don't instinct* — was in both their minds, but he wasn't instincting. She was good for this race. He was tapping it, but a safe distance from transformation, or there would be amber in his eyes. He would never risk that for a race. "Let's see," she said.

"Overcoming barriers," Nathan said, louder than he intended. "Sorry." He quirked a smile at Rosalind's raised eyebrow.

"The race obstacles had me thinking about barriers to work progress. The species testing case is scheduled," he said, watching her face and then continuing when she gave no response. "I requested the patient's MRI reports from Pittsburgh in Earth's Third Sector. I don't have the reports yet."

"I'll see what I can do," Rosalind said.

"Thanks," Nathan said, grateful. "One phone call from Rosalind slices red tape."

I pay a high price for that power, she thought. There was a lot of red tape between the Earth Sectors and the Galactic Core Station. Everything went through the Universal Bureau of Negotiations. And surprisingly, the vast population of Earth, with its sector divisions, didn't even know it existed. *Will that all change after this week?* She recalled her conversation with Xenos. As UBN security director, she served as an adviser to the Scholar's Council. The UBN was the pinnacle of the triangle that balanced the Tokoleh and Earth Alliance, and the UBN director stood at the top of that pinnacle. *Pinnacles are precarious things*, Rosalind thought.

[17.2]

The gun cracked, and Nathan bolted from the line. Rosalind must have been lost in thought because he was in the lead and carried the lead into and out of the cul-de-sac that led to the horse barns for the hotel guests who wanted to experience nature on the GCS but were uncomfortable on the back of a Griffon. Rosalind was close. The familiar hum of her robotic legs warned him and urged him on. She was one of the strongest women he knew. He managed a small but firm lead on her as he negotiated the first obstacle. There were other runners in the race, but he and Rosalind separated from them and battled for first. They exchanged the lead through several obstacles, but he came out of the last turn and could finally see the finish line. Then, as quickly as he saw it, it disappeared as he felt his foot angle into a divot. He tumbled and rolled but was unable to regain his feet. Rosalind gave his hair a flip as she moved ahead.

"Galactic dice!" Nathan stood, glad his roll had prevented a bad twisting injury to the ankle, but his pride would hurt soon as Rosalind charged forward to the finish line. She seemed to be running faster than usual as he stood and struggled to make up the distance.

[17.3]

"You better move before Jenny and Shavar catch up," Rosalind shouted over her shoulder to Nathan with a grin. She sensed the separation from him like an influx of energy. She was moving faster, but her mind felt foggy. Her vision was sporadic and fast, catching glimpses of everything at once: the race, the crowd, the barriers, and...the woman. Rosalind sensed the fogginess now in her mind more clearly — someone was touching her mind, and in that moment, she knew it was this woman, though the woman was unfamiliar to her. The woman gripped the rubber barricade, squeezing it in rhythm to her own robotic foot strike. The woman's blond hair was up and her eyes were closed as Rosalind closed the distance to the finish line. Rosalind searched the tangle of silver in the back of her mind and saw the transparent shimmer of another tangle atop her own.

"Hey, watch where you're stepping!" a woman shouted at a large man backing into her.

Rosalind was pulled from her thoughts by the loud voice. The voice belonged to a dark-haired woman fifty feet away on the opposite side of the raceway. Rosalind tried to put her thoughts back to the race but sensed still the fog of her mind.

The fog was now gone, but unease pulled her eyes back to the blonde. Rosalind noted how others crowded in and smashed her against the barrier — not with malice, but indifference. The woman's jacket and scarf were fashionable but not trendy. Rosalind followed the woman's line of sight as if her mind still laid over her own. The sun was just starting to warm the April morning, and Rosalind saw the woman's face contort when the dark-haired lady moved in her direction. Rosalind watched the dark-haired woman's face and caught a flash of her eyes when the woman looked directly at her. It was as if she knew the blonde had touched her mind.

There was a blinding flash of crimson behind her eye. Rosalind stumbled with the pain of it just as she heard the woman's voice scream in her mind.

Forget the race, Rosalind thought, glad her tangle — or at least the Oscult of it — had a functional anteroom that prohibited connection to the rest of her mind. Even with that, she felt nauseous as she stumbled then righted herself just as Nathan moved past her in a blur.

Nathan didn't stop. He pushed fast and hard, making the finish line to the sound of a crowd given to cheer for whoever crossed first.

"Bragging rights for a year," Nathan shouted as he turned.

His smile faded as her gaze met his after pulling herself away from a stare-down with the woman in the crowd. Rosalind picked up her unsteady pace and crossed the line as Jenny and Shaver made the final turn at the evergreen to come into view. Rosalind grabbed Nathan in an unusual show of affection and whispered in his ear. "We've got a Sahaja Intuit here. Do you know about it?"

Rosalind felt a prick at her hip as Nathan shifted to look. His rotation had shifted her near the crowd. Rosalind sensed the warmth at her hip but did not have time to speak as the man with the casted arm slipped the needle back to its hiding place. It was the last thing she saw. Rosalind squeezed Nathan's neck, then the world fell away.

[17.4]

Nathan sensed Rosalind's dead weight and clasped her waist to ease her to the ground, characteristically checking her pulse out of habit. "Rosalind! Rosalind! You, by the tree, call EMS," he ordered as he checked for a pulse and began CPR. "You in the STAFF shirt and cast, get the AED from the first aid shelter." Nathan continued rescue breathing, shouting commands while he performed chest compressions in between. "Hang in there, Rosalind, come on!"

[17.5]

Sylvia rushed to the stranger and knelt. "Slide to her head. I'll take over chest compressions."

"They need to be centered over the sternum."

"I know CPR. Breathe for her, and stop telling me what to do."

The man, unperturbed, continued his rescue breathing and his commands. *The natural outflow of a man accustomed to crisis,* Sylvia thought and felt a ping at her core. *No, no, no. That has already caused you enough trouble on the Orbiter. What is it with you and take-charge men — or women, for that matter?* she thought, recalling she'd been distracted equally by Tessa's protective streak for Jezel and Michael's competent investigation.

"Jenny, turn off her stimulator and get the robotics off her legs."

Bossy Man's words pulled Sylvia back to the job at hand just as the staff guy returned.

"The AED is missing a pad," he reported, out of breath. "One of the race coordinators on a Griffon flew to the start-line-first aid for the other one."

Sylvia directed the young man while Bossy gave the woman another breath. "Get the keys out of my coat pocket." She nodded down toward her pocket as she continued compressions. "There's a gray rental vehicle parked in the second lot. Inside is a military medic bag. Bring it to me." She noted the swollen, bruised hand in the cast with the unbearably crooked-looking fingers as the man approached.

"Sure," he said, easily lifting the keys from her pocket with his good hand, then turning to head down the hill toward the parking lot.

"You might want to send someone after him," Sylvia said as she watched the man stumble and adjust as if the tree balanced him, though he never touched it. "I'm going to get the AED."

"The staff guy just said…" Bossy began between rescue breaths as he smoothly took over compressions.

"He's lying, and whatever has your friend on the ground was in the needle he stuck her with right after she crossed the finish line." Sylvia didn't wait for Bossy's reply as the lady removing the robotic legs glanced up with her own concern and spoke.

"The override on her manual stimulator remote is password coded," she said, working frantically to try another number.

"314159265," Bossy said, and Sylvia noted a look in his green eyes that said he hoped to hear the woman rant at him for having to change it. *A lot of people care about this woman; maybe that was why she felt so connected.* She raced off, still hearing the man shouting directives.

[17.6]

"Get them off," Nathan growled.

"Okay," Jenny said, punching in the code. "Her stimulator is off." She wrapped the small wires, barely visible, around the code panel just as the stranger knelt back at Rosalind's side to take over compressions, the AED between her and Nathan.

"Give it to Jenny," Nathan said, continuing compressions till the AED passed to Jenny, then he paused to check her pulse. "Unpack the AED, Jenny. I'll put the pads on her." Nathan pulled his hand from Rosalind's neck. "Come on, Rosalind. Damn it!" Nathan placed the pads, working around as the stranger continued CPR and Jenny took over rescue breaths.

"It's ready," Jenny said.

"Stop CPR," Nathan announced.

"Scanning for shockable rhythm," Jenny read aloud from the screen.

"What is PEA?" the stranger asked, leaning over to see the screen.

"Pulseless electrical activity," Nathan answered, simultaneously sliding back to give a rescue breath. "The only treatment is proper CPR till we can reverse the cause."

"EMS is climbing the embankment. Go tell them what we've got," the stranger said.

As if her calm triggered his physician report mode, Nathan stood and stepped toward the group, climbing with equipment. "We have a twenty-eight-year-old female with pulseless electrical..." The paramedic removed his hood and faced Nathan. "Marcus!" Nathan's relief was palpable. "It's Rosalind. PEA — I think it's a toxin. Do you have the Delta725 to scan her?"

"Jeremy, get the O2 on her and take over CPR," Marcus said. He slipped the Delta725 on, already loaded with the fluorescing laser. He slid the eyepiece down over his right eye as he knelt. "It is a toxin. Bala, bring the injection kit and the chemical binders. I want to get something IM while you get a line."

"IM?" Nathan heard the stranger whisper to herself, not realizing Bala was close enough to hear her. He noticed her for the first time, leaned back on her heels, her blond hair falling around her face.

"Intramuscular injection," Bala answered. "Marcus can give the injection in her muscle to initiate the toxin reversal and buy me time to get an IV line," Bala said as she moved easily to slide the needle into Rosalind's exposed vein.

The blonde swallowed hard and moved away to let the team work.

"I'll do that, Jeremy," Nathan said, offering to take over compressions but not moving to interfere when Jeremy indicated he had it under control.

"Nathan, I know how important she is to you. We won't let you down. Whoever gave her this brought it from one of Earth's low-tech facilities — its chemical binding is weak. We'll have it reversed before she is in the back of the squad."

"I've got a pulse, Marcus," Jeremy said, adjusting his position. "It's faint, but it's hers."

"Get the pacer on her," Marcus and Nathan said simultaneously.

"We got this," Marcus said with a gentle touch of his big hand to Nathan's shoulder.

Nathan relaxed. "Her stimulator is turned off," he said, his tall frame stooping to lift her robotic legs. "I'll bring these."

"She is not going to be happy," Marcus said, turning to his patient strapped to the air gurney. He gestured at Rosalind. "When she wakes up, just know I'm blaming you for removing them."

Nathan tried to smile, but the lifeless metal robotics at his fingertips made his lips tighten, and Marcus went back to work.

Nathan's fear twisted into anger at the blonde. "Why did you give your keys to that criminal? Your car will be long gone, along with the chance to catch the man who did this!"

"My rental car will be right where I left it — with my publicist, who is coming to pick me up. If *your* criminal kept my keys instead of tossing them, the police can track him down. They have a locator device. Meki knows I lose my keys on tour, so he had circuit stickers with locator devices put on my keys."

Nathan adjusted the robotic legs under his arm. "I'm sorry. Forgive me," he said, dropping his eyes to stare at them before looking back to this woman who had helped. "I should be thanking you for your help."

"Don't thank me. Thank your girlfriend. I think that injection was for you."

"What? How do you know that?"

"I'm not sure. It all happened so fast...I'm not even sure I saw it," she answered, twisting her necklace back and forth. Nathan imagined she was replaying the last moments of the race in her mind. "Did you see how easily he picked my pocket for the keys?" She dropped the necklace and rubbed her forehead.

Nathan wondered if she had a migraine by the way she squinted, as if bright color flashed at the edge of her mind. *I can't worry about her right now,* he thought, chastising himself for talking with a beautiful woman while Rosalind was en route to the hospital.

"He's probably a common thief hired for his slick hands. I doubt he even knows what was in the needle, but I didn't trust him standing over us."

Regaining his professional composure, Nathan shifted his weight. "Are you okay?"

"I'm fine. Just a headache. I'm still trying to acclimatize. It's my first experience traveling light-years away for work. You look around here..." She gestured at the evergreens at full height, though they appeared stunted, and the crocuses pushing through the ground in their partial shade. "Nothing is changed from Earth, but everything is different." She rubbed at her temples.

"So, you're here for business, staying at the GCS Hotel?"

"GCS Hotel?"

"The Galactic Core Station Hotel. The only place to stay unless you Sim-beam to Replica Earth."

"Oh, yeah, business," she said as if he didn't need to know her personal business.

"I'll talk to the police." Nathan extended his free hand. "What's your name in case they need to contact you?"

"I'll have Meki take me there. He'll know where it is." The woman flipped the charm at her neck back and forth as she stared past him at the shadow cast by the evergreen from the sun reaching higher at her back. "The day feels identical to a cool April morning back home. It's a little creepy to be so similar to Earth yet be so far away." She paused, as if she had been talking to herself. "I've got a busy schedule and would rather get it over with now. If I find the keys, I'll take them by for fingerprints."

Nathan dropped his outstretched hand. The woman was anxious and hadn't noticed it. "It's worth a try, but keys are usually covered with half prints and ridgelines from the owner's hands that can make the process difficult. They may be in luck that you don't have a GCS ring. Most people store their door code in their ring while here, but guests without them have a keycard. They may be able to get prints from it." Nathan rubbed his chin in thought.

"Thanks," the woman said, moving down the embankment toward a car pulling into the lot.

"Some people don't have fingerprints, though," Nathan added, thinking of Rosalind and a few other Intuits he knew, but the blonde had disappeared.

CHAPTER EIGHTEEN

"MAGGIE, CALL MS..." NATHAN squinted to read the name. "Sylvia Debair, and have her come to the clinic today at one o'clock." Nathan activated the hands-free phone earpiece, muted the television screen in the limousine, and maximized the abnormal section of Sylvia's MRI on the hologram displayed by the laser from his ringphone.

Nathan smiled, picturing the eighty-two-year-old spitfire as she checked the schedule on her desktop computer in the clinic office. It was ancient Earth tech and Nathan hated it, but Maggie liked it, so he had asked Rosalind's people to install the upgrades to keep it working with the Replica Earth technology.

"Move her from the seven p.m. to the one p.m. slot?" Maggie asked, mumbling under her breath. "You have the injured Immortal from Orbiter C13 at one fifteen."

"I know." He enlarged the MRI on his screen. "I want a neurologic exam before the Species Imaging, and I can do that between the treatment protocol for the Immortal. If this is another celebrity wanting Replica Earth technology testing for the PR benefits of species connection, I'm not wasting my time or the RE resources."

"I don't think she wants 'RET for PR.'"

"Maybe not," Nathan answered, his focus distracted as he typed a text to Rosalind in a small window at the hologram corner. She'd left the hospital against medical advice in the early hours of the morning and he knew she would be in her office to prove to everyone she was fine. She'd refused to stay with him, so he'd slept on the sofa in her suite which was annexed off the Archive. *Have you found the woman from the race? I want to see her this evening before Houseman ties her up with the race investigation.* Nathan was still watching the text box when a sphere flashed to his left on the hologram screen, indicating more images from Maggie were loading.

"The final file just uploaded," Maggie said. Nathan could hear her deftly typing the twenty-five-character UBN code. "Damn RE tech," she said as the rest of the MRI files pinged to Nathan's secure phone. "Getting her here early may not work — ouch!"

Nathan grinned. He knew she was bracing the phone between her shoulder and ear as she shuffled sticky notes on the clinic wall, searching for her personal calendar.

"Make it happen, Maggie. Don't worry about my schedule."

"I'm not talking about your schedule."

The chauffeur opened the door, and Nathan snarled at the blast of cold air. "It's April, not November," he muttered, buttoning his suit jacket.

[18.1]

Maggie traced her finger through the week on her National Geographic calendar. She was so glad the Tokoleh kept that historical resource protected through the war — they made the best calendars. Earth Day became an entire week celebration at the GCS, the hub of a Replica universe that fed Earth, twenty-five light-years away. "Earth Week," she mumbled, her fingers roving the calendar blocks. She had traveled the world more than once when she lived on Earth, but the jet lag of a lost day on a flight from DC to Beijing was nothing compared to the time you lost traveling from Earth to the Replica system here. But, she refused to relinquish her National Geographic calendar, and she just corrected the holiday dates when the calendar first arrived. Maggie found what she was looking for. "Ms. Debair has a book signing."

"Oh, and Maggie text me with confirmation of her appointment time. I may be in a meeting."

Maggie rolled her eyes and wished someone was there to appreciate it. Nathan was one of the kindest men she knew, but when he set his mind to something, he was a train running full steam, so she repeated, "Ms. Debair has a book signing."

[18.2]

"Hold on, Maggie," Nathan said as he stepped from the vehicle.

The chauffeur tugged his coat so tight the hotel insignia disappeared. "Do you want me to wait for you, Dr. Renner?"

"That's not necessary, John." Nathan tapped his ring once, and the laser MRI image disappeared. "I'll take the Local Tram inside when I'm finished." Nathan then noticed it wasn't John, his usual chauffeur. He had really been distracted this morning.

The man nodded. "Yes, sir, but there are shutdowns in the green line."

"Maggie, does the green line shut down before the clinic?"

"Yes, I rode the green back to the GCS-Transfer-Tram to take the yellow."

"Okay, let me know when you confirm the appointment. I'm here at the GCS Hotel. I planned to take the green but may have to use the car."

"I'll try her now," Maggie said, giving up.

"Thanks, Maggie." He tapped a glowing icon on his ring band to disconnect, then twisted it around his index finger once. The blue hue of the resonance earpiece over his left ear disappeared. The slight electron static tingled, and he rubbed his ear, dislodging a wave of brown hair. He checked the ring as he moved toward the stairs. No response from Rosalind yet.

Nathan surveyed the massive columns of the hotel resort entrance. The light from the rising, distant sun reflected the shadow of his six-foot-six frame on the white marble. The clinic he managed near the rear wing of the ten-square-mile resort was only a small piece of this architectural masterpiece built as a tribute to the technology and beauty humanity had almost lost in the war. *Imagine how much farther humanity could be now if we hadn't had to practically start over almost seventy years ago.* Nathan pushed the thought away, pleased that RE technology had allowed him to regain ground. It was hard to believe it was 2116 and Earth's last world war ended sixty-some years ago when there was nothing left to fight with but sticks and stones. The Tokoleh managed to keep the Earth from complete annihilation and saved much of its history and a cluster of its people here. The rest that managed to survive on Earth had rebuilt it with the almost invisible assistance of the Galactic Core Station at the hand of the Tokoleh. Many on Earth still didn't even know the Replica Universe existed here twenty-five light-years away.

Climbing the stairs, Nathan shifted his briefcase to avoid bumping a woman descending in a battle against the wind and her scarf. Her orthotic shoes were worn and slipped on the step edge.

She regained her balance on Nathan's arm. "Dr. Renner?"

"Yes, are you alright?"

She tugged the scarf free from her face. "I'm fine." She squeezed Nathan's arm. "You saved his life."

"Mrs. Barrett, hello!" Nathan said, recognizing her. "The surgeon did that."

She held his eyes with hers. "My husband's a stubborn old fool, but he's mine, and he's both alive and not a transformed Griffon because he mattered to you."

"That means a lot to me, Mrs. Barrett," he said with a grateful nod. His injection had halted the man's transformation, allowing neurosurgery to clip his aneurysm before he had a stroke. "The donation of his blood and surgical tissue for research will help many Griffons."

Maybe even the Griffon who showed up at my lab, he thought. "You're headed back to Earth Sector Three, right?" he asked, gratitude in his smile.

"Yes, last day at rehab. We're headed home."

"Tell him I bet fifteen Tokee his team doesn't make it to the Superbowl."

Mrs. Barrett laughed and turned.

Nathan climbed the six steps. *I need to update my fantasy football,* he thought, glad the Earth Alliance and Tokoleh had aligned to save sports of entire nations during a war that destroyed the world. Nathan's ring vibrated. He tapped the side to laser the hologram screen across the back of his hand. He read the incoming text as he finished the stairs and entered the ornate hotel.

MAGGIE: Ms. Debair not answering phone. I had hotel operator try her room. Should I try her emergency contact? He has his locator on.

NATHAN: No. I will check on her.

Nathan headed toward the elevators in the sixty-five-foot domed ceiling lobby.

MAGGIE: Do you need her room number?

Nathan hesitated when the elevator opened. He backed away and turned toward the lobby area, realizing how impulsively he had made his initial decision. His beast was more apparent in his everyday decisions — impulsive, primal, and dangerous. He had no reason yet to think the woman needed his help. "Be rational," he muttered to himself as the elevator door closed.

NATHAN: I'm not going to her room.

MAGGIE: Room 416 Diplomat Wing

NATHAN: You said her emergency contact has his locator on. Where is he?

[18.3]

Sylvia slumped against the headboard and traced the raised emblems of her book on the hotel nightstand. In the darkness of space, with only her confused mind to see the symbols, she had almost believed it was real. Now, she was rethinking everything. *Anyone can pick latitude or longitude numbers for a place and scribble them down,* Sylvia thought, then recalled the Tokoleh book she and Kinley had been transcribing. He had said some of the translation had to wait till he could access books in the Archive that had the older Tokoleh language.

Tessa had said the glyphs in her book were an ancient Tokoleh language someone had translated for the coordinates. *I don't know any Tokoleh language. So, I can prove the numbers are not a translation of my work. I need to get into the Archive.* Her laptop pinged in the kitchenette just beyond the little bedroom where she lay. She had left it on last night to video conference with her publicist. However, Meki was an early bird. He mistakenly thought mornings were better. She still had a headache from the charity race yesterday and neck pain from the tension of bracing in her seat when their Orbiter had to manually dock the day they arrived.

"This is ridiculous," Sylvia mumbled, squinting her eyes almost closed against the light coming into the kitchenette despite the heavy drapes in the sitting room. She tilted the glowing laptop screen down after she tapped a key and reached for her coffee cup. "You're too bright, too."

"You know, Sylvia, I can't see you with the satellite cam facing the counter-top," Meki said from the tilted screen.

"Believe me, that's a good thing. I haven't had my go-juice yet, and I'm going to need my energy if I know the schedule you have planned."

"And I know you. You're already planning how to change it."

Sylvia banged another stylishly modern cabinet. "Why is it that Hotel 7 charges eighty-nine a night and I can always find the coffee maker, but here it's ten grand, and they hide it from me?"

Meki sighed heavily. "It isn't ten grand to stay here."

Sylvia muttered, but Meki continued. "I have a meeting to finalize some details for your courtesy two-week stay here at the hotel."

"I'm only staying a week." Sylvia plugged in the single-cup coffee maker. "It took us a week to get here. I have dogs. I'll be down in an hour." She tilted the laptop screen back up.

Meki's distinguished face appeared on the screen. He removed his glasses in thought, then slid them back on. He smiled as the black frame hinges nestled in the only patch of gray in his otherwise perfectly groomed black hair. "Volun-teering to walk the dogs at the shelter once a week does not constitute having dogs."

"Yes, it does. I'm not staying here an extra week to see their clinic research facility, their casino, their high-end shopping district, their museum...okay, I might stay a day for the museum. Who are you meeting?"

"Rosalind Mathing — the Universal Bureau of Negotiations is based here. Rosalind is the UBN security director. Your escapade to save her life may be an opportunity to secure some less creative work for the next year."

Sylvia stopped moving, and the silence spoke the concern they both held about the changes developing in Sylvia's mind. *Is Meki trying to find me some writing work in case things get worse?*

Meki broke the silence. "The least she can do is foot some of the bill for you to relax while they try to woo you to the academic drudgery of writing their policy manuals."

So, that was his ulterior motive — he wanted to find some work she could handle in her "new condition." She had sensed he was up to something, hiding something, but pushed it off to one of the many variances of her own mind. "I could use some drudgery after this past year," Sylvia said as she mindlessly rubbed the laptop's edge.

He is trying to help; don't be ungrateful, Sylvia derided herself, but her frustration still sounded in her words. "So, back to my reality. Kita — I think that was the name you told me for the woman who appeared at the signing in Pittsburgh — wanted coordinates and grand secrets to my book, then another stranger shows up at the next signing fearful his life was in jeopardy if I didn't give him the coordinates to pass on to God knows who..." Sylvia's voice was escalating. "Then my book becomes part of an altercation on the Orbiter that ends in injury and death..." Sylvia paused, considering. *Should I tell Meki about the translated coordinates?* Michael had said not to reveal anything about the book's involvement with the coordinates to Jezel's manor because it was now a UBN issue. Sylvia bit the inside of her lip. "And the UBN wants me to help write policy manuals. It sounds...bad."

"I told you not to worry about the accident on the Orbiter. The Marshals said the investigation discovered no connection with your book. It was a coincidence."

Sylvia twisted her necklace. She knew Michael was still investigating. She remembered Michael's plan to re-question Max. "Yes, but they still don't know what the scribbled numbers were for, do they?" Apparently, a picture with a couple of numbers scribbled in the book had surfaced on the Rompnet. *The picture had to be taken before Jezel's injury because there was no blood covering them, and the full set of numbers was not there.* She thought about Kita again and the fact that she hadn't told Meki that the woman had accused her of working with the Separatists and given her a photo. Her guilt at keeping so many secrets won out. She fingered the photo in her robe pocket. "I have something to show you. It hadn't seemed important then, just strange," she began. She had looked at the photo again last night. She loved the tree on the far right side of the photo, but it meant nothing to her, and she had decided to tell him. "Kita gave me this photo.

Should I recognize it?" She held the photo near the camera so it filled the screen for Meki to see.

Meki rubbed his chin and examined the photo, then leaned back, and his face went out of frame. "No," he said off camera, and Sylvia pictured him leaning back, still rubbing his chin. "Did she say anything?"

"No," Sylvia lied. She didn't trust her memory of what Kita had said.

"Does it bother you?"

"I'm fine," Sylvia said, twisting her necklace back and forth till she noticed Meki scowling at her. She dropped the charm, making a mental note to change to her longer chain so it would lay lower under her shirt where she couldn't reach it so easily. She picked up the six packets of sugar for her coffee.

"Very well. See if channel five is running your promo. I've got to go."

"Will do." Sylvia lifted the remote and her coffee to forge into the sitting room of the suite, glad to have a mundane task to start the day.

"What is that electronic music?" Meki questioned. "Is the TV on channel five?"

"That's the ringtone for my room phone. You can set them, and I toyed with it when I couldn't sleep last night. The TV is on mute," she added, pointing the remote at the news anchor on the screen and ignoring the ringing phone. *Why answer to tell someone they dialed the wrong number?* Sylvia thought. "I hope they have a history channel," Sylvia said, hearing Meki still on the laptop screen. "See you shortly." Sylvia sighed, enjoying the warmth of the coffee snug in her hand.

Meki disconnected. He never heard the coffee cup shatter.

CHAPTER NINETEEN

R OSALIND STROKED THE GARDENIA leaf, lost in thought and the heat of
the sunlamp. *The Dalen Overseer had been in the lockout room,* Rosalind
thought, even while she spoke to the speaker phone. "No, I'm sure the injection
was intended for Nathan, not me," Rosalind repeated. "You're an excellent investigator, Houseman, which is why I asked you to take the lead on this, but chasing
down my enemies could take a lifetime. Check the groups opposed to Nathan's
research, and if we don't find a lead, you can start on the list for me." Rosalind
closed the connection to Houseman. The hum of her computer system running
a diagnostic she had written almost blended with the buzz of a single bee out of
place in this room buried beneath the Earth. "I'm going to alter your structure,"
Rosalind said, speaking to Stinger.

"Alter my structure?" an AI voice returned with disdain as the bee landed on
a shelf at eye level with Rosalind.

"Yes. Stone has a new smaller circuit board I can utilize. As a fly, you can bring
me intel on the Dalen work project."

"A fly? Disgusting. I won't have it. My AI circuits reject your offer." The phone
line beeped.

Rosalind pushed the speaker button on the landline phone, holding the corner
of the blueprint on her desk. "Make it quick, Harry," Rosalind said to her UBN
dispatcher, watching Stinger pace on the shelf.

Stinger muttered as he paced, "Who will ever believe my name is Stinger if I'm
a fly. It's ridiculous!"

Rosalind tried not to smile and focused on what Harry was saying. "I still have
security systems down in two of the hotel wings."

"This better be something Marie can't handle." She hoped her voice held enough emphasis for him to think she was trying to find the glitch shutting the main security systems down. She had shut the system down herself, but that was her secret.

Stinger stopped pacing.

Rosalind could hear Harry tapping and turning his pen. She pictured him staring at his screen in the UBN main office, unaware of his distracting habit. "I think there may be damage in one of the energy-generator rooms."

Rosalind smoothed the old-fashioned blueprints out on the desktop and took a seat, clicking open the remote screen. Harry usually stopped his fidgeting when she was watching him.

"Oh, hey," he said when her face filled his screen.

Stinger landed on her middle knuckle while she traced the symbol representing the Portal in the energy enclosure of the energy-generator room.

"Damage in the energy rooms?" Stinger asked.

Rosalind ignored him. She knew he was running an algorithm through his AI system.

"I'm listening," Rosalind said, leaning back in her chair and watching Stinger and Harry. She liked working in this antiquated office.

She had technology at her fingertips, and she loved it — even designed some of it — but when things got personal, she always came here.

Harry double-tapped a sensor on his pen, and the computer screen shifted. "I can't usually see much in the diplomat wing because of the privacy haze before eight a.m., but it seems worse in that energy-generator room. I thought you might want a look."

She pressed her thumb to the computer screen to open the secure view of the Bunker energy-generator room off the diplomat wing. "By the way, Harry, secure two Archive level-three passes for Xenos and his Governor Protector Kinley. I was going to take them in, but I'm not going to be available." Rosalind rocked forward in her chair and picked at the thigh latch on her brace as the screen opened a hazy view of the energy room. "It is worse." She scanned the screen. "I'm going down to check it out." *Humidity?* she thought as her mind plotted every option. Rosalind stood, running her index finger over her right eyebrow, the signal for Stinger to join her. She hadn't disconnected before standing, and she groaned with the motion.

"Do you want the wheelchair brought up? I could go with you." Harry waited.

Rosalind winced. She had left the hospital AMA, and the staff knew she should still be there. Rosalind squeezed the latch on her brace, a reminder of her fragile freedom. "You just want to see a security site you don't have access to. Get back to work."

Harry laughed and disconnected.

"I'm shutting down the main security systems of the hotel so I can review everything with the old system," she said as Stinger buzzed at eye level. "The Dalen are here. I haven't seen their work permits, and there was an incident on the Orbiter that brought them here. I need you to be my eyes on them. Nathan said there was another death at Piano Cave, so I have a feeling they came in for a project there."

"Great!" Stinger said. "This is my test. If I succeed, you agree never to make me a fly!"

Rosalind sighed. She felt pressed for time, seeing every event, even the minor ones, as a threat. She didn't have time to check out the energy-generator room, but no one else had the security clearance to do it. "Fine. Report your information to Michael and me."

She tapped her ringphone and noticed a text from Nathan. She would read it in the elevator. He probably wanted to know if she had found the girl from the race yet. To be honest, she hadn't tried. She had planned to start her security shutdown process yesterday after the race but instead spent the evening in the hospital. The downtime had her watching Orbiter C13's landing again.

Orbiter C13 had been forced to make a manual landing two days ago. C13's pilot, Major Tom Haddock, was an arrogant show-off. She hadn't given much thought to it as accolades of his skill escalated, but now, no one could find him. Her sixth sense told her he wasn't here. A look at the old security system cameras would tell her who climbed out of the pilot's hatch, but she had to check the energy-generator room first.

[19.1]

Meki crossed his legs and relaxed in the wingback chair in the diplomat lounge as his fingers scrolled the portfolios. He checked the archway to his left, considering the hidden door just beyond it where he needed to be after this snag was released. The Earth Alliance Representative would be here soon; the Tag-Baran EAR had pull in the Scholar's Council, but Meki disliked him.

"Mr. Hunew? Hello, I'm Dr. Renner."

Meki startled from his thoughts. "Dr. Renner," he said, standing, his thoughts resistant to leave his Intuit portfolio review for the energy-generator room project. "You're doing the Species Imaging for Sylvia this evening. Call me Meki."

"Meki, I apologize for the interruption. I'm sure as Ms. Debair's..." Nathan paused. "Emergency contact," he continued, "I figure you are very concerned about her MRI and what we plan to do for her here. I would like to see her sooner for a neurologic exam."

"I'm Sylvia's friend," Meki said, sensing Nathan's curiosity. "I would love for her to be seen sooner. However, as her publicist, I will have to consider our appointment this evening sufficient. She has a signing today from three to six, and other engagements prior to that obligation."

[19.2]

Nathan realized now why the name sounded familiar. The girl from the race had mentioned her publicist.

He smiled. *Thank the Source*, he thought, glad he wouldn't have to rearrange his schedule. Now, he just wanted to see her. Nathan frowned as Meki stared at him. If her publicist was with her, it probably was a PR stunt, and they were wasting his time.

"She will be meeting me downstairs in about an hour. Can I give her a message?" Meki asked when Nathan's lips formed a hard line.

"Meki!" A boisterous voice rocked the chandelier just above Nathan and Meki's head.

Nathan's hands fisted at the sight of the EAR from Tag-Baran, Griffern's capital. *Earth Alliance Representative, my ass,* Nathan thought. The man had fought his research for the Earth Alliance as well as the Griffons at every turn. "A message isn't necessary. I will see you both this evening."

"Very well. It was a pleasure to meet you."

Nathan didn't shake Meki's offered hand. *I'll see her now,* he thought, questioning the connection of Meki with this man. Meki turned to face the bull tramping across the large lounge toward him. He had entered from the main corridor just behind the wingback chair.

"Representative Faraday," Meki said firmly but with quiet enthusiasm. Their voices became the conversation of two people, and Nathan left the way he came. *Room 416 is on this floor in the opposite wing,* he thought, extending his stride with purpose.

[19.3]

Faraday sat at the checkered game table, his back to the arched, floor-to-ceiling windows. *The only thing good about meeting in the diplomat wing is the access to the bar,* Faraday thought but realized it was best not to move straight toward it. "I can meet your request for personnel." He lifted the Prism-Light game piece and the Prism-Shadow game piece, tapping the base of the two pyramids together. "In addition, I can upgrade your Intuit portfolio."

"Any problem with the restrictions?" Meki asked.

Faraday shrugged. He knew Meki needed an upgrade of his portfolio options for an Intuit, and he had that ace in his pocket. He'd let Meki control the conversation for now. "No problem. Ninety percent of them are Dalen."

"Recruit or bred?"

"It's a mix."

Smack!

Faraday's face burned with the contact, and he gripped the game table to resist attacking the man. He was in this for the bigger win. Meki would get his soon enough. "A Dalen is a Dalen," Faraday said, smiling and spreading his hands wide, dangling the white and black pyramids back in his hands. "They're all just pieces in the game."

"No. They are not. A recruit knows a freedom a Dalenborn has never known." Meki lowered his voice and leaned into Faraday's space. "A recruit, Dalen, is your worst nightmare. I don't care if you have to search all Five Sectors. Fill the order with Dalenborn only."

Meki moved away from the table as if he were dismissing him.

Faraday watched as Meki pressed a small icon on his ring. He saw his watch blink with a synchronization flash, and Meki double-checked it. *Something is wrong with whatever he is watching,* Faraday thought. *Not my problem.* Faraday stood. "That makes the deadline harder to meet." He walked to the bar on the opposite wall and poured Scotch from the decanter. "And the cost increases," he continued when Meki ignored him and stared at his watch.

"Then you have a problem," Meki said, manually overriding something between his ring and his watch. "This job is key. We will keep the deadline with or without you."

Faraday was sure that was true, but Meki didn't realize Faraday took his real orders from V-Kasana, and Meki himself was only a piece being used in a bigger game. V-Kasana had communicated that Meki would pay well for an Intuit of high caliber for his project. "So, what about the Dalen Intuit I offered for your portfolio of applicants? Are you interested in him?"

Meki looked up from his watch, appearing only half-interested. "Is he Dalenborn?"

"Of course," Faraday lied. It was some loser recruit that had managed to get himself half-killed on Orbiter C13, but he was an Intuit, and every job could use those.

"Send me his information."

"Very well, he is at the job site in Piano Cave. They'll arrange for payment if you decide you're interested," Faraday said, then added, "I'll make the adjustment for the order of all Dalenborn — no recruits as a gesture of good faith." He clinked the ice in his Scotch glass. V-Kasana would probably tell him to change their records and send them anyway. He'd never seen the man in person, but his communications never indicated he would be bothered by such trivial details. What did it matter if they were recruits or not for Meki's project to shuttle book crap back and forth to Replica Earth? *I don't care as long as I get paid,* he thought, rubbing his throat. The Scotch was not very smooth, but he'd take it back to his room anyway. It was free.

[19.4]

Death by Dismemberment scrolled across the news feed on the wide-screen television in Sylvia's hotel room. Tears blurred her vision, and blood smeared the marble inlay on the hardwood floor from the cuts on her hands as she scraped up shards of porcelain, desperately gathering every shattered piece of the coffee cup. Sylvia's eyes darted across the floor. "I need every piece," she murmured between quiet tears. Her shoulders shook with the weight of the death. She rocked back and forth till a voice pulled her to awareness.

"Ms. Debair. Sylvia?"

Sylvia paused, sitting back on her heels at the controlled voice that matched the tailored button-down shirt she could see through the cracked hotel door. She ran her fingers along the corner of her silk robe, then she was back on her hands and knees collecting the broken pieces.

[19.5]

"Sylvia?" Nathan said again, stepping into the sitting area after several knocks didn't elicit a response. He swallowed hard when he saw the tie of her robe draped across her bare legs just beyond the sofa. Her cry registered to his brain, and he pushed away the line of thought that traced up from her shapely leg to the body just beyond his view. He berated himself at the primitive thoughts that plagued him about this woman after only meeting her once. He took two quick steps and knelt beside her.

Sylvia placed the splintered pieces on the napkin she must have brought in to protect the furniture. "I've got to put this together," she said.

Nathan covered her hands and lifted them from the debris. It wasn't uncommon for patients to overreact to small things when they faced the condition that was shown on Sylvia's MRI. *I just have to figure out if it is good or bad,* he thought. "You can't," Nathan said gently. "Pieces are missing."

New sobs racked her words as she collapsed back on her heels. "I know." Her knee-length robe fell open when she placed her bloody hands on her knees and focused on the television. Nathan pulled his eyes up quickly. She lifted her necklace, twisting it at the V-neck of her chemise.

"So many pieces missing," Sylvia said, rubbing away a tear with the back of her hand.

Nathan folded the napkin around the fragments and wiped the blood from the floor. He aborted his efforts at cleanup when he noticed her watching the screen and not the floor, her cut, bleeding hands now back on her bare legs just below her silk sleeping shorts. The TV screen flashed a bloodied sidewalk, then shifted quickly to a body covered, followed by a photo of the victim.

"Is that someone you know?" Nathan asked, touching her shoulder with his empty hand as he stood to find a trash can. Sylvia looked up at him, and he could see the face of the blonde from the race, but the tears had stripped away the confidence.

"Yes," she said, her eyes never leaving his face.

Nathan squatted next to her. "I'm so sorry. Who is it?"

[19.6]

Sylvia pushed the curtain of long, spiraling blond hair behind her ear. "I don't know his name. He asked me to sign a book for a reader named Kita."

"You remember that?"

"I remember because it has been at the forefront of my thoughts for the last few days. I'm not sure Kita sent him, but Meki thinks she did." Sylvia rubbed at the blood on her hands. "He said he would be killed if I didn't..." Sylvia paused. Her intuition about people was usually pretty good, but could she trust this man she'd only met yesterday? Of course, the man had been saving someone's life when she met him, so he had that going for him as well. "People are asking for information I don't have. My work is fiction, but people keep asking for coordinates. He..." Sylvia reached toward the screen and felt fresh tears. *People are dying. How can I stop this if no one believes me that the places aren't real?* She had to trust someone. She had to get all the collecting pieces out of her head. The idea of pieces made her look down. Her blood still streaked part of the floor. Meki was busy and Michael was already working on one mess her book had made. She looked up at this stranger crouched like a protector at her side. She sensed both danger and safety with him, then she made her decision. "The man on the screen was at a signing. He told me to write the coordinates to the Lost Cities and sign it. I explained to him it was a book of fiction and that I didn't have coordinates, but he pressed me till security had him removed." Sylvia covered her face with her bloodied hands. "I didn't even sign the book."

Sylvia jerked at the knock on the door and wondered for the first time how Nathan got in.

Meki's voice came with the second knock. "Sylvia, I added an interview."

"Tell him I'm in the shower," Sylvia mouthed silently, pushing off her sense of comfort with him as secondary to recognizing him from the race.

[19.7]

"Just a minute, Meki." Nathan moved to the door. "Sylvia's in the shower," he said, watching her pass through the kitchenette to the bedroom before disengaging the lock.

"Damn it. She saw it," Meki said, noting the TV screen to his left as he plowed through the doorway. He removed his glasses, squinting at the screen.

"Hello, Meki." Nathan pushed the door closed. "She should be out shortly."

Meki ignored him. "I wanted to tell her first. She will be devastated. It's ridiculous what they show on television."

Nathan repeated himself, hoping to halt Meki's tirade and get some information. "She will be out shortly. What do you know about her condition?"

Meki turned and replaced his glasses. "No more than she knows. That's why we're here."

"No more than she knows about what? I'm right here." Sylvia stepped from the bedroom to the kitchenette and placed her clean hands on the countertop, a bandage on the only cut that refused to stop bleeding.

"I didn't want you to see that." Meki pointed at the television.

Nathan tried not to stare at her fitted turquoise blouse. These two were up to something, but she was beautiful.

"I can spin your connection to the death into a positive," Meki said, and Nathan took the opportunity to appear distracted by the news report while he monitored their conversation from his peripheral view.

Meki touched Sylvia's hand across the counter. "Someone did mark the book, as you mentioned. It's only two numbers, but three major networks have contacted me via BEEcom for interviews this morning." Meki looked at Nathan as if irritated that he was here. "All the major stations have connections with the UBN. Their staff are here already for Earth Week, and they know we're here."

"I can't do an interview." Sylvia looked past Meki to the living room, where her book was open on the TV screen, one of the elongated map pages unfolded, displaying several hieroglyphs. "This is not a PR opportunity — a man is dead!" Sylvia stared at the TV.

Nathan noted the hieroglyph on the screen was the Ankh the Tokoleh used in their ancient texts.

"Opportunity is just that," Meki said. "A set of circumstances, good or bad, that open a new door. You just went from 'some author' to a household name."

Sylvia's slim eyebrows pulled down, narrowing her crystal-blue eyes. "I'm not doing it." Her small nose wrinkled with a look Nathan's primitive instinct registered as disgust rather than anger.

"It's not your fault he's dead."

Sylvia's face softened.

Why does she feel it is her fault? Nathan thought.

"Maybe doing the interview would help keep it under investigation..." Sylvia said, pausing thoughtfully. "And not swept under the rug."

"Exactly," Meki said. "It might help them find her. She did this, not you."

"You know who did this?" Nathan interrupted, pointing at the screen.

Nathan watched Meki's jaw clench, and Sylvia answered. "He doesn't know, but he suspects Kita, the reader I mentioned earlier."

"Look, I know this is awful, but when bad stuff happens, your job is to deal with it. My job is to spin it."

Nathan folded his arms and felt his shirt stretch tight across his back as the anchor continued the story. "This is coming your way whether you want it or not, Sylvia." Nathan pointed at the screen. "Your book's been banned in Earth's Third Sector by the Earth Alliance Representative there."

"What?" Sylvia asked, moving toward Nathan.

"The glyph symbolizes the five species," Nathan said, tapping the four corners of a stone version now magnified on the screen with some writing or additional glyphs at the center. "But some say it marks the Lost Cities." Nathan gave a final tap at the middle where a circle lay with a rectangular box at its center and the two lightning-like seats at either end. "What is your book about?" Nathan turned, his arms still crossed.

Sylvia shuddered and leaned back.

Nathan relaxed his arms. He'd seen that posture before. His beast created a primal energy of dominance he didn't always intend, and he had startled her. There was something very triggering to his beast when he was around her. *I should keep my distance,* he thought, even as he felt something unexplainable pull at him.

"Her work is..." Meki said as they both watched Sylvia move closer to the TV. "...complicated."

Nathan could read nothing in her faraway stare.

Nathan's suspicion about Meki had needed no push, but it heightened now. If Sylvia was a Sahaja Intuit and didn't know it, Meki had kept more from her than just hieroglyph history. If she wasn't Sahaja, then both were playing him. Every species had some small connection to the Rainbanes. It was the thread of their Rainbane heritage that held their single-species network DNA wrapped to their human spinal cord, allowing connection and signaling. Few had enough of their species DNA to train, and even less were Sahaja. The testing would be perfect PR for her on the heels of this galactic exposure of her book. *The latter seems most likely.* "Meki is right," Nathan said, pulling his cuffed sleeves free of his forearms. "It appears you are more important than the dead vagrant."

Sylvia's shoulders slumped, and Nathan felt it like a slap in the face. *Sometimes you're an ass,* he thought.

She touched the screen, and the pixels jumped. The dead man's photo was tucked up in the corner, miniaturized as if unimportant, while her book took the full screen. She slid her hand to the side and fumbled with the buttons, turning it off. The screen seemed to swallow her when it went black behind her. "How can no one care?" Sylvia asked.

Nathan could see her struggle to dispel her own guilt about the man who lay dismembered, broken, and now neglected by the focus on her book. *Maybe she wanted some of this, but it went too far?* he thought

Nathan stepped toward her and cupped her hands, turning them palms up. Her moments of frailty and strength were exhausting, but he whispered, "What do you need?"

Sylvia straightened at the words. "I need that man not to be dead. I need to know this isn't my fault," she said, then stared at her hands. She rubbed her thumb over the fingertip cuts and the injection site of the immigration chip before speaking. "I need to know how a stranger I met once at a race has access to my room." Sylvia held Nathan's eyes.

"I'm the doctor scheduled to do your imaging this evening. I stopped by to see if I could do a neurologic exam before your appointment." *So I don't waste my time,* Nathan thought but was pleased he'd kept the fury from his voice. *She is technically a patient, one more reason to keep her at arm's length.*

"Is my MRI abnormality a disease like Meki thinks, or..."

Nathan watched Sylvia's face as she decided on her words. She was hiding something for sure.

He cleared his throat, feeling the low tone that was stuck like a growl that pulled deep in his chest at the dilated blue eyes staring earnestly at him. *Just great,* he thought, pushing away the desire to pull her in when she pulled her hands free. *Be honest with yourself. She agreed to come because the publishing industry doesn't like uncertainty. She is in a contract with them, and coming here for special testing will, at worst, be good PR for them and, at best, be much, much more.* "I'm here to be your doctor. I'll answer that question when I have more results," he said, finding a tone that sounded professional.

Sylvia nodded and turned to Meki. "I'll do the interview. I want a preliminary question list from your final choice. Cancel my luncheon with the Mayor. I'll do the interview then."

"I was going to just cut time from the signing."

"No, my readers come first."

"But—"

"I'm dealing with it. The Mayor goes. You put a spin on it."

"That's the Sylvia I know. Done!" Meki said, already at the door before turning. "How did you get in, Dr. Renner?"

Nathan started at the use of his professional tag but spoke to Sylvia's stunning blue eyes more than Meki's request. "You didn't answer your phone when my staff called."

Sylvia's eyes told him she knew he was embarrassed, but she didn't speak, leaving the silence for him.

"I was concerned when you didn't answer your door. MRI results like yours can be associated with blackouts. I used my in-house physician override to get in."

"I've read about the blackouts," Meki said, not looking at Sylvia. "But with the additional interview, there is just no way to do the exam now."

Sylvia stared past both of them, her fist at her chin, her elbow propped on the arm clenched around her stomach, and her thoughts now appeared to be a million miles away. Nathan realized for the first time just how much she had on her plate.

"Maybe you could find time to come with me for fifteen minutes," Nathan said. "I have a friend who can get you fitted with a ringphone. It will monitor your vital signs and call me if you have...any problems before I see you this evening."

"What kind of problems?" Sylvia asked, and Nathan saw a layer of fear in her eyes before she shifted her gaze to her phone and lifted it as if unconsciously considering his offer.

"Blackouts and seizures are common but not frequent. The ringphones are practical." Nathan stepped over, took her phone, and touched her healing finger. "They can connect with the chip you had injected at arrival and give you immediate access to your accounts."

"You mean my bank accounts twenty-five light-years away..."

"Literally at your fingertips," he said, rotating the solid gold ring on his index finger. He could feel his own smile matching hers.

"The rings have locator technology," Meki said. "It could help me keep up with you since you've lost your keys." He grinned but grumbled something about her spending her advance before it was even advanced and pulled the door closed behind him.

Nathan felt relief when Meki left. He'd wanted to identify the gap between what Sylvia knew about her condition and what he would need to explain. "Sahaja are rare," he said, pointing to the barstools. "May we sit?"

"Certainly," she said. "What is a Sahaja?"

"They are the closest genetic coding to their original species form, and the few we have diagnosed have come to us in all kinds of conditions."

Sylvia squeezed her hands in her lap. "You say that as if some of them couldn't be helped."

"That has happened. For example, a Sahaja EvP maintains approximately ninety-eight percent of the original DNA in their EvP network from the first pairing of their ancestors with the Rainbanes. Yet if they are walking around on Earth, they probably do not know other EvPs even exist and that there is something incredible about what makes them different."

Sylvia leaned forward. "Can you tell me more?"

Nathan shifted in his seat. *Is she looking for an angle to use if she doesn't get the results she or the publication team want to see?* "When did you first realize you were Sahaja?" Nathan asked a renewed firmness in his voice. If she was lying, he was her enemy, and if she was not, he was her doctor. Either way meant she was off-limits.

"So, Sahaja aren't a separate species like an Intuit, EvP, Griffon, or Immortal?" Sylvia twisted her charm, then picked up her phone. "I still have trouble keeping them apart, but they're fascinating," she said, curiosity in her voice. Sylvia laid her phone down and looked at him intently.

"Correct. There are Sahaja of every species type." Nathan narrowed his eyes, watching her. "And technically, Immortals came before the Rainbanes, but that history is a lot to absorb in one setting." Nathan sensed her eagerness to know more, *but why?* He was compelled, but still hesitant. "The testing I provide is specific for Sahaja evaluation." Nathan watched Sylvia's face, but he could read nothing there. Nathan tapped his ring discreetly with his thumb. His hand was folded under his arm, but it would record his words to a text even as he spoke them to Sylvia.

NATHAN: No one comes for Sahaja testing the way you have.

Nathan double-tapped the ring to send the message to Rosalind's phone.

Sylvia blinked and wiped her eyes, "Your eyes are distracting. They seem to get this amber burst inside the green."

Nathan pushed his chair back and closed his eyes.

"Sorry," she said. "That was inappropriate. I shouldn't be appreciating my doctor's eyes. I don't...I don't know about the Sahaja you're talking about," Sylvia finished, clearly taking care not to stare at his eyes.

"Never mind," he said. "We'll talk about it this evening at the clinic." He had no intention of doing the imaging tests on her without the neuro exam first, no matter what Rosalind said happened at the race. This woman could be manipulating them all. He wanted to monitor her biometrics with a ringphone. "Let's go fit you for a ringphone."

"You go ahead. I'll meet you in the lobby, say, half an hour."

"Twenty minutes," he said, determined not to be her pawn. "I have to leave for the clinic soon. I can introduce you to the ring maker before I leave the hotel," he said, closing the door as he left.

[19.8]

Sylvia circled her finger on the phone, causing the calendar page to turn indecisively as she stared at the closed door. *What just happened?* She touched her fingers and remembered Nathan's concern. She shouldn't care, but she did. She walked back to the bedroom for her briefcase and sat down on the bed. She slid out the picture Kita gave her, recalling everything that brought her to this point. She felt the tears and wiped at them. "I'm so afraid," she said to the distant ceiling. She looked back down at the photo, then opened her book and slid her hand over the emblem that Nathan said represented the five species. She let her finger trace along the glyphs inside it. Hieroglyphs that Tessa said could be translated to numbers from ancient Tokoleh writings. She closed her eyes. She gave up her dream of archaeology because of fear. She apparently blocked her own memories out of fear, and now she was here alone because she hid her condition from family and friends out of fear. "I can't run anymore," Sylvia said, opening her eyes.

"What was it Nathan said?" she murmured as her hand skimmed the lines of the house near the large tree in the photo. "Sahaja?" Sylvia blew out a long breath, thinking about what it was going to take to face the rest of this week. For that matter, the rest of her life, because it was never going to be the same. She felt a chill as she noticed something in the photo and moved toward the window to see it better. There was a finger in the upper left corner of the picture. A flash of the vision that blocked her memory made her stumble. The red eyes made her short of breath, and she reached for the windowsill. The sun, now a giant orange, peered over the ridge of the mountains beyond the hotel. "It's a new day," she whispered. She checked the clock to her right on the nightstand. "I'll ask Nathan more about Sahajas downstairs." She outlined the shape of the mountain through the window, seeing her own reflection in the glass as she promised this change to herself. "I'll use my archaeology knowledge to find answers, not be buried by the questions." She pressed her hand to the glass, feeling the warmth of the rising sun. "I'll be honest with myself about the changes in my mind and face them." A flash of orange raced behind her eye, and Sylvia gasped as the vision formed again.

The red eyes gleamed when the vision spoke: *"It will kill you."*

Sylvia trembled as if her body was struggling to find the surface of a deep lake, one hand braced on the sill and the other still pinned to the glass warmed by the sun. She pressed her face to her hand and felt the wetness of her tears. She gritted her teeth. "And I'll face the demon that guards my memories."

A sound behind her caused her to spin, but there was nothing. She imagined the dead man with his glowing eyes in the doorway to the kitchen, but she blinked, and the image disappeared. She reached for the closet door and opened it in search of her robe. She slipped the picture inside the pocket. She didn't want to leave it in the book — she was taking that with her. This way, she would remember to review the photo after her shower tonight. She turned back to the window to let the sun warm her face and push away the nightmare that tugged at her memory. A spark of yellow-orange danced toward her eyes from a silver tangle that seemed to glow faintly in the back of her mind. "Nathan..." she whispered as a million questions flooded her mind, and she traced a design on the window. "Can a doctor help me?" The words seemed contrary to the tightness in her chest at the thought of seeing him this evening. Why did she feel afraid and attracted to him at the same time? She took a deep breath and let it out controlled. "It's okay to be afraid. You just have to carry on."

CHAPTER TWENTY

Nathan bumped his knee as he shifted the chair. The tables around the indoor pool, with their round, delicate glass, were too low for him to sit comfortably. "Thanks for meeting here, Xenos. The tram lines are a mess, and the Sim-transport is a nightmare with the influx of travelers using it for transport to the planet."

"Not a problem. Thank you for extending my treatments so I can postpone the regeneration for now. Kinley and I have a lead to follow on a case."

Nathan closed his eyes and took a deep breath, turning his head toward the waterfall to his left. He should encourage him to regenerate. *He shared his reasons with you. It's his choice.* "The medication has increased risk if taken for more than two years," Nathan said, turning back to the man who sat across from him. "I can't guarantee I will have any answers after working with your fellow Immortal from the Orbiter. I'm bringing Jezel out of cryo today. Her LC agreed to let me share select information with you. It seems you know one another."

"Thank you. I'm indebted to them and to you."

Nathan nodded. "You support my work and have helped me help others. I couldn't ask for anything else. I'll let you know if I discover any answers for how she retained her memory through her first regeneration. I do know it occurred roughly four years ago. They have described it, but I cannot explain it scientifically." Nathan paused, pursing his lips when Xenos steepled his fingers in thought. "I am, however, working on a project that may reveal a descendant of the Rainbane Reborn, bloodline."

Xenos sat forward. "Are you certain?"

"Not at all," Nathan answered honestly. "It is most likely tampering artifact."

"Tampering artifact?"

"Yes, some of the preliminary MRI results are so interesting I worry they've been tampered with, which is why I wanted to speak with you. Rosalind tells me you were on Orbiter C13. Can you answer a few questions for me?"

[20.1]

Outside, the morning sun had done little to warm the air, though it was nearly nine a.m. Meki dropped his phone in the pocket of his briefcase as he sat down on the bench. The Earth phone had limited function here, so he used it to check the Earth time. His watch was set to Replica Earth time, while his ringphone ran a check on the energy-generator room. The GCS was a nice place to stay till their Sim-beam to the planet was available. Many of the Earth Week celebration events were planned here for that very reason. However, the signing wasn't one of them, and he needed to have things finished here before they headed down to Replica Earth.

"Do you mind if I sit?" an elderly gentleman asked, breaking Meki's reverie.

"No, crack on. I need to head inside." The ground shifted like the roll of a wave, and Meki fell into the man. "Pardon me," Meki said, regaining his balance.

The man waved off the apology. "Twenty-five light-years away, and it feels like home."

"The mountains?" Meki asked.

"No." The man tapped at his chin. "California. I'll be damned if that wasn't a tremor."

Meki barely kept his feet from running as he raced back into the hotel. The GCS Hotel was a ten-square-mile facility that functioned similarly to a Tokoleh fuel cell here at the Galactic Core Station. The Tokoleh had *engineered* or *adapted,* depending on who you spoke to, the replicated solar system. It was considered an incomplete terraform project, initially planned for the inhabitants of the Tokoleh's first merge with humans, but that had brought about The Void and left the Tokoleh struggling to save themselves and Earth's entire solar system. Biagio's toast to begin Earth Week, before the charity race, recounted the terraform history, the Tokoleh's scramble to salvage life from each of the planets within Earth's system. Meki recalled the history, and his purpose for a better future flashed through his thoughts. He wanted to run but slowed his pace as he neared the hotel entrance. The Bond of Five Tower had held on Earth — uniting the multi-planetary species for a while — then came the Great Splintering. Meki felt another tremor as he climbed the stairs. The energy of the Replica Solar System generated the magnetic field around Earth via the Portals from the GCS. It was more than important; it was the life protection for Earth. Tremors should not be occurring in the biodome that housed the GCS. Meki continued inside the hotel, tapping his ringphone for a holographic screen.

Did I not calculate for the pressure shifts? Meki asked himself as his mind ravaged through the data on his holographic screen. This project allowed for little variance. He had told them to let him focus on Sylvia during this trip, but their only sense of focus was what they wanted right now. And he had to agree it needed to be done. Soon. If he didn't feel so strongly about humanity's ability to destroy itself and everyone else with it, he would have refused. He preferred being less visible.

[20.2]

Nathan frowned at the crack in the resort emblem near the pool's waterfall. The shudder he had felt move through the ground seemed minimal, almost contained. Except for the chair across from him tipping over and this crack that ran right up the middle of the rectangular box on the resort emblem, there was no evidence of the tremor. Nathan ran his hand along the stone edge, moving to the opposite side of the pool. A woman sat at a table that had been invisible to him from the other side. He gave a professional smile and returned to the stone.

[20.3]

Kita stood to leave and didn't return the stranger's smile. She didn't want anyone to remember she had been here. She doubted he would. He was too busy checking the crack in the stone, or maybe it was just the glyph that had him intrigued. She remembered her heart racing the first time she saw the glyph in Earth's Third Sector. It was almost identical to this one, but she had been five at the time and wasn't supposed to be there.

The hotel emblem displayed the glyph design — with a simplicity that spoke of power — everywhere here, but it remained hidden on Earth. The thought reminded her of why she was here, and she increased her pace. She hesitated a moment at the thought of Mr. Tall and Curious finding the tab she placed on the doorframe lock in the pool storage room.

She decided it was unlikely he would go plundering in the pool storage room. Few people knew of the old connections between the energy-generator rooms. Most of them dumped out into places that had been turned into storage with the recent renovations. They were closed now but not sealed, and you could still move around through their antiquated passageways if you didn't mind the darkness or the time it took. She had been using them since she arrived.

[20.4]

Nathan probably wouldn't have noticed the woman, except when she pushed her braided dark hair back, her jacket sleeve pulled up, and he noticed the dry half-inch rash at her wrist.

He had been seeing it more and more frequently from the Fifth Sector. It was a dramatic contrast to her otherwise perfect bronze skin. She had striking features with her transparent green eyes and a confidence that seemed purposely subdued by tattered clothes and a grunge look that wasn't in style in any sector anymore.

Nathan tapped his ringphone and called Rosalind when the woman disappeared into the women's changing rooms.

"No, Nathan," Rosalind said. "I haven't found her. It's been a day, and now I'm having to use my security code to restart the elevator, which has stalled for some reason. I haven't even—"

"I don't need that. I found her this morning, and she's possibly a fraud. I'm calling to remind you to check your data on the Fifth Sector. I saw another person with that same rash."

"That is the least of my worries right now, Nathan. You're fixating. What's going on?"

"Nothing. The tremor reminded me that you were checking the data on the sector atmospheres. If something is changing with Earth's atmosphere and specifically in one sector, maybe one of the generator-energy rooms needs evaluation."

"What tremor?"

"You didn't feel it?"

"I'm in an elevator," she said, and Nathan could hear the sounds of elevator doors opening. "I've got to go. I'll call you when I'm finished here, and just for the record, I think you're wrong about the girl. What's her name? I'll check some things if I get time."

"Sylvia Debair," Nathan said and disconnected as he moved toward Stone's place to meet Sylvia. He touched the one-letter text he had sent to himself from Sylvia's phone. Her number showed on the holographic screen. He'd canceled a few appointments at the clinic since he'd have to take the car to the clinic after his meeting with Xenos. He tapped the icon on his ring to turn on the eye remote. Neon blue traced around his right eye, forming the laser link, then disappeared. He let his hand fall to his side as he entered Stone's shop. He could control the interface to the phone with his eye now, and the holograph screen projected just in front of his eye. He blinked twice to dial Sylvia's number.

[20.5]

The cell phone in Sylvia's room vibrated. Her bedroom was unchanged by the tremor, except Sylvia Debair lay motionless on the floor, her thumb hooked in the gold chain of the charm around her neck.

CHAPTER TWENTY-ONE

S YLVIA GROANED, ROLLING TO her knees. She squeezed the carpet at her palms, but the room continued to spin. *Why am I on the floor?* She stood gingerly, feeling the rush of a headache behind her eyes. She tried to move and felt groggy. She touched her nose and mouth — they tingled. Bracing against the nightstand, she pushed the drawer in with her knee and stared at her book and phone. She didn't remember bringing it in. Maybe she should have Nathan test her before this evening. A feeling of déjà vu wrapped around anxiety as she tried to remember what she had been doing. Had she passed out? Her phone vibrated, and the sound flashed color to her brain. A tangle of silver at the back of her mind surged and pushed an orange tendril of light that licked like a flame behind her eye. Her head throbbed, but she lifted the phone. "Hello."

"Where are you?" Nathan blurted.

Sylvia could hear his fingers drumming, and she envisioned him standing at a glass case with rings on display. *What time is it? Is he waiting for me?* She didn't like being late, but this had been a spontaneous plan to meet. The reminder of that pushed a surge of warmth through her. She pictured Nathan with his shined brown leather shoes contrasted against the cream-marbled tile of a high-end jewelry store. Nathan called it Stone's Communication Shop, but everything in this hotel screamed high-end. "I think I passed out," she said, her thumb pressed to her right eye where it met the bridge of her nose. If she pushed hard enough, maybe those ribbons of color would retreat to that tangle in the back of her mind. It had to be coming from the migraines. She'd never had it before. "I'm fine, but I think I hit my head. What tremor?" Sylvia continued as Nathan's voice spoke over hers. "No," she finally said firmly. "It's not necessary for you to come up, and

I can't meet you now." She checked the time on her phone and confirmed it with the clock on the nightstand. A thin ribbon of red raced to her left eye, pushing the headache there. "I have to be in the lobby," Sylvia murmured as she shifted toward the clock. She had looked at it just before... *Before what?* she thought, missing what Nathan said. The ribbon of red thinned to orange, pushed back to the tangle, and tingled down her spine as she reached for the clock. "I was supposed to meet Meki no later than ten thirty."

"What? I can't hear you," Nathan said, his voice loud as if speaking louder would help him hear her.

"Sorry, stop shouting," Sylvia said, pulling the phone back to her ear. She noted a spark of static electricity between her hand and the clock when she brushed its face. She moved back to the window. *I feel better.* The headache was easing but not gone. "I'm headed down to the lobby," she said, grabbing her briefcase and walking around the foot of the bed toward the doorway. Her keycard was on the countertop in the kitchenette, and she grabbed it, pinching the phone between her ear and shoulder as she passed through. "Fine," she answered, not sure exactly what Nathan had said but ready to be off the phone.

Sylvia closed her hotel door and took a calm breath in the hallway. The corridor was silent, and she double-checked the outside flap of her briefcase where she had dropped the new keycard to her room, tucking her phone in her pocket. The police still had her keys. She smiled, remembering Meki's frustration. She was going to worry the man to death. She touched the leather flap, feeling the shape of her book inside, as she started down the corridor. Today, she'd deal with the book. Tonight, she'd let Nathan test her atypical mind. Tomorrow, she'd find the archives. *Then,* she thought with a shudder, *I'll find a quiet, safe place to face the demon of my memories.* Lost in thought, she missed the hallway to turn for the elevator. Sylvia stopped walking and backed up, colliding with a body.

Sylvia screamed, releasing a panic in her she had been denying since awakening on the floor of her room. "Let go!" Sylvia's words were muffled by the hand over her mouth. Her momentum to back up pushed her closer to her assailant.

"Don't scream," the voice behind her said.

Sylvia's self-preservation kicked her fear to action, and she stomped hard with the heel of her right shoe, but the assailant's foot was gone.

"Listen to me," the voice said, and Sylvia registered a familiarity she couldn't place. The assailant released her and stepped back just as Sylvia's foot planted hard to the floor again.

"Tell me the coordinates. I'll leave without you."

Sylvia whirled, eyes wide, fists up — but too low to protect her face, she realized when she noted she could see the woman's face. "You." Sylvia swallowed hard, backing out of the alcove. "Meki was right. You sent him, then you killed him." She couldn't fight this woman. "It was you. Oh my God!" Flashes of standing pools of blood and a dismembered body stripped her anger to fear. Sylvia bolted down the hallway, bypassed the climbing elevator, and hit the stairs. *She's right behind me*, Sylvia thought, too afraid to risk a look over her shoulder. The steps jolted her spine as she hit them two at a time, skipping the last three to the landing. Her momentum propelled her too quickly for the turn. She twisted her wrist as her hand caught in the banister when she used it to regain her balance, never stopping as she hit the next flight of stairs. Two more flights and her breathing grew faster, but still not keeping up with her racing heart. She could see the metal door to the lobby and panicked with the thought of stopping to open it. The metal stairs rang with the sound of footsteps, and with her heart pounding in her ears, she couldn't tell where hers separated from Kita's.

[21.1]

Kita's left hand dropped the skeleton key, with the severed Gordian knot, back around her neck as the knob to Sylvia's hotel room twisted open. She had not been certain the old lock system would override the technology, but she realized her tension when she released her held breath. She had hologram-webbed the security camera, but anyone paying attention would notice and demask it. She had to convince Sylvia to help her — at least give her the coordinates. She could find another Intuit to help her with other parts of the mission. Sylvia wasn't the only Intuit, but finding one with Sahaja ability was difficult, and that was the reason Kita needed her...mostly. Only a Sahaja Intuit or someone like Aarunya could turn the relic lock in the Earthside Portal.

Kita pushed away the pain in her chest. *Aarunya is dead, and that is my fault. This woman is not her.* Kita grimaced, holding her chest. She blamed the quick fix of her dislocated shoulder for the pain that lingered in her chest, but she only half believed that. Kita tapped the ring on her hand twice and twisted the band inside its specially designed gear mechanism to create a secure connection. Jo wouldn't be at the Earth Alliance Cryptography office now, but she could leave a message with Hope.

The line pinged. "Hey, Kita, Received your quanta packet, passed it on to Jo. Where'd you get the information?"

"Hope, great! Listen," Kita said, ignoring the question even as she remembered figuring out Motorcycle's hint and getting the data on the second mission. "The book on the news — it practically begs someone to take up the search for the relics, but the author refuses to divulge her information about the locations. Convince Jo the two of you can work your magic on it and the packet quietly. Let me know what you find."

"Did the Earth Alliance ask you to remove the author?"

Kita closed the line. None of her friends understood what it was like to return from a killing place and try to be normal.

[21.2]

The stairwell felt like another dimension as Sylvia burst through the door to the lobby and looked back to see the heavy metal door close behind her. No sign of Kita. Sylvia almost tripped on the carpet as she peered back over her shoulder, afraid to stop watching. Finally, Sylvia scanned the lobby. The resort had its own police force, fire, and ambulance, but she was uncertain where to find them. And what would she tell them? "One of my readers attacked me in the hallway." They would think she was a writing diva who had lost her marbles. She checked the massive clock at the entrance: 10:45. The agenda this morning was interviews scheduled to start at 11:30 a.m., then a long conversation with herself before the Sim-beam down to Replica Earth for the signing this afternoon. She would tell Meki that Kita was here, and they could go to the police. Sylvia's thumb hovered over the call button on her phone, and she took the moment to appreciate the fact that her heart was finding its normal rhythm, even if her headache was worse. Meki would believe her.

Boom! Sylvia jumped and turned as another crash followed a screeching feedback sound that set her jaw in lockdown. A gangly man stood and unwrapped a cord from his leg. A swarm of activity overtook her.

"Bob, get the microphone ready. We're live in minutes."

Sylvia shifted in an attempt to get away, but a crowd of people formed a ring around her and the gangly man with the microphone. Someone whispered near her ear from behind, and Sylvia jumped, then registered the familiar temple gray hairline and glasses. Her body relaxed. "Meki."

"I'm sorry Sylvia, the place is crawling with news teams here for Earth Week. We should do this now. Then we can tell the publisher we've made a public statement, and they can use some of their local personnel to deal with the other news teams. It's the best way to use the publicity in our favor. We may need it. The police want to speak with you at noon. They are trying to cancel the signing this afternoon. The Earth Alliance is making allegations that you work with the Separatists, so I've got my hands full. If we do this now, I can cancel the interviews."

"The who?" Sylvia whispered, half facing Meki, half watching the man with the microphone chatting with his crew.

"They've banned your book in Earth's Third Sector, where that man was murdered."

"Banned *The Recollectors*?" Nathan had mentioned it earlier. "Why?" Sylvia's mind raced. "I expected an investigation with everything that happened, but why ban the book?" *Because it isn't fiction, and two solar systems are willing to kill you and others to get its truth.* The thought made Sylvia freeze with the sense of growing possibility it was true.

"Don't worry about it. I'll handle that. Just keep your composure. It is a work of fiction, and you have nothing to hide."

Sylvia twisted her necklace back and forth. It was a work of fiction — she had imagined it herself. But why did Meki say it as if he needed to convince her?

"Live in three, two, one."

A microphone jabbed into the space between her and Meki.

"Good morning, Ms. Debair. I'm Alex Jenkins with NET News. Why do the police suspect you for murder in Earth's Third Sector?"

CHAPTER TWENTY-TWO

SYLVIA'S FIST CLENCHED, AND she dropped the chain at her neck. Alex pressed her. She sensed he read it as a reaction of guilt, but Sylvia had noticed Kita in the crowd.

"She is not a suspect," Meki inserted firmly, but Sylvia knew now that "suspect" was precisely why they were scheduled with the police.

Sylvia took a deep breath, as much to calm herself to speak as to try to push back some of the pain in her head. The headache pulsed, and the ribbon of color snapped like a whip at the back of her eye.

"Can you tell us more about this page that was ripped from your book and found with the murdered man?" Alex flashed a photograph of the page with the two handwritten numbers to the camera before handing it to Sylvia.

Sylvia glanced at it with only her peripheral vision as she watched Kita move closer in the crowd. The ribbon of color in her mind, now almost an orange glow behind her eye, threatened to obscure her vision as the headache worsened. She turned her focus to the page. Kita wouldn't attack her here in this public place with cameras rolling. "It's a picture of the lock key in Warenow Manor, an imaginary place from my book's first Lost City." She avoided the two handwritten numbers printed below the illustration of the lock, letting her eyes drift to the four-square-glyph she had designed to be beside every page number. The TV anchor's words this morning nagged at her, seeing the Griffon form in the bottom right square of the glyph.

Alex pulled the microphone back to himself and repeated the question. "Did you write those numbers when the man appeared at your signing in Earth Sector Three the night he was murdered?"

Sylvia pushed at the color in her thoughts, now yellow, a flicker as she envisioned the Griffon's talon touching the circle that lay in the center of the four squares of the glyph. "I didn't..." she stammered. "The book is a work of fiction." She shuddered, imagining the Griffon talon piercing the circle to dip into the rectangular box with its lightning-shaped Guardians on either side of the box. "I don't know where these numbers came from."

Sylvia's phone chirped with a text. "The headache is worse," she whispered, sensing Meki now standing to her right. "And Kita is here."

Meki searched the crowd then took over the microphone space, putting Sylvia at his back.

Sylvia checked her phone while Meki spoke.

KINLEY: Have to cancel our meeting tomorrow — your information about the stolen painting has opened a new lead.

Sylvia's shoulders sagged.

SYLVIA: It's fine. I understand. Good luck.

"The relic keys to the Earth Sector locks belong to us!" a voice blasted near the back of the crowd. "We deserve to know where they're hidden."

"What are Earth Sector locks?" Sylvia muttered, looking up from her phone. "Relic keys?" she continued when Meki didn't answer, his eyes on Alex, who leaned toward the crowd with the microphone. Sylvia knew Meki wanted control of the impromptu interview. She just wanted out.

KINLEY: I'm really sorry. Has Michael received the results from the willow bark testing? If so, ask him to reach out to Xenos. We've tried to reach him. Xenos thinks he is on a project for Rosalind, which means he may be unreachable for days.

SYLVIA: I haven't seen him.

The willow bark, Sylvia thought, wringing her hands. *Another reminder someone is trying to kill me.* She chided herself for being dramatic, then recalled Kita's attack this morning.

SYLVIA: Why did you ask me on the Orbiter about the five species glyph I used as my symbol for the Final Lost City?

Alex pressed the microphone close. "How do you answer the people of Egystan and other Earth Sectors who connect your book of hidden cities with the lost relic keys to the Earth Sector locks?"

"It is a work of fiction," Meki answered for her. Sylvia let him. She hadn't agreed to this interview. Not like this.

KINLEY: I asked because I'm familiar with the Tokoleh history that ties the glyph to the Lost Cities and wondered if you were using it as some code?

Not intentionally, Sylvia thought, but then she didn't know anymore. She sighed at the text. *Cities — Not city, singular, and not species as Nathan thought, but...* Sylvia paused in her thought, realizing if she could just get to the Archive, she'd know more. Maybe she'd seen a Tokoleh carving during college. She'd interned on several small digs before the one that destroyed her. *Do my trapped memories hold the keys to connecting it all?* Just like the anchor had said. Had her imagination held some partial truth? *I won't know till I can get to those memories.*

Sylvia reached for her necklace and released it when the colors of the numbers written in the book swirled through her mind anew. Sylvia froze. It was the first time the numbers she often saw when she touched the charm were in any order. The colors seemed to disappear deep in her brain as if they could bury themselves, but they stirred feelings she couldn't explain. Feelings of rejection she thought she had overcome but now felt anew when she wondered about a family she couldn't remember and who had abandoned her.

KINLEY: I saw the news, Sylvia. I'm so sorry. I don't believe the reports.

KINLEY: Sylvia. I know you had nothing to do with that man's death.

Sylvia didn't respond, and her phone began to vibrate with Kinley's call. She quickly typed a response. Kinley had become a good friend.

SYLVIA: I'm fine. Can't talk.

Sylvia stored the phone and stepped forward. "It's a book of fiction," Sylvia said, interjecting her support to what Meki was already saying and using her anger to prop up the brokenness she felt. She would not share with them the tattered memories, dreams, and nightmares that inspired a book that seemed connected to a galaxy larger than what she knew existed.

[22.1]

Rosalind pinched the bridge of her nose. With her eyes closed, she could picture the blueprint of the energy-generator room. The elevator in the UBN building pinged and opened. Rosalind stepped into the elevator typing notes from her investigation of the energy-generator room with a laser keypad displayed from her ring to the back of her left hand. Her phone rang, and she tapped the side of the ring once and continued to type. "Yes, Nathan."

"I think Sylvia may have had a blackout. I'm convinced she is not—"

"Nathan, I have humidity in the energy-generator room that shouldn't be there, a security system I'm behind on review. I don't have time for this. She is, or she isn't. That's your job to figure out."

"I don't want to waste my resources on a spoiled Third Sector celebrity."

"If you thought you were wasting them, you wouldn't be talking to me. You would have canceled her appointment." Rosalind pushed the elevator key with an elbow, still typing her report. "I might lose you. Come by my Archive office later if you want to talk. I'll be there late." She liked the office she kept separate from her UBN main floor office. Her second office was in the Archive with hidden access to her home in the annexed portion.

"Alright. Hey, maybe the tremor caused the energy-generator room problem. I was at the pool, and it was enough to crack the stone."

"Maybe," Rosalind answered. "The old underground tunnel system door was ajar — the most likely cause of the moisture in the energy-generator room and the fluctuation of energy measured in the room due to dissipation into the tunnel."

"A lot of energy lost? Will the UBN have to shut the energy Portal to fix the problem?"

"I don't think so. The energy loss is minimal, and I secured the door, but I want to get in the old tunnel system and check it out. That's been a back-burner project for a while."

"Could the tremor jar the door open?"

Rosalind pursed her lips. Maybe she was overthinking things. The tremor may have jarred the door open, but something just felt wrong about it. She wanted to spend time in the old underground tunnel system, but it was too easy for her to get lost in the symbols and history carved throughout it. "Don't forget the G125."

"Have it."

Rosalind stopped typing and stared at her elevator steel encasement. She pushed the phone disconnect and pulled up the application screen as a secondary window. She tapped the eye icon, and the silver resonance piece formed a halo around her eye just as the elevator opened. She closed the door and hit the security lock. The elevator was as good a place as any to view this old blueprint.

The resonance eye tracked the movement of her biological eye as she scanned the blueprint displayed on the elevator wall. Her ringphone chirped. "Open text on screen," Rosalind said, and the text typed at the bottom of the blueprint image.

MICHAEL: Accessed logs for lockout rooms Orbiter C13. The Dalen Overseer was the last one to use Lockout Room A and Jezel the other.

ROSALIND: &

Rosalind scanned the blueprint as she awaited Michael's response. The tunnel's diagram left the energy-generator room but was cut off on the blueprint after two inches. "Upload tunnel blueprint."

UNAVAILABLE IN DIGITAL FORM flashed on the hologram screen just above Michael's text response.

MICHAEL: Jezel reported using it. The Dalen Overseer failed to mention it. I need UBN push to let me question him again.

Rosalind sighed, collapsed the hologram, unlocked the elevator, and stepped out, hitting the call icon on her phone and selecting Michael's number. "Get a GCS investigation inquiry from Houseman. He is investigating the race attack. Marcus identified the drug from my system following the attack. I'm forwarding you the report on that and the willow bark. Make sure you give Xenos a copy of the results. I think he will be interested."

"Sure, I'll reach out to him. Do you want me to ask Xenos to contact you?"

"Yes."

"If you're crossing the Orbiter investigation with the race attack, you're looking for something," Michael said.

Rosalind smiled but kept it out of her voice. "The drug was manufactured by a pharmaceutical company near Pittsburgh where this Dalen team is housed. That's enough to get you an inquiry with the Dalen Overseer for your questions...and get a Nitpati to grant you access to the Dalen work permit."

Static crackled her phone when she disconnected then dialed the main UBN security office one floor up. "Harry, I'll be down here in my Archive office the rest of the day. Keep an eye on the energy-generator room temperature and pressures for me. Contact me with a change of more than two degrees. Oh, and get me the hard copy blueprints of the tunnels."

"Roger that. I've got extra eyes on the lobby — just a heads-up."

What is going on in the lobby? She didn't even ask; extra eyes usually meant someone being a general nuisance. Harry and the crew could handle it, but her gut worried about everything these days.

[22.2]

Nathan watched the lobby crowd escalate to a mob. Sylvia's fisted hand twisting and releasing that charm didn't go unnoticed by him. *If I save her from this, maybe she'll give me the time to do the exam.*

There was a primal energy when he moved through the crowd — he was a lion parting high grass on a plain. He bumped Meki's shoulder as he stepped between Sylvia and Meki, which was the straightest route to Alex.

Nathan ignored Meki's wide eyes, which narrowed as he moved between them.

"I disagree." A woman's voice penetrated the argument of voices in the crowd. Alex was struggling to keep control of the interview. Sylvia had turned away, and his microphone was picking up pieces of argument in the crowd about the Tokoleh, the Separatists, and the Earth Alliance. Each, in turn, was blamed for any number of recent events.

"You can blame that man for keeping the truth a secret — his lab keeps the Tokoleh in power!" The man's voice was gruff with that edge of conspiracy fervor that bred panic. Nathan ignored the accusation. It wasn't the first time he had been blamed when he was trying to help.

[22.3]

Sylvia waited as Alex tried again to save the derailed impromptu interview. The lobby was a torrent of heated discussion. She registered a new frustration on his face when Nathan appeared. Her focus on Nathan made her unprepared for Alex's question. "Can you clarify if the Final Lost City in your book exists, Ms. Debair?"

"It. Is. Fiction. The Lost City isn't real..." Sylvia lost her train of thought as a word interrupted — *Sahaja*. The word pulled from that reservoir of darkness buried in that silver tangle. The word circled itself, wrapping with new words. *Centerworld* — a thread of red twisting into red eyes and the vision from the Orbiter. Sylvia bit her lip, feeling a bead of sweat at her temple as she forced herself to pull at the thread of memory even as the bloody hands grasped her blouse. She could feel the sticky blood, but she wouldn't stop. "Sahaja's Risk," Sylvia murmured as the small success boosted her purpose, and she pressed for more. She was falling into a sea of water. Sylvia panicked. The vision of a checkered gameboard erased the man with red eyes as she released the memory, and the lobby came into focus. She was panting and grateful the chaos of the lobby distracted everyone as she wiped her forehead, feeling sick. She felt she was drowning, but she had this tiny memory. She and her father played the game — not the man she called father now, but another man, another life. Sylvia bumped something and startled from her own thoughts. Nathan towered between her and Alex. Nathan's six-foot-six frame blocked the camera, and he placed his hand firmly on Alex's shoulder.

"We have to get to another appointment now." Nathan's tone was business-friendly and adamantly curt.

Sylvia smiled. Something about Nathan made her both cautious and reckless. Her breath caught when he turned his green eyes to her. Reckless trust tempered by a failing caution that said she should not.

"Thank you. The book signing has been canceled for today," she said and raised to whisper in his ear, "I'm afraid, but I need to get to the archives." Sylvia bit her lip, then remembered how vulnerable it made her look and released it.

Nathan stiffened, and Sylvia sensed his tension. It seemed to express itself even in his eyes, like starbursts of amber at the iris that pierced the green and threatened to overtake it. Sylvia berated herself for being so open. *He's a stranger.* What was she thinking? She turned to find Meki but realized her finger held Nathan's belt loop. She had used it to leverage herself to his ear.

[22.4]

"We need to get out of this crowd," Nathan said, relieved when she released her touch at his waist. Nathan caught a glimpse of himself in a mirrored wall. The Griffon amber sparked from his iris bright against the human green of his eyes. *How can this woman so easily trigger my Griffon instincts?* "UBN security wants to speak with you, and the Archive is there," Nathan said, focusing his thoughts on the professional role he had with this woman. *Get her to Rosalind's office. I can do the exam there. She can get you access to the archives.* Nathan's ring vibrated. He tapped it, and a flare of blue wrapped his ear. "Hi, Maggie. What is it?"

"Tessa Danquah called from the regeneration prep wing at the hospital. Jezel wants to postpone regeneration. Your new adaptive cryo has helped her, and she is wanting to leave the hospital."

"What? She can't be that well."

"That's what I thought, but they are adamant. Of course, she won't leave AMA because it will jeopardize—"

"Yeah, I know." Nathan said, interrupting. "Let me call them." Nathan dropped the call and dialed the hospital, watching Sylvia scan the lobby. "Let's move toward the door," he said.

"What about Meki?" Sylvia asked, stopping to look behind them.

"Don't stop here," Nathan said, fighting his initial instinct to touch the small of her back to guide her and deciding to press her elbow instead. *Damn it,* Nathan thought, seeing a whirlpool of light circling in layers as it flowed from the depths of his brain's limbic system toward his network. He and Jenny had unpublished data that identified this area as a region of histone modification of the Griffon genome. Sylvia's energy expression was breaking down the G125 if he was getting network signal. A connection dial tone pulled him to his call. "Lisa, yes, put me through to regen prep wing room thirty-one." Nathan turned, using his height to help locate Meki. "There," Nathan said, pointing to where Meki and Alex were speaking. "You can contact him when we are free of the crowd."

"We could also wait for him," Sylvia said, her brow furrowed as she looked down at his hand pressing at her elbow. "Besides, I thought you were taking me to get a ring, er, phone."

"That was before you ruined my schedule," Nathan said, then started to correct his words at the rotation of her neck and raised eyebrow.

"Ruined your schedule!" Sylvia stopped shy of the door and jerked her arm away.

Nathan stepped slightly away. They were clear of the crowd now.

"Tessa, hi, it's Dr. Renner." He waved a hand at Sylvia, palm out in apology and protection. He thought she might punch him. He was surprised when she froze as if recognizing the name, but he continued to speak, careful his words did not reveal patient information. "Tessa, I'm concerned Jezel is not—"

"Yes, we know," Tessa interrupted. "Jezel has agreed to come back tomorrow, but she is feeling better, and we have some pressing matters to discuss with the author who was on the news this morning. We plan to attend her signing, and then we will return to complete treatment."

"Her signing has been canceled, but she is standing right here with me. If I let you speak with her, will Jezel stay?" He let the words *in the hospital* remain unspoken

There was a pause, then, "Yes."

"Tessa and Jezel want to speak with you. Do you know them?" Nathan asked, his eyes narrowed.

"Yes," Sylvia said, lifting her chin.

Nathan wondered if it was true confidence or bravado. "I can transfer the call to your phone," he said, searching for her number on the laser screen display. He needed Jezel to stay in the hospital; leaving would delay her care, and he could tell Tessa knew it and was pleased with this alternate option.

"You have my number?" Sylvia asked, her hands pausing as she reached for her phone in her pocket.

Nathan grimaced, pausing with his finger above the number. He had a number in the clinic computer from when her appointment was scheduled, but he didn't know if it was her cell number, and he didn't want to lie to her. *What is wrong with you around this woman?* Nathan could kick himself for half of his behaviors this morning. He was acting like the primal beast who knew only how to gain what it wanted at any cost. "I sent your number to my phone in your room. I was afraid something might happen to you before we had a ringphone for you," he said, feeling the anger at his beast heat his ears. *She is not property, not something to obtain or protect,* Nathan thought with a force that made his Griffon network glow gold and amber.

"You show up in my room uninvited, show me kindness and indifference, offer me help and rejection, steal my phone number, shove me around by my elbow like I'm a prom date you don't want to see the next day, and I've ruined your schedule." Sylvia pulled her phone out. "Send me the damn call."

Nathan could see more anger in her blue eyes than her words and felt a surge at his network. *What the hell?* Nathan stepped away from her, turning toward the concierge desk to hide the amber he knew she would see in his eyes. It was as if the emotion she stirred in him was eating up the injection molecule by molecule. "I'll call for the car and grab my jacket." He moved toward the concierge desk and tapped the record feature on his ringphone. "Increase the dose of histone deacetylase in the G125." Nathan slowed his pace. He wanted to record this information to share with Jenny later at the lab. "Whatever Sylvia Debair is..." Nathan paused, thinking. "It seems to alter the breakdown of the deacetylase in the G125, allowing the Griffon DNA to unwind and be exposed for expression."

The concierge reached out the jacket as he approached, and Nathan took it and turned. Sylvia was where he left her and appeared to be finishing her call. Nathan twisted his ring to turn off the recording feature and took a deep breath to face Sylvia.

"Your car is here, sir." The valet stepped back out the door and motioned the limousine to pull forward.

"I'm sure Meki knows where UBN security is located. He can take me," Sylvia said, turning away from Nathan and heading back toward the crowd that was breaking up.

"No," Nathan said. "I mean, listen, I'm sorry," he continued, surprising himself and feeling his own sincerity push something back.

Sylvia paused but didn't turn.

"I'd like you to talk to Rosalind. You helped me save her life the other day." He breathed out a relaxed breath, and the human effort required for rational thought helped. He'd give himself a dose of the G125 he carried when they reached the security building. *By the Source, I just gave myself a shot this morning.* He usually only required one injection a day to maintain the tight, closed, unreadable form of his Griffon DNA. "If I take you, I can ask Rosalind to grant you access to the Archive," he said.

"The police want to speak with me at noon."

"Rosalind can probably help with that." Nathan took a slow breath. "I sincerely apologize. I can be overprotective in general, though not of everyone so blatantly," he said, surprised at his own confession. "I know Rosalind is the best person to help you if you are interested in the Archive."

[22.5]

"Rosalind Mathing?" Sylvia asked. She rubbed the notch of her neck. *Is this the same lady who wants to meet with me and Meki about my writing her procedure manuals?* Sylvia thought as she waited for Nathan's answer. His eyes appeared distant, and unease tightened his shoulders. "Your girlfriend is Rosalind Mathing, the director of UBN security?" The strain on Nathan's face registered, and Sylvia shifted the conversation. "Maybe they were after her and not you after all."

"We still don't know that yet," Nathan answered. He seemed distracted. "As the Chief Director of UBN security, she is a reasonable target. Houseman is investigating it."

Sylvia had given up her effort to find Meki in the crowd but only realized now that she and Nathan had walked out the lobby doors. The April sun warmed the patch of space where they stood. They shifted from the limited shade of the valet dropoff area, moving toward a limousine that crept forward toward them.

"Thank you for coming with me," Nathan said, reaching for the limousine door to indicate for the chauffeur to just stop here. He held the door open against the wind that channeled through the breezeway as Sylvia climbed in, sinking into the leather seat. Nathan was in quickly behind her and neatly folded his coat between them. "I don't want you angry with me. Let's talk about something neutral till we get to security."

"Fine," Sylvia said, watching Nathan send a quick text by tapping the back of his hand. She stifled her envy at the technology and wondered about the design of his ring but didn't ask. "What do you think about the numbers in the book?" Sylvia said wanting to talk to someone with a different perspective. Tessa and Jezel had given her a challenge with some new information, and she had at least one page in her book to focus on once she had Archive access to the Tokoleh ancient texts.

"I don't know, I didn't see them." Nathan pressed his ring. A hologram screen appeared, and he tapped an icon. "Hold on. I'm sure someone posted a picture of it." Nathan enlarged the screen so they could both see. "Is that your book?" he asked, seemingly shocked at the nesting pattern of the hotel glyph-emblem on the book's front cover at the center. The glyphs that appeared as chairs seated to either side of a rectangular box formed the hotel emblem and could be seen everywhere

here. The glyph represented seated Guardians at the Source. Yet, Sylvia's design, with its steeper angles, looked like lightning bolts to either side of the box and seemed more ancient. The Tokoleh species glyph appeared in the four corners of the book cover. The four squares united by the circle at the center reflected power, with the hotel emblem repeated at its center.

"Yes, and the picture beside the cover is the page that was torn out." Sylvia began reading the article beneath the picture.

"I don't see any numbers."

Sylvia stopped reading and dropped the charm around her neck. "Someone wrote those in."

She touched the hologram and scrolled to a picture below the article she had been reading. *I look startled*, Sylvia thought, seeing herself in the picture. *Not startled — afraid.* She felt like part of a team through the entire investigation on the Orbiter when she had the support of Xenos, Kinley, and Michael. Now, she felt alone again. Her eyes roved between her turquoise blouse and the paper she gripped in the photo, Alex holding the other end. The zoomed-in picture of the page showed the numbers written in pencil, but her mind saw the blood-covered numbers from the Orbiter. Sylvia leaned back against the leather and took a deep breath with her eyes closed. A ribbon of color retreated to the tangle in her mind, and the blood-covered numbers disappeared with it. She opened her eyes and realized Nathan was watching her.

"A man is dead, I'm alive, and my book is the single connection between them." Sylvia shifted to peer out the window, the pain in her chest uncomfortable. "The numbers are not in the original. Someone hand-wrote them in."

Nathan bumped her elbow as he shifted his arm to bring the screen close and enlarge the picture again. "I can see that now," he said as he typed the numbers on the laser keyboard on the back of his hand.

Sylvia watched as the numbers written in pencil popped up on a text in the corner of the screen as Nathan typed them on a document he titled "Sylvia." She squeezed her eyes closed again, then opened them, forcing herself to reread the two numbers. She was rubbing the charm at her neck and tracing the engraving on the back: HEA. *Maybe it means Happy Ever After. Yeah, right.* She let her fingers move along the black that covered the back of the charm. Even the hues of black seemed to have numbers. "Is synesthesia a common problem with people who have an MRI like mine?"

Nathan stared at her, back at the screen, then twisted in his seat to face her.

Sylvia thought he looked as if she had asked him a trick question.

"Can you describe your synesthesia?"

Sylvia licked her lips. His hard stare made her uncomfortable. *Does he think I'm going to lie to him?* She tilted her head to look at him. That would be absurd. *Who would lie about colors having taste and numbers having color?* Sylvia explained her symptoms, and Nathan listened with rapt attention. His focus made Sylvia look away to the screen with the book and its numbers.

"Do you know what they mean?" Nathan asked once she finished speaking.

"I think..." Sylvia paused. *Two men are dead, one in a coma, Jezel is in cryo, and the single component between them is my book.* Was this the real reason why Rosalind wanted to see her? Sylvia decided not to tell Nathan about her speculation that they were the beginning coordinates to cities and that she was going to the archives to research a page of her own book. Instead, she asked, "You didn't answer my question about the synesthesia. Do you and Rosalind think I had something to do with the attack at the race?"

Nathan's lips formed a line, and Sylvia felt again the weight of his stare as if he was trying to read something in her face as he spoke. "Yes, we can see that occur. However, it is unusual, and it is possible the changes on your MRI are due to a chemical."

"A chemical?" Sylvia asked, feeling her eyebrow practically reach her hairline.

"Yes," Nathan said, finally looking down in thought. "And no, Rosalind doesn't think you were involved with the attack." He caught his balance as the car made a turn. This close to her, his nose flared. "Jasmine and rain," he whispered.

Sylvia barely heard it, but the words and his low tone made her shiver.

"How can you be sure?" Sylvia asked, swallowing hard at the dilating pupils in the rich green of his eyes before he regained his balance. Someone had attacked the woman she and Meki were scheduled to meet about a "proposal for procedure manual writing." Now Nathan wanted to take her to meet the same woman. Procedure manual writing suddenly seemed a mundane cover for something more.

"She wanted to thank you, and it helped you escape Alex. I'm hoping it will give us time to do that neuro exam and give us a few answers," Nathan said, and Sylvia tilted her head. Something had changed.

She took in his broad smile. Maybe Nathan could give her some answers before they arrived. She used his technique and watched him as she spoke. "I dream of Lost Cities. The dreams are so vivid I often put them in my book."

"Does your book use numbers to identify the cities?"

"No, there were no numbers on the locks," Sylvia said, then realized he had asked about the cities. She associated the numbers she had seen in her dreams with the locks, not the cities. *I thought my mind was creating numbers as combinations for the locks,* Sylvia thought, feeling an uncomfortable foreboding. She had deferred adding the numbers, thinking they were unnecessary, and instead only used the dreamlike glyphs from her imagination. *The glyphs, Tessa said, were ancient Tokoleh numbers. Numbers that might be coordinates to cities. Cities that might possibly be from memories I can't reach except through my imagination.* Sylvia's mouth went dry.

"Were there numbers in your dream?" Nathan asked, sounding interested.

"They weren't important." She wanted to push open the door and jump out. "The numbers in my dreams, that is. They were always hazy and without meaning, and..." She pointed at the screen he reopened. "Someone else wrote those." She reached for her necklace. *But I've seen them in my dreams,* she thought, being fully present as the vision reached for her from the ribbon of thought that made dreams a nightmare. She faced the window, releasing the thought. Facing the demon that guarded those memories was for another day. First, the archives, and Rosalind was the key to that. The day was now gray as the sun hid behind clouds darkened more by the tinted glass. The numbers now seemed more real than these dwarf trees and starved evergreens. "Nothing here is quite as full as Earth," she said, more to change the subject in her mind.

"It's better when you are planetside. The core station is a biodome." Nathan leaned toward her with interest. "So, your book has Lost Cities and locks somehow associated with those cities?"

"Indirectly," Sylvia answered, toying with the door and its hidden handle. She wouldn't have found it if she hadn't seen a color flash in her mind when she touched it. "It's a standard fiction story of Lost Cities and relics. I didn't even expect it to do so well."

"Relics?" Nathan said with almost reverence.

Sylvia looked at him. From this angle, that starburst of amber appeared in his eyes again. There was something primal and attractive about it. She took a breath and turned to trace her hand along the hidden door handle as she spoke. "The relics open the locks, but the relics have been lost as well..."

"You wrote a book about Lost Cities, relics that open Portal locks in them, and you think it is fiction?" Nathan's tone was incredulous.

"It is fiction!" Sylvia said, pulling her thoughts from the landscape, which mingled with the colored thoughts in her mind. She had a pressing desire to be back home. She glared at Nathan. He seemed to choose his words carefully, as if part of him wanted to protect her and the other wanted to push her to some unseen confession.

"Do you know what these so-called fictional relics are called here?" He twisted his ring a half-turn, and the screen turned ninety degrees so she could see the picture of the lock in her peripheral view.

Sylvia didn't answer, but she gave her attention to the picture. She sensed Nathan watching her. She touched the air displaying the hologram as if it could take her to another time, another place.

Nathan spoke in a quiet voice. "This is a picture of the relic associated with the Umbilical lock in Egystan, the region you know as Earth Sector Four."

Sylvia didn't bother to explain she'd only learned of the sectors in flight and was confused by the multitude of names used for places on Earth. She closed her eyes, pushing away the bright thread of yellow that seemed to race from the tingle in her fingertips back to the tangle in her mind. "It isn't real."

Nathan swiped the screen, and a new picture appeared, an illustration from Sylvia's book identical to the photograph on the previous screen. Nathan's voice was a whisper of thoughts.

Sylvia couldn't make out the words. "I'm sorry. What did you say?"

"In your book, you call this the 'Relic of Mastery.'" Nathan pointed. "Do you expect me to believe you don't know 'Mastery' is the English translation of the ancient Tokoleh name for one of the relic keys?"

Sylvia swiped the screen between the two pictures. The full-color photo was identical to the one she had drawn from her dream and had enhanced as an illustration in her book. She had never seen the photo before. She did not know it existed. *It is only fiction if you don't believe.* The words reverberated from somewhere in her mind, and Sylvia's gut twisted.

"They call them Circle Relics here because of their shape," Nathan said. "This picture shows a Circle Relic game piece for a game we play here. It is an old game that's been taught to children here since before anyone can remember."

"What do they call the game?" Sylvia asked, fearing the answer.

"Sahaja's Risk," Nathan said, his eyes leaving the screen to look at his hand as he spun the ring on it. "Chemical triggers are not the only cause for the abnormality I see on your MRI." He leaned back against the seat as if there might be guidance in the roof. "Sahaja realignment is a differential diagnosis."

"A differential what?"

"An alternate cause for what I am seeing. Some of your history and symptoms fit, but others..." He paused. "To be honest, some of what I see is suspect," he finally said, as if realizing it wouldn't hurt to just put his cards of skepticism out at this point.

"I see," Sylvia said and bit back her anger. *What kind of doctor doesn't believe his patient? Not one I can trust,* she thought, realizing she would need to gather as much information as she could without getting too entangled with Nathan or Rosalind. "Can you tell me more about the game?"

"Every child and adult player in the game tries to demonstrate their selected figure is—"

"SuryaChaya," Sylvia whispered, interrupting Nathan. "My mother called it that." She closed her lips tight, determined to hold on to this memory if it would lead to her mother. *A Sahaja requires balance.* The thought circled like a whirlpool. She was underwater. She couldn't breathe. Red eyes glowed just beyond the water above her.

"I think the Immortals call it that, but no one here does. Sylvia? Sylvia! Do you have seizures? Sylvia, look at me."

[22.6]

Sylvia could hear her name beyond the water, distant. The tangle in Sylvia's mind sparked, and a vision of a girl waving a game piece appeared. The child held the metal-crafted figurine of a female warrior. A dark orb glistened like a marble in the figurine's plated abdomen. Sound attended the vision, interrupting the distant calling beyond the water. She couldn't see to whom the child spoke. Her lungs were burning. She needed air. "I want to be an EvP this time," the child said, waving the figurine in the air. The vision vanished with a tug. She sensed the red eyes of her earlier vision trying to form, but she mentally pushed it back toward the tangle. She gasped and jerked as if her face had just broken through the water. Sylvia gasped several more times before her breathing evened out. It was as if that vision with the red eyes had become part of a trap around her memories, a twisted gatekeeper of her mind. "I don't feel well," Sylvia said flatly, the pain in her chest finding purchase and climbing to strangle her voice as the landscape beyond the window blurred through the tears she refused to let fall. *Take a deep breath, be strong, focus on the positive.* She almost laughed at her own advice. She had friends who were optimists, but she was a realist.

"I know the game," she said, covering Nathan's hand to make the screen from his ring disappear. "Or rather, I'm starting to remember it." She pushed his hand to his leg and tried to breathe through the ache in her chest. "My parents..." Sylvia paused. She didn't want to say they didn't want her, which sounded like self-pity. "I just don't remember anything about them." Sylvia hesitated. She remembered nothing prior to her life with her adopted family. *How does someone forget the first seven years of their life?*

[22.7]

"I'm sorry," Nathan said, looking away when she bit her lip. Her scent was vulnerable, and his Griffon instinct was to protect her. *Not an instinct I can trust,* he thought, since to a beast, to protect was to have. To own. He closed his eyes. *I am not an animal.*

Nathan pinched the bridge of his nose. He was certain Sylvia had caught the starburst of color flash in his green eyes before he closed them.

"Am I giving you a headache?" Sylvia asked it with such sincerity, he laughed.

"A little. Though not truly your fault," he added.

"Tell me more about the relics," she said, and her eagerness restored his discomfort and raised his skeptical barriers.

Nathan shifted in the seat and tapped his ring microphone. His words would be converted to a text he could covertly send to Rosalind as Sylvia gazed again at the changing landscape. Nathan spoke to Sylvia, and his words formed a line of text he would send to Rosalind.

NATHAN: Do you expect me to believe you have such blind knowledge to write a book describing the lost relics of the Five Sectors, yet not know of them?

Nathan covertly tapped the send icon on his ring. Rosalind would receive the text, and she could help him decide about Sylvia objectively. The instinct and primitive limbic emotion this woman made him feel was the Griffon, and that couldn't govern.

"I thought my dreams and nightmares were born of my imagination," Sylvia said quietly, still facing the window. "I studied archaeology in college, so the glyphs seemed a natural adaptation of that exposure." Sylvia turned, and Nathan leaned in when their eyes met and her voice became a whisper. "I don't know what I believe now."

Nathan took a shallow breath, trying to avoid the scent of her. The lost look in her eyes made him want to put an arm around her. Instead, he folded his arms. He needed to ask these questions directly. *If she is lying, she'll weave the web to trap herself.*

"Do you know of the lost relics of the Five Sectors?"

"No. I don't, but I can show you the relics in my book. I have a copy in my bag." Sylvia reached to the floor, the bandage on her hand falling. She had worked it loose playing with the hidden handle on the door. Sylvia sat back with a sigh, her head collapsing against the cushion of the seat. "I left my bag."

"Being banned in Earth Sector Three will not keep the book off the Rompnet," Nathan said. He glanced for a moment out the window, reminded by the landmarks as the driver made a left that they were almost to the UBN building. "Do you know where the Lost Cities are located?"

"No."

Nathan waited, but she offered nothing else. He remembered Rosalind didn't know he was coming with Sylvia. He hadn't lied to Sylvia — Rosalind did want to see her. She just didn't know it was going to be now. He tapped his ring. "Text Rosalind: Headed to security now. Meet us." The phone chirped when the message sent. "Text Stone: Sylvia's ring needs key coding capabilities."

A pleasant AI voice balked, "Error. No Stone in contacts."

Nathan huffed at the glitch. "Text Eli Stonebridge: Bring ring with key coding capabilities."

He felt Sylvia's eyes on him. Her focus made him conscious of his own body. He was sitting in profile to her, his thumb under his chin and his index finger over his lip.

"Does the ring microphone have to be that close to your mouth?" Sylvia asked, then braced herself against the door when they took a turn and stopped suddenly.

"No, just thinking," Nathan said, bracing his hand against the seat in front of him.

"Sorry, Dr. Renner, for the sudden stop," the chauffeur said, catching Nathan's eyes in the rearview mirror as he coasted forward to the barricade. "I wasn't expecting a roadblock here."

Nathan tilted his head when the chauffeur removed his hat and laid it on the passenger seat. *That's odd,* Nathan thought as the chauffeur looked away to roll the window down and speak with the guard approaching.

CHAPTER TWENTY-THREE

"I 'M SORRY," THE GUARD said after the chauffeur relayed their purpose and destination. "Dr. Renner and his guest will have to walk from here."

Sylvia, glad for the fresh air, engaged the handle to step out just before the chauffeur clicked the locks and pulled a handgun from the passenger seat. The pop of the gun didn't register with Sylvia till the guard collapsed against her half-opened door.

"Run," Nathan said, his large hand against the tinted glass as he shoved Sylvia and the door. The chauffeur turned and fired into the empty seat above Nathan's back. Sylvia scrambled to her feet, Nathan right behind her. The air whipped through them as they raced behind the car, headed for the cottage-style housing. Nathan took the lead.

"We're a block from the security building."

The gun fired again and they both ducked, but the ping of it made Sylvia suspect the driver had shot at the second guard still behind the blockade. Sylvia turned her head as she ran. The driver backed the car, turned rapidly enough to smoke the tires, then gunned it toward the main road of this block. She didn't know the area but assumed he was going to try to beat them to the security building so he could get another shot at... *Who? Me or Nathan?* "What's going on?" Sylvia gasped between breaths when Nathan pulled her between two cottages. "It was you and not Rosalind they were after at the race."

"I don't know, but the security building is the next building. I want to make sure Rosalind is there. The roadblock could mean it's been compromised, but more likely, Rosalind is ahead of whatever just tried to happen." Nathan had tapped one word by text and received an immediate response. He answered even as he pulled Sylvia to the back of the house. "And, after hearing about your book, I'm not so sure it isn't *you* they are trying to kill."

"I can run on my own," she said, jerking from his grip. "I don't need your input adding to my fear. It makes an orange ribbon of light flare near the silver tangle in the back of my mind."

Nathan flashed a look over his shoulder at her.

Sylvia stopped dead in her tracks at the ferocity of his eyes. She realized he no longer hid the glow of amber that flared in them when he looked at her, but it didn't manage to stop her mouth. "Listen, someone has tried to kill me twice today, and each time after being with you. Forgive me if I don't feel like following your every lead."

"I don't have time to convince you— What? Twice?" He continued interrupting his own words. "Tell me later," he said, grabbing her hand. "Let's go before someone tries again."

"Call Meki for me."

Nathan balked.

"If you want me to trust you, let Meki know where we're going."

"Fine. Here. Text him." He tapped the ring, pulled up the screen, and reached out his hand as he scanned the area. "I have limited military knowledge, but a few of the Earth Alliance Special Task soldiers shared some basics with me when I completed a military internship at their field hospital."

Sylvia reached for the ring and he grabbed her hand, half pulling, half lifting her around the back of the cottage. "Stop it, let go."

Nathan paused, but Sylvia didn't think it was due to her command. Rather, he seemed to crouch at a sound. "This is a gated community and all the roads are blocked. The chauffeur will have to ditch the car and come after us on foot."

Sylvia watched him breathe the air as if tasting it. The way he moved sometimes was so intense and primal. She closed her eyes against the thread of attraction. *No, absolutely not,* she thought, but her body was already ignoring her.

[23.1]

"Listen," Nathan said, his voice hard and his hand tight. He looked at her, then away, scanning the area again. "The relics in your book — at least the one I just saw — are real and have been missing for a long time. It's hard to believe you know nothing about them." Nathan noticed a sun-reflected glare from a rifle scope in the distance, and he felt his anger rising. *Whatever game you are playing, woman, is going to get us both killed.* Nathan intentionally relaxed his grip on her hand. He could forget his strength when he was angry. He didn't want to hurt her, but damn it, trying to protect her was going to steal his mind and replace it with a beast.

"I don't know about the relics!" Sylvia shouted, then followed with a whisper as if she remembered there was someone with a gun out there. "It's a coincidence. I'm sure pictures of them are on the Rompnet. I must have seen it in passing and pulled the image into my dreams." Sylvia twisted her hand in his and tugged the ring from his finger.

She was quick, and he growled a reprimand to keep her from running away. It was unnecessary as he watched her lean against the wall and slide the ring on to manage the screen. She typed what he presumed was Meki's number.

"At UBN security. Come get me!" Sylvia said as she typed.

The reflection on the rifle scope shifted. They hadn't been noticed yet. However, the fact that he could see it at this distance meant the Griffon genes near the DNA promoter code were unfolding. He had to be careful. The rest of his Griffon DNA was still buried for now, but he walked a fine line. He leaned his head back against the wall and closed his eyes. Talking would help — that was a human thing. "What did you mean when you said someone tried to kill you twice?"

Sylvia looked up from her text and held his gaze.

Nathan watched her face. She was experiencing the fading amber in his eyes. *It's just the light,* he thought, preparing the lie. But why lie? She was probably going to see the full-on Griffon before this day was done. He could sense it, like the beast itself rattled a cage he had held it in for too long.

"Your eyes are like the statue on the Orbiter," she said, her eyes never leaving his. "A large Griffon poised in a leap near the banister, its amber eyes cut with precision to catch the light."

Nathan noted her shudder before continuing.

"Those eyes were fixed on the fragile people who passed beneath it in the shadow of its broad wings and massive claws." Sylvia blinked once and darted past him toward the white brick and steel building.

Nathan dove after her, taking her to the ground, rolling with her even as the crack of a rifle rang in his ears and a bullet zinged above them. Nathan kept them rolling till they fell over the small embankment, then scrambled back up it on the far side, both moving fast toward a door on the abandoned side of the building. He punched the buzzer three times, whispering something between each one.

"Why did you do that?" Nathan pulled her against the wall behind him, and Sylvia tried to see his eyes again. The door buzzed, and Nathan jerked it open, pulled her inside, and collapsed.

The lock engaged, and Sylvia stumbled on top of him.

You smell like sunlight, and your heart is racing with the speed of fire catching wind. Sylvia hadn't spoken, but the words registered in his brain as if she had. She pressed her palm against his chest to get to her feet.

"What?" Nathan said, then froze, his body stunned when a jolt of energy cracked into his chest. His body jerked, and he heard his own moan. He shook his head. "What did you do?" He asked aloud. *And how did I hear your thoughts?*

Nathan considered the events and gritted his teeth at the possibility. *How can she speak along the Griffon network?* "Are you a Griffon?" Nathan managed to get the words out in a low growl. *Don't let it change you,* he thought, reaching to form the thought into human sound. The word *don't* came out like gravel crushed over large stone. Nathan sighed — the single word meant success. Words were human. He opened his eyes. *Human,* he thought. *Not this beast that paces closer than ever before.* He had heard her thoughts about him. Brief, but definitely there in the Griffon network where he could hear them.

"Sorry if I hurt you," Sylvia said. "I shouldn't use your chest like a wall."

"It's fine," he said, feeling sweat trickle at his back. He had been closer than he realized.

Sylvia seemed to sense something was off and tried to smile. "What could you possibly do as a doctor to get ripped muscles like what I felt beneath your shirt?" She seemed to recognize how her words sounded too late.

Nathan watched her blush despite the dark of the corridor.

"You could support two or three of me, I mean." Sylvia seemed to decide to stop trying to fix it and dusted her pants, then wiped her palms.

Nathan took in their surroundings, seeing them from her perspective. They were in a stone-walled corridor with a dirt floor that looked older than the newly renovated outside. Nathan pushed to a seated position against the wall and leaned his head back.

He looks exhausted, Sylvia thought.

"Please don't talk to me through the Griffon network. It pulls me to it."

"What?" Sylvia asked. *It's you,* Sylvia thought in a flash. *You're exhausting.* She touched the opposite wall, the heaviness returning to grip her chest.

Nathan braced his hands on the floor and gritted his teeth. "How do you not know you are spilling your thoughts into the Griffon network?"

"I'm...I'm not trying to do anything," she finally said, unable to say more. She squinted, and Nathan let her study him as he pushed up the wall, beginning to regain his human focus.

His ringphone pinged with a familiar sound.

"It's from Rosalind," Sylvia said and removed the ring from her finger. She reached to drop it in his outstretched hand as if both were mindful not to touch the other, but his right leg gave way, and he pressed his hands to the wall to stabilize.

"Tell her we're in, and I need a drink," Nathan said, nodding for her to take the ring back as he tried to stand on the leg again. He'd left his G125 syringes in the limo in his jacket.

Sylvia slid the large ring on her thumb. She read the text but noticed Nathan's struggle to balance. "Are you okay? What happened?"

Nathan looked at her and took a deep breath. Had she exchanged energy with him using an EvP network? Part of him didn't believe it was possible. No Sahaja of any species, much less a Rainbane Reborn Sahaja with all five networks, could make it to her age without being found by the Guardians or the Watchers. He'd originally thought it was just force that had pressed his chest, and that maybe she was a Griffon. Many Griffons tried to hide what they were out of fear, but that inevitably turned out bad. *You mean like now,* he thought. He watched her face to see any sign that she knew what it was she did. *God knows I'm not certain,* he admitted to himself. It seemed she could both push him toward the change and pull him back. Nathan ran his hand through his hair. *Don't lie to yourself,* he chastised. *No one ever comes back.*

"I'm fine," he said, managing to stand on his own, braced against the wall in the narrow hallway. "Let's move."

"You must feel some better. You're back to bossing me around." Sylvia smiled when she said it.

Nathan felt some of his tension ease. "Tell me what you know of the game, and I'll fill in the rest." *It's a safe place to start a discussion about Sahajas and the fact that you might be one,* Nathan thought.

"I had forgotten about the game," she said, her voice as dark as the hallway. "I just held on to the broken memories of childhood, I guess." She slowed her pace as if thinking. "You say the lost relics are real. Have any of them been found?"

Nathan dodged the question. "I scanned what I could find of your book on the Rompnet in the car, and...some of what you mention is here."

Sylvia stopped walking. "Like what?" she whispered.

Nathan stopped and turned. "The relic keys are still lost or hidden…" Closer to her than he realized, he took a step back. "But the Tokoleh Portal locks are here."

Sylvia stepped forward, shrinking the gap between them. "So, the Portals for the lost keys are here?"

"No, those Portals are on Earth," Nathan said, stepping back again. He had started to recover, but for some reason, his Griffon species surged to dominate and force the DNA change when she was close. If she was doing it on purpose, she was cruel. If she was a Rainbane Reborn Sahaja only now finding her strength to connect, heal, and destroy, and she didn't know it, then she was dangerous. Nathan ran his hand through his hair, the brown waves tangled with debris from the roll down the embankment. He leaned his shoulder against the stone wall and thought about the Tokoleh energy Portals in the energy-generator rooms. He had only seen one other page of her book on the Rompnet post, but it was enough to make him still uncertain about her motives.

[23.2]

Sylvia stared at Nathan as he leaned against the wall. His suit shirt fit perfectly across his chest, the cuff pulled snug to his forearm with his hand in his hair as he thought. She wondered how he had ever looked frail, but there had been a brief moment — pale and trembling, with a bead of sweat at his lip as if he fought a secret demon. The thought reminded her of her own demons, and she shuddered.

"Maybe Rosalind can explain," Nathan said, motioning for Sylvia to turn. "Roz, this is Sylvia."

Sylvia spun, taking in the gorgeous redhead with silky straight hair standing before her. She looked different from the day at the race. *Was her hair straight that day?* Sylvia tried to recall, then realized she was staring. She felt that connection with her again. *What is that?* she thought, tugging on the crimson haze in her mind. Her body felt as if it was just awakening, and she was feeling the world and everyone in it for the first time. Sylvia shuddered. *You felt that way in college before everything crumbled,* she thought, pushing away the memories of how literal that thought was to what had happened during her final year.

"Pleasure to meet you," Rosalind said.

Sylvia stuck out her hand.

Rosalind ignored it. "Please come with me. I came up to get you through security quicker, but it's busy. I don't have time to chat."

Okay, Sylvia thought, dropping her hand. *No time for manners.* Then she took in Rosalind's business-casual-meets-recon-soldier attire and remembered someone was trying to kill one or all of them.

Rosalind's microphone crackled on her Kevlar jacket. "Director Mathing, we have a fire in quadrant E."

"Well, it seems you are pretty busy," Sylvia said, wondering at the humor that laced her words. She never talked to people like that.

Surprisingly, Rosalind laughed before speaking into her lapel. "Lock down D and E, and check for electrical sources. Once clear, send maintenance to check it out. Send one of our guys with them. Use your protocol. Call me if—"

"I'm calling you."

Rosalind tapped the holographic blue haze around her ear, and a semicircle ring wrapped around her neck. The microphone went silent to Sylvia's ears, and she recalled Michael using that same blue ring when he took his secure calls on the Orbiter.

The blue ring disappeared, and Rosalind quickened her pace. "You two will have to come with me. I can't leave you here without transferring your custody to someone else, and I'm not going back to my office right now. Here, Nathan." Rosalind passed a syringe to Nathan.

Sylvia watched Nathan quickly slip it into his pocket. Rosalind had brought him his "drink"? Maybe, but she made no effort to hide what she had given. She apparently had no patience for hiding his struggle...or was it for something else?

Sylvia watched as Nathan squeezed the syringe now in his pocket. *Is that for me?* Sylvia thought as Nathan squeezed his pocket again and looked straight ahead. "I'm not a piece of evidence to be transferred and labeled," she said, determined she had gone far enough with these people. She should wait for Meki.

"Yes, you are," Rosalind said without hesitation or sympathy. "Nathan, make sure she keeps up."

[23.3]

Nathan nodded, thinking Rosalind had considered what he said and felt the risk of Sylvia was real. So, why did he feel so disconnected at the thought of not moving forward to discover more? His vision remained beast, though his thoughts were his own again. He used the eyeshine to enhance the limited light in this dark hallway. It had to come from pinhole light of compromised stone up ahead because it was meager. He gripped the syringe in his pocket at the reminder of the beast, but he didn't want to use it yet. *I want to be free of my cursed Griffon DNA, and Rosalind would give anything for her Intuit DNA to work,* Nathan thought, letting his mind wonder about how opposite they were while being so close. Rosalind knew every corridor in the building and was moving faster than them, especially now that Sylvia had slowed to a walk and started to turn around as he came up behind her.

He could see Sylvia's hands trace on the stone to his left as she tried to orient as they moved. Her fingers were long and delicate but had a strength he felt when she blasted that nervous energy into his chest. He couldn't figure her out. Nothing was consistent. He needed that neuro exam. Her synesthesia made him think she was an Intuit, but that blast of energy to his chest needed EvP direction, as the human network connection to the world was not that powerful. Further, he was certain her thoughts had touched his Griffon network, but she'd have to be a Griffon to do that. Nathan shook his head, trying to clear the haze. He would make sense of it when he regained focused thought. The neuro exam would help him clear coincidence from actual species skill. Then, he could determine if there was enough evidence to warrant an evaluation for Sahaja. *I haven't seen any specific species skill great enough to make me think Sahaja*, Nathan thought, not happy with what that meant. *She's an impostor, and her MRI abnormality is chemically induced.* Nathan felt his lips tighten with anger before almost laughing with his next thought. *Or she's...*

Nathan stopped dead in his tracks. *There is only one bloodline that could hold all five networks. Don't hope for that, Nathan. There are no more Rainbane Reborn descendants, not after the war.* Nathan increased his pace to narrow the distance between him and the impostor. Rosalind was counting on him to keep Sylvia cooperative till they could sort it out.

[23.4]

Sylvia could see the cold in the stone-like blue sheen across her mind. The warmth she had felt in her hand was gone, but her spine tingled. She must have pulled a muscle pushing up off Nathan after her fall. "Where are we going?" she asked. She sensed Rosalind didn't like her. The woman had probably noticed Sylvia's attraction to her boyfriend. Girlfriends had that sixth sense. Nathan had to be her boyfriend. They were too close not to be. She would keep her distance.

"What did you say?" Nathan asked, slowing.

"Where are we going?" she repeated, dropping her hand from the wall to walk faster now that he was striding beside her. She couldn't go back to the door. It probably had some security lock, and someone was outside shooting at them. Nathan appeared to see better than her in the darkness. He probably knew the corridor. She would trust him for now if he answered her questions.

"There is a fire in the Bunker energy-generator room," Nathan said.

"The Bunker! Oh no, you don't. I'm not going down there. This is down far enough for me. Bunkers are not safe — not at home, not here. I've read stories about them during the war," Sylvia said.

"Be careful what you believe," Rosalind's voice echoed back to them from ahead. "And speed up."

Sylvia didn't want them to hear the panic in her voice, but she had no intention of going into any area below the Earth. The tomb of her last archaeological dig almost killed her. "I can wait for you guys here. I've heard the stories of death in the war bunkers, and I'm already uncomfortable this far underground." Sylvia stopped moving. "I'll be..."

Nathan stopped and turned. His long stride had carried him well beyond her once she stopped. "It's not a bunker," Nathan said, moving back to her. "It's actually an energy-generator room on the Bunker level of the hotel."

So, it's still underground, Sylvia thought. She bit her lip. *You are being ridiculous. What happened in the tomb—*

"Rosalind can help if someone is after you. It's better to stay on her good side," Nathan said, interrupting her thoughts and standing by her side.

Sylvia thought his smile looked forced, but then he relaxed. This would be okay, she told herself, but the memory of what happened, the energy she had felt in that tomb, the Earth had felt alive in that dark place... *And intent on destroying me*, she thought with a grimace as Nathan spoke again.

"Several people want you dead. You don't want Rosalind pissed at you, too," Nathan said.

Sylvia would have thought it was an effort at friendliness if his smile hadn't disappeared when he actively started backing away. "What did I do now?" she said, frustration edging her voice.

Nathan paused as if considering. "I'm just pushing a thought to the Griffon network."

We will destroy each other — you with what you don't know, and me with what I can't control.

"Well, that's cryptic and scary. What is it you can't control?"

Nathan spun, leaving her in two strides. "You can hear thought communication tagged for the Griffon network. I need to do your neuro exam as soon as possible," he said from the dark distance between them. "But I'm going to need Rosalind."

"What?" Sylvia asked, staring at the darkness. "Sure," she mumbled into the resulting silence. She felt the isolation and separation so completely she braced her hand against the cold of the stone to stave off the pain of it.

CHAPTER TWENTY-FOUR

"SEVERAL PEOPLE WANT YOU dead..." The reality of Nathan's words gripped Sylvia's thoughts, and ribbons of orange and red raced from the tangle at the back of her mind. *The energy of fear and something else,* Sylvia thought. *The colors now seem to connect with emotions.* She let her eyes close as she listened to Nathan racing away into the darkness. His eyes held more amber. She had seen them flash just before he stiffened and began his retreat. They beckoned her now like a gem caught in a dark stone, and she stepped forward. She couldn't stay here; it felt too much like being trapped. "I can do this," she muttered. "It's not real." She reassured herself with that calming whisper with each step, bracing her hand against the cold stone to see the blue coolness of it in her mind. However, Meki's words — "It's only fiction if you don't believe" — haunted her memory and fanned the ribbon of color in her mind. It raged and flashed with every step in the darkened corridor that seemed to close in around her. *Like the tomb,* Sylvia thought, the memory flooding to her without restraint. She and her best friend had been trapped for hours. Sylvia felt the tears and pressed her back to the wall, wrapping her arms around her waist. Her best friend had died only two feet away, and Sylvia had been unable to reach her.

"I'm not going!" she shouted, and her words echoed on the stone. Sylvia stared into the darkness of the narrow hallway. "I don't believe any of this," she whispered, her arms squeezing tighter to her waist. "I don't believe a man was killed because of something I know." Sylvia sank to the floor, her back tracing every variance of the stone wall. "I don't believe someone is trying to kill me. I don't believe a world exists that gives real meaning to a book I wrote twenty-five light-years away." She pulled her knees to her chest, glad the darkness hid her tears. "I. Don't. Believe!" Her voice cracked with a brokenness she could no longer hold.

[24.1]

The halt of distant footsteps, the crackle of microphoned voices, and the staccato of Rosalind's robotic legs were background noise to the heavy breathing she now noticed in the ten feet between her and Nathan. She didn't realize he had returned.

"Nathan, take the G125 injection," Rosalind whispered, low and cautious, and Sylvia noted the amber glow of his eyes.

"Damn it, Nathan," Rosalind said, then halted at the sight of Sylvia crumpled on the opposite wall. "The fire is contained per the last report, but I still need to get to the energy-generator room. I don't have time for this." Rosalind looked at Nathan and then Sylvia.

Sylvia watched Rosalind move slowly toward her. "I should have thanked you for helping Nathan save my life," Rosalind said calmly.

"It's not necessary," Sylvia said, her chin propped on her knees and her arms wrapped around her legs, wishing she could breathe without her chest hurting. "Anyone would have done it. I just can't help you now. I'm worthless like this," she said, looking up in the dark. "Ask Nathan. There's something wrong with my brain. He has it on MRI. I didn't believe it, but now it's all I believe. There's something...really wrong with me. I feel like fire is spinning through my spine just sitting here. My head hurts so bad I can hardly bear to keep my eyes open even though it's dark, and things almost get brighter when I close them. Go do what you need to do. Meki is coming for me. We'll figure this out, and I'll meet Nathan at the clinic this evening."

"Why didn't you tell me this?" Rosalind said firmly, turning to Nathan.

Nathan nodded, but the gesture appeared to be an effort to clear his head. "I..."

Rosalind seemed to recognize his struggle to find words and let her question remain unanswered. "I've got to clear the energy-generator room and get the two of you back to my office where we can sort some things out." She knelt.

Sylvia closed her eyes, but when she closed them, she could see Rosalind more clearly, like seeing her through a plate of magnified glass with color. Sylvia wanted to explain that it had just started in little pieces, but it hurt her head to talk.

"Look at me," Rosalind said, her tone even but commanding. Her voice told Sylvia she couldn't afford to waste time.

Sylvia opened her eyes, not trying to hide the tears as they fell.

Rosalind nodded at the response. "You can believe it or not, but what you believe impacts your choices. Not only what choices you make, but what choices you have. Now, get off your ass and move. I don't care where. I don't have time to waste. You believe something, everyone does. If you don't want to know any more, then head back to the door. I'll let you out. Meki is probably waiting at the front of the building, and I have an EvP creating a shield of protection four feet around the building till they find the shooter. But, if you want to understand what you are, you will have to come with me."

Sylvia stood gently, using the wall for support. Her back still felt on fire, but it seemed to ease as she moved away from them, stepping back toward the door. Rosalind was right. Meki was probably waiting. She could go back to the hotel. He could help her sort things out. Sylvia twisted her necklace. All her life, she had despised being overlooked, stepped on without apology, her ideas dismissed without hearing. But now, under the steady gaze of Rosalind Mathing, all she wanted was to be invisible. Yet, the farther she moved toward the door, the more lost she felt.

Rosalind turned to Nathan. Sylvia realized his eyes didn't have that amber glow any longer, so they must have returned to their rich green color.

"Let her out," Rosalind said and didn't look back. Her steps increased till the pace of her robotic legs was a hum.

[24.2]

Rosalind's anger edged her forward. The ribbons of light from the tangle in her mind raged down her spine till they hit the dead structures that breached the connection of her Intuit networks. *She has a network connection that works,* Rosalind thought as she ran, and she was confident the woman had touched her mind with her Oscult at the race. *That can't be...* Rosalind's thoughts were interrupted by a buzz.

Stinger hovered as Rosalind approached. "Where's the pterodactyl and the dame?"

"You know he hates it when you call him that."

"Of course he does. That's why I do it."

"And dame? That's not very creative."

"Well, I need ample exposure to the woman to determine a properly annoying one. Till then, dame will do."

Rosalind nodded as if that made perfect sense. She continued her pace toward the energy-generator rooms. "Nathan will be with us soon. Sylvia's leaving."

[24.3]

Sylvia closed her eyes, listening to the sound of the robotic legs, but they had grown too distant now. *I want to know,* Sylvia thought, taking a tentative step back toward Nathan's quiet breathing and Rosalind's lost footfalls. *I decided I would keep going even when I was afraid,* she thought, even as the step back was small and insignificant. It was all she could manage. *I will do this.* Sylvia took another step and opened her eyes abruptly at the wave of nausea that came over her.

"Your girlfriend is bossy, too," she said, trying to abate the growing sense of fear and loss as Nathan moved closer and Rosalind moved farther away.

"She's not—" Nathan stopped. "We know our fields. I trust her calls here, and she trusts mine at the clinic. I hope I see you at the clinic this evening."

Sylvia watched him finger the syringe in his pocket as he moved past her to unlock the door with the keycard Rosalind had given him. He hadn't taken the injection yet, Sylvia guessed, and she wondered if the thought of her seeing him do so unsettled him.

She glanced down at the charm she twisted back and forth. *"Sometimes what you fear is the next step."* Her heart ached with the memory of the man who taught her the game. *The words of my father,* Sylvia thought with both longing and loss. *Why can't I remember?*

Nathan returned to where she stood when she did not follow. He reached for her elbow, then stopped.

Sylvia noticed his hesitancy and looked directly at him. "This thing that is wrong with me..." She hesitated. "It makes me dangerous to others, doesn't it?"

Nathan nodded but didn't speak.

Sylvia faced the dark stone corridor, her back to the door, and started down the hall. Her walk became a run, and the fire in her spine pushed her to follow the madness that moved ahead of her on mechanical, robotic legs, down a darkened hallway to what she feared the most.

Despite her steady swimming habit, Sylvia struggled to keep the pace Rosalind's robotic legs set. She pushed, and the three of them finally reached the energy-generator room.

Rosalind's retinal scan opened a vault door, and Sylvia coughed with the first rush of air. According to Rosalind's report to them as they ran, the fire was contained, but there was smoke inside the vault. It wasn't thick, but it took her by surprise as her shoes, thick with mud and debris, marked the concrete floor when she stepped inside.

[24.4]

"Stay put. This will take two minutes." Rosalind pushed aside the conflicting thoughts and emotions at Sylvia's return. Part of her was eager to know more. To her knowledge there had not been a Sahaja Intuit on the Galactic Core Station since she came here as UBN director. She closed her eyes at the remembered disappointment when the reality of the injury in her own network demonstrated the hopelessness of fully using the Intuit tangle in the back of her mind. She had been physically disabled since birth, but the hope of her Intuit network functioning once she had found it, followed by the disappointment of its dysfunction, had almost destroyed her. She had turned her focus toward her physical body and left the research of her network to lie in the dust with all the books she had accumulated with her work.

Can I help this woman? There was a pain in her chest at the thought.

Rosalind touched the screen on the inside wall, and a field of energy rose in place of the vault door behind her, Nathan, and Sylvia. She stepped forward out of earshot from the two of them before speaking to Stinger. "Something about that woman makes me uncomfortable."

"She's like you," Stinger said.

Rosalind didn't know if he was implying that she was jealous because Sylvia had a network like hers that worked and that made Rosalind uncomfortable, or if he was talking about her stubbornness. She had created the damn bug with an adaptive learning artificial intelligence program, so it had been her design for about a week before it had begun to be something altogether its own.

"Why are we here?" Stinger asked, landing on her shoulder to avoid the lull of the smoke on his insect programming. "The fire from quadrant E is out, and they have the accessory vent systems on reverse to remove the smoke."

"I need to check the area near the old tunnel entry, Stinger. It was open before the fire, which makes me suspicious. I want to take a better look." She made the turn to move down one of the nine-foot-high rows of electronics and generators that stood near the wall where the old tunnel entry was hidden. She glanced back toward Nathan and Sylvia. Sylvia was taking in the room and Nathan stood stiff. Rosalind's phone rang. "Make it quick, Michael," she said, frustrated.

"There are restrictions on access for the Dalen work permits. Houseman has Dranjo appealing it."

"Suri Dranjo?"

"Yeah, I know. The work permits are signed by Biagio, so Houseman said it would take her skill to get access."

Rosalind closed the call. "Stinger, I need you to get information on the Dalen now and get it to Michael. Houseman had to call in the Tokoleh's best attorney."

"I can't leave you with pterodactyl ready to transform at any minute."

"He's a Griffon, not a dinosaur, and he will not hurt me."

"Their bodies are Griffon, but their instincts are ancient. If he transforms, he will be feral and won't give two duck balls about you."

"Fine. Help me get the data on the Dalen at Piano Cave, and I'll take care of Nathan. I know what's going on."

[24.5]

I can do this, Sylvia thought to herself, taking in the surroundings. Her fears from previous underground experiences were dampened by the lack of visual cues that they were underground. *I still sense that energy I felt in the tomb.* Sylvia swallowed and focused on the modern things in the room to ease herself. *This is a generator room, not a tomb.* Her stomach growled, and she smiled at the connection to something normal. "Nathan, not to complain, but it has to be at least noon or later, and I'm hungry. There's a fire in here, and your girlfriend just locked us in."

"We are fine," Nathan said, carefully forming every word.

Sylvia nodded. He had said his mind still did not feel completely his own. On the way down here, he had tried to explain the line he walked with the Griffon that was a part of his DNA.

[24.6]

"Rosalind knows what she's doing, and despite her current disposition, she wants to help you." Nathan patted the syringe in his pocket and took a deep breath. He hadn't had to use it. He had kept his distance even as they talked, which helped. It took everything in him to overrule his original instincts. He wanted to hold her. His rationalization said he wanted to protect her. Griffons in their feral form were unique — as protective as a lion to his pride or lioness to her cub, yet as selfish and predatory as an eagle when ready to hunt.

"What is it like to be a Griffon?"

Sylvia's question pulled his eyes to hers. They were so blue in the unusual ambient light down here. "I'm human. I just have Griffon DNA in the network intertwined with the human spinal cord," he said, holding Sylvia's stare. The heat in that stare made his restraint falter. He pulled out the syringe. "If I transform, I will not remember my human form. You will not be safe." Griffons did not protect for the purpose of love, only the instinct of an animal protecting what it claimed as its own.

"Is the injection to prevent it?"

"Yes," Nathan said, placing the syringe back in his pocket. Rosalind had moved down an aisle of equipment. He was embarrassed Sylvia had seen his weakness. He wanted to change the focus. "The room is structurally a generator room," Nathan said. "There are five of them. This one they call the Bunker."

"It's dark and loud."

"That protects the energy Portal." Nathan pointed at the columns that touched the ceiling.

"They appear too beautiful to be down here," Sylvia said, moving ahead and to the left where she could see them fully.

Nathan wasn't sure what Rosalind was looking for behind the walls of tall equipment that spread out to the right from where they entered. He had stopped here, not wanting to go past the large fuse box panels on the left till his eyeshine had reduced. He knew the columns just behind them, with their iridescent rolling color shield blocking entry to the Portal section of the room, would be painful to his eyes in transition. Nathan heard Rosalind's voice. She had knelt at the far end of one of the aisles; he was familiar with the sound of her robotic leg movement. *She must have found what she was looking for,* Nathan thought, recognizing her quick commands to Stinger, though he couldn't quite make them out with his senses returning to human standards.

Nathan squinted but didn't see Sylvia. He suspected that she had moved to the other side of the fuse box panel so she could see the columns fully, and he had been grateful for the distance between them. However, his comfort at her distance was now uneasy. Surely, she wouldn't mess with the columns. The smoke hazed the space still, and Nathan scanned the room as he moved to go around the panel boxes. "Sylvia?" He followed the equipment's dark lines back toward the columns hazed in blue. His pulse increased as the scant light became increasingly useful to his human eyes. *Oh no...no,* Nathan thought when his eyes landed on Sylvia knelt by the base of a column. She was touching the glyphs at its base and paying no attention to the vibrant shifting color shield that splayed between the column and its twin. *This woman is going to get herself killed or trigger the opening of a network system we've not seen in years.* Nathan felt his fear for her tugging the beast forward again. He pulled the syringe from his pocket. He didn't think he could stop it again. "Get away from the columns," Nathan said, hoping she would just listen and not argue with him. His words were a rumble. The colors in the shield were shifting. He wanted to be firm, but the words came out harsher than he intended.

She's mine to protect. Nathan squeezed his eyes closed as if doing so, he could push back the force, pacing like a beast in the back of his mind. "I'm her doctor," Nathan said, but the words came out a whisper. "And her friend." He realized how real that felt, but these words weren't even a whisper as they slipped into the smoke haze like a prayer.

"Look," Sylvia said, not turning back to Nathan. "These markings are similar to the ones I saw in the Rendera temple." She shuddered and Nathan tried to recall what she had said about her fear of a temple, tomb, or something underground, but his mind couldn't focus.

"Why does this woman pull me so?" Nathan murmured through gritted teeth. He just wasn't strong enough. He removed the cap from the syringe, a sense of failure at needing another dose.

"What the hell?" Sylvia wiggled her fingertips. "Something just tugged at my hand."

Nathan dropped the syringe. Glyphs glowed deep violet at Sylvia's fingertips, causing her to finally look up at the sheen of color that flowed across to the other column. Panicked, Nathan lunged for her, yanking her away from the column as a hiss of sound vibrated and pulled the air around them. Nathan closed his eyes and turned away to avoid the flash of light that would burn his eyes with eyeshine. He held tight to Sylvia with one arm, reaching with the other for the low stone wall that marked the walk area where they had entered. The air popped in his ears, and Nathan felt the release of the vacuum's pull. It only reached three feet out from the columns, so they were safe now. "Could you just do what someone asks for once?" Nathan squeezed the stone wall with his right hand, mentally trying to force the amber to surrender to green again so he could open his eyes without the eyeshine. He still held Sylvia with his other hand. He could feel her shaking.

[24.7]

Sylvia trembled. Nathan's grip on her was loose now, but he gripped the stone wall like he could break it. *I'm underground,* Sylvia thought, both afraid and angry. She grabbed on to the anger. "No. I'm tired of doing what everyone asks." If she grabbed the fear, she would collapse. Her heart was racing. She knew she shouldn't have come. "I'm hungry. I've been attacked, shot at, pulled into a fire, and when I finally find something I connect with and understand, you drag me away."

"It's not a museum piece to be admired, and you obviously don't understand," Nathan said. He opened his eyes, and Sylvia saw almost complete amber before he forced them closed again. "Maybe if you remembered we were attacked, you would listen!"

"I do listen!" Sylvia snapped, shoving Nathan's arm, still in her personal space, though his hold was tenuous.

Nathan gripped the low stone wall with both hands, his back to her. "If you connect..." he started through gritted teeth.

"I didn't connect," Sylvia said, but her voice was low and distant as ribbons of color fluttered like northern lights near the silver tangle at the back of her mind. Nathan shuddered, and Sylvia wondered if it was rage or illness. He tremored like her neighbor back home who had diabetes. Regardless, she wanted to check the rest of the column, but what had happened? Had he stressed his body somehow trying to save her? She felt guilty, then remembered how rude he had been in the hotel. *He has medicine*, she thought. She saw him put the syringe from Rosalind in his pocket, and he said it would help. Her back was burning where he had jerked her up, but for a moment, she glanced to see if it was the fire behind her. There was nothing there. Fear sparked a memory of darkened Earth collapsing around her. A ribbon of orange-brown hazed through her mind, wrapping the tangle of silver in her mind till its light winked out like her lantern did years ago 150 feet into a tomb. Sylvia gasped.

"Your network is reopening," Nathan said. His head bowed as he braced with both hands on the cement slab that held a relief pattern Sylvia couldn't make out blocked by his body. "Touching the column to the Portal area opened your network, and your fear is pushing energy through your network," Nathan roared. "The scent of you is overwhelming, jasmine and rain like the forests of Griffern's Elysian." Nathan closed his eyes as if it required effort for him to find words.

Sylvia stepped back, her low heel catching on broken concrete. Nathan's shirt stretched taught against his back. "Jasmine and rain?" Sylvia asked, the melody in her voice unintentional, but she noticed his shoulders relax. Some.

Nathan took two deep breaths with his head tilted toward the haze of smoke still above them. "Elysian is a revered place on Griffern considered the truest replica of our original Griffon home." Nathan's head dropped to his chest as if words required too much effort. "It always smells of jasmine after the rain. You smell like home when you push that much energy through the network."

That sounds beautiful, Sylvia thought, and a hint of yellow flashed then disappeared in the now brown ribbon of her mind. It was faint. Maybe she could help. Sylvia reached to her necklace but stopped and forced her hands to her side. She stepped toward Nathan but halted when his head reared back, and he bellowed at the lofted ceiling.

"Go. Away!"

Nathan's head dropped again to his chest, and his hands squeezed the angled corners of the concrete slab. His voice whispered in a broken command, "Don't. Touch. Me."

Rosalind's voice echoed in the large room. "Nate?" The tinge of fear in Rosalind's voice escalated Sylvia to panic and Rosalind bolted from the aisle. She shoved Sylvia away.

"What's wrong with him?" Sylvia asked.

Rosalind worked Nathan's white-knuckled grip from the frame. "Sylvia, get to the door. Nate. Look at me."

"I'm not leaving him," Sylvia said.

"You're the problem. Go to the door."

"I didn't do anything. I want to help."

"You can't help, you're afraid."

"I'm not afraid."

[24.8]

Rosalind wheeled on her. "You are afraid. Afraid of failing those who depend on you, afraid you won't be smart enough, strong enough, brave enough to be what you need to be." Rosalind knew she was spouting her own fears, but she needed Sylvia to leave.

"How...how do you...know that?" Sylvia stammered, backing away, swatting at an insect that landed on the panel near the door. "I can't be buried again...below the Earth in a darkened tomb."

Rosalind could see the weight of her words in Sylvia's expression, but she couldn't worry about that. The woman was rambling. "You know something about you is different, but you're too afraid to find it. Face it."

Rosalind stood between her and Nathan, but she could still see the tremor shake his shoulders, and the syringe of medicine half slid under the fuse panels.

"The energy field at the door is down." Rosalind pointed. "Get out of here."

CHAPTER TWENTY-FIVE

T HE ELECTRONIC BLUE HAZE at the vault door was gone and Sylvia raced through to the corridor. The elevator wouldn't open, and she headed for the emergency stairs. *I've got to get away from here, get home.* Sylvia shoved the door, hitting it at a dead run. She almost fell into the stairwell.

She caught herself as the lock on the door popped in place behind her. She tried the door, but it wouldn't open. She noticed the retinal scanner to the right of the door when she finally paused to take a breath. *Exit only.* Sylvia leaned her head on her arm against the cinderblock wall. A man was dead, Nathan was fighting demons she seemed to make worse, and Kita wanted something from her she didn't have. She needed to get away, far away. *Where? The world is so different now. Not even home is the same. Earth Sectors? How did the Tokoleh even decide that? Just do a raffle for longitude and latitude lines?* Sylvia pulled her necklace, ready to break it free as she gripped the charm. She gritted her teeth, trying to release the anger. She would sort it all out. Then she could help. Sylvia closed her eyes, evaluating the tangle of silver wrapped with tendrils of color glowing at the back of her mind. What had she made happen at the columns? Why had it tugged at this network inside of her? *Rosalind is right. Leaving is the best way for me to help.*

Sylvia climbed two flights of stairs two at a time, struggling to breathe as her chest constricted with guilt. She tugged on the door at the next landing, but nothing. She fought back tears. She had been able to forget, almost. Pieces of memories flashed in her thoughts. She faltered as she turned and started the next flight of stairs, collapsing on the metal and concrete. *What am I running to?*

"Sylvia?" Rosalind's voice echoed in the stairwell.

Sylvia closed her eyes and felt calm resolution. She stood. Whatever she was, she didn't need any of Nathan's tests to tell her that she was a liability. Maybe her parents hadn't abandoned her. Sylvia doubled over at the pain in her chest. *Maybe my parents are dead.* A wave of nausea came with the next thought: *Because of me.* Her back burned, and it seemed determined to come through her chest. She gripped the banister, and blue-white light lanced down the metal rail like an electric current. Sylvia pulled away from the rail, staring at her hands. The burn in her back and the pain in her chest were gone, but her head pounded as she raced up the last flight of stairs. She was determined to get back to Meki and be on the next Orbiter home.

"Sylvia, Nathan is fine," Rosalind said. "Well, he's better than he was. I'm coming up by elevator to escort you back to my office. Wait for me in the lobby. You don't need a retinal scan to exit there."

Sylvia didn't answer. The door clicked with her effort, and she stepped through and paused in the hallway that led to an expansive curved gallery. Sunlight streamed in through the floor-to-ceiling glass on the right, where the corridor made a sweeping turn. She could hear voices but couldn't see past the turn. The hush of quiet, inquisitive interaction made her hesitate, and she tried to regain her composure. It was a front desk conversation at the entrance. She stopped briefly and feigned interest in one of the prints on the brick wall opposite the glass. She strained to listen but missed the conversation. She dropped her necklace, the charm a heavy stone when the glare from the light shifted to reveal a portrait of a woman, unfamiliar, wearing a similar charm at her neck. Sylvia turned away and covered her mouth. She blinked twice and realized she was staring at the inlay of brick on the floor, her hand still over her mouth. She started walking, keeping her eyes on the floor because the walls seemed to spin.

Sylvia raced down the corridor into the foyer and burst through the glass doors, breathing the windy, cool air deep into her lungs. She hadn't cried in years about the things lost to her, and now, every day here brought more evidence of lost things. "Crying doesn't help," she scolded. *Or maybe it does.* She sank to the ground, letting the tears fall.

Something wrapped her leg and she jumped. She crab-walked abruptly two feet before realizing it was a cat and now it sat staring at her. She relaxed and the cat moved toward her hand still braced on the ground. She scratched its ears and was grateful for company that required her to give no words of greeting.

"Can you come back inside?" Rosalind asked, surprising Sylvia with her presence but even more with the measure of concern in her voice. "My EvP-Intuit team still holds a shield four feet out from the building, but it's not safe this far out." Rosalind touched Sylvia's elbow, lifting her first and then the cat. She pulled them both back within the shield perimeter.

Sylvia looked up at the man standing near the roof's edge. His posture seemed casual, but she could see the strain in the lines of his face as he scowled at the disturbance. He relaxed at Rosalind's nod.

The cat reached a paw to her and Sylvia released an exhausted sigh.

"Of course the rescue cat everyone calls Scratch, who only likes three people on the whole Galactic Core Station, likes you," Rosalind said, placing the cat in her arms.

Sylvia smiled. The cat reminded her of the shelter at home and how much she missed the animals. "I promised myself a change, a determination to keep moving forward even when I'm afraid. I tried that — following you into the Bunker room — and things got worse."

"It is necessary to face your fears, and I commend you for pushing through your underground fears after your experience in the tombs of Turkey."

Sylvia's eyes widened. *How does she know about that?*

"I looked into your history after the race," Rosalind said as if reading her mind. "What you did not do well today was evaluate the safety of your environment for yourself and others. That means, yes, you put us and yourself at risk. For you, it may prove positive. an Nathan, I am still uncertain."

Sylvia blinked back the tears collecting in her lashes and steadied herself with a deep breath and the rubbing of Scratch's soft ears. "You certainly don't pull your punches," she said with a weak smile. "I appreciate your honesty."

"A mentor once told me leadership without honesty is a lack of courage."

Sylvia thought about that, letting Rosalind's words sit with her. "That means honesty with yourself as well," Sylvia added, to which Rosalind gave a thoughtful nod. "Who..." she started, prepared to ask about the portrait, then let the question trail off. Rosalind had challenged her to figure out this new environment; she would do that. Rosalind had been right to tell her to leave. "I need to go home. Is it possible for me to borrow resources from the archives and return them via Orbiter shipment?" The sun was high in the sky now, and its warmth beat down on them, though she thought she sensed a difference within the shield. *I'm beyond my knowledge of reality here.* Her thoughts reminded her of Rosalind's words. "You said what happened may be positive for me, but you were uncertain about Nathan. Why? And what does he mean when he says I smell like...home to him?"

[25.1]

Rosalind stepped forward, answering none of her questions. "You almost killed Nathan — well, almost triggered his Griffon transformation, which is as good as dead." *Does she really not understand what she is doing, or is she here for exactly that?* Rosalind shifted on her robotic legs, decision made. "The burning in your spine earlier was the energy racing in your network," she said, monitoring Sylvia's reaction. "It does that if you don't store it in the tangle or release it." *I'd show you, but my network...* Rosalind cut the thought off. "The column opened up your network, allowing you to release the energy into the electromagnetic field between the columns that protects the Portal side of the energy-generator room." Discussing the theory of a skill she so thoroughly knew but could not use brought more pain than she wanted to deal with right now. However, if the stolen relic key was in the hands of the Separatists, they would need a Sahaja Intuit who could help. And, if her research and gut instinct were right, Sylvia was more, but she needed to be sure. Her heart couldn't bear the loss if she discovered one more dead-end trail to the Rainbane Reborn. Not even Nathan knew the full truth of what she left buried in her work collecting dust in the Archive's basement. "Each network represents a species' DNA, which allows energy exchange between the species-specific network and the human network..." Rosalind paused. "Let me explain inside. I have some models in my office that will help you understand," she said, turning to head back into the building. "Bring Scratch. He must have run out from the front desk when you left."

Sylvia looked but didn't move. "Thank you, but I can't go back inside." Her words were a whisper but Rosalind heard them. She paused at the door and waited, though she could tell Sylvia was talking to Scratch rather than her by the smiles, pats, and rubs she gave the traitorous cat. It seemed nothing would be hers anymore with this woman around, and yet a part of her felt glad she was here.

"Since my decision to come here, two people have died," Sylvia said, adjusting when the cat turned its head back for her to scratch beneath his neck. "I did something terrible to Nathan without even trying. What if I killed my parents?" Scratch flipped completely to expose his belly for rubs.

Rosalind shifted at the door, uncomfortable with the vulnerability Sylvia was exposing when she thought Rosalind was too far away to hear. "You realize we call her Scratch because she has wounded more people with those claws than a Griffon in transition."

Sylvia looked up at her words as if only then remembering she had asked her to come inside. "I can't stay here." Sylvia rubbed her temple, then set Scratch down. "I need to go home, but I would like to borrow some resources and do what you recommended — figure a few things out about this new environment before plunging forward."

Rosalind unfolded her arms and lifted Scratch, who now circled at her feet, into one arm. "You can't help anyone there..." Rosalind stepped closer, touching her shoulder. "Yet."

"Help anyone?" Sylvia gave a hollow bark of laughter. "I'm going home to help myself. Going home to not hurt anyone else. I don't know what is real anymore. I'm remembering things that are painful, forgotten things tied to my imagination of places that appear to really exist."

Rosalind watched as Sylvia's face clouded. "What is it?"

"Nothing, just a pattern I recognize now. Something that occurs with any effort to recall my past."

"You've seen something that is here...before?" Rosalind stepped back, unsure if it was suspicion or curiosity she felt. "Come back inside and we can talk about it. It's not entirely safe for you out here. There are ways to take down the EvP shield."

"It's not safe for you guys if I'm in there. You said so yourself. Can I just use your ringphone and ask Meki to come get me?"

"He was already here. The front desk told me. He left to look for you back at the hotel."

Sylvia wrapped her arms around her middle, turned her back to Rosalind, and stared at the sky.

"Listen." Rosalind nudged Sylvia's shoulder gently to get her to turn. "I have the network model in my office, and Nathan needs to do his neuro exam. This will explain a lot for you, then you can decide what you want to do. Nathan has already admitted his responsibility in what happened today. Please don't think either of us lay today's events only on you. Let's just say that until now, I was uncertain of your motives, and there is definitely a chemistry between the two of you that seems to heighten things."

[25.2]

Sylvia blushed. *Rosalind knows I'm attracted to him,* Sylvia thought, realizing this might be worse than everything else. *And Nathan admitted his responsibility — what does that mean? Did he feel something similar?* Now Sylvia felt hot all over and was more embarrassed.

"Are you alright?" Rosalind asked. "He said you were hungry. He ordered lunch from the UBN cafeteria. I'll notify Meki. The front desk has a secure line."

Sylvia really was hungry, almost ravenous. She bit her lip.

"Don't feel guilty. The hunger is common after a connection."

"You know what's wrong with me?" Sylvia asked, both hopeful and afraid. *Do I really want to know?* Her hands trembled with the memory of the red-eyed vision warning about the cost for finding herself. *Will more people die?*

"I don't know," Rosalind answered thoughtfully. "an I have a photo, along with the other things I've mentioned, that may help us figure it out."

Sylvia nodded and headed toward the building. "Speaking of photos," she started, then twisted her hands together to keep from reaching for the charm at her neck that had slid beneath her blouse. *I have to know.* "Who is the woman in the portrait holding the charm necklace?"

Rosalind motioned for her to enter the elevator as she looked past her toward the hallway where the portrait hung. "We don't know who she is, but the charm she wears is thought to be the original one made when the relic keys were crafted at the Tower of Drumming centuries ago."

In the elevator, Sylvia braced herself in a corner. "Is it lost, too? The charm?"

"We don't know. There are so many replicas floating around, from cheap tourist recreations to handcrafted beauties, that it would be an exercise of true statistics just to calculate how long it would take to weed through the plethora of charms designed to replicate that one."

Sylvia rubbed her blouse where the charm lay underneath, unable to resist the calming habit even if she refused to pull the charm free. "You said it's common to be hungry after a connection. My 'connection'..." Sylvia made air quotes as she spoke the word. "Is that what hurt Nathan?"

Rosalind looked thoughtful before she spoke. "In a way. If what I'm thinking is correct, your Griffon network flared wide open and had enough pull to impact Nathan without you touching him," she said. "What are you remembering?"

Sylvia focused. *I have a Griffon network?* She stared at her muted reflection in the stainless steel wall behind Rosalind's head. "That game Nathan mentioned. I remember playing it as a child, with my father. Little things are coming back to me." Sylvia paused, now prepared for the familiar vision of red eyes that faded when she released her pull at memory.

She noted Rosalind's wide eyes. She figured her fear was palpable. Her last episode with the vision had left her exhausted and certain that she had almost drowned.

"Oh, you don't recall much of your childhood, and pieces of it are returning to you with this exposure?" Rosalind asked, shifting.

"Yes," Sylvia said with a smile that felt better than it looked when she saw it reflected back from the stainless steel wall. She looked down at the floor. "It was like he wanted me to remember the game forever...and be good at it, too." Sylvia paused. The words registered purpose in her mind, but with the familiar delay of forgotten things.

"Were you ever in cryo?"

"No," Sylvia said. "I didn't even know about cryo till coming here." *You didn't know about a lot of things before coming here.* "Maybe a better answer would be, I don't know. I don't recall being in cryo."

"Many families use the game to train their children when young, hoping to enhance any residue of their species. If identified, it can be properly trained. Showing you the game may help—" Rosalind stopped speaking when the doors opened, and two men stepped in.

"Rosalind."

Sylvia startled at Michael's voice. Despite their agreement to be friends after their one-night tryst, they hadn't spoken since she left the Orbiter.

He nodded at her, then turned to Rosalind. "Houseman's team investigated the lockout room, and there are...developments."

"Speak freely," Rosalind said. "I understand from Xenos that Sylvia was an effective part of the Orbiter C13 investigation."

Sylvia warmed at the words but hesitated at Rosalind's knowledge. She wanted to talk with Xenos and Kinley, but they were leaving Replica Earth. *Maybe there is a way to reach them if I get one of those ringphones.*

"Stewart was the UBN representative on the team," Michael said, waving toward the man with the shaved head. "I'll let him tell you."

"There was blood and tissue found, though the place had been cleaned. The team is running the DNA against the registered DNA for everyone on Orbiter C13."

"There hasn't been a match yet," Michael added.

"Have Houseman call me when the DNA runs are finished."

"Roger that," Michael said as the elevator pinged.

The two men exited, and Michael's gaze landed on Sylvia. Sylvia bit her lip, recalling Michael's words to her the one night they had spent together: *Women who look as soft and quiet as you draw me with their inner strength.*

"You're not invisible," Michael said as if knowing her mind was recalling his words. He held Sylvia's eyes before the door closed between them.

Rosalind gave an eye roll as if Michael said that to all the girls. Sylvia sensed that wasn't true, but regardless of Michael's words, she no longer felt invisible, even if she did feel alone.

Sylvia patted her face as they stepped from the elevator, realizing her cheeks were still wet. Crying didn't answer questions. She knew things, things that had helped her write a book that now had people killing each other and chasing her. She had to face the truth. A part of her was missing, and Rosalind and Nathan might help her find it. *But what if I hurt them in the process?* Sylvia let her eyes roam the hallway, taking in the features beyond the glass walls to her left. The room looked like a museum of books and artifacts that extended for miles. *Surely there are answers there,* Sylvia thought, but they continued to walk. "Why are you helping me?"

[25.3]

Rosalind slowed, letting Sylvia catch up. "The network, the part of you that is so dangerous, is also the missing piece for the Earth Alliance if you are Sahaja." She noticed Sylvia's unwavering gaze at the Archive room. "I can grant you limited access." Rosalind let her gaze rove over the stacks of books and artifacts as their pace synchronized. The room was even larger than it appeared, with an access room reaching down into caverns beneath the building, but Sylvia didn't need to know about those. The Archive was her baby. Rosalind had spent years endeavoring to restore her own network, and much of what she had learned she stored down there with the rarest of resources. *Maybe by teaching Sylvia, I will find something I have overlooked*. The thought helped Rosalind suppress the weight of another responsibility. "The relic keys you illustrated in your book — did you draw them?"

Sylvia twisted the chain at her neck but dropped it before Rosalind could focus on it. "I drew the originals from my imagination and dreams but had an artist illustrate them for the book." Sylvia chewed her lip. "They are real, aren't they?"

"The relic keys are real and fit the locks of the TEA Portals on Earth. Their counterpart on this side are called Kukshi Portals."

"TEA?"

"Tokoleh-Earth Alliance Portals..." Rosalind said, pursing her lips. "The TEA Portals Earthside and the Kukshi Portals here, though twenty-five light-years away from each other, are a single door through the Simultaneity. The keys only fit Earthside and have been lost for many years." She slowed her pace to extend Nathan's recovery time before they arrived. He was a good man, and the beast in him would be an avid protector of Sylvia if he transformed under her network, but he would be lost to a primal beast that knew only instinct. More problematic was the connection he seemed to have for her in his human form. Perhaps Nathan had been right. Was it possible this woman was trying to push Nathan into the change? Intuits were excellent manipulators if they wanted to be. *But she is more than a species Intuit. You know it despite your questions.*

[25.4]

Sylvia tried to walk with a confidence she didn't feel. Her stomach growled, and she clenched her arms around her waist. She needed Rosalind and Nathan's help. Her written world was shifting from fiction to reality as painfully as the ribbons of color in her mind seemed to untangle memories of her past. The opaque doors before them opened with a swipe of Rosalind's ring. "Your office is inside this huge library?" Sylvia asked, unable to contain her pleasure at the prospect of being in a world of books again. A memory of sneaking peanut butter crackers and water in her purse at the local library so she could spend the day made her stomach growl again. She paused, noting there was no vision with this memory. *So, the vision is only linked with my early memories?*

Rosalind nodded in answer to her question as they stepped through the doors into an anteroom. "This entrance gives me control of who comes and goes to my low-tech office on the other side."

"Is it the only entrance?"

Rosalind stiffened, then seemed to relent. "If I want you to trust me, I have to show some trust in you. This office allows me the luxury of working alone with antiquated systems that can run under the radar even while I cross-work with the high-tech security systems everyone associates with me."

Sylvia's sense of connection disappeared as they stepped through the doors into a small space with trash bins and shelves of folded paper suits and masks. Through a second set of clear glass doors, a clean room bustled with a handful of workers.

"Put this on." Rosalind handed Sylvia a paper suit, sliding one on herself.

Sylvia toyed with the white hood. "Your office is a clean room?" she asked, almost putting her foot into the wrong leg.

"No, my office is on the other side, inside the archives."

"Ohhh," Sylvia said, her happiness at the thought shifting to awe. *Archives! This is where I need to be. I could stay here for a week,* she thought.

They moved through the aisle that separated two sides of the clean room. People in the white paper suits seemed to blend into the white walls. Their faces were masked, with only their eyes visible as they hovered over stainless steel tables working with technology, lasers, and a few pieces of equipment Sylvia didn't recognize, but the colors from one of them danced on a back wall. And, at a glance, she would have sworn water hovered in the air as if suspended in the corner to the right. *Probably a hologram image*, she thought as they moved out of the clean room into an exit chamber and discarded their paper suits. Sylvia stepped through to a breathtaking library. "Archive," she whispered, correcting herself. The room expanded beyond what she could see, making the Vatican Archives and Library of Congress look like children's libraries. Those libraries were two of only a handful restored after the Earth War of 2050.

"This way," Rosalind said, never pausing as she turned right and headed toward a door.

Sylvia followed, her breathing deep and relaxed at the smell of old books despite the tinge of processed air she sensed being circulated to protect the vast history that lay out before them. Rosalind had offered no further explanation for the clean room or the archives as they walked toward the office door. Sylvia decided just to take it all in for now. It at least helped her forget how hungry she was. Well, almost.

"The door is heavy," Rosalind said.

"Umph," Sylvia grunted, turning at Rosalind's words and getting her hands up quickly enough to catch the heavy wooden door closing toward her.

If the Archive was tastefully aged, Rosalind's office was just old. It looked more like a scene from a police precinct of the 1970s films they watched in college than the technologically advanced society surrounding them here twenty-five light-years from home.

"Ahhhhhh, pizza. Just what the doctor ordered," Rosalind said, grabbing a slice and folding it as she moved to her desk.

[25.5]

"Schedule Jezel for another treatment tomorrow and..." Nathan turned, realizing the women were within earshot of his phone conversation. He winced. Nathan was careful about patient confidentiality, especially regarding his work with Immortals. He had hoped to get this call done before they arrived, but his earlier call to Jenny had tied him up about the blood samples on the Griffon in the lab. *Glad they didn't walk in on that conversation.* He looked Sylvia's way. "I can notify Ms. Debair of the schedule change."

[25.6]

"This is nice," Sylvia said, taking in the office and letting her mind wander to the challenge Jezel and Tessa had given her to translate the page in her own book in exchange for information. Now, she was here at the archives. Sylvia smiled. She was finally putting a few things together. The small accomplishment felt dim now against the onslaught of failure the day had brought, but she was here now. She glanced over her shoulder through the glass wall beside the wooden door. The combination of technology storage and antiques that created the view beyond this office told her there was more in that library than a thousand miles of shelving could hold.

"Don't get too comfortable," Nathan said.

Sylvia turned at his voice. Nathan leaned against an old wooden desk with a landline phone she had only seen in recordings of prewar TV shows and old movies.

"You can't stay." Nathan continued, nodding toward the food. "But please eat. Your network is still humming."

Sylvia glared at him.

"The hum in your network is energy hunger and creates a vibration that is different from what I felt when your network was wide open pulling on me. It's unsafe for us to be too close together until we sort some of this out." He blinked, holding his eyes closed for a moment, and Sylvia considered that had probably been hard for him to admit. He opened his eyes and glanced down at the phone on the desk. "It's actually the original phone from the cop scene in the movie *Terminator*. Rosalind's office down here is more broke than Baroque. Her predisposition for collecting beautiful is evident in the Archive." Nathan pointed at the glass wall, and Sylvia glanced again over her shoulder.

Nathan pushed off the desk and walked toward Sylvia.

[25.7]

Rosalind watched Nathan, wanting to let her mind relax for just a moment, but she was afraid — and not just for Nathan. She could sense the struggle in him. He would do his best to be the doctor she needed, even if it pushed his risk. This day — rather, these last few days — had pushed her as well. Her recent stay in the hospital was a vivid reminder of her vulnerability, and she was not surprised her mind treacherously returned to her childhood.

"This is her fifth surgery, Dr. Pelrose, and she is not yet even seven years old." The woman's broken words were a whisper to her ears as she lay recovering from anesthesia. She hadn't opened her eyes, though she had been awake long enough to overhear her mother's discussion with the doctor.

"It will require two more surgeries, and she still may never walk."

Rosalind shook her head as a familiar buzz pulled her from the memory but not quite back to the focus in her office. She could remember the shadow of her mother near her bed after the doctor left. She had watched her through the smallest slits in her closed eyes. Her mother rubbed the casts that wrapped her twisted legs. She couldn't feel the touch, but the movement of the shadow was familiar. She squeezed her eyes tight and relished the wetness of the tear that rolled past her temple before it dropped to the sheet. At least she could feel her tears. How strange that she could remember thinking that. Her mother had been so strong, always fighting for her and her brother to have every opportunity possible to succeed despite the poverty of a single mother in the Fifth Sector.

Rosalind tore her thoughts from the past when Stinger landed on her robotic legs as she sat in her office chair. Nathan and Sylvia stood in a discussion at the glass facing the Archive. Rosalind ignored Stinger when he displayed a hologram screen above him, hidden by the desk. The sight of him reminded her how the past had become the future. A surgeon brought into her care because of his medical technology had married their mother, and she, as a child, began designing robotics with him, creating more significant projects, including the legs she now wore. *I literally ran with it,* Rosalind thought, flipping the latch at her thigh and noticing Stinger's hologram message· "Not work permits. The Dalen are in desensitization chambers." Rosalind's eyes widened. *I've got to move on this.*

"I can tell from here it's a Rendera temple piece by the glyphs," Sylvia said.

Rosalind moved to stand behind the two, staring past the glass. "It seems your competence in earth archaeology is significant," she said.

[25.8]

Sylvia blushed at the compliment. "Thank you. Too bad I can't remember the history that matters the most to save it."

"You will," Rosalind said with confidence, then turned to Nathan. "I have some information on the work permit issue, and I need to check on it. I recommend you do your exam before I leave."

Sylvia wasn't sure how long Nathan and Rosalind had been together, and she was having difficulty not being jealous of the woman's sway over him. She tightened her arms at her side to keep from bumping Nathan as she turned. She still wasn't sure what it was, but she could sense him. It was like he was touching her core with heat.

"Grab some pizza and come over here." Rosalind pointed at one of the seats before her desk as she moved back to stand behind it, pulling a rectangular box from her drawer.

"Those look like blueprints," Sylvia said, watching Rosalind set the box down and flip the latch to open it. Sylvia stepped toward the pizza at a small table near the wall. She watched Rosalind place a photograph from the box on top of the blueprint. Sylvia bumped the cardboard pizza box that hung partially off the table, and Nathan turned from where he stood now next to the desk. Sylvia flushed and looked down at the pizza. Her back was on fire again. *Rosalind said the heat in my spine is the energy in my system, but what do I do with it?* Sylvia glanced again and noted Nathan removing items from a leather satchel. She watched his shirt tighten across his solid chest when he lifted it back to the floor. The heat lanced along her spine.

"What are you doing?" Nathan said in a forced whisper, pushing his hands into his pockets. "You're moving energy in the network again."

"I'm not trying to," Sylvia said, chasing the ribbon of yellow racing around her mind.

"She's pushing every button," Nathan said through gritted teeth, then pointed at the photo. "That should wait till I've tested her. She could be using us." Nathan relaxed his jaw, then continued. "She has to feel what she is doing. It is too strong for her not to." Nathan leaned in toward Rosalind, his hands bracing the desk. He lowered his voice and his head, but Sylvia could still hear him. "She knows what she does to me."

Nathan's words made Sylvia shiver, and the ribbon of yellow raced like heat along her spine.

She watched as Nathan raised his head and met Rosalind's eyes. "She is either careless or criminal."

Rosalind looked Nathan in the eye and then touched his hand as if she could give him peace. With her other hand, she dumped out several small metal pieces from the box and splayed the box open, its back exposed as a gameboard. "Set this up over there," Rosalind said, pointing at a table beside the chair positioned behind Nathan. Rosalind waved her hand from Sylvia to the gameboard. "The game of light and shadow. Sahaja's Risk," Rosalind said, her voice soothing.

Nathan stood straight and stepped back as if ensuring each piece was perfectly placed.

Rosalind's words pulled Sylvia from watching him.

"This is what I wanted to show you," Rosalind said, motioning for Sylvia to come to the desk while Nathan bent to adjust a piece on the board. The movement brought her closer to Nathan, but she could no longer see him.

Sylvia sensed rather than saw Nathan finish and take one of the chairs behind her. The tingle in her spine made her turn.

His eyes were fixed on the tools for the neuro exam he had laid out. "My emotions can't be trusted. Your exam will have to wait." He crossed his legs, propped his elbows on the chair's arms, and pressed his fist into his open palm, leaning his chin against them. Sylvia could see the sheer will in his face. "Let Rosalind explain the academics of what *might* be going on with you."

Sylvia wanted to reach out to him. She sensed the ribbon of yellow-like energy that tried to touch him. He was disappointed in himself, and it was her fault. *Not my fault*, she corrected with a thought. *This evolving connection with my world is exhausting*. She turned to Rosalind, who opened her hand, exposing a metal game piece. She tossed it to Nathan. The marbled abdomen of the miniature piece flashed familiar in her mind just before sticky, bloody hands pushed her and her memories below the water, and Sylvia struggled against the vision that trapped her every time she reached for this place in her mind.

CHAPTER TWENTY-SIX

MEKI DUCKED INTO THE energy-generator room from the hotel side, shoving the Dalen ahead of him. The fact that Faraday had found a Dalenborn Intuit hadn't surprised Meki. After all, his own father had been Dalenborn, not that he had let that secret out. Great effort and expense suppressed that information. His mother had been Immortal, and that was the bloodline he claimed, rather than the EvP line of his father.

"Move faster, Dalen," Meki said, giving the man a directional push. *I fought to keep free men from the captivity of the Dalen.* His work destroying a smuggling ring that trafficked free EvPs into the Dalen was what had brought him to Biagio's attention. It's why he spoke out about the difference between Dalenborn, Recruits, and Captives. He had experienced the pain of stolen freedom; that was slavery. He had no tolerance for the ones who ended up on the hazard crews running death-wish missions just to get the next hit of whatever ruled their minds. That's where this one came from. "You have an opportunity at redemption," he said as the man staggered forward ahead of him. His body still bore the bruises, cuts, and severe injuries from his last mission with the hazard crews. Faraday had been vague about that mission, and Meki didn't care. His preliminary test demonstrated a capable Intuit.

"Stop!" he said when the man continued to walk past the stone carved with the glyphs indicating the stone of capacitance. *The man can't recall his own name,* Meki thought, remembering the nondescript history he had been given about the man. "Your Intuit ability kept you alive," Meki said, again regarding the man's injuries. Whatever he had been through would have killed someone with less ability. Meki turned the man and lifted his chin, wanting to see the eyes again.

The man was taller than him by a head, but with his head bowed, his eyes were hidden. The eyes remained glassy and distant.

"What we are doing today is a first step to setting all humanity free. That will be amazing," Meki said.

"I am..." the man said, his eyes focusing for a moment of lucidity, then returning to a lost place.

Meki paused. "You're what? Amazing?" He gestured for the man to move to the stone. He had already been given instructions of what he was to do.

"No," the man said, then touched the capacitance stone. "I am free."

"Give me the picture you took from Sylvia's room before you align with the capacitor," Meki said, ignoring his words. He wouldn't argue with the man. He agreed Dalenborn were free, but he spoke of freedom of all humanity from the decision-making they were not built for, decision-making that should be left to Immortals. For a moment, Meki considered the possibility that the man meant he was a free man who did not choose to be Dalen. "Recruits are free men who choose to be Dalen. Captives are, well, just that — captive. Are you one of these?" Meki asked, feeling angry if Faraday had lied.

The man didn't respond.

"Are you a Recruit or Captive?" Meki asked, holding his frustration in check. Faraday knew his stance.

"I didn't choose this," the man said.

Meki's lips drew into a hard line. *Faraday lied. Now I'm stuck using a Recruit or Captive.* he thought, recalling the coffin-sized spaces in Piano Cave filled with liquid as Dalen clawed at their walls. It was not the best use of desensitization chambers.

"We will discuss your status when we are done here. For now, you work for me." Meki checked that the photo was the one Sylvia had shown him. The thought tempered his hostility. "You're certain she didn't see you?"

The Dalen nodded and pressed both hands against the stone.

Meki noted the stone. It was situated opposite the Portal and between the columns on the left and right side to the UBN and hotel, respectively. He could see all four columns from the capacitance stone in the V point of the room. He had left the shield down on the hotel entrance side in case the Intuit was too fatigued to take it down again when they left.

"Speak," Meki said when he noted the Dalen had only nodded to confirm he had not been seen by Sylvia.

"She didn't see me," the Dalen replied in monotone.

"Dalenborn are the best of humanity. Unlike Recruits or Captives, they know their place and value it." Meki prided himself on granting speech to his tools; to mute them by removing their tongues, as some did with their Dalen, showed a lack of control over their tools. The moment of command was like the hammer's thump of power as the nail drove its claim into submitting wood — one must hear the compliance to truly appreciate it. It was best to have a free, obedient tool. "If you are not Dalenborn, I will release you once the job is complete."

Meki noted the man's eyes widen and felt the anger in him double. Faraday would pay for what Meki was now forced to do. "Very well, take your place on the capacitor. I need your best effort. Diverting the flow of energy from the Portal will shut the sector Umbilical down. You must keep energy level readings steady at the capacitor, or the UBN will know we are here, and you will die."

The Dalen's now bare feet found purchase on the relief pattern as he climbed.

[26.1]

My name is...my name is... The framing on the stone and two hieroglyph features seated at each end of a rectangular box meant something to him, but he had forgotten and didn't care. *Cajal is safe. The* random thought made him pause, and memories began to flood through cracks in his mind. *My brother. My name is Wesley.* He closed his eyes as a tear rolled down his cheek. *I remember. He will live free, be educated in the best school, and with financial resources.* Part of him had secretly known it would cost his life to see that happen. Being away from the torture of the caves had allowed recovery of enough pieces of himself to know part of him was broken, and he wouldn't survive this last project. He was grateful for the respite to allow a few clear thoughts into his mind. *The paperwork...at the school. Yes, resources in place for Cajal.* "I am free," he said aloud as he lay back to take his position on the capacitance stone. Wesley let his head rest against the hard stone, and locks wrapped his limbs.

[26.2]

The man is insane, Meki thought at the Dalen's whispered words. He checked the camera security system — the self-propagating holographic webbing held its place over the camera. He tried to focus, but the man's words worried him. He would get more details from him when this was over. Free men could be killed but not enslaved. If he was telling the truth, Meki would see him free, and Faraday would pay with his life. Meki felt better, and he refocused on the camera. The holographic webbing would last a day. He smiled, wondering who was watching his artificial feed on the other end. He checked the time: 1:10 p.m. They could start. The UBN standard report went in on the hour for each

Umbilical. Meki tucked the photo away. The man's skill as a thief had come in handy. The photograph could be useful or dangerous. Meki had no intention of leaving the direction of that to someone else.

[26.3]

Sylvia jumped in the chair when the phone rang in Rosalind's office, almost dropping the photo Rosalind had given her. She pulled her free hand away from her chest. She had not expected the landline phone to actually work. Minutes ago, she had slumped into a chair adjacent to Nathan, touching the photo. Sylvia had barely contained her reaction. Rosalind seemed content to mark the blueprints on her desk as she scrolled through video screen from security cameras while Sylvia viewed the photo and Nathan repacked his bag.

"Yeah, Harry," Rosalind said, pinching the phone between her ear and shoulder as she continued tracing something on the blueprint with her finger.

"I know you can see the hourly reports as good as us," Harry said loud enough for Sylvia to hear, "but the Bunker's energy-generator room, although steady, still shows lower pressure and energy leak."

"Thanks, Harry. Check it every half hour instead of hourly until I return to the office."

Rosalind hung up the phone, and Sylvia sensed her eyes on her as she traced the photo with a trembling finger.

[26.4]

Rosalind found it hard to divert her attention along multiple paths. She liked focus, but it was a luxury she couldn't afford with the energy-generator room problems, Earth Week security pressing, a possible Sahaja Intuit — or worse, Rainbane Reborn descendant with no training, Nathan on the brink of transition, and... She glanced away from Sylvia to the video of the old camera system, a possible security breach. No one but her knew the old camera system was still in use. *A potential breach through the old tunnels,* Rosalind thought, taking a deep breath and reaching to rewind the video. It was just a shadow, but... "One thing at a time," she said, speaking to herself before turning to Sylvia. "I thought it might jog your memory. The house is considered an important landmark for several reasons."

"I've seen this before," Sylvia said, hesitation in her voice.

Rosalind slowly sat back in her chair as Stinger buzzed near her ear and landed on her shoulder. "You recognize the house?" she asked, tapping her finger twice on the desk, a signal for Stinger to record the conversation.

Sylvia wiped her free hand on her pants and seemed to watch Rosalind's face before dropping her head back to the photo. "No."

"What?" Rosalind said, frustrated by the woman's vacillations. Her peripheral vision caught another shadow in the running video to her right. She hit pause. "Wait," she said just as Sylvia opened her mouth to speak. *One thing at a time,* she thought to herself again. "I want you to have my full attention when you explain," she told Sylvia. *Yes, she'd seen it before, but no, she didn't recognize the house. The woman is exhausting.* She dropped the corner of the blueprint she was tracking as she watched the video feed on a monitor mounted on the bookshelf. *I need to get this security camera review done and restore the main screen cameras. If someone is moving through the tunnel passages, I need to review the new and the old systems together.* At present, she had to shut one down to see the other. A few simple lines of written code would run them together with time stamps. "Let Nathan explain about your MRI while I review this security video." *And rewrite a program to get both systems running simultaneously.* Rosalind sighed. It required time she didn't have. "Then we can talk about the photo," she said, looking at Sylvia before turning her back to her and Nathan to pick a few dead leaves from a plant under the sunlight. Stinger followed her cue as Nathan and Sylvia's voices rose in hesitant conversation.

Stinger landed on a healthy leaf. He found the memory in his AI circuit that allowed him to connect with Rosalind's Oscult and spoke into the anteroom of her mind. "I think her uncertainty is catching. You can't make up your mind! Record a conversation. No, wait, we're not having it now. Sheesh."

Rosalind ignored him but sighed lightly at the use of her Intuit Oscult, one of the small pieces of her Intuit network that functioned. She had shared the memory of her building Stinger with him once his design was complete. The memory allowed their connection in the anteroom of her mind. "Get your information about the Dalen desensitization chambers to Houseman, then go back to the EG room from this morning and see if we overlooked anything in the commotion."

"Sure, send the only sane creature away when things start getting curious." Stinger huffed but lifted into the air and out the vent near the ceiling.

She had been right to show Sylvia the photo, but now she didn't know if she wanted to know the woman's connection to it. The photo held her dream of answers. If they belonged to this woman who could not remember, then her search was a dead end again. She turned back to the security feed.

[26.5]

Sylvia tried to shift her chair as Nathan pointed at the hologram screen. She grunted, but the oversized chair didn't budge, so she leaned to see the holographic screen Nathan had opened on his ringphone with her MRI.

Nathan slid his chair over with ease and enlarged the holographic screen.

Sylvia stared for a moment at her brain and spine on the multiple MRI pictures Nathan had clustered together. "These are the places my doctor back home pointed out."

Nathan cleared his throat when Sylvia turned her eyes to him. "Um...the MRI shows a few places that could be read as demyelination—"

Crash! Rosalind's chair tipped over when she stood quickly. Sylvia jumped at the noise. Rosalind didn't bother to lift the chair but grabbed the old security camera video she had stacked on the shelf. She was thumbing through the old VHS tapes, mumbling dates and times.

"I can't believe it," Rosalind said, selecting two tapes and returning the others to the shelf to look like memorabilia.

"What is it?" Nathan asked.

"Nothing yet," Rosalind said, setting her chair upright as she hit replay on the VCR.

"Like I was saying," Nathan said, pointing to an area on the MRI. "These areas are sometimes read as demyelination, but in a Sahaja Intuit, it can be an indication of original Intuit mutation under strain, IMUS. It's not exactly correct terminology, but it's what we call it."

"How do you know if it is demyelination or IMUS?"

Nathan seemed to relax as the conversation turned toward medicine and science. "Demyelination is permanent damage to the sheath around the nervous system in humans. IMUS is uncontrolled/unbalanced use of the species-specific network and can heal if not severe. I often do the neuro testing at thirty-minute intervals, looking for improvement to help me discern who may benefit from the scan testing. It is an expensive scan and can't be done just for people's PR stunts."

"PR stunts?" Sylvia asked. "People do that?"

"Yes, among the people who are aware of the Tokoleh and the status of Replica Earth, having a species scan here, even if it is negative, comes with a prestige of influence that doesn't make sense but happens. Each species has a single network that wraps around the human spinal structure. Each network has a spectrum of color that the scan can pick up to identify the species. Often, the ribbons of the network are thin, which makes them appear as demyelination against the human spinal structure when actually they are ribbons of residual species network, which can be developed if identified. However, recently, we've seen the demyelination mimicked by chemical manipulation, which is exposed with the species scan."

"So, people use medicine to try and create a positive MRI test result that will give them the prestige of coming here for species testing?"

Nathan shrugged, and his shoulders sagged. "It's happened. There are those who really don't know, which is why there is a push for legislation in the Scholar's Council this year to reveal the Tokoleh fully to Earth. The more people know, the sooner children can learn their skills with simple things like this game." Nathan lifted a miniature piece from the board to his left. The figure held iridescent colors in lines of color that formed between its hands. "Instead of expensive tests when they are adults..." Nathan paused as if rethinking his words. "...and less capable of learning control."

In that moment, Sylvia could see the weight of these decisions on him, trying to determine who needed help, who was playing the system, and who could be at risk for a major human illness, only to see many of them be too damaged by years of imbalance and poor control. She didn't need a doctor to explain the scarring process when things were repeatedly injured and tried to heal. She reached to touch his arm but paused. She was one of those adults unable to understand and control the network awakening in her.

She knew then the truth was in her memories. There were answers in her book if she could discover the clues she had used to hide them from even herself to avoid the pain of battling the Guardian of her mind. Sylvia twisted away from Nathan and let the weight of the personal discovery sit inside her. She took a deep breath, allowing the wetness behind her closed eyes to exist. She watched the ribbons of color dance around the tangle with another deep breath. When she focused, she could see five colors distinctly, as if all the chaos of colors had coalesced to give her structure: red, blue, green, yellow, and orange, each pulsing with energy before braiding around one another as they danced like a glow around her spine before racing back to the tangle at her mind. She reached out with her eyes closed and took the game piece from Nathan's hand. She watched in her mind as the line of colors held by the game piece arced as if she bent the very light they represented.

"I have all five networks," Sylvia said, opening her eyes and seeing Nathan focused on her and Rosalind focused on the game piece in her hand, whose arms now held the iridescent colors in a stunning arch, her hands now supporting the light rather than pressing the lines of light together in a straight line the way they had appeared originally.

"We thought you might," Rosalind said. "Who taught you how to do that?" she asked as if she had seen it all happen on Sylvia's face rather than the game piece.

Sylvia looked down at the photo. "I don't know, but I think this helps." She paused, holding the photo tight and reaching for a memory. She gasped when she immediately felt submerged. Within seconds, her lungs were burning with the need for air, and red eyes glowed beyond the surface of the liquid just out of reach. Sylvia released the memory and gasped, collapsing back in the chair. Nathan gripped her chair as if ready to shred its wood to pull her free.

Nathan looked at her, and she saw it in his eyes. He was tired yet driven with a curiosity that wouldn't let him give up.

Sylvia felt her disappointment that maybe the picture represented a safe place where she could find the peace she would need to wrestle back control of her memories. "Maybe this doesn't help," she said, waving the photo, the failed attempt dampening her earlier heightened mood at seeing the five networks coalesce. "I don't even know what I did," she said finally. "I just know I was able to see those five colors braiding around my spine. What does it mean?"

Nathan and Rosalind both appeared hesitant as they stared at her, then Rosalind turned and spoke to the video screen. "Where are you?" she said, one hand poised over the VCR pause button as she scrutinized the screen, leaving Nathan to answer.

"We need the results of your species scan before discussing what any of it means."

Sylvia felt the blow harder than she would have expected. They didn't trust her. Maybe some, but there was enough doubt for them to hedge.

Nathan tried to continue by offering to try her neuro exam now, and Sylvia sensed he felt a new weight at her revelation.

"Dang it, nothing." Rosalind popped the tape out and slipped in the second one, causing Nathan to jump this time. Sylvia felt too numb to move.

[26.6]

Nathan barely resisted slapping the desk with his palm. He knew Rosalind reviewed the old security camera system. She kept them operational for when she thought someone might be screwing with the new tech stuff installed with the renovations. But he was getting pissed at her throwing him under the bus with Sylvia, and he was curious as to what she was searching for.

Rosalind gave no commentary, and Nathan stole a glance at Sylvia. She was staring at the MRI, twisting her necklace back and forth. "This test is why you are here, right? You want to know if you are Sahaja or if you should seek treatment for a human disease."

Sylvia dropped the chain but didn't answer, leaning forward, propping her chin on her fist as her elbow perched on her knee, staring at the MRI screen and knowingly or unknowingly flexing the Griffon network about every five seconds.

Nathan gripped the chair. Sylvia's movement brought her too close to him. He could hear her steady heartbeat. *Hear her heartbeat?* Nathan swallowed. Griffon *hearing.*

"Show me where you're going," Rosalind mumbled.

Nathan gritted his teeth to keep from yelling at Rosalind to help him deal with Sylvia rather than fool with security.

Rosalind, usually attentive to Nathan's moods, reached overhead to the shelf and retrieved another tape. "Surely, you're not going..." Rosalind's words trailed off as she finally glanced over and seemed to register Nathan's exhaustion.

"Shit, what is up with you two? You're like magnets with dual ends. You think you've lined them up to repel each other only to find their ends flipped and stuck together."

Nathan forced himself to move toward the desk away from Sylvia, picking up the spinal model and turning back to Sylvia.

[26.7]

Rosalind popped the third tape in the buzzing VCR. "Just a few more minutes," she said, recognizing the isolation in Sylvia's stare. *Why couldn't this woman be a Sahaja who knew what she was doing? That would be helpful,* Rosalind thought, even as she felt a pang of guilt when Sylvia looked away. Why did all of it need to be done while she should be managing the security of the Galactic Core Station, which at this point appeared to have a security breach and a malfunctioning energy-generator room?

[26.8]

Sylvia sat back and focused on Nathan. "Can you show me with that how I can make it safe for you to do my neuro exam?"

Nathan didn't answer for a moment, then tapped the base of the skull on the model where the networks seemed to wrap into the brain. "If you can store the energy inside the tangle, it decreases the risk for injury to someone."

Sylvia looked down at the charm she had lifted again absently. The memory of the burn in her back earlier today almost brought tears as she realized it was worsening. It wasn't painful, just building like heat on a day with no relief. Somehow, she knew whatever was wrong with her was connected to her parents' death. The photograph in her hand seemed to make that feel very real, but she still wasn't sure why. *I don't want to hurt anyone else,* she thought, but she could feel her fear and anger mounting as she touched the photo.

Rosalind pushed away from the desk. "I hate to do this, but I need to get the security camera film from the old system monitoring the Bunker EG room. I'll be right back."

"What?" Nathan said, jumping away from the desk where he'd been leaning. He barely had time to beat Rosalind's quick robotic leg movement to the door.

"No," Sylvia said, standing. Fire laced through her spine.

Rosalind and Nathan froze.

Nathan visibly struggled with what moved in her spine, but she couldn't help it. "I want to know how you got this photo out of my room."

Rosalind and Nathan looked surprised. "You have this picture in your room?"

"Yes."

Rosalind began backing up to her desk. "I'll get the security camera film shortly."

"Why did you steal the photo from my room?" Sylvia asked, panic fueling her anger.

Rosalind didn't answer but instead pulled a magnifying glass from her drawer. "Are you sure it's identical?"

"Yes, I'm sure!" Sylvia said, pacing to the desk. "I was just looking at it this morning before I passed out." A hint of a smell tugged at her memory as she remembered waking up on the carpet.

Rosalind passed her the magnifying glass. "Are you sure? Check it again."

Sylvia scanned the photograph with the magnifying glass as she described to them how Kita had given it to her at a signing during the tour.

"So, there are two photos like this?" Rosalind asked.

Sylvia wanted to trust them, but it was evident Meki didn't like Nathan. "Meki thinks Kita killed the man we saw on the news this morning because I didn't write the coordinates to the Lost Cities in his book," she finally said.

"But there were numbers written in the book." Nathan tapped the hologram above his ring, and several pictures and articles appeared from the Rompnet. "Remember, the ones from this morning." He sat on the arm of the chair and scrolled.

"But, I didn't write them," Sylvia said, looking up at Nathan, closer now that he leaned forward from the arm of his chair.

"Why would this Kita kill him? Why not just take the book?" Rosalind asked, her robotic legs crossed as she leaned against her desk.

Sylvia shrugged her shoulder. "The man told me he would be killed if I didn't write the coordinates in the book, but security had him removed before I even signed it." Sylvia squeezed her eyes closed at the flash of memory from the morning's news report. She gripped her head in her hands, her elbows braced on her knees.

Nathan finished scanning the article. "Who put the numbers there in the book if not you?"

"Whoever killed him?" Sylvia said absently, her head still in her hands, then recalled they were the same two numbers written in the book from the Orbiter. *Did the man copy them down from the Rompnet and get killed for it?* "I don't know."

Rosalind shifted her weight, squatting to be eye level with Sylvia, though her head was still bent in her hands. Nathan slipped back into his seat.

Sylvia felt a shiver of vibration in her spine but didn't look up.

"Are the Lost Cities in your book actual places? Places where the Portal keys are hidden?" Rosalind asked, her monotone careful.

Color twisted at the tangle in the back of Sylvia's mind. With her eyes closed, it seemed the ribbons of color stretched toward one another, almost blending like the colors of a rainbow, then slipping from her view to wrap around her spine. Her voice seemed distant to her as she answered. "I don't know," she said honestly. "But I don't know the coordinates. Everyone seems to think I do." Sylvia ran her hands through her hair but didn't lift her head. "I can't recall all my memories. I wanted to use the archives to see if its resources could trigger recall that might help."

"But why would Kita give you the photo?" Rosalind and Nathan asked together.

Sylvia lifted her head and looked at them, seeing the answer for the first time. "She wants me to remember. She thinks I know the coordinates." Sylvia felt a new conviction about Kita's guilt in the murder as she stroked the photo still in her hand. "And the photo," she said quietly, her eyes distant. "The photo is personal. I think she wants me dead, so I can't give them to anyone else." Sylvia leaned back against the chair leather, letting her head lull against it while pieces fell into place as she recalled Jezel's words to Tessa.

"Even Jezel thinks I have coordinates, or rather, my memory has the coordinates for where the relic keys are hidden." She closed her eyes. "Kita looks about my age, so she couldn't have done it, but maybe her family or whoever she works for..." Sylvia opened her eyes, but she seemed to be unable to see anything but the tangle in her mind. "Somehow, she is connected to my parents' death." Red eyes appeared, and she was drowning. Sylvia pushed back at the vision, unable to breathe. "Parents I can't yet remember." The words came out in a burst from her held breath. Sylvia blinked twice, and the tangle vanished, pulling with it the vision as the room reality flooded in. "But...I think when I remember them, I will remember many things." *That is, if it doesn't kill me to do it.*

Rosalind gave a low whistle as she stood.

Sylvia sensed Rosalind's...fear. She looked down at her hands. She could feel the heat in them. Nathan stood as still as a predator in high grass and backed against the wall to her left. She felt the heat again in her spine. He stood rigid, his eyes looking at her but slightly past her, unwilling to meet her eyes. Sylvia spoke cautiously. "I didn't know the locks and relic keys I imagined for my book were real till Nathan explained it today on the ride over," Sylvia said, her voice quivering with the weight of the whole day. "Kita attacked me in the hallway this morning." Her vision blurred as she tried to focus on the photograph.

"That's who that was? I was wondering why you hadn't told us."

"You knew about it?" Sylvia asked, looking up from the photo with suspicion.

"I just saw it on the security camera footage. I fast-forwarded through several floors' film to approximately the time she would have arrived on any given floor, and I found her in your wing."

"Really?" Sylvia said, surprised. She realized she had begun to think she was imagining events and felt relieved to have proof she wasn't losing her mind. Maybe.

"Someone, I suspect her, placed hologram webbing over the camera feed in that hall. The new camera and old camera system do not work together. The old camera system is often overlooked, which is why I still use it." Rosalind pointed at the VCR machine on the shelf behind her. "The hologram webbing she placed on the new camera system is good. It would be difficult to notice the glitch if I didn't know where to look for it from the recording. I pulled footage from the old camera system and matched the time stamps. The old camera recorded the events in the hallway."

Sylvia rubbed her eyes, and the tangle at the back of her mind twisted as if trying to fit a different pattern. She shuddered. *She wants me to remember.* Sylvia froze as the tangle settled, and the iridescent light wrapping down her spine was visible in her thoughts. "I can see it now." Sylvia met Rosalind's eyes. "It's almost complete."

Rosalind stared at her as if a shadow of something terrible had just passed through her mind.

Feeling exposed, Sylvia closed her eyes. The vision of the man with the red eyes flashed in her mind, and she gripped the chair. *Familiar.* "There is a part of my life still disconnected from what is reawakening in me," Sylvia whispered. "I just have to find a safe place to face it."

CHAPTER TWENTY-SEVEN

R OSALIND STARED OUT AT the Archive, recalling the collection of years of
work begun in childhood. A struggle to surmount the tragedy that left her
unable to do what she was about to teach someone else. Rosalind closed her eyes.
"I can help you reconnect and complete the network if the species test confirms
you are a Sahaja Intuit," Rosalind said, moving closer to the glass wall. *All your
work will pay off*, she thought to herself. *You will have a Sahaja Intuit network
to train. It just won't be yours.* Rosalind wanted to lean her head on the glass and
weep. Instead, she removed the glove from her hand and touched the glass briefly
with her fingertips. The tangle in her mind brightened with the sensory ribbon
of color. She had the heightened sense of a Sahaja Intuit in her hands, but the
damage in her spine made translation across to the human network inconsistent.
She wore the gloves when she could because the heightened sensation didn't serve
its purpose with the network not functioning, and it was distracting, sometimes
painful. Her medical records documented it as Raynaud's phenomenon, so people assumed it was the cold intolerance associated with that condition when she
chose to wear them. Only Nathan knew the truth. The thought made her wonder
if he had noticed she was wearing them more often.

[27.1]

Sylvia sensed Rosalind's reluctance but could not determine if it was still her
disbelief of Sylvia's motives or something else. She lifted the photo, tired of only
getting pieces of help. "Why did you take this photograph from my room?" she
asked again, risking a glance at Nathan, who had moved back to the desk as if
focused on the hologram screen of her MRI, but she saw the tension in his back.
She felt the burning along her spine that she had come to associate with his spells,

but she was starting to get angry. She was not responsible for his problems. She knew something was changing in her, and she was trying to figure it out. If he couldn't help her without jeopardizing himself, he should keep his distance and stop blaming her.

"Rosalind," Nathan said, closing the MRI screen and walking toward her. "The tests are scheduled for this evening,"

"Why are you both treating me like I have some secret agenda?" Sylvia said. "You break into my room, steal from me, drag me around to dangerous places, tease me with bits of information after I expose my weakness, then treat me as if I am the one who can't be trusted."

"If you can be trusted, then why are you and your publicist, Meki, working with a man like Senator Faraday? The man is unscrupulous and known for his leanings toward the Separatists."

Rosalind interrupted as if to balance the growing heat in the room. "I initially found her, this Kita, when I started the security film review. She is the one who manually landed Orbiter C13 earlier this week. From there, I was scanning film trying to find her again since she obviously stole Major Tom's ride and had some purpose for not wanting to be found."

Sylvia had returned to the photograph and was focused on the edge. Rosalind must have noticed her picking at the corner.

"I didn't steal the photo from you. I have had it for years. Did you find something?"

"I'm not sure, but I think so," she said, wiping the corner. "I thought my photo had a fingertip in this corner." Sylvia tapped the photo. "Here near the lens when the picture was taken. I need to go back to my room to get mine for comparison."

"You can't leave," Nathan said, and his dominant tone pushed Sylvia's last nerve. She glared at him, but he continued. "It's not safe."

"You need to make up your mind." Sylvia clenched her jaw as she spoke. The photograph felt cold in her hand compared to the heat cascading through her spine. *Why does it do that?*

"And stop doing that!" Nathan growled low.

Overwhelmed and feeling angry, Sylvia stepped toward Nathan. "You told me I couldn't stay when I came in. Now you're telling me I can't go. What's wrong with you?"

"You know what you are." Nathan paused, and Sylvia sensed his conflict as he selected his words. "What is your purpose in touching Rosalind's mind at the race and pushing me to transform?"

[27.2]

Rosalind touched Nathan's hand. She waited to see his shoulders relax before turning to Sylvia. "Each species has a specialized network intertwined with their human network. The specialized Intuit network pulls in from the external world. This is the network you are default opening when you feel that burn in your spine." Rosalind reached over the desk to where Nathan had placed the vertebrae model. She opened it to show several colored layers wrapped like a braid around the spinal cord that then ran through a hole in the bottom of a skull. The skull separated into four pieces to reveal a model brain inside.

Sylvia stroked the braid. "Each of these different colors represents a species network," she said, gently separating the threads braided around the spinal cord.

"A species can have variant thicknesses of the network twined around the human spinal cord, and a Sahaja of that species will have a thicker one."

"These look full but not significantly thick," Sylvia said.

"This model shows the network for all five species. The Rainbanes were said to have all the networks in balance and therefore had no greater thickness in any one network." Rosalind sat on the desk and pointed at each color. "Your MRI is unusual in that it shows only patchy areas of network braid and demonstrates that patchiness along an atypical distribution."

"Rosalind," Nathan said, his voice controlled.

"So, that's why Nathan thinks I'm an impostor and here for the PR. Use a chemical to mimic a species network so I can make a big buzz about getting species testing on Replica Earth," Sylvia said, and Rosalind noted how Sylvia's eyes locked with Nathan's.

"Yes," Rosalind said, touching each of the colored braids as she spoke. "The atypical distribution of the patchy areas appears to represent all five networks, not just one." *Galactic dice,* she thought, catching a glimpse of Nathan's eyes as she toggled her vision between him and Sylvia. They both stood stiff, eyes locked. A Griffon's instinct to protect was as natural as its instinct to mate. That's what she had missed. *These two are attracted to each other, primal, unconscious...* Rosalind stopped thinking; she had to act. "Sylvia," Rosalind said quietly, seeing fear win the mix of emotions in the woman's eyes. "When you are afraid, you open that network that pulls on the world around you. I need you to relax. Your fear draws him toward transformation to protect you."

[27.3]

Sylvia nodded slowly, frozen where she stood. Why did she feel this clash of emotions for this stranger? Her mind told her she would feel better in his arms,

protected. *No*, Sylvia thought. *Not just protected. Wanted.* His eyes stared back
at her, the green almost wholly gone. Sylvia blinked, and he looked down as if to
gain his strength. What was she thinking? The man's girlfriend was right here in
the room. She had almost transformed him once today. If she had any decency,
she would leave, find an Orbiter, and get home as soon as possible. The thought
sent fear and loss racing in a mix of colors through the tangle at the back of her
mind.

"Nathan," Rosalind whispered, her tone firm. "Is your mutation compromised?"

Nathan didn't answer, and Rosalind moved gently to step around the desk, as
if careful not to startle the animal now partially with them.

"She can't be real!" Nathan roared.

Sylvia somehow instinctively knew his anger was at his own failure. She saw the
ribbon of yellow flare, and she heard Nathan's thoughts.

I'm beyond return, he thought, and Sylvia watched the words disappear within
the network of yellow as if seeing the words fade like mist in his mind.

Nathan's low, pained growl startled an already moving Sylvia, and she backed
toward the door. Her movement triggered the Griffon's instincts, and he looked
up with new eyes. The green was gone, and the gold starburst exploded from the
pupil. Nathan spoke, but his words were a low growl.

Sylvia paused at the sound. To her ears, it had been a beastial growl, but
her mind heard the words: *"I won't hurt you."* She swallowed hard as Nathan
approached. Her heart pounded. She needed to leave, but she wanted him closer
even as she crossed her arms to muffle her thundering heart. Her back was hot as
fire, but it didn't burn. Rosalind was speaking, and Sylvia was trying to listen but
couldn't make out her words.

Nathan reached Sylvia. She gasped at his proximity but didn't resist when he
took her eyes with his. He touched her arms at the elbows where she had crossed
them to her chest. She saw his promise to protect her in his eyes, but it flickered
with a sense of failure. She wanted to close her eyes and try to find an emotion
she could trust.

Sylvia let her eyes blink once, then close. She now seemed to hear Rosalind.

"If he transforms to protect you, he fails another."

Sylvia shuddered. The muted colors twisted then glowed from the tangle in
her mind. Rosalind's voice reverberated in her head, the words both a statement
of fact and a warning. Sylvia's lips parted to speak, but when she opened her
eyes, the words fell away. Nathan's eyes were closed, but she knew they glowed

amber beneath, and his hair had grown two inches. He was changing, trans-forming. She pushed her hands against his chest. "Nathan. Stop. You can't do this." Now that she had decided, she wondered why it had seemed like something she wanted. Then she remembered how unconscious the whole process had been. Fear gripped her. *I'm doing this*, she thought, realizing Nathan still stood gently gripping her arms above the elbow despite her hands pressed to his chest. *He isn't listening.* Sylvia struggled, trying to break free, but Nathan didn't release her. He just opened his eyes, those gold-amber eyes. There was something extraordinary about him, and she wanted him for herself, but he belonged to another. Her anger at him for not helping her fight raged with her deep recognition of how he wanted her. *How can he feel this way with his girlfriend right behind him?* The two emotions collided into a single fear. "Stop it!" she commanded and flinched at the current that arced between them. The heat pulsed once exploded in her mind and burned fast, disappearing as a jolt at Nathan's chest. Nathan jerked, his arms extending with the force. Warm tears found their way down Sylvia's cheeks, and she braced against the door.

[27.4]

Nathan shook his head and looked at his hands as if waking from a dream. His mind felt foggy, and he glanced up at Sylvia, a flash of memory at the sight of the shelves of books beyond the glass wall. He couldn't find the words he wanted. They seemed farther away than ever before. His hand trembled at the thought. How had she done it? She had kept him from transforming. He let his head drop when he saw her eyes. She was breathing heavily. It had taken a toll on her.

Nathan tried not to notice the rise and fall of her chest as she gradually slowed her breathing. He focused on her eyes. It was the best he could do with that primitive need still edging his mind.

[27.5]

Sylvia placed her palms firmly against the door at her back. Nathan looked at her, and her breath caught. She still felt the ache at her core. She wanted him. It was primitive and selfish. *What is wrong with me?* she thought, glad she could feel the cool of the door at her back. She needed to leave. He had a girlfriend — right here!

"Sylvia, I..." Nathan looked up from his hands to find her eyes. "I apolo-gize. I will do the test this evening because I'm the only one who can. Then, I'll hand your care over to a colleague."

Sylvia shuddered at the clear green of his eyes. He was the same man, but he felt like two. She needed the doctor, and she craved the...Griffon. Now, she couldn't have either.

She turned, grasping the doorknob.

"Sylvia," Nathan offered gently.

"Let her go, Nate. She'll be back. She needs the archives," Rosalind said, and Sylvia knew Rosalind was glad to have avoided the tragedy but appeared too shaken to deal with more right now. She turned to her desk. "Leave the picture, and bring yours."

"It's on the desk," Sylvia said and pulled the door open. What did she expect? She had almost kissed the woman's boyfriend right in front of her. And there was more. Sylvia had felt something feral, seen something unfettered in his eyes. She almost pushed him to transform into some wild beast from which neither of them would see him return.

[27.6]

Nathan let her go but stood watching through the glass as she braced against a shelf just beyond the door to the clean room antechamber. She hadn't entered it, choosing instead to go around the protrusion to remain in the Archive room. If she noticed the doors on the other side, she could leave without going through the clean room. One could exit that way, but getting in through there required Rosalind — her little safety feature to keep people out. Nathan tapped his foot as he watched her. Part of him wanted to run after her. She probably didn't realize he could still see her. She had waited till she passed the protrusion of the clean room before leaning against the tall wooden shelving of books, then stepping between them. He could tell she had her arms wrapped at her waist, though all he could see was her elbow as she leaned back against a collection of books well over 200 years old. *Good thing Rosalind is at her desk*, he thought. He forced his finger to stop tapping his leather belt, realizing it would draw Rosalind's attention and might bring her over. She would more easily let Sylvia transform him into a Griffon than let her lean on the books in the archives. Sylvia pushed away from the books and stepped out of the aisle, never looking toward the glass. *She must have noticed the doors*, Nathan thought, watching her head away from him. With his hands still on his hips, he tapped his belt again, caught himself, and stopped. He turned back to Rosalind once he saw the Archive doors close behind Sylvia. He would make things right this evening at the clinic. *What if she doesn't come?* He needed her help to get Elizabeth back, yet part of him worried she would make him forget

Elizabeth, and even himself. *But she kept you from transforming*, he reminded himself, then spun, pushed the door open, and raced for the Archive door.

Nathan caught her in the hallway with a few easy strides. "Where are you going?"

"To get my picture and figure out what's going on. Go back to your girlfriend. If she will have you after the stunt you pulled."

"She's not my girlfriend." Nathan took two strides and turned in front of her.

She dodged to go around him.

"Sylvia, please." He resisted the urge to take her arm.

She stopped and turned.

Nathan's gut twisted with the full attention of her crystal-blue eyes, but he had to decide at some point whether to trust her. He held her stare. "Do you recognize the power you have...over me?"

Sylvia almost laughed. "Power? The power to turn you into a beast and feel like I'm burning inside myself. It's not an upside."

"I know," he said, realizing she didn't know that she had saved him. "I understand." His words carried weight beyond today. She didn't understand what she was, and he couldn't be around her much till she did, but he could trust her. He could stop treating her like an impostor. He could do the species test. *But, damn, her MRI showed telltale signs of chemical tampering that I've seen in several impostors.*

"If you understand, then let's just leave this alone," she said, moving her hand in a circle between them, then turned back toward the elevators.

"I don't trust myself with you." His gentle touch to her arm asked her to stop without the dominance so familiar to him when the Griffon pressed his mind.

She paused as he spoke, her back to him.

"That's why I can't...be your doctor."

"I guess Rosalind is safe?" Sylvia said, sounding bitter, then sighing as if feeling guilty.

"Damn it. She's my sister."

The elevator dinged, and doors whisked open before Sylvia could speak. A short, thick man stepped out and, as if purposely ignoring them, shouted at Rosalind, who was coming out the Archive doors.

[27.7]

Sylvia watched the stout stranger exit the elevator.

"Tell Nathan I'm not speaking to him anymore," he said. "I just spent an hour with your security staff, unwilling to disturb you because they said Nathan's not here, and they had to verify my credentials before they would even call you."

"Sorry, Stone," Nathan said, speaking to the man's back. "Rosalind brought us in the back way. They didn't know I was here. Did you bring the rings?"

"Do you hear anything, Rosalind?" the stout man — Stone, apparently — said, looking over his shoulder, pretending he didn't see them standing there.

Rosalind smiled despite the tight face she had worn when she had stepped from the archives. "Come on, Stone, I'll let you in."

Rosalind is his sister, Sylvia thought, not wanting to wrestle with why that made her happy.

"Go get your copy of the photograph and get back here," Rosalind said.

Her openness about the photograph in front of Stone told Sylvia Rosalind trusted him, but she had come out to tell them more than that. She already knew Sylvia was going to get the photo — she had said as much to Nathan in her office. So, Sylvia waited, watching the woman with a new mix of emotions.

Rosalind turned to the Archive door and opened it with a touch of her palm to the glass wall at the right. There was not even an electric panel or scanner there. Sylvia blinked, thinking she had missed something, as the door opened for Stone, whose thick hands held two briefcases. "You can put them on the desk. I'll be in. I know what she needs." She let the door close behind him and walked to Nathan and Sylvia. "The chauffeur and Kita are in custody. I just got a call from Houseman. Get the photo and get back here."

"What puzzle pieces did Houseman find?" Nathan asked.

His familiarity with Rosalind had a new slant to Sylvia now that she knew of their familial bond, and she felt more relaxed. She noted the contrast of Rosalind's paler hand as she touched Nathan's olive skin. It was a wonder the woman had any color at all working this far underground all the time.

"I'll tell you when you get back." Rosalind turned back to the Archive door. "Stone isn't one for squandering time, and I need to run the pressure and energy measurements on the Bunker EG room from my high-security system. The numbers Harry just called in are a problem."

Sylvia felt a twinge of envy at the easy swing of the woman's straight, silken red hair as she pushed through the Archive door. *She must straighten it some days*, she thought, wondering if the woman ever slept. Sylvia watched her as she moved past the shelves of books inside the Archive and disappeared. Sylvia pulled one of her own blond curls straight. As much as she felt connected to the woman because of their equal appreciation of books, they were very different. She could barely keep the frizz out of hers, which is why she so often wore it up.

"Come on. I'll walk you up."

Despite Nathan's effort, Sylvia knew her MRI gave him mixed ideas about what she really was and why she was there. But, she knew the why now, better than she had when she agreed to come. There was part of her missing, and it was an important part. It might be small, patchy areas of network, but it connected her to her past. A past that held answers for more than just her.

CHAPTER TWENTY-EIGHT

"**D**O YOU NEED INCENTIVE?" Meki fingered the box in a soft leather pouch strapped around his belt just inside his suitcoat. He rechecked the dropping energy levels showing on his screen. "Manage your energy!" Meki shouted, losing his temper. He preferred to use pain incentives for training. It could be too distracting during actual projects, but this Intuit was testing his patience. Meki absently reached again for the leather pouch and the blade that was clipped next to it.

[28.1]

Wesley's body dripped with sweat, and his hands gripped the stone as he braced his arms to stabilize his torso and help him breathe. "The energy keeps disappearing," he gasped out. He had removed his shirt because of the metal in the buttons, and he watched as his ribs expanded in an effort to create more room for air, but the energy he held condensed the air to vapor. His lungs were drowning in a mist of his own making. He pressed his chin to his chest and gritted his teeth. "When...I cycle the energy, it's less." Wesley converted the stone's energy through his network to modify the energy loss in the room. If someone found them, he would be taken into custody, and DNA testing and investigation would destroy his plans for Cajal's new life. He had to do this. He had trouble recalling his recent missions. Each of them had been prefaced and followed by such incredible torture his mind felt disconnected. Somehow, the room was losing energy despite him replacing all the stolen energy from the Umbilical Portal. He was good at this. Years as a thief gave him precision in energy exchange. He knew exactly how much was coming in from the Portal, and he was sending equal amounts out into the room from his fifth network to maintain levels even as his third network pushed the stolen energy into the fuel cell attached across the arch of his bare feet. He had a moment of intense sadness that he had not had the opportunity to train with other Intuits. His skill was good, but hard earned. He had been surprised at the few he had contact with had lacked his precision, but not everyone could do the refined work using the human network like he could. However, today it wasn't enough.

"You're not focused," Meki bellowed as the screen revealed another drop in the room's energy.

Wesley shook his head, trying to focus. There had to be a leak in the room. Energy was escaping somewhere. He couldn't think. He had planned to hold enough energy to down the man who brought him here, but he was into his reserves, and his thoughts were getting foggy. "I'm down to my reserves."

Meki strode to the stone, grasping Wesley's strapped hand. He touched the nub on his left hand. Wesley jerked, a memory of pain and torture flashing in his mind, but even the pain of losing the finger was nothing compared to the suffering of the desensitization chambers in the caves.

"You were a quick learner," Meki said. "Perhaps too quick. You only lost one finger in training, but then again, I'm not sure Faraday's techniques have training as their endpoint." Meki slipped out the blade he kept at his side. "I use pain to teach. There is a difference."

The sound of blade on sheath brought Wesley up taut against his wrist and ankle restraints. "It's not me." The words were wet, and Wesley coughed as he spoke.

Meki dropped his hand and stepped to Wesley's feet. He slid the blade lightly across the small toe of his right foot, just enough to break the skin.

"No. Please," Wesley whispered, squeezing his eyes closed and fighting the exhaustion of breathing through the growing fluid in his lungs. *I can do this. We just have to find the leak*. Still gasping, he managed, "Check. The. Room."

[28.2]

Meki returned to the screen to see if the small incentive had helped. The numbers still dropped. If the Dalen was right, he would die trying to maintain the energy level. Meki ground his teeth. He disliked uncertainty, but he had to decide. Faraday's people had or had not trained this Intuit properly. His instincts told him Faraday was indolent and had not. *If this man is a Captive...* The thought recalled his conversation with Faraday, and Meki pushed away the idea. "Focus, Intuit," he said, removing his blade. "I'm doing this to save your life. Better to lose a toe and improve your focus than lose your life." *The man has skill*, Meki thought. *If he is not free but a true Dalenborn, I have a solid tool to refine.* The thought made him briefly forget his anger at Biagio for the shift of plans and restore his purpose.

The Dalen screamed but the effort worked. There was a blast of energy into the pattern that cycled back to the energy monitor. It cycled for two patterns with increased flows from his brief glance. "Good," Meki said, glancing again to confirm the surge on the screen, but he couldn't see the numbers. "Focus. Let the pain keep the energy aligned," Meki said, moving back to read the numbers. "Yes. That focused effort helped." The numbers spiked. Meki leaned forward when the numbers began dropping rapidly. He turned, but the man was no longer gasping. Meki dropped the severed toe tip in a small chemical incinerator tucked in a soft leather pouch at his waist. The room temperature shifted. The stone was losing its heat. *Cold,* Meki thought, knowing his error before he reached the man's head. "Bloody Galactic dice!" The blank stare of dead eyes pushed Meki's anger, and he shoved the man still strapped to the capacitor stone. Biagio had rushed this project, and Meki had lost a good tool. He slipped the chemical incinerator loop, and the knife now clipped again at his side, around to his back where they wouldn't be seen. He moved to his computer. "Damn it, Biagio!" Meki cursed. These numbers would raise the alarms and have the UBN checking the room before the routine hour. Meki tapped out several commands, and the Umbilical Portal was back open and running. This would buy him some time to figure out where the leak was located, finally realizing there had to be a major one. He cursed Biagio again. He would have checked these little glitches if he hadn't been in such a hurry. Now he had a body to get rid of.

Then he remembered Kita was here. The police were already suspicious of her thanks to a fraudulent accusation he had mentioned to them when he called about picking up Sylvia's keys. *This might work in my favor, after all.* Meki checked the computer screen. The numbers wouldn't be back up before the UBN hour check-in. He needed to be gone.

[28.3]

Rosalind's mind slipped away to the unrealistic Bunker EG room numbers Harry had given her. She efficiently selected two ringphones and paid Stone. "The extra is for wasting your time," she said, scanning her finger across the payment holograph screen displayed above Stone's own ring. Her ring chimed once, indicating the accounting was complete and money had been moved from her account to Stone's. She could have used her ring to pay, but it required an extra password step of confirmation.

"Thanks, Rosalind. I know you're more than busy this time of year. Leave it to Nathan to create more work for both of us. Tell him he still owes me fifty Tokee on that last football game."

"You tell him. You know he will call wanting to add bionetics to her ring." Rosalind smiled, and Stone found his way to the door, shaking his head. The click of the door was the only sound in the silence as Rosalind popped open her secure screen for the Bunker EG room. Stone would see himself out. She usually watched people as they left to walk out through the Archive room. People didn't understand what it meant to be careful around historical things, but she had let Sylvia leave and now Stone, too, distracted by the mounting security issues. She checked the time. "Where is Stinger?" she said aloud, fully aware she often talked to herself out of habit from him usually being nearby. "He should be back by now." Rosalind checked the time on her ring and leaned back in her chair, tapping her chin. "The numbers aren't as bad as Harry indicated, but I'm glad I had him checking at half-hour intervals because the numbers are down. Stinger will have more information when—"

"Of course, he will," Stinger said, landing on the blueprint and circling to note that everyone was gone. "Stinger always has the information you need. Granted, he misses all the fun intrigue of a crazy new Intuit who doesn't know her own strength. Instead, I get to spend my time listening to muffled vibrations of sound through a shielded vent near an energy room. You do realize the new renovations make it impossible for me to get in."

"Yes. I know. I just wanted you there in case anyone went in or out."

"Not on the UBN side, but there was someone in there. I circled to the hotel side when the noise ceased, and no one left on the UBN side, but it takes a while to get to the hotel side, even if you can fly. Whoever was there is gone, but I didn't see them leave. Maybe on the cameras?"

"Noise? What kind of noise?"

"Voices, though the vibration was difficult to translate. I have the recordings if you want to try your amplifiers to see if we can make something out."

"Let me talk to Houseman. I may not need the recording yet. It will take a lot of time to decode the vibrations, and Houseman has Kita. If he picked her up near the hotel side of the Bunker EG room, I may already have the culprit but not the evidence. I'll phone him and ask him to release her so I can test my theory about why she is here."

"Great!" Stinger said. "Another opportunity for me to find this man's flaw."

Rosalind rolled her eyes as she picked up the landline phone. "Houseman's just a good man, Stinger."

"No," Stinger said, lifting off the blueprint and circling her head as she spoke to Houseman. "He has a deep, dark secret. I just know it." Stinger circled in a figure eight pattern just above eye level.

Rosalind raised an eyebrow, and Stinger landed on her forehead. "Thanks, Houseman. Rosalind said, hanging up and swatting at Stinger. He laughed. It was a static sound, but Rosalind recognized it. "Come on, I have to go back in there." But, thanks to following Kita on the old security system, she had an idea why the numbers were down, and Kita had unknowingly shown her where to look. She hadn't thought much of it initially. "I thought the door to the tunnel had been left open by accident. However, I think Kita left a micro-fuel cell with an attracter somewhere in the room. Now I just have to wait for her to come back and get it."

"Why would someone do that? A micro-fuel cell is barely a distraction in a room with that much energy. Why not steal more if you want energy?"

Rosalind stood and headed for the door. "I know, that's what doesn't make sense. But a micro-fuel cell is the only thing I can think of to create this consistent leak." She paused, grabbed her taser, and clipped it to her belt. *Why bring a micro-fuel cell?* Rosalind thought.

Stinger buzzed off her shoulder to fly in front of her, backward. "If she accessed past the iridescent shield to the Portal area, there are replaceable fuel cells at the stone capacitor where the Intuits circle energy during maintenance. Why not use one of those?"

"It would be hard to get one of those out — they have trackers on them — but it still doesn't explain why she wouldn't bring one of her own if she was here to steal the energy." Rosalind continued to walk. She bit the inside of her lip as she thought. *What does the micro-fuel cell do that the others do not?* "That's it!" Rosalind jerked to a halt. She needed to get down to the Bunker energy-generator room now. "She'll definitely return to the Bunker EG room to check the fuel cell is functioning and then escape through the tunnels. I plan to have our own conversation with her." Rosalind tapped the taser.

CHAPTER TWENTY-NINE

NATHAN KNELT NEAR THE bed, the covers lifted and his ring light on. "I don't see it. Did you check your other books?"

"Yes, but I had it out. I was looking at it before I passed out this morning." Sylvia checked the robe in the closet. Her hand rummaged the pocket nearest her. Empty.

"Wait." Nathan stood, bumping his hand on the nightstand.

Sylvia closed the trifold closet doors that faced the bed so Nathan could get past her. He knelt by the leg nearest the door. The small room reminded her of hotels in Paris — tastefully tiny.

"Did you find it?" she asked as he knelt, reaching blindly near the leg. She leaned over to see.

"Maybe."

He pulled something white from underneath. "No," he said, dramatically dropping the tissue and scratching his nose with the back of his hand as if to stave off a sneeze. "Well, you didn't drop it under here. Where were you when you fell?" Nathan stepped to the bathroom to wash his hands.

Sylvia opened the closet again to check the other pocket of her robe. "I didn't fall. I passed—"

"Sylvia!" Nathan shouted, and Sylvia jumped. "Don't touch anything else."

"What is it?" Sylvia said, her hand over her chest.

"Someone was here." Nathan's words were muffled as she saw him reflected in the mirror. He smelled his hand and quickly started the water running in the bathroom.

"What?' Sylvia asked, not really listening as she reached back to the robe's other pocket. *So, they didn't clean the room well, and he touched someone's snot rag.* "I found it," Sylvia said, waving the photo as she turned.

"Someone was here," Nathan repeated as he stepped closer to look at the photo.

Sylvia stopped waving it. A new fear crept through her when their eyes met. She shifted her eyes to the photo and noticed the smeared writing on the back. The picture faced Nathan the way she had pulled it from the robe pocket.

"You didn't pass out," Nathan said, reaching to touch the hand that held the photo. He paused and let his hand fall to his side.

Sylvia read the truth of the pause in his eyes. Touching her made the connection stronger, and her fear already had his heart rate up. *I can see it in the pounding pulse at his neck.* "It's not the photo like Rosalind's, is it?" Sylvia asked, letting the photo slip from her hand. She sat down on the bed and buried her face in her hands. There had been no writing on the photo Kita had given her. She didn't understand everything yet, but she knew she had to control her fear around Nathan to avoid pushing whatever buttons threatened to transform him. Nathan was silent, and she sensed his struggle. *I can do this,* Sylvia thought, taking a deep breath and standing to walk toward the window to put some space between them.

"Do you remember anything before..." Nathan paused, and Sylvia tried to read him. "Before you...lost consciousness?"

He doesn't like the thought of me being vulnerable, Sylvia thought. *It draws on his need to protect.* "No, I'm — I was in such a rush this morning." *What had been so important?* "It's funny how the signing for a fictional book I wrote seemed so important this morning." She blinked. "Now the signing has been canceled, my book is banned, and..." Sylvia looked up to meet Nathan's eyes. "I don't believe it's fiction anymore." She felt a moment of imbalance and reached for the windowsill.

Nathan stepped toward her, then hesitated as if judging how close would be tolerable, as he spoke. "There is chloroberiotoxin on that handkerchief." He stepped backward to the door. "It makes me sneeze when I use it in the lab. I have a terrible allergy to it." He showed her his hand, irritated with red welts despite his quick effort to wash his hands. Nathan measured his step from the bumpout that formed the closet back to the door of the room. "I recognized the smell and felt my hand start to itch before I washed my hands in the bathroom. It would be easy for someone to hide here."

Sylvia watched him physically push the anger out of his face as if trying to calm himself. She wrapped her arms around her middle and stared at the afternoon sky, trying not to recall the moment from the morning when she'd thought she had heard something in the room. She tried to divert her thoughts as she faced out the window. She envisioned the GCS like Meki described it. *Like a diamond perched on a ring band,* he had said when describing the Galactic Core Station nestled in the ring of docking ports that circled Replica Earth. Part of her was relieved they wouldn't be doing the Simultaneity Transport from the GCS to Replica Earth, but she was disappointed about the signing cancelation. The hotel and elaborate self-contained environment were more than lavish and comfortable, but she couldn't feel farther away from home. "Why would someone want that picture, Nathan?"

I don't know," he said, stepping toward her and catching himself before he took her shoulders. "I'll let Rosalind know, and she can send an investigative team. Do you mind if I do your neurologic exam while we wait for them?"

Sylvia tried to ignore the ping of anticipation, but her back started to warm. She was beginning to associate it with Nathan's proximity, which she knew was too simplified an explanation. She turned to him. *I can understand this, control it.* "You said I helped. Is that true?"

"Yes, you kept me from transforming, but..." Nathan's lips formed a tight line. "It could be a fluke. Your network is patchy from...well, it just may not work a second time."

"I thought one of your colleagues was going to be my doctor," Sylvia teased, then appreciated the flush of heat in her back that matched the flush on his face as he pretended to look for Rosalind's number.

"I'm reconsidering," Nathan said hesitantly.

"Really?" Sylvia leaned toward him.

Nathan stiffened, and Sylvia froze, watching him. His tempered words matched the amber restricted by the strain of green surrounding his pupils.

His hands fisted, and the amber starburst flared then receded as Nathan forced his eyes to focus on the closet beyond her. "Damn The Void," Nathan said, taking a deep breath through his mouth like an animal stirring his instincts with the smells of his environment.

With the smell of jasmine and rain, Sylvia thought, wanting to stand close at the thought of what she would see in his eyes. Fire licked Sylvia's spine, and she blew out a breath. She had almost forgotten she was a danger to him, even if she didn't understand it. She was selfish to want to see that hunger in his eyes again. She forced her hand away from her necklace as she leaned against the closet frame. "It's no big deal. I can see someone else."

"I can do it," Nathan answered. "It will get easier as you learn to hold the energy in your network or store it in the tangle."

Sylvia sensed talking helped. "You say network, single. Why do I see the colors of all five networks?"

"That is one of the reasons I wanted to do a neuro exam before the testing. Your MRI shows patchy areas on what appears to be five networks. However, having five networks is impossible."

"Impossible? Then what is it?"

"Yes, impossible. Only the Rainbanes and the Rainbane Reborn had all five networks, and their bloodline has vanished. However..." Nathan looked at his shoes as if he didn't want to answer. "As I said, it has been recently found that chemical manipulation can mimic that appearance."

"So, you still think I'm taking drugs of some kind to trick you into doing the scan test so I can promote my book?"

"I'm not saying that. I'm just telling you what the data has shown. I'm sure you have at least one network, just from..." He paused.

"Just from the trouble I've caused," Sylvia added for him.

Nathan cleared his throat. "I'm just not sure. That's what I'm saying. Have you been exposed to any unusual chemicals?"

"Just the cloroxberry toxin you mentioned."

Nathan pursed his lips. "The chloroberiotoxin will not do it. It just knocks you out, fast. It may not be a healthy network due to your difficulty balancing it, but you said all of this was fairly new. A chemical makes the most sense."

"Well. I don't use drugs. I don't even take vitamins." Sylvia frowned, afraid. *What if I don't have the ability to help or even survive whatever this is?* The fear worsened her anger. "Well, like I said, I don't do..." Sylvia stopped mid-sentence. "The poisoned willow bark," she whispered, then looked up at Nathan. "How long would a drug have to be in your system to create what you describe?"

"It depends on the drug. What are you thinking?"

"Nothing. Something I need to talk with Kinley and Xenos about," she hedged. "What is The Void?" she asked, trying to laugh as she repeated his curse from earlier.

Nathan grinned. "I'm usually more cautious with my language around patients. You set me at ease even as you trigger my greatest change." Nathan ducked his head and leaned against the doorframe between the bedroom and kitchen. "Most scientists date The Void to about a hundred and fifty thousand years ago. The Great Splintering is the most recent event in Immortal scientific history."

"The Great what?"

"I forget you were raised on Earth. The schools established at the expanded space station have taught the history more thoroughly for those joining the Earth Alliance since the war, but it still isn't taught in Earth's educational programs. When were you born?"

Sylvia turned, glancing back out the window. "I'm not sure. I was adopted at about age seven. My adoptive parents don't have any information about my past, and I don't remember it. We celebrate my birthday as the day I was adopted, March fifteenth. They do not know what year I was born." Sylvia bit her lip. *There is probably a good reason I don't remember it*, she thought, recalling the photo on the bed face down where she dropped it. "What about you?" she asked, turning back to Nathan and sparing a glance at the bed. She needed to look at the photo but couldn't convince herself to do it.

"Actually, I was born several years before the war in 2050."

"Don't be funny, I'm serious," Sylvia said, pushing the photo away as she sat on the bed. "You sound old and crabby sometimes, but it's April 2116, which would make you close to seventy-one years old, and you can't be a day over thirty-five."

"Thirty-five! I look that old?" Nathan asked, running his hands through his hair. "I'll turn twenty-nine before the end of the year." He smiled at the look of confusion on Sylvia's face. "Rosalind and I were both in cryopreservation for years as children. We came to the expanded space station that orbits Earth to seek specialized medical care for Rosalind, and I got a boost in my education. It's a long story, but you don't age when in cryo. So, we didn't grow up till we came out of cryo."

Sylvia traced the bedspread near the photo, another clash of the familiar with the unknown. Cryopreservation wasn't an unfamiliar term, but she had never thought it was really used. The space program on Earth stood out in Sylvia's mind because it was a prominent part of the news during her first year with her new family. Morgan watched the news about modifications and renovations to the already expanded space station, but it had seemed a distant thing to her. Sylvia closed her eyes at the memory of her adopted father. She had called him Morgan rather than Dad for a while but couldn't recall an exact time when that had changed.

"What are you smiling at?" Nathan asked.

"Just remembering Mom, Mimi, tell the story of how I decided to call her Mimi and Dad Morgan because they were names in my favorite book." Sylvia laughed then looked up, a little uncomfortable, but Nathan's interest made her continue.

"Morgan loved space despite his expertise in archeology. He watched all the news stories during the space station expansions. Now here I am light-years beyond that Earth-orbiting system." Sylvia dropped her hand from her chain and glanced again at the photo. *Wondering who I am and if I want to know why my birth parents are gone.*

"It sounds like you were very loved," Nathan said, using the bedspread to push the photo away so he could sit. "We probably shouldn't touch that more till they can check it for prints."

Sylvia bit her lip, wanting to seize the photo and be done with it.

Nathan watched Sylvia's face. "Rosalind will be able to help teach you about the energy of your network. I suspect it is Intuit." He wiped a wrinkle out of the bedspread. "I don't know how much Rosalind is comfortable with me sharing with you about her damaged Intuit network, but you need to know there are answers."

"How do I hold the energy of the network?" Sylvia asked, remembering something Nathan had said earlier.

"I don't know exactly," Nathan said, standing and walking to lean against the door that went into the kitchenette area. "My knowledge of the system is as an integrated structure of the original Rainbane system which doesn't exist anymore. My research specializes in the Griffon network and the Immortal DNA. It's my understanding of the integrated networks of the Rainbane system that allows me to determine a lot from the neuro exam. The chemical impact doesn't allow the flow through between the networks like the Rainbane system — rather, you get spurts from each like epileptic firing without guidance."

Sylvia watched the excitement in his eyes as he spoke of something that intrigued his curious mind.

"In the original Rainbane system, the fifth network is the one that connects your energy to the outside world. The EvPs have that single fifth network. That's the one you used to stop me from transforming. The jolt of energy is like..." Nathan paused. "Directed power. Rainbanes were able to give purpose to the energy. You can read stories about it in the old Tokoleh histories because that control part goes through the Immortal network." Nathan ran his hand through his hair as if trying to think of something more familiar to her Earth sensibilities. "Have you ever seen someone cardioverted with those pads that shock a patient's chest in the ER?"

"Um...on TV, and in a training video when I took CPR."

"Well, that's kind of what you did, but the energy triggered a methylation process that shuts off the expression of genes. It's complicated and acutely triggers transduction signaling that ultimately impacts gene expression, but that's a concept of it."

"If you know this, you must have Rainbanes to study. How can they be extinct?"

Nathan shook his head and leaned his elbows on his knees. "No. We re-create it with chemistry." He held her eyes with his. "We make drugs that do it. That's why I'm the expert at determining when drugs — chemistry — tries to masquerade as something it isn't."

Sylvia stood, anxious about the chemical Xenos had identified on the willow bark. She had been excited at the fact that somehow, maybe, her intent played a role, even if she didn't understand what to do with that. Now, she realized it might all be the misfiring of bad chemistry. She took a deep breath. Maybe she could try controlling it. Then she'd prove it wasn't the poison triggering sporadic responses in mimicry. She pulled at the bedspread to straighten it, planning to head into the kitchen. The photo fell to the floor on the other side of the bed, where Nathan had pushed it toward the edge. She paused and looked back toward Nathan. He was watching her, so she forced her gaze to meet his.

Nathan stepped backward into the doorway. "We should probably leave this room so Houseman and Rosalind can check it. I can tell you more about what I know clinically of the Intuit network."

Sylvia knew he was right, but someone had taken the photo Kita had given her and replaced it with this one. *Maybe Kita herself,* Sylvia thought, for the first time remembering that Kita hadn't followed her down the stairs. Sylvia stepped toward the bed.

"There is a tangle of threads in an Intuit's mind called the Oscult," Nathan blurted.

Sylvia figured he was trying to distract her from the photo she now felt determined to see. "Fine," she said, turning her back to the photo.

"The test we will do this evening in clinic tells me the function of the Oscult and the network." He leaned his back to the doorframe rather than stepping through to the kitchen.

Sylvia could tell he felt bad that a part of him still didn't trust her completely.

"The MRI indicates you have the tangle, but the specialized test clarifies if the network is capable of Sahaja-level function."

"Sahaja," Sylvia said, "I remember you mentioning that. So, there are different levels of ability?"

"Yes, only Sahaja Intuits have both a functioning Oscult and network. Standard Intuits have a functioning network but can't use the Oscult."

"Is that a big deal?" Sylvia asked, closing her eyes to see the silver tangle she had come to consider her "complication." "What does it do?" She still felt the burn at her back, and she watched the tangle in her mind as a ribbon of orange coalesced around the silver, as if pulling it in and forming a border. She felt the burn in her back dwindle. Sylvia smiled. Was this closing the network? *Did I do it?* Sylvia thought. The orange all but disappeared. The headache she had been managing all day disappeared. She jumped with excitement. "I did it!" Sylvia opened her eyes and, unthinking, took Nathan's face in her hands to soften the hard line of his jaw as he watched her.

It was a mistake.

CHAPTER THIRTY

S YLVIA FELL AGAINST THE doorway. Her thoughts flashed crimson. The tangle in her mind seemed to be unwinding like a spool of thread, only more than one color of thread. Sylvia braced against the door and pressed her head into her hand. The ribbons of iridescent color broadened to form pictures. Dual images of the Bunker energy-generator room and her hotel room lay over one another like transparencies as she saw both simultaneously. The two pictures danced like a hazy dream, shifting from real to unreal and back as she struggled to claim just one as her own. She blinked, trying to push back the visions and focus on what she could see with her eyes, not her mind. Somehow, intuitively, she knew this was important, but she found it hard to think. Her headache returned with a vengeance, and she pinned her temples with her fingertips, bracing against whatever was at her back to keep her balance as she tried to focus.

[30.1]

In the Bunker EG room, Rosalind stumbled and took a knee, quick to scan the sector of the room before closing her eyes to look at the flickering crimson in her synapses arcing like electric current to the silver tangle that writhed in the back of her mind. Sylvia had touched her mind, which shouldn't be possible. *She has a functional Oscult*, Rosalind thought. Sylvia's dormant synapses opening too fast, without her having the skill to control them, could kill her or someone else. *Damn it, Nathan, I don't have time to save your ass.* Rosalind left the thought full of its unspoken energy, hoping it would connect to Sylvia's thoughts. Oscults were bidirectional regardless of who established them. *How did she enter the Oscult anteroom of my tangle without a memory? She must be Sahaja.* Rosalind bit back the remorse at the reminder that her network did not work properly. She must be careful if she taught Sylvia about the Intuit network and Oscult. She hadn't dealt with a Sahaja Intuit in years, and with her system flawed, she could accidentally give Sylvia access to her own mind. Rosalind consciously rejected the nudge from Sylvia's thought that tried to enter her mind. The thought circled in the Oscult anteroom of her memories, but she could not see it. She mentally paused, grateful her Oscult held. Nothing pressed into her tangle. Her Oscult functioned, for now, though her network never would.

First things first, Rosalind thought, standing to move past the wall of generators and electronics. Kita had been moving around through the old tunnel system. Rosalind stopped by the tunnel door. It was slightly ajar and tricky to perceive if you weren't looking for it. She didn't bother to lock it. She expected Kita to come back through and had more than a few questions. She rolled the small micro-fuel cell in her hand. Kita had placed it at the backside base of the column that formed the entry to the Umbilical Energy Portal section of the room. The fuel cell was full; it should no longer be pulling energy. She tapped her phone and pulled up the screen to check the pressure and temperature numbers while she waited. *Nathan, please don't get yourself killed or transformed,* she thought, frustrated at having to choose between her duty to the populace of two solar systems and her brother. Two message notifications flashed on the screen, and she checked them before opening the temperature and pressure readings. One was from Nathan, which she popped open and read as she walked back toward the corner to hide and wait. She had authorized Kita's release, but it would take a while for her to get here, so she had a few minutes. Rosalind squinted to read the text.

NATHAN: Someone stole the photo. Need you to investigate the room. We will wait for you here.

At least he's alive, Rosalind thought, preparing to respond to the text, then noted the time stamp. He had sent this before Sylvia had touched the Oscult in her mind. "Galactic dice!" Rosalind cursed, then touched the screen to open the second message. It was from the police at the hotel, probably letting her know Kita was released, so she left it to read later. She shifted her gaze from the hologram screen, checking the tunnel before risking more time with her screen up. The tunnel door was still pushed almost closed, just as it had been when she checked it earlier. She glanced past the tunnel door. From this back corner, she could see the iridescent shimmer of the security field between the columns that led to the energy Portal. There was a flicker on the other side. *What is that?* Rosalind closed the hologram screen to allow her eyes to readjust to the dark room. She squinted to see beyond the sheen of iridescent color fifty feet away.

Rosalind stood from her squat in the corner and passed the partially ajar tunnel entrance, uncomfortable to have it at her back. She shuddered but kept moving. She had planned to check this area after neutralizing Kita. However, the hair raised at the back of her neck as she approached, and her instincts pulled her to the columns. She twisted the ring she wore so the decorative triangle that allowed her to drop the column shield was now on the palm side. She squatted and placed her hand on the column base where the nested glyph glowed. The iridescent colors of the shield shifted as if flipping through a paint catalog. Each color flashed vibrantly, then disappeared, layer after layer. Rosalind fingered the taser at her waist but didn't remove it as she stepped between the columns to the energy Portal section. It created the base of the V-structured room. The Portal glowed with the usual blue light. However, looking to the left, she could see what caused the flicker she had noticed. The identical columns that shielded the room from the hotel side flickered orange and red, failing to form their usual shield of layered iridescent color. It was as if a fire glowed there instead, casting a strange flickering glow across the space. Her mind refocused. Something lay beyond the capacitor stone. The capacitor was solid stone with an enlarged version of the glyph pattern. It represented the First Energy of the Universe. *The Source*, Rosalind thought, touching each nesting pattern as they repeated one inside the other till they seemed to disappear at the center. The edge of the outermost design lay hidden beneath a torn strap.

The straps were there for Intuits to hold, not to be held — a physical connection for their human output from their Intuit transfer of energy. Rosalind's stomach lurched at the thought of what might have happened here, even as she moved toward the far end of the stone. The smell of sweat caught her first, then the body came into view, shoved completely off the back of the stone. It caught the flicker of the fire-colored light from the damaged shield. Rosalind rechecked the columns to make sure no one waited there. The columns flickered the residual colors of their failing shield. She, too, had failed. Her investigations now seldom involved death, but she never forgot the smell. It was acrid and grew stronger as she knelt at the capacitor. The blue haze of light from the Portal that cycled at her back cast an eerie shadow. It created a macabre dance with the orange column light that dappled the man's bare chest before her. She raised her T-shirt neck to cover her nose as she stepped around the stone capacitor and squatted to examine the body. The arm on this side had broken when this restraint didn't give with whatever force had shoved him. Rosalind fought the urge to release it and bowed her head.

What is going on? The ancient iron loops formed at the head-edges and foot-edges of the stone had been usually just used as braces by the Intuits when they had held energy to allow maintenance on the rooms. No one used the Rainbane straps anymore, as energy room calibration was a standard procedure now. *Not when energy is leaking from the room.* Rosalind shivered with a wave of thought. She squeezed the micro-fuel cell in her hand. She had failed. Kita had already been here. The entry had been from the hotel side; she would have to bring in the hotel police. Rosalind punched in the numbers for the hotel police department, then paused, clicking the second text that she still hadn't read. She scanned it as the call went through.

"Hello, Core Station Hotel police department..."

Rosalind didn't even let him get his name out. "This is Rosalind Mathing with UBN security. Get Lieutenant Houseman."

"Yes, ma'am."

The text appeared on her screen as the phone line hummed with music as the officer put her on hold. Rosalind scanned the text twice, glad she had opened it before Houseman came to the phone. The second text earlier had been from him.

HOUSEMAN: She refused release. She states she is a Tokoleh-trained EvP working with the Earth Alliance. She wants to speak with you. Either she trusts me and you to share this much info, or it's a trap. She is lying about something. Regardless, her refusal makes it your call.

"Rosalind."

The sound of her name from a familiar voice pulled her from the text, but her mind was still on it.

"Are you headed over?" he asked.

"Houseman," Rosalind replied, using his last name. She realized they had worked together so often and so long she would be hard-pressed to remember his first name. "I have a dead man in the Bunker EG room, and it sounds like my number one suspect is still in your holding cell."

"You got what?"

"Yeah. Get the intersectoral squad down here. I'll meet you on the hotel side to let you in. We're going to have to shut down the Umbilical. I can't risk putting a trained Intuit on that capacitor to regulate the energy in here till I know it's safe." *Is Nathan safe?* Rosalind thought even as she considered that she would have to postpone helping him if she followed this lead. *Everyone has to do their job right now,* Rosalind reminded herself as she moved toward the failing shield between the columns that should have blocked the entrance to the Portal from the hotel side. Despite its apparent failure, it still flickered with enough energy to hinder the intersectoral team.

Intersectoral teams were small, fast, and built with the talents that represented each species. Rosalind met Team Four at the hotel side vault lock. Houseman took Rosalind's report, now complete with temperature readings, pressure fluctuations, and a first-on-scene description. This gave Houseman a head start on the investigation but kept Rosalind connected to it.

"You don't have to bring in the intersectoral team to stay in the loop," Houseman said. "You're almost as good of an investigator as me. I don't mind sharing."

"Please. Like you could tell the difference between a crime scene and your office desk without me."

Houseman laughed. "At least you cut through the jurisdiction red tape."

Rosalind nodded, understanding the implied request. "I'm going to speak to this 'EvP' you have in custody," she said, making air quotes around the term. "Keep me posted."

"She refused to answer our questions," Houseman said, growling when his glove tore. He reached for another. "She wouldn't even give us her name but said if you didn't want the Umbilical from the Fifth Sector shut down, you better come see her. I didn't press her because I knew you had a plan, and you usually respect mine." The second glove tore as he placed his large hand in it. "Now this..." he said, waving at the scene before them and pocketing the torn gloves. He reached for the X-large glove box.

"I'll head there now," Rosalind said, knowing what Houseman was getting at. He had left some rope for Rosalind by offering to release the woman, and he hoped it didn't hang them both. She pushed her fear for Nathan and Sylvia to the back of her mind again. She hoped leaving them together didn't end with one or both of them dead. Rosalind looked again at the crimson hue of the synapses Sylvia had touched in her mind. They still hummed with the excess neurotransmitter, but the color was gone. She didn't want to think about what happened. *One piece of the puzzle at a time,* she thought as she strode from the room and into the hotel.

[30.2]

Sylvia's hands pressed to her chest as if by force she could slow its beat. Her breathing was better now, but she still leaned against the doorframe with her eyes closed. The red-layered vision of the Bunker room was gone, but her head swam, and she felt nauseous. She opened her eyes to focus her thoughts on the hotel room. She replayed the moment she had touched Nathan's face.

Heat had flashed in her hands and burned in her mind, streaming like lava in her spine. Nathan's hungry eyes glowed like an amber sun. Sylvia held the burn in her spine. She had savored the fire, though she was certain she was going to die. Nathan's hands had taken hers, pushing them to the small of her back as if they could recapture the heat that ran in her spine as he pulled her to him. His neck had smelled clean, with the hint of leaves and earth. Sylvia had breathed him in when her cheek brushed his neck. It all happened so fast. She had reached for the tangle, trying to touch it even as her lips brushed Nathan's neck. The low, needy growl from Nathan she had felt as a vibration against her lips made her core tingle even now. Then, the pain. *Not my pain*, she recalled with the thought. *Nathan wanted me. Why did that cause him pain?*

Then the cascade of crimson had happened, the shadow of the Bunker room in her thoughts, and Rosalind's words had come back to her: *If he transforms to protect you, he fails another.*. In that moment, Nathan had jerked away, lunging into the kitchen.

Sylvia looked for him now, finding him gripping the raised tile edges of the kitchen floor, panting and drenched as if a fever had broken. Nathan looked up at her. She stood in the doorway now, staring at her hands, thinking she would see the fire in them because it had left through them as quickly as it had come, tearing from her like recaptured life as it circled back to Nathan. He hadn't jerked from her. She had pushed him, shoved him with the energy in her hands. Tears formed, and her hands blurred as she covered her face. "What did I do? I'm so sorry."

A knock at the door pulled their attention. *Great, Rosalind's here just in time to see us wrecking her investigation scene.* "I'll get it."

[30.3]

Nathan shifted to stand as Sylvia crossed to the door. "It's not your fault. You're still learning how to move and hold energy. I shouldn't have..." The words were lost in the shame he felt at his inability to fight his attraction to her. *It's my fault. That kiss brushing my neck,* Nathan thought, closing his eyes. *It can't happen.*

Elizabeth had transformed into a feral beast trying to save him. He had to find a way to bring her back, and he needed to be a doctor to Sylvia. *Damn it.* In many ways, she was so much like Elizabeth. He often felt she was near when Sylvia had her network open. *Strong Sahaja Intuits can do that because their pull on the external world is so strong,* Nathan reminded himself as he regained his focus. *But what she does still feels different somehow.*

"Oh, hello?" Sylvia said, then her voice dropped to a more quiet conversation.

Nathan watched as Sylvia leaned her shoulder on the open door as she peered at whoever was on the other side. Her surprise pulled his attention. *It's not Rosalind.*

Nathan moved to stand beside Sylvia and was startled to see a boy, probably ten or eleven years old. His hand tapped the top of the book that Sylvia's hand now held with almost reverence.

"Okay. I understand. Thank you, Cajal." Sylvia pulled the book to her chest. "Why did they send it by you?"

"Tessa wanted to stay with Jezel for her treatment."

"Yes, but I thought you said you helped in one of the labs. Is Jezel in a laboratory, not the hospital?"

The boy started to fidget, and Nathan wanted to help him out. It could be difficult to explain how the hospital was connected to the research facility labs. Then, it dawned on him that he didn't recognize the boy. "Which lab do you help in?"

"I'm new, so you wouldn't know me." He pulled on his cap, snugging it down on his head and making the curls spring out beneath it. "I'd better go."

He turned and almost sprinted down the hallway.

"That was strange," Nathan said, leaning out the door briefly.

"Yes, maybe he was just nervous." Sylvia turned from the door, tracing the spine of the book. "It was a big responsibility Tessa gave him to deliver an Archive book this old."

Nathan pushed the door closed.

"Why did Tessa—"

Sylvia held up a hand. "Can I just have a few minutes?"

"Certainly, here, sit down." He pulled out the barstool at the counter. *She is not Elizabeth, and she can't help you return Elizabeth from her Griffon form if you forget that.* Nathan stepped clear of the counter so that she could get by. *Why does the pull to her have to be so strong?* He carefully entered the bedroom, deciding to grab the picture and her book without disturbing anything else. Rosalind had not responded to his text. Sylvia was powerful even having only patchy areas of her network functioning. She could possibly turn the tide of his research. She was certainly unique, and that, in any species, usually created discovery for everyone.

[30.4]

Sylvia was seated on the barstool. Her legs dangled, free of the rungs.

"Here is the picture and your book," Nathan said, placing the photograph on top of the book and sliding it across the granite counter. "I need to shower.

When I come out, will you tell me why an Immortal and her Life Companion are sending you books they have secured from the archives?"

It was only then that Sylvia realized how hot the room was. She bit her lip. "I did this, didn't I?" she asked, dodging his question. "Created this heat, I mean."

Nathan cuffed his sleeves again, then looked up at her. Sylvia could see the sweat at his back. "The uncontrolled release of energy creates a lot of heat." Nathan paused. "It's common when Intuits are learning to move energy between their network and the human one that allows all species to touch the world. Lucky for me, you don't have all five networks functioning. If that much uncontrolled energy came through an EvP network able to touch the external world, I'd be dead." Nathan walked through the doorway to the bedroom.

"Did I hurt you?"

Sylvia heard Nathan pause and sensed he was near the bathroom. She could no longer see him but could picture him standing with his arm braced at the bathroom door, that serious thoughtfulness on his face.

"I'm fine. It's my fault, too," he finally said.

Sylvia felt a tear and wiped it with a napkin from the counter, glad when Nathan changed the subject.

"I've ordered a suit, but I'll come answer the door. I'll have to sign for it since I'm in your room."

Sylvia heard the familiar beep of the room service panel to the right of the bathroom. Everything here read the biometric codes from the injected chip.

"Okay," Sylvia said, her elbows and arms on the granite as she leaned over the counter to view the picture. *He's my doctor*, Sylvia reminded herself. The conflict she felt reminded her of the hope and fear she had after meeting with Tessa and Jezel. The fear of learning more almost forced her to turn away from her book and the photo. *What would be in a picture left for me to find?* Sylvia paused in her half lean over the counter, feeling the Archive book in her hand press almost painfully into her stomach. *Nathan is a species specialist. That's why he is treating Jezel.* Sylvia felt the panic grow with her racing heart. The picture had been left in her robe pocket to find when she was alone. *Maybe I should wait for Nathan*, Sylvia thought, then chastised herself. "Only you can do this," she said, then sat back on the stool when she noticed she was shaking despite her words. *No wonder I keep pushing Nathan's buttons*, she thought, looking across the counter at the book with the photograph visible but not viewable from her seat. *I feel so vulnerable here.* Sylvia twisted the chain at her neck, hearing some noise from the bathroom. *I've got to do this before he comes out.* She laid the Archive book down gently and reached out to pull her book toward her, letting her eyes focus on her book and the Archive book, sliding the photograph to the side out of view. *One piece at a time.*

Tessa had marked a page with a sheet of paper and some notes, and it was strange that despite the evidence of the intrusion upon the book, the dust was not disturbed. *Feels like my life.* So much of her life had been poked and exposed, but it seemed as if a veil, like the dust on the book, remained over all that was her, and even she was afraid to disturb it. The thought of a veil reminded her about the woman in the tight astronaut suit she had felt so connected to. She opened her book to the page where she had tucked the veil map. She pulled it free and placed it over the unfolded map in her original book. This was where she had hidden things, even from herself. Now, it was time to find answers. *Why am I so afraid?*

She opened the Archive book to the page Tessa had marked and ran her finger along the glyphs. She watched a ribbon of color flow from the tangle in her mind. The first glyph was familiar, one she recalled from the corner page drawing for one of the Lost Cities in her book. A Lost City that might be Jezel's home. It was a number, just as Tessa had said, and she typed it in her phone. She felt nauseous but pressed on. She flipped from the map page in her book to that very page that held the hieroglyphs Tessa and Jezel said could be translated from the Archive's ancient Tokoleh book she now held in her hands. The vision flooded her mind: red eyes, white teeth, and a feral smile. The face was distorted as if she was underwater. *I can't breathe!* Sylvia's mind protested, but she pressed on translating the next three glyphs to numbers with one hand on the Archive page and one steadied on the page in her book. *I can hold on. I can bear it.* She matched the Tokoleh glyph from the Archive book with the glyph she had drawn in her book. *Another number.* She felt her chest tighten.

I need air, please! The voice in her mind was her own, but that of a child, and she felt the tears. "I can't." She shoved the books away, and the ribbon in her mind snapped back to the tangle, pulling the red-eyed vision with it as if it had been the very band around her chest. Sylvia gasped for air as her hands braced on the countertop. Sweat beaded at her neck and forehead. She took two heaving breaths and tapped out the numbers on her phone so she wouldn't forget them. Her arms trembled, and she mistyped twice. She blinked back the tears. Five numbers. She cautiously pulled her book back to her. Two more glyphs remained.

She reached to her left, where her laptop from the morning lay. She turned it toward her and typed in the numbers from her phone. If Tessa was correct and she had written down the latitude lines for the manor, then there was more hidden in her mind than she realized. *Five numbers,* Sylvia thought as she typed them in, asking the Rompnet to find the coordinate. The computer pinged, but it was obvious the five digits would not be enough. She would have to finish the translation to know if what she had written from her imagination was actual coordinates for a place Jezel called the manor — a place where one of the Portal keys had once been hidden. She didn't want to do this. There was such incredible realness to the experiences that came with the vision. *It is okay to be afraid; just find the courage to move forward.* The voice that she heard in her mind was her father's. She knew it now. She breathed deeply and traced her hand along the page from the top corner to the bottom corner, where another set of glyphs taunted her with the effort it would take to finish the entire translation. "It has to be done," Sylvia said to herself. The ribbon from the tangle in her mind began to unspool, but she was pleased to get the final number and N for north translated from the top glyphs before the weight of the vision engulfed her again.

Sylvia focused now on the glyphs in the lower right corner of her book. Two were glyphs similar to numbers she had already translated, so she skipped over those, pressing her hand and her focus on the Archive book to help her translate the rest. She blew out a steadying breath, prepared for the onslaught as the ribbon of color formed the whole vision in her mind. She was screaming, her hands flared against the sides of a stone basin, her feet too short to reach the bottom of the liquid that covered her to her waist. Red eyes glowed so close to her face that she couldn't distinguish the features. She turned her head toward the hand that pried her fingers free. Her eyes seemed to focus on the tattoo, or maybe it was a burn on the wrist of the arm that pulled at her fingers. She could feel energy coursing through her, and for a moment, it was as if she could use the power to fight back, but it wasn't enough, and then she was beneath the liquid. The numbers came fast in her mind like they were pulled through her memory, not even requiring translation as if sucked into her thoughts by the vacuum her body made in the liquid. The red eyes glowed again, distant and beyond the liquid she now instinctively knew was not water. Sylvia let the liquid surround her, let it take her. It became part of her, and she no longer breathed. There was no way to cry, but her heart felt the tears. She was alone and afraid.

The scream was more energy than sound, and Sylvia shook her head as she fought the last tendrils of the vision. The room was hot and as foggy as a steam room. *Did Nathan leave the bathroom door open?* Sylvia looked down at the granite where she gripped the counter edge, fingers splayed atop the stone. There was new veining in a pattern that ran from her left hand to the Archive book and from her right hand to her book. Both books were open, with pages flipping in a movement of air that only now seemed to be settling. Numbers circled in her mind as if released by a wild ride and bouncing around aimlessly but in an order that was consistent. She quickly tapped them into her phone before turning to the laptop, prepared to plug them into a search engine for latitude and longitude lines. She traced the new veining on the countertop. She didn't understand it yet, but she had done that. She had impacted her physical environment with her energy.

She slumped back on the stool, feeling the weight of it. She had altered stone. How much more dangerous would she be to people? She closed her eyes. The remembrance of the vision caused a shudder along her spine, but it seemed distant right now. "You made progress," she whispered to herself, though she felt hollow with the discovery. She found the fear that held her memories captive and took a slow, deep breath. "But it's a fear that threatens to break my mind if I try to navigate the pain of it." Sylvia closed her eyes against the tears that threatened. And that was it. There was real danger in it. *Only I can face it, and I have to choose.*

Shuffling sounds from the bathroom reminded her of Nathan's proximity, and she remembered the photo. She didn't fully understand her pull to Nathan, her instant connection with the astronaut, her concern for Xenos and Kinley, and her guilt over the people who'd lost their lives searching for coordinates, but these people mattered to her. She had made an unconscious decision to be invisible, and in doing so, people were dying. *One must accept something in order to change it.* Sylvia crumpled to the floor at the words. The voice was undeniably her mother's, and she knew it now like her own. "I haven't heard your voice in years," Sylvia whispered as she traced the design in the wood of the island bar's wall. She accepted that she had made decisions that kept her hidden because someone had found her once, and it had been painful. If she pushed through to find herself, it would draw attention. Now, she had to decide whether she was willing to face the risk. She put her back to the wall, feeling sheltered for a moment by her mother's voice and the overhang of the granite countertop. "Am I willing to change myself and let my life follow that change?"

Sylvia pressed her palms together, feeling the press of her own strength, then relaxed them to lie open, palm up on her lap. There was no tremor now. "I'll be afraid again, Mom. And I'll find the courage to press on, Dad. Thank you for loving me enough that the kernel of its truth remains even when squeezed and hidden by pain." Sylvia reached for the barstool to stand. *My book isn't fiction. The coordinates are real.* She hadn't plugged the numbers in on the laptop, but on her phone note, it was evident the numbers were a latitude north and longitude west. It was just a matter of typing them in to see if they brought up Jezel's manor.

There was more distant movement now in the bedroom. Sylvia stood carefully and turned, searching the counter for the photo. "There is a spare robe in the closet," she said, realizing he had probably been taking extra long in the bathroom waiting for his suit to arrive.

She fingered the photo without looking at it, then pulled it into view. She relaxed a little as the scene formed, and she recognized the large machine that seemed to occupy the most space in the photo. It appeared similar, but not identical, to Jezel's cryo-regen. Her stomach lurched. "Is this something I should recognize?" Sylvia fingered the photo and relaxed a little. There were no dead, twisted, or dismembered bodies. An arm was reaching from the corner of the photo, but it appeared to be attached to someone just reaching in while the photo was being shot. Sylvia scanned the photo from right to left, the cryo-regen tanning bed. Sylvia smiled, recalling Tessa's laugh at her first calling it that. The glyphs were familiar. "Why did someone leave this photo for me?" She forced her eyes back to the arm in the photo.

Sylvia lifted the photo, tilting her head. The arm reaching into the image was lifting something from a small box located on a nondescript table near the cryo-regen. Sylvia pulled the photo closer, then dropped it, and half fell, half stumbled off the stool away from the counter.

CHAPTER THIRTY-ONE

S YLVIA JUMPED AGAIN WHEN the doorbell buzzed. She buried the squeak with gritted teeth. She could not be afraid. "Nathan can't test me if I can't control...what had he called it?" Sylvia's words were a whisper to herself as she thought, *emotional energy*. She took a deep breath, recognizing the burn in her spine. She had new determination, but changing behavior was challenging. *The Griffon network's strength is its connection to the limbic system. It is primitive passion and drive.* She recalled Nathan's words from their conversation on the way to the room. Sylvia bit back a laugh, remembering Nathan catching himself mid-sentence: *"Fight, flight, or fu..."* He had not finished the sentence. Sylvia figured he realized he was simplifying the network's strength a little too much for a doctor-patient relationship, but she needed to understand the Griffon network better. She considered texting Kinley, but she was standing near the wall in her effort to escape the picture and her phone was on the counter.

Nathan appeared at the bedroom doorway and walked past the kitchen toward the door. Sylvia was glad he had told her he would answer it. Maybe she didn't look like such a fool for just standing here.

"Did you find a connection?" Nathan asked, his back to her as she stood near the wall, feeling the curtains brush the back of her pants. The sensation sparked a color in her mind, but it evaporated before she could fully see it. The burn in her back was easing, but every moment made her feel a ripple of each network, not one. Maybe there was something in Nathan's hypothesis about drugs. *I need to speak with Xenos about the effect of wolfsbane.* The thought made her absently touch her pocket where she kept her phone. She was grateful to see that habit must have made her lift it from the counter when she startled. *Kinley will be with*

Xenos. "Um, let's discuss it when you're done. No rush," she said, swallowing. *I need you to have clothes on.*

Nathan looked briefly at her over his robed shoulder, "So, you did?" He sounded excited, then turned back to scribble a signature and tap the holograph screen in the man's hand with his chip-injected finger. The man disappeared.

Nathan's hair was drying fast. Waves of curl slipped from behind his ears as it dried. Sylvia tried not to notice. "I'm...not sure, but I think I recognize something in the photo," Sylvia said, recalling the image. *Had it actually been...* The question collapsed in her thoughts, and she realized she was staring at Nathan's smooth chest, partially exposed by the complimentary robe, open to the waist where it tied.

Nathan stared back at her from the door. "Sorry." He lifted the new suit hanging in its clear plastic bag.

"Did you recognize the photo?" Sylvia asked, trying to change the subject. He had seemed excited, but now he was guarded again.

"No," Nathan said, moving into the bedroom. "I recognize the equipment, but I didn't get a good look at the picture."

Sylvia leaned at the counter, not seated, tapping a text on her phone before reaching for the photo.

SYLVIA: Can an Intuit hear thoughts dropped in the Griffon...

Sylvia paused, trying to recall the word Nathan had used

SYLVIA: ...commune? And will you ask Xenos if wolfsbane can cause the human network

to mimic the five network species? Nathan wants to do a neuro exam and...

The clank of a hanger drew her attention, and she hit send. She looked up. Nathan's visible arm slid into the crisp white shirt, and he had two buttons fastened when he stepped into the doorway in his black pleated pants.

"I'll wait till you're dressed," she said, looking down at the photo and feeling hot again. She covered the small box just inches from the hand, reaching into the picture. *How do you control emotion when every sensation is so intense?*

"Go ahead," Nathan said, pulling the jacket from its hanger and laying it over one of the bar chairs when he stepped into the kitchen.

"What does this look like to you?" she asked, pulling her finger away from the photo after tapping the area where the chain dangled from the box's rim.

Nathan cocked his head to see it better as he rounded the counter. "A necklace of some kind," he said, then froze.

Sylvia's hands, so accustomed to twisting the chain at her neck, defiantly gripped the counter's edge.

Nathan took the photo, and Sylvia kept her eyes glued to him.

"There are probably lots of chains and charms like that. But..." He glanced at her neck and back to the photo. "Do you think it is yours?"

Sylvia didn't answer, but she had the charm in her hand as she focused on the counter.

"I want to do your neuro exam while we wait for Rosalind," Nathan said quietly. "The chaos has us behind schedule, and I want to get your scan in this evening." He laid the photo down. "We can look at this closer with Rosalind's magnification lens."

Sylvia sat and squeezed her legs at the ping of feeling she had with the thought of him touching her. It mixed with the uncertainty of the photo, and she almost collapsed on the counter.

Nathan reached to touch her but pulled away.

Color danced across the tangle in Sylvia's mind, pulling to her spine. She gasped as she watched the color shift up her spine and roll out of view as if it had fallen into a well. *The tangle. The color pulled into my tangle.* Nathan had reached for her then pulled back. She was starting to recognize patterns in her network and tangle. *What is it you want, Nathan Renner?* Sylvia thought. She recognized the chemistry between them, but she still sensed there was something — rather someone — that held Nathan, though he said Rosalind was his sister. *Find out what he wants,* Sylvia thought, just as her phone pinged.

Nathan was laying items on the counter. Sylvia suspected they were for the exam, so she checked her phone.

KINLEY: A Sahaja Intuit can sometimes connect with the Griffon commune via an individual Griffon, but Xenos wants to speak to you and Nathan if you are willing for Nathan to share your medical information in the context of the conversation.

The text hit her like a ton of bricks. *Nathan needs to know my skill as an Intuit because of the connection I seem to have with the Griffon network.* The cold sensation of being used for his Griffon research rather than wanting to help her coursed through her, and she felt nauseous. *Two can play that game,* Sylvia thought, forcing herself to sit straight in the bar chair, then berating herself for her feelings of rejection that spurred the anger. The luxurious fabric cushioned her back, and Sylvia closed her eyes when it caused color to trace the sensation through her spine and to the tangle in her mind. "Xenos wants to speak with us.

Will he be able to call my phone from Amrita?" Sylvia asked, opening her eyes and noting Nathan's gaze as she rolled the planet's name over in her thoughts: *Amrita*. She sensed once again a forgotten familiarity.

Nathan looked away and cuffed his sleeve. "If I share the satellite signal from my ringphone, he can," he said, tapping some feature on his ring.

Damn it. I see it in his eyes, Sylvia thought, reevaluating her analysis. *He feels what I feel.* "Where is Rosalind?" New worry about doing this without her as a buffer made Sylvia swallow hard.

"She should be here shortly," Nathan said as Sylvia typed Nathan's answer to Kinley.

Nathan paused, straightening the Q-tips on the counter. "What is Xenos calling about?"

Sylvia started to hedge when her phone rang. She tapped the green button and hit speakerphone. "Hi, Xenos. Nathan and I are here. Are your concerns about the wolfsbane?" Sylvia asked, wanting to ensure Nathan knew she wasn't hiding anything.

"Hello, Sylvia." Xenos cleared his throat.

Sylvia wondered how much the man suffered from both his cancer and its treatment.

"Yes, I wanted to mention a detail about wolfsbane to Nathan."

There was a pause as Kinley spoke in the background. "Also, let Sylvia know Michael confirmed that it was wolfsbane on the willow bark."

"Correct." Xenos said, repeating Kinley's words and adding, "The batch that arrived with your books had a significantly higher concentration."

"Why?" Sylvia asked immediately, her mind racing through what it all meant. Her mom had given her the willow bark for her headaches that started after her friend died in the tomb. "My mom is a botanist at the university. She wouldn't have added anything to it to harm me."

Nathan spoke up. "Wolfsbane could have naturally contaminated the willow bark if your mom was collecting in an area where it grew."

"That is certainly a possibility for the first batch," Xenos added, sounding hesitant. "However, the batch you found stored with your books had a concentration high enough to block network activation regions." Xenos paused, and Sylvia sensed he was letting her and Nathan process the information before saying more.

She didn't understand what that meant entirely, but the wide eyes and step back Nathan took from her made Sylvia wrap her arms around her waist and stare at the picture on the counter. "The wolfsbane blocks the activation of my network, and now that I'm not using it, my network is activating."

Nathan gripped the counter. "They used it in the war, didn't they?"

"Yes," Xenos said, his answer quiet and solemn.

Nathan looked at her, and Sylvia reached for her necklace but stopped, recalling the photo and feeling like she could trust none of her patterns.

"It would explain why it appears you have patchy areas along five networks."

"Five networks?" Xenos and Kinley said in surprised unison.

Sylvia watched Nathan's eyes, determined to read what was in them as he spoke. She was grateful he didn't look away but held her stare.

"I haven't completed her scan. I was preparing to do a neurologic exam before we headed to the clinic this evening. We have to consider the possibility..."

Sylvia watched his lips form a hard line, her eyes willing him to continue. Instead, he asked. "How soon will you and Kinley be returning from Amrita?"

"Sylvia," Xenos said.

Sylvia stared at her phone lying on the counter near the simple items Nathan had laid out for her neuro exam. She swallowed hard, thinking about the colors she would see at the touch of the feathery wisp of cotton and wondering anew what it all meant. "Yes, I'm here." Sylvia closed her eyes and braced her hands against the cold of the granite countertop, letting the cool sensation flow through her. This testing of Nathan's would help her know more about what was evolving within her. Yet, the thought of him so close when she felt so vulnerable made her sick with fear of what she might do. The worst was not knowing. "What is it that Nathan does not want to say?"

"We've found a link to Coriolis here," Xenos answered. "One of the reasons it has been so important to me to track down one of the most notorious criminals of the war is the almost certain extinction we were sure he caused in his vendetta against the Rainbane Reborn bloodline."

When Xenos paused, Nathan added, "The only bloodline to carry all five networks."

What if I do have five networks? I can't control even one. What if I just kept hurting people with this...brokenness, Sylvia thought, realizing for the first time that though she knew now her synesthesia wasn't a complication of some terrible disease, it was the hallmark of a power she didn't understand. "You don't know for sure, though," she said quickly. "It still may just be one network and not even a good one, right?"

"It is possible," Nathan said, but his tone was flat, as if his mind didn't even know it had given an answer.

"We can be back at the GCS in twenty-four hours," Xenos said.

"You are a good person, Sylvia," Kinley added as if he could see through the phone and sense her fear.

Sylvia stared from the phone to the photo, realizing she knew little about who she really was. Sylvia sat back on the chair, her initial excitement about learning more of herself collapsing in her previous thought about Nathan wanting to use her skill. *Is that even more real now? What is his interest in helping me? Who would try to block my network activation?* Sylvia let the thought hang as she snuck a glance at Nathan as he worked to shift a few of the items on the counter. She tried to recall the day's events. Rosalind's words about Nathan being unable to help someone else if he helped her. *What does that mean?* The answer seemed to be there when she looked at his eyes as he approached her. *He loves someone very much and...I am dangerous to that even if I can help him, and even as he tries to help me,* she thought, a little ashamed that the thought made her feel good because it meant he wasn't using her. And then, the question was there. "Am I a lot like her?" Sylvia asked.

CHAPTER THIRTY-TWO

ROSALIND PUSHED AWAY FROM the stone wall in Kita's holding cell, where she had leaned with one robotic heel pressed to the wall. The holding facility Houseman had used for Kita was a three-sided Prism-Light room with only one solid stone wall. They usually used it to restore energy for their own EvPs. Houseman hoped to prove or disprove the woman was an EvP. It was difficult for EvPs to resist taking in the light, especially if they were exhausted from mass shifting. However, Kita had not so much as even touched one of the lines of light. She still sat on the cot, her elbows on her knees with hands hanging comfortably but at the ready.

Rosalind nodded at Kita and left the cell, sliding the steel framed door closed, careful the lock didn't engage. The steel framework of the room ran around the floor and ceiling like a track and projected the Prism-Light. Kita had given her a lot to think about. She was either not an EvP, or she was a Sahaja EvP and one of the strongest she had ever met if she could sit that calmly in a three-wall Prism-Light room. Regardless, what Kita did now would answer the rest of Rosalind's questions. It was a considerable risk, but it had to be done. Now, she needed to investigate Sylvia's room. She quickly texted Houseman for a status report on the Bunker room. Sylvia's keys were looped over Rosalind's right index finger. They bumped her left hand as she tried to type on the laser-projected keyboard on the back of her hand.

She headed to the elevator. Nathan would be fine. He had a healthy respect for what an Intuit could do.

[32.1]

"We can do this at the office later," Nathan said, covering the items on the counter to slide them off and put them away. A pattern glowed on his ring, indicating a message.

"No. Do it now." Sylvia reached to stop his hand but paused before touching him. She looked down at her hands as if they were foreign, then reached for the copy of her book, pulling it to her on the counter. She opened it, flipping through the pages, intent. It was difficult to realize she had written this book, drawing relic keys and locks, creating imaginary places, and designing glyph art, not knowing consciously that it already existed. No wonder people didn't believe she had no coordinates for the Lost City. *Cities,* she thought, pulling her phone close to review the text she had received from Kinley earlier but had refused to believe.

KINLEY: Xenos says the proper translation of your glyph is cities, not city.

Sylvia closed her eyes. *Jezel's story of the manor must be true.* She stared at her palms, now turned up in her lap. She willed them to reach out and open the book. She reached the page, unable to look at the glyphs drawn there. She took a deep breath and scanned the page. She needed the text from the archives to translate the rest of the glyphs, but her gut told her Tessa was right. She had the latitude and longitude lines, and she would translate the rest later. She pulled the photo over and let out the groan that had been trapped in her throat. She may not have recognized the picture, but Nathan said it was a room here at the Galactic Core Station. The question was, had she been there before? She looked up at Nathan, "I...I need to call my publicist." Sylvia said, closing the book with the photo tucked inside.

"Meki?" Nathan stammered, shoving his hands in his pockets.

Sylvia watched him, seeing their progress of trust take two steps back.

"Damn it," Nathan cursed under his breath. "What does Meki have to do with this?"

"I showed him the other picture. Now that it's been stolen, I'm afraid I may have forgotten..." She looked down at the chain she twisted back and forth at her neck. "He can help ensure I don't forget anything about it when Rosalind arrives." Sylvia looked up at Nathan, asking for understanding. Asking him not to lose his trust in her.

Nathan's ring chirped. "It might be a message from Rosalind." He tapped the ring to see the message. "Rosalind is on her way now." He reached out to Sylvia, stopping just inches away. The pain in his eyes was a visible weight she could read as easily as she could see the amber. He wanted to trust her, but there was doubt.

She looked down at his hand on the counter, inches from her arm. He lifted his hand and closed the distance.

"I want us to be friends, at least."

White-hot fire leapt through Sylvia's thoughts, racing through her spine at his touch. "Nathan." She gasped with the sense of heat and loss. She pulled back on the energy with her thoughts, closing every outlet of expression down.

Nathan gripped the counter, his chest heaving once as he bore the force of the small, quick energy release. "That wasn't as bad."

Sylvia knocked the barstool over in her haste to get down and back away. "I'm afraid of what I've forgotten." She felt the wall at her back and savored it as she forced back tears. She clenched the fabric of the curtain in her right hand and could feel her pulse pounding in her neck. "Afraid of who I am."

Nathan regained his poise. "Meki knows these things?"

"Meki has been my friend, publicist." Sylvia paused, realizing how strange much of her life really was. "He knew my family — my adopted family, before..." Sylvia let her eyes focus on the wide crown molding around the ceiling and door behind Nathan. *What had Meki told me when he offered to be my publicist?* Her name had come up in a publisher's meeting. He had asked to meet her because he had known her adopted family. Had he known her father, Morgan? She paused, trying to think. It wasn't a memory barricaded by the vision. She just never really thought about it.

"He knew your adopted father before the family adopted you?"

"He knew Morgan's brother before he died," Sylvia said, finally recollecting the information and wondering for the first time at how quickly he'd become a friend of the entire family. It didn't matter now. He had, and she was glad. She let the rest of the story fall away. "He can help me put this together without hurting anyone."

"Is that why he came with you?"

"I think so," Sylvia said, her elbows on the counter and her head in her hands.

"You don't know?"

"I don't know anything!" She gestured with her arms wide, but her moist eyes belied her anger. "Someone wrote on the back of the photo, and all I can make out from the smudge is 'home,' but I've never seen the place before, and who would call cryo home? I think Meki thought coming here and seeing you would help."

Nathan sat the stool upright and adjusted the seat. "I'm sorry," he said. "I realize how harsh my words must have sounded. Come sit down. The exam will help us understand some of it."

"We can't," Sylvia said, backing farther into the wall. "Every time you touch me, I feel...I...don't even know what it is, but I can't."

"I think you have opened your Oscult and all five networks now," Nathan said.

His tone was matter-of-fact, but she felt she was standing between two worlds, with one represented by the wall at her back with a curtain that brushed her elbow. She wanted to hide behind it like a child who thought everything would disappear if she couldn't see it. Another world seemed represented by the seat Nathan tapped. The former beckoned her to hide. The latter asked her to trust. The two worlds diverged like paths that would never cross again — she had to choose. Sylvia soothed her brittle nerves and reached for the soft texture of silk upholstery that swathed the stool. *Am I trusting you, or me?* Sylvia thought as she stepped toward trust.

[32.2]

Nathan's ring pinged. He tapped it, and Rosalind's voice spoke.

"You answered, so you're alive?" Rosalind said, and the line clicked off.

Sylvia stared at Nathan's green eyes. "You're struggling. I see the flux of amber in your eyes and your grip is about to crack the counter."

Nathan closed his eyes and relaxed his grip on the counter. "I've been doing this for years. I'm better than this beast that lurks in my DNA."

"Why do you consider the Griffon part of yourself as less? We're just in over our heads right now. That doesn't make some part of you unworthy of connection."

Nathan focused on his ring. He couldn't listen to her words. They needled at a crack in the walls he had built. He tapped his ring, and Rosalind's voice sounded on the other end.

"Five minutes," Rosalind said and disconnected again before Nathan could answer.

"Let's get started," Nathan said. His professional smile was forced, but he could do this. He had to do this. He felt more comfortable knowing Rosalind was on her way, but Sylvia's unanswered question hung in his mind: *Am I a lot like her?*

She was, in some ways, Nathan considered. Things like his initial, almost instant attraction to her, which had happened the same way with Elizabeth. Her quiet strength... Nathan shook his head, realizing the memories of Elizabeth the thought fostered. He wanted answers — Sylvia proved there were things about the different species they still didn't understand — but would that get Elizabeth back, or was she lost to him? Researching Sylvia and her condition, just like the other species, would give him answers, but could he get those answers and survive without transforming or wanting her more than he already did? Nathan stared at the counter. *You are a professional. You swore an oath to help each species.*

He felt guilty for not answering her question, but what do you say? *Um, yes. And I'm very attracted to you and have been from the first moment I saw you, but I happen to love a woman who is now a feral beast.* It was too much for him to reveal, let alone something Sylvia could handle right now. He needed to temper his protective instincts and focus on the work. His mother's words strengthened his thoughts: "Make good choices, son," she would say with a soft smile when he found himself in a hard place. Just her belief in him that he would had always made him feel better able to do just that. He ran his hands through his hair. He wished she were still here. He reached for the wisp of cotton to test the level of Sylvia's sense of touch and felt the pull from Sylvia as her network flared.

CHAPTER THIRTY-THREE

S YLVIA TRIED TO FOCUS on the team of people that bustled in her suite and not notice Nathan standing so close. The first few tests, he had told her, were neurologic exams. She was glad Rosalind had arrived. She had a calming effect on Nathan and, thereby, indirectly, her. She closed her eyes, watching the colors in her mind that reflected the sounds around her. The colors danced between the tangle at the back of her mind and her spine.

"Sylvia," Nathan said. "You're focusing on the sounds in the room. I can tell by the change in your facial expression."

"Sorry," Sylvia said, opening her eyes, pleased to see Nathan had stepped back a little. His face was drawn, and his eyes appeared distant. She didn't think it was her this time. Her network felt better. She made a mental note that focusing on sounds and watching the colors they produced seemed to help her network find a balance. Sylvia scanned the room, associating people with the sounds she had been hearing. The soft rustle of fabric to her right had been the man on the floor just beyond the sofa. His white coat looked like the material she had seen in the clean room. It brushed the floor where he worked on his hands and knees with blue gloves contrasting the bright white of his coat sleeve. She scanned toward the propped-open door just as it fully opened, and Meki walked in. Sylvia smiled. "Give me a minute," she said to Nathan as she slipped off the bar chair.

"Is that smile for me or the coffee?" Meki said, raising the cup in his hand.

"The coffee, of course," Sylvia said but gave him a sideways hug as she took the coffee. She froze a moment of hesitation at the fact she had touched him without any problem. Maybe trust played some role in helping her control the network. "Thank you," she said, raising the slitted lid to her lips. He had changed clothes and smelled like he had just showered. Sylvia glanced down at her dirt-stained pants and the debris at the hem near her shoes. She needed a shower and to change herself.

"You're welcome," Meki answered. His eyes moved from her to the buzz in the room as he continued. "Enough cream to make it khaki and enough sugar to make it diabetic." Meki's slightly English accent made the comment sound like it came from a displeased butler. "What's going on?"

"I'll let Rosalind explain." She waved Meki to follow her as she moved toward the bedroom.

"Rosalind Mathing?" Meki asked. "What is she doing here?"

Sylvia waved for him to follow her. Rosalind could answer all his questions. Sylvia thought his features were suddenly hard, but Meki didn't like surprises.

"Rosalind, this is Meki, my publicist," Sylvia said, sticking her head into the bedroom where Rosalind was working. "He saw the missing photo."

"Don't come in!" Rosalind said abruptly, not turning from her place at the window. "Wait in the sitting room. I'll be right there."

Meki's lip lifted in a sneer at Rosalind's dismissal, but he cut off his retort. "Your photo is missing?"

"Yes, it looks like that is all that was taken."

"But why Rosalind? Wouldn't the GCS Hotel police be called for that?"

Sylvia sensed Meki's agitation. He was accustomed to giving orders, not taking them. "Nathan could probably use your help documenting the rest of my exam, Meki," she said.

Meki stiffened, and Sylvia realized she'd made it worse. "He keeps having to stop to write stuff down," she added, trying to make the recommendation sound less patronizing. Sylvia touched her lips to force herself to stop talking.

"I'm sure he wants to make his own notes, and I need to finish arrangements for our trip home." Meki navigated from the tile to the hardwood floor, his eyes glued to his ringphone.

Sylvia breathed out a sigh. Meki thought she should go home. Just a few hours ago, she had felt the same. Now, she was uncertain. She was so close to getting answers.

Nathan's scowl indicated his dislike for her idea of Meki's help. When she noticed him, he turned back to the counter. Sylvia returned to the bar chair and climbed up to let her feet dangle. Sheesh, sometimes being short made her feel like a child, and the context of the moment didn't make it any better.

[33.1]

"Thank you," Nathan said when Sylvia settled back on the stool. He was glad Meki had not been interested in Sylvia's idea. He needed the pauses between each portion of the exam to gather himself. Her pull on his energy was incredible. He had only completed visual fields, pupillary reaction, and accommodation before Rosalind had arrived. They would have been further along, but a discussion about how his testing movements for her visual fields looked like "air quote" movements led them to an analysis of book quotes. Galactic dice, he enjoyed talking to her. He and Elizabeth seldom discussed books, but they had other common interests. He had met Elizabeth when she redesigned his office. Remembering her balanced like a lynx atop a ladder as she measured for drapes caused him to smile. She had been so strong and vulnerable at the same time. *Something similar between her and Sylvia,* Nathan thought, watching Sylvia cross her legs to keep them from swinging. "I need you to hold your head still, close one eye, and follow the movement of my finger with your open eye."

"Okay," Sylvia said, adjusting in her seat to place her back firmly against the chair. "This is still the neurologic exam?"

"Yes, testing for nystagmus." Nathan held his index fingers up side-by-side about a foot from her eyes. He stepped back just a little to make the process more comfortable for him — looking into her eyes made the pull of her energy stronger. She couldn't push or pull his energy without touching him, but newly opened synapses were like a vacuum — the pull was so strong that there would be chaos until she learned to control it. Sylvia was a strong Intuit. Regardless of what else she might be, if she learned to direct that energy, she could be helpful. Nathan closed his eyes. *Maybe find a way to save Elizabeth.* She had been his greatest fan and defender. Damn it, he missed her. He needed her.

"Good," he said, swallowing hard when she opened her one eye and focused both on him. He couldn't ask Sylvia to help without telling her about Elizabeth. Her question earlier deserved an answer. "You are like her. A little," Nathan said, moving his hands to test her regular eye movement and taking her eyes off him. "She isn't dead, but as close to it as a Griffon can be and still have a heartbeat."

[33.2]

Sylvia followed his fingers, careful to keep her head still. She was surprised to realize it was the answer to her earlier question, and she felt a tinge of bitterness yet comfort that he was sharing the information. This was difficult for him. She would do her best not to make it worse. She focused on his fingers, determined not to fail these tests. *He is being honest with me,* Sylvia thought, realizing it meant more to her than she had expected. She didn't notice Rosalind come through from the bedroom until she heard her speak to Meki, sitting on the sofa in the sitting area to her right.

"Can you describe the photo for me?" Rosalind asked, standing beside the couch.

"You get right to the point, Ms. Mathing," Meki said, standing to face her.

"I apologize, Mister..." Rosalind paused, as if waiting for him to fill the gap rather than use his first name to keep the formality he started. Sylvia was certain Rosalind knew his full name, But, she had probably realized how uncomfortable she made people feel when she seemed to know them before being properly introduced.

"Hunew. Meki Hunew."

"Please sit, Mr. Hunew, I apologize. I know we are both accustomed to working in an environment of precision and efficiency. I prefer to dispense with the niceties when speaking with a professional. I apologize my staff had to cancel our earlier meeting." Rosalind waved for Meki to sit and nodded at Sylvia.

"No problem. We appreciate you diverting our meeting with the police today."

Sylvia smiled when Nathan rolled his eyes. She, too, recognized his sister's overtly ego-stroking shift in voice, and Sylvia recognized it after just a day with the two of them.

"Watch my fingers, not me," Nathan said, wiggling his right index finger as he continued to make the right side of an H in her peripheral view. "I'm testing extra-ocular movement."

Sylvia raised an eyebrow. "Extra what?"

"The eye movements controlled by muscles that pull on the eye," Nathan answered. "If the neurologic exam demonstrates no failure in your human nervous system, we can proceed with the specialized scan to evaluate for alternate species variants to diagnose the MRI changes." Nathan's lips drew into a line.

Sylvia wondered what he wasn't saying. He didn't mention the heightened sensations and whether that was good or bad. *It was probably part of the test at some point,* she thought and felt a twinge of anger that he wasn't telling her all that the test evaluated. "Oh, okay," Sylvia said, stealing a glance at Meki as his conversation with Rosalind took her attention. Meki had returned to his seat on the sofa, and Rosalind had shifted the linen upholstered Queen Anne chair to an angle where she could see Meki, Nathan, and Sylvia.

Mr. Blue Glove had finished his work on the floor and had moved to the bedroom. Only two people were left of the team that came in initially after

Rosalind — Blue Gloves and the one that had been in the bedroom working with Rosalind. The room had quieted.

"Can you tell me about the photo Ms. Debair was given while on tour?" Rosalind asked.

[33.3]

Meki focused his eyes on the tapestry drapes behind Rosalind. He didn't see any problem answering her questions, but it never paid to be hasty; today's events proved that. He was still angry Biagio's plan had pushed him to be careless. Also, a part of him worried about whether the man had indeed been a free man taken captive, not a born Dalen as he had been told. Meki spoke even as his thought lingered on the man dead in the energy room. "The photo was a Polaroid, the old, unusual kind that printed right from the camera. There was a little farmhouse in the center. A large tree, probably eighty years old or so, to the right of the house as you face it." Meki pulled his thoughts back and let his eyes meet Rosalind's, resisting the urge to touch his breast pocket, where the photo now rested. "A very plain photo. Why are you interested?"

"Sylvia says Kita gave it to her, and since she was attacked by her this morning, I thought it might be important."

Meki jumped to his feet. "She attacked you? Why didn't you tell me?"

Sylvia jumped at the force of the words directed at her and shook her head. Her eyes were still crossed from following Nathan's finger to within an inch of her nose. Meki noted the flush that rose from her neck to her cheeks when Nathan's hand lingered close to her face.

"That's it. We're going home." Meki let his rage flow. This would work out — the perfect excuse to get out of here and have the opportunity to train Sylvia himself. "I'm getting you out of here." *If Dr. Renner is doing her neurologic exam, her synapses are not only open but functional. No one would risk touching an Intuit in an exam like this if she didn't have control.* She was a Sahaja Intuit. He was sure of it now. The question was, did he wait to see if his other speculations were right? She could help their project move forward, and her book was real. He had told Biagio it was and the fiction was that she believed it was all in her mind. With a fully functional Sahaja, the Separatists would support his plan to expedite the transition of Immortal power. The energy stolen here would support the small group of humanity the Separatists were fostering under their rule in the Andromeda Galaxy. Sylvia would be his greatest tool. Meki looked at Nathan and then Rosalind with a disdain he didn't have to feign. "I thought this place would help you, not kill you. It isn't safe for you here."

Meki watched Rosalind's scrutiny as Sylvia faced him and then turned to her.

"Meki has been my publicist for several years. He even left his job with his prior publisher to help me. He can be a bit overprotective."

Meki smiled.

"Really?" Rosalind said, holding her chin with a thoughtfulness that made Meki uncomfortable. "How long have you been a Guardian, Meki?"

"He's not my guardian," Sylvia said before Meki could reply.

"Not a guardian in the way you are thinking," Rosalind started. "Guardians are part of a group selected by the Tokoleh to protect and monitor people who demonstrate potential with species-specific capabilities." Rosalind looked from Meki to Sylvia. "People like you."

"Xenos told me about them on the Orbiter. They're the good guys, right? I had trouble remembering which worked for the Tokoleh." Sylvia closed her eyes as if remembering Xenos speaking, then kept her eyes closed while repeating the words as if it helped her to remember them exactly. "The Guardians were established as a counter group to the Watchers, who were formed by the Separatists to hunt down and destroy anyone with species skills." Sylvia opened her eyes. "Did I mix them up, or is that right?"

"You're right," Rosalind said, looking back at Meki. "But, he hasn't done a very good job." Rosalind's eyes locked with Meki's, and he looked away. "If Kita is a Watcher, he has done a lousy job of protecting you."

"She's right, Sylvia." Meki sat, then slouched on the arm of the couch, allowing his relief to ring through as remorse. "I've done a terrible job of protecting you, and now that your synapses are open, you are at more risk than ever before."

"What do you mean?" Sylvia half sat, half braced herself with her arms seeking purchase behind her on the bar chair. She felt the truth would be more than what she wanted.

Rosalind nodded at Nathan. "Do the hearing test."

"I don't like skipping parts of the exam," he said, but made adjustments.

Meki sensed Nathan was equally aggravated and relieved. Perhaps there were parts of the exam that were more revealing or dangerous, considering the tension in the room. Sylvia looked truly frightened as her eyes darted around the room. "It's okay," Meki said, not moving from the sofa arm lest he frighten her more. This was a difficult time of transition, but he wanted to see for himself that she was functional. She would want to help him once she knew what was at risk.

Nathan rubbed his fingers together to get Sylvia's attention. "I'm going to have you close your eyes, and I'm going to rub my fingers together like this at each ear. You tell me which ear you hear it in?"

Sylvia swallowed and looked at Meki.

Meki smiled gently. "You'll do fine."

[33.4]

Sylvia bit her lip and then slid back to be comfortable on the stool. "Okay," she said and closed her eyes. Crimson flowed in her mind, jetting through her synapses, then slowed as if someone had cut off its flow. She pinched her eyes closed to fight the urge to open them.

"Relax," Nathan said.

Sylvia's shoulders dropped, and she took a small breath through her nose. She focused on the movement of light through her synapses. She felt she could see every scent and sound in the room like it was dancing, changing color and direction. She could feel a smile pulling on her lips.

[33.5]

Meki noticed Rosalind rub her head, but she didn't appear to be in thought. *Could Sylvia be trying to touch Rosalind's mind?* Meki tried to control his excitement. If Sylvia had a functional Oscult along with her network, she would be indispensable in his plans.

Nathan rubbed his left thumb back and forth across the tips of his fingers at Sylvia's right ear. She smiled but said nothing.

"Can you hear that?" Nathan asked.

A wisp of her hair slipped from behind her ear with the movement of his fingers, and Meki noted that Nathan squeezed his fist, digging his nails into his palm. Meki grinned. *The Griffon doctor sees a mate. He is fighting the urge to push that strand of hair back behind her ear. I can use that.*

"Hear it?" Sylvia asked in a mesmerized tone. "I can see it, even. The sound has a color and a...I can't think of the word."

Nathan rubbed his fingertips on the other side, still using his left hand because he had placed his fisted one in his pocket.

"I can hear it in my right ear now, but you're still using your left hand."

"How do you know that?" he asked.

Meki was certain all three onlookers already knew the answer.

[33.6]

"It's as if I can hear...no, *see* the metal from your ring." Sylvia's eyes bolted open, and her smile disappeared. "Was I right?" she asked, her eyes shifting about the room again. Excited at this new connection to the world, she grinned. The idea that each network connected to a tangible human sense like sight or sound made shifting through them a bit more understandable. Reality replaced ecstasy as she noted the impact of her revelation on the faces in the room. Each face was familiar yet changed. Nathan's face was shadowed with a mix of hope and fear. Meki's hard face held an eagerness she had never seen. And Rosalind... Rosalind looked hurt. Sylvia closed her eyes. She had just reminded Rosalind of the pleasant part of a functional network, and it made her gut twist. There was something genuinely different. She felt a power she had never felt before, and the responsibility scared her.

"Of course. You did very well," Rosalind answered quickly.

"I'm sorry, Rosalind," Sylvia said.

"Don't be sorry. Never be sorry. It is a gift that was wasted on my broken central nervous system."

Sylvia was surprised at the brutal honesty. Then again, she reminded herself, Rosalind was brutally honest with everyone, herself included, apparently. Sylvia focused on Rosalind's blue eyes. She filled her thoughts with hope, not sympathy, and it was as if the woman could read even that.

"Not even my robotic legs and spine stimulator could give me the gift you now hold — five running networks surrounding your central nervous system that allow you to push and pull energy for every species that lives." Rosalind held Sylvia's gaze. "Don't apologize for the power, and don't shirk the responsibility that goes with it."

Sylvia saw something flash in those blue eyes, and she shuddered, looking to Meki just in time to see him tame his smile.

"This is wonderful, Sylvia. You did great!" He had his ringphone screen back up and typed as he walked to the door.

Nathan spoke up. "We don't know the truth of that yet."

Meki shrugged. "As you know, the signing was canceled. I'll coordinate to get us on the next Orbiter home. The additional tests aren't necessary. I can convince the publisher that your health is not at risk."

"No." Sylvia jumped from the chair.

"Wait a minute," Nathan added. "I still want to do the species testing to see if the Oscult is functional and set up a series of tests to monitor that the demyelination is reversible."

"Leaving won't be possible," Rosalind stated, focused with resolve on Meki. "There's been another murder, this time here. No one comes or goes till the investigation team releases transportation."

"What?" Nathan and Sylvia both chorused. Rosalind hadn't mentioned it when she arrived.

Rosalind looked at Sylvia, then down at the floor. She tapped her ring as if discarding a message and looked up to find Sylvia's eyes. "I may need your help."

Sylvia tried to breathe but felt her chest tighten. *Another death.* She closed her eyes at the reminder that the signing had been canceled due to the dismemberment earlier. The new realities of her book seemed to make everything more intense. She staggered around the counter to put it between her and everyone. "I...There's..."

"That is ridiculous," Meki said, answering Rosalind and not listening to Sylvia's efforts. "I'm responsible for her."

"So am I," Nathan said, facing Meki, who had turned from the door.

Rosalind moved behind the couch to stand closer to Meki and Nathan with her hands on her hips. "She's an independent woman and she can decide—"

"No," Sylvia yelled over the three of them, then held her forehead, trying to squeeze the headache away. Her voice softened. "Not right now, I'm not." Sylvia pressed the heels of her hands into her eye sockets with her elbows propped on the counter. "Right now, I'm a caterpillar hanging from a precipice with my insides squished to goo." She lifted her head but looked toward the sliver of orange light squeezing through the curtain. The sun was setting. "I'm too far gone to be a caterpillar anymore, and there is no guarantee I will grow wings. I'm transitioning, immobilized by the process, and nothing useful till it is done." Sylvia looked down at her hands and turned them palm up, tracing where the chip had been placed in her fingertip. *No fingerprints,* she thought and didn't stop the tears at the sense of empty, unknowingness of herself that seemed to be as blank as her fingertips. "I'm not anyone else's responsibility, and I've yet to find all of myself." She looked up at them and returned to the most familiar thing in the room. She touched the silk upholstery of the second bar chair and saw it in her mind as sound, color, and movement all at once. "I'm a mutation," she said, not with pity, but reality. "A transition that can't continue to exist." She sat down and stared through them. "Nathan, you want me in the clinic." She never looked down but reached to the counter and picked up the unstruck match. *What was he going to use this for?* She twisted it between her thumb and index finger. She could sense its potential energy.

Nathan cleared his throat.

His discomfort pulled Sylvia from her thoughts. "Rosalind, you want me to help you, though I don't know with what." Sylvia laid the match back on the counter when she registered their concerned looks. "Kita wants me to come to a sector she says is my home, though I have never known it — or can't recall it." She gave Meki a look that asked if he had withheld information from her, but he just removed his glasses and placed the tip in his mouth as he folded his other arm across him in a way that made him appear thoughtful. She finally looked away from them and lifted the necklace from her chest. She tucked it in her shirt. "Meki wants to take me home...to wherever, whatever that home means to him." Sylvia looked up from where her necklace now lay hidden. "It doesn't mean anything to me anymore. I'm too different to be what I used to be and still not what I'm meant to become."

Sylvia's pumps clicked from the tile to the hardwood floor as she moved from the kitchenette toward the door.

Nathan stepped back, and Rosalind moved to the counter and picked up the match.

"You can't leave. How will I find you?" Meki asked.

"Let her go, Meki." Rosalind stepped between Meki and the door, unceremoniously moving him with her height and purpose. She pulled Sylvia's keys from her pocket. "If you don't mind him finding you, take these with you. Kita is in UBN custody and being held at the hotel police department. You should be safe. She agreed to an examination by Nathan. That will help us a lot. I'll send him down there while you take some time."

[33.7]

Meki looked at his watch. Kita's arrest must have been the message Rosalind read earlier and discarded. If his plan worked, Kita would be the suspect for the death in the energy room. If so, they might be able to make a morning Orbiter headed home. If Kita was in custody, that might give him time to test...Meki's thoughts trailed off as his mind planned, and he half-heartedly listened when Rosalind spoke.

[33.8]

Rosalind tapped the door in thought. "I need to tidy up loose ends with the Bunker energy room investigation." She didn't want to discuss the new photo, her findings in Sylvia's room, or the Bunker murder till she was in her office. Meki hadn't indicated any interest in what was happening in the Bunker energy room, and she didn't like that. Sylvia had a lot to digest already. She could bring her back to her office for questions. "We have time. You're farther along than you realize, mutant." Rosalind dropped the keys in her hand, and Sylvia smiled.

"She's right, take some time," Meki said.

Sylvia stared in turn at each of them, then opened the door and stepped into the hallway.

CHAPTER THIRTY-FOUR

S YLVIA HAD KNOWN EXACTLY where she was going when she left her room. Her foot wrapped and unwrapped around the leg of the museum bench as she repeatedly sketched the city's glyph from her book on the brochure. *Not one city*, Sylvia thought, and the vision of the man with red eyes threatened. She took a deep breath and pushed it back toward the tangle in her mind. She smiled at her slight improvement suppressing the vision when she retrieved memories. *It's 4:30 — the museum closes at 5:00*. She unfolded the first-day welcome brochure. The painting had caught her eye, but she had thought no more about it till today. It carried the movement of a Van Gogh. The swirling night sky circled out from the moon as color transformed from white to yellow to green, then moonlight abandoned light to dark of night at the edges. Two center figures united a black silhouette against the color-shifting haze of sky. The suited silhouette blocked an onslaught of wind. Something about the movement of the wind seemed familiar. *The missing Rembrandt storm painting*, she thought, tilting her head appreciating the similarity. *Did my lead on the painting help Kinley and Xenos?* Sylvia hoped their hunt for Coriolis proved more successful than her hunt for herself had been. She looked at the painting again. The wind raged from a rectangular carved stone not visible in the cropped brochure picture.

She left the bench and moved toward the ten-by-ten-foot painting, shoving both hands in her pockets to fight the urge to touch the textured oil on canvas. The wind cleared space on the canvas as if the torrent whisked the oil back like waves to reveal a hieroglyphic replicating relief pattern on the carved stone. Two glyph figures facing across a rectangular box were carved repeatedly in the center of each box. *So familiar, this pattern inside a pattern.* Sylvia closed her eyes, pulling at the energy in the tangle. She bit her lip, anticipating the pain of the memory. *I lost my best friend that day.* The memory of the tomb, the glyphs, and the darkness unfolded in her mind. Sylvia suppressed the vision of the red-eyed man using her human network. It was the easiest to access and had the strongest connection to the tangle.

Sylvia stood. She hadn't thought about the Rembrandt painting since college. Critics and curators claimed one figure looked out from the painting, and they claimed it was Rembrandt in self-portrait. However, Sylvia saw three faces looking out. She smiled, recalling her three-by-two-foot print hanging in her study at home. "Yes. Three faces looking out at me in the wind-tossed storm painting," she said to herself, pulling the details of the print from home and the museum piece here fully into her mind.

She closed her eyes and watched her mind follow the movement of the wind. It pulled her in toward the stone on the museum painting, dragging her toward its center, then twisted and raged, pulling her onto a ship. The ship's wood groaned with every blast of wind and sea wave. She stood inside the lost Rembrandt painting, tossed about on a ship at sea. Then she hovered above it and descended as if becoming the view that drew the focus of the three faces. Each face was different in feature and age, yet the eyes...the eyes of each man were the same.

Red eyes flashed, and Sylvia stumbled back so fast she bumped the bench. She caught herself with an outstretched hand and pushed upright.

Sylvia shuddered. Her exposure to the art hadn't been in childhood. *Are the red eyes bleeding into my newer memories?* Sylvia's shoulders slumped, and her body felt too heavy to move. The thought of more loss made her want to scream, yet she felt stripped of the energy to make the effort.

She pulled her shoulders back. *I am strong enough.* She worked the knot of memory like a knot in a thread. Maybe her insight on the painting as it tugged through her archaeology-laden mind could help Xenos and Kinley. Beads of sweat glossed her forehead. This nesting glyph on the stone painted before her appeared to be where the wind originated. It seemed to push and pull on the silhouettes and had pulled her mind to the ship of the storm painting. *What does that mean? Does it mean anything other than the loose association of a creative mind loving art?* She studied the glyph on the stone. It was definitely similar to the glyph representing cities in her book, which...

Sylvia stopped, her limbs frozen. "The glyphs were in the tomb," she whispered. She was almost killed there. Diane *was* killed. Sylvia shrank with the memory of her best friend but tried to see more. *It wasn't an accident.* She huffed out a held breath, and the tangle of memory recoiled. She could feel her body trembling with fatigue. *If it takes that much energy to unravel just one knot in my memory, I may never remember anything valuable.*

"Can I talk to you?" a voice whispered too close to her ear.

Sylvia jumped, chastising herself for not being more alert to her surroundings. "No," she said, scrutinizing the painting and lacing her hands behind her back to create space between her and Meki. Everything felt different, but she had no right to take it out on Meki. He was trying to protect her. "How long have you been a Guardian?"

"I'm sorry I wasn't forthright with you," he said. "There was...uncertainty when I was assigned to you."

"Well, tell whoever assigned you you're no help at all." Sylvia kept her back to Meki. "I'll take my chances with Kita. At least she intends to show me something."

"Are you certain?"

Sylvia's huff was loud in the quiet, and the high-ceiling room felt cold. She wrapped her arms around her middle, but there was no comfort. It only made her back feel more exposed. "Yes. She offers something from my past. Maybe she's a Watcher, and it's a trick, but I'm taking that risk."

"Risk can pay off," Meki said. "What impresses you about this painting?"

Sylvia turned to face him. She wished she had brought her jacket. The cold enveloped her. "Nothing really. I've seen that nesting pattern...in my dreams and associated each pattern in my book with separate areas of the world — Earth, that is — but now..."

"But now?" Meki pressed.

"In my book, each pattern is different but has similarities." *Likeness with five variations.* "The fact that the nesting pattern glyphs are identical on all the glyphs I've seen here so far makes me more confident some of my book is fiction." Sylvia pointed at the painting. "One repeating identical pattern." She returned to the bench. "It doesn't matter. It was just a dream." She waved the brochure over her shoulder, her back to Meki. "This is just a painting, and parts of my book are fiction. Imagination, conjured stories, probably from pictures I saw as a child." Sylvia crumpled the brochure and headed for the exit. She didn't want Meki to know she knew more. He would worry. "I don't need a Guardian anymore. I can't risk you getting hurt."

"Where are you going?"

"To speak to Kita," Sylvia said, increasing her stride.

"Kita's gone. She escaped." Meki's words paced as fast as his feet. "Nathan called and told me to find you. He was searching for Rosalind. He couldn't reach her by phone."

Sylvia stopped and turned. She held the fear before it slipped to show in her eyes. She raised her chin. "Then you really should keep your distance, Meki. You can't protect me from her, and I'm..." She searched for the words to convey how dangerous she felt she was to those she cared about. "I'm still changing," was all she could manage. She turned back toward the entrance connecting the hotel to the museum.

Meki reached for her.

Sylvia sensed it and stepped toward the side wall. "Please don't touch me, Meki."

Meki let his hand fall and leaned against the wall. "I know this is all new, but you are doing sodding well. I can help you."

"How?" Sylvia asked, glad her chain was inside her shirt out of reach.

"I can help you find Kita." Meki crossed his arms. "Bring her to justice."

"Then talk to Rosalind." Sylvia pulled her phone from her pocket and headed down the hall. Her keys fell and smacked the marble floor, reverberating sound around her words. "She's the one seeking justice."

"What are you seeking?" Meki asked as they both reached for the keys.

Sylvia looked at Meki, keys in hand, as they both stood. "The truth."

The two stared at each other before Meki stepped back slightly.

Meki removed his glasses and tapped his chin with them before replacing them. "I can give you truth..." Meki's lips pursed. "And you can help me with my project. Would you do that?"

"If I can."

Meki smiled and waved his hand back toward the museum. "All the nesting patterns from your book are real. Each represents an energy Portal that feeds Earth's sectors from the GCS. There's one right here."

CHAPTER THIRTY-FIVE

ROSALIND STOOD FROM HER squatted position in the energy-generator room. She was glad she made it back before Houseman and his team left. Beside her, behind the capacitor, she gave the human representative of the intersectoral team a nod of respect as she watched the woman tag the evidence she collected. She was a keen observer, and Rosalind liked her work ethic the few times they had worked together. "Did you help Houseman track the race assault back to a Separatist cell group in the Dalen?"

"Yes, forensic evaluation of the chemicals in the injection were linked to several Earth factories. A group of Dalen workers had been at each site. I reviewed the factory logbooks and corroborated missing chemicals reported while the Dalen workforce was at each location. The man who attacked you is still missing, and the Separatist link disappeared."

"I see. The Dalen are saying it was a Separatist cell group that developed within the Dalen and not orchestrated by the Dalen. However, you don't have any links to the Separatist chain of command?" Rosalind clarified.

"You got it." The woman tilted her head, her observant eyes trying to read Rosalind.

Rosalind hadn't shared her suspicions yet and wouldn't till she had all the facts. She stood to move toward Nathan, who paced as he spoke to Houseman. Rosalind knew what had brought him here.

Nathan saw Rosalind and escaped Houseman. Dr. Enders, the medical examiner, had left to autopsy the body, and Houseman had cornered Nathan with medical questions about the scene. Nathan jerked his head toward the generators as if asking her to join him. "Kita escaped. She wasn't at the police station when

I arrived. They have no idea where she is. I let Meki know. I told him to meet us at the UBN front entrance lobby."

Rosalind nodded distractedly at the news. "Did you notify Sylvia?"

"No, Meki was going to find her and let her know."

"We've got to find Sylvia before he does."

"What? But...you gave her the keys so he could find her."

"No, I gave her the keys so he would feel comfortable to leave her alone. I removed the location sensor. We may still have time."

"What do you mean, we may still have time?"

"Meki is a Watcher, not a Guardian. He's been with the Separatists for years, according to what I've found, which wasn't easy."

Nathan's hands fisted. "Why didn't you tell me?"

"There wasn't time. Do you have an extra injection with you?" Rosalind asked, then turned and barked a command to her lieutenant, the UBN liaison with the hotel police special team. "Send any new info to my secure line and contact Harry. Tell him to start scans on the other energy-generator rooms every ten minutes."

"Yes, I have extra G125." Nathan seethed through gritted teeth, but Rosalind was already moving. "You said she was safe," he pressed, catching her in one long stride.

Rosalind moved quickly through the energy-generator room to the hotel side, pulling up the screen on her phone. "I switched locator signals so we could find her. She's in the museum. I checked on her earlier."

"Is she still there?" Nathan asked, looking over her shoulder at the holograph tracking screen above her ring finger.

"Yes, but she's moving." Rosalind's robotic legs whined when she leapt into a dead sprint.

"Rosalind," Nathan shouted.

"She's headed toward the Museum energy-generator room."

Nathan felt the hair rise on the back of his neck. He squeezed the syringe in his pocket. He had found the one he had dropped earlier and used it. Yet, still, he felt he needed to use this one before the day was over. He felt the weight of his decision as keenly as the day he lost Elizabeth. Access to the G125 had made him push the lines of transformation to touch his Griffon genetics. He'd been toying with how much of his Griffon DNA he could expose to be faster, stronger, and more cunning before he had to halt the process with medicine. Now, facing the need for a third injection made him very concerned he was too far gone already. Nathan breathed deeply as he sensed the distance between him and Rosalind shrinking.

He could control it. He would use his medicine when they reached the Museum EG room.

[35.1]

Meki watched Sylvia's hand trace the concrete block wall. He knew she could feel the cold seeping into her from them.

"Thanks, Meki, for being open with me and helping me find answers. I need to do this. I remember the nesting patterns on the columns," Sylvia said, pausing as if fact-checking a memory. "Nathan's concern pulled me away from the column in the Bunker energy-generator room, but I remember the pattern, and the nesting patterns on the Bunker columns are identical."

Meki noted Sylvia's reluctance for detail and suppressed his interest. "Correct. The columns mark the entryway from the energy-generator room into what we call the Umbilical." Meki tried to keep the excitement out of his voice, but he was so proud of her. "The Portal, some call it," he added, wondering what Rosalind and Nathan may have explained. *Here she is, ready to reach her full potential — with me.* He used his universal key to unlock the door to the energy-generator room, discreetly covering the camera with the hologram webbing as Sylvia curiously found her way into the room. She would have to wait for him to see the columns. A glass door locked access to the energy-generator room on all the hotel side entries, unlike the UBN side, which required biometric entry to log who entered the energy-generator room's main exterior door.

Meki stepped up behind Sylvia.

She shivered and stepped aside. "What did you do?"

"Nothing," he said, dropping the small light-collecting prism he had touched her with into his pocket. He moved to open the glass door. *She's full of energy,* Meki thought, smiling as the glass door began evaluating the number sequence passcode he entered.

[35.2]

Rosalind finally slowed her pace when they reached the stairs leading down to the concrete-walled corridor. She wouldn't get a good signal down there, and she wanted to check her phone for a report from the scan Harry was running.

Nathan didn't stop, but Rosalind's hand grabbed his cuffed sleeve. Nathan rounded on her. "Why are you stopping?"

She didn't answer, letting her silence, as she checked the screen, be a background to his hostility.

Rosalind could sense his tension dropping and didn't bother to check the amber waning in his green eyes. Nathan released the death grip he had on the syringe still in his pocket. "I can do this," Nathan said, and Rosalind saw that he was allowing himself a moment of reprieve in that he reached for his medicine rather than lash out at her. For all its strengths, the Griffon species was often primitive in its decisions, but this time he won.

Rosalind watched Nathan inject himself. His struggle was evident, but his control hadn't wavered. "Harry didn't see anything on the security camera with the first check," Rosalind said, breaking the silence. "They're probably close. I'll check the locator."

"I'm going down to the door where there is more light." Nathan wiggled the second syringe.

"Okay." Rosalind tossed him the universal key for the metal door. You'll have to wait for me to enter the glass door."

Nathan shivered when the key struck his hand. "She will be fine," he whispered to the cinderblock wall. "They're not here yet."

[35.3]

Meki reached for Sylvia, then hesitated. He didn't hear Nathan turn the key in the primary entrance lock behind him and enter the four-by-four entryway between the main entrance and the glass doors. Meki watched the pearlescence of the colors shifting on the electromagnetic field before them as each layer of the EM field cascaded vibrant colors between the columns. It reminded him of the Prism-Light Cells the Tokoleh provided for EvPs like him and Kita. "This is Kita's world, you know?"

"The Galactic Core Station?" Sylvia asked.

"I mean the entire world, including this Replica world."

"Because she's a Watcher?"

"No," Meki said, stepping closer to the EM field. "And stay back until I'm with you. This is the last layer." Meki could feel his impatience and set his jaw, angry again at the lack of planning Biagio had forced him to navigate in this mission. Sylvia had reset the EM field to red twice when she had gotten too close. She could definitely connect her network to the external world. Meki relaxed at the thought. "Being a Watcher, or even a Guardian, is just a job," he said, his voice softening. "It's Kita's species type that matters."

"So, what is she?" Sylvia asked.

"An Escape velocity Puller," Meki said. "But it's her caliber that makes her so dangerous. She's a Sahaja EvP, just as you are a Sahaja of your species." Meki watched Sylvia's eyes go distant, then wide. He glanced back toward the door as he thought about how to describe her ability. His eyes caught Nathan's through the glass. *Sod it!*

[35.4]

A growl, primitive and deep, echoed through the door along the cinderblock wall. A sound Rosalind recognized. *No matter how human we look, we're all animals.* She opened the steel entryway door in time to see Nathan's hands fisted, crushing the syringe with the needle still buried in his thigh. She was careful not to speak as she watched him fight his first senseless, primitive urge to bolt through the glass. His educated mind struggled to convey reason to a nearly awakened Griffon species.

[35.5]

"Why is Nathan here?" Sylvia jerked her head back at the snarl on Nathan's face. She couldn't hear his words through the glass but she could feel his fear in her gut as he bared his teeth and fisted his hand against the glass.

"I need more time," Meki said.

His voice was a mutter and Sylvia looked from Nathan to Meki. "More time for what?"

Meki stepped toward the violet sheen ahead of them and Sylvia felt the oppressive weight of chaos and panic when Meki wrapped his arm tightly around her waist and pulled her close.

"More time to show you what you are." Meki pulled them closer to the rolling color between the columns.

Sylvia could feel the energy this close, as if it wanted to arc to her. Her back was on fire and she turned back toward Nathan.

"Nathan doesn't want you to understand your potential. He is a beast who thinks only of himself. You can reset the electromagnetic field as we come through. That will give us some time."

Sylvia sensed in an instant it was a bad idea. "No!" she screamed, her mind flashing crimson with a fear that was both hers and not her own. Everything in her burned white as phosphorus, like sunlight in its purest form, alternating between the hottest white then recasting the shades of color from the columns through her mind. Every nerve burned and hummed with energy.

They collapsed against a second set of smaller columns with Meki's arms still wrapped tight around her. Energy arced from the entryway columns into the five loops of Sylvia's central nervous system. "Let go, Meki."

Meki didn't respond, but his grip tightened.

"What are you doing?"

"Showing you the truth — what you are."

Sylvia thrashed, but her energy was leaking out where he touched her.

"It's an EvP world," Meki whispered almost like a song, lost, alone. Near ecstasy stretched his voice. "But it's nothing without an Intuit to hold the light."

Sylvia sensed the great emptiness in him, the part of him that was necessary to do all Xenos had said EvPs could do. It came at the cost of this deep, empty space inside of them.

He's lost his mind, Sylvia thought and pulled hard to the right to escape his grasp, but it was as if the light flowed through her, reaching Meki and pooling in him to fill an empty spot he had carried for way too long. Seeing it, she paused.

"That's it," Meki whispered. "Stop fighting. Be quiet and feel the energy in the room. Intuits are conduits for energy."

Sylvia shuddered, closing her eyes. The ribbon of her thoughts glowed in full color. She watched the energy in the room start to replace what she was losing to Meki. She reached up, putting her thumbs to her brow as the familiar light glared even to her closed eyes, but there was no pain this time. The light seemed to pass through her.

"Now stop holding the light," Meki commanded.

Sylvia heard him, but the light grew, and she tried to open her eyes. She could see, but her eyes were still closed. It was like seeing energy without the lens of the human eye.

"Let go!" Meki shouted.

The light moved like dust particles in sunlight, dancing in an uncertain pattern.

"I can't," Sylvia screamed, trying to arch away from him but pulling more energy from the room.

[35.6]

"Stop!" Meki shifted his thoughts, trying to find a place for the overflow of energy. He held Sylvia like ecstasy and death in his hands, and he couldn't let go. *Had that fool doctor been willing to risk his life? Sylvia can't control the light!* Meki fought to breathe, but his lungs were unwilling as the excess energy seemed to compress them.

[35.7]

Nathan paced as Rosalind tried an alternate sequence to open the glass door. "We've got to get to her. He's going to kill her, and she doesn't even know it."

"We're not getting in this way. Galactic dice!" Rosalind spun, almost knocking Nathan against the wall in the small entryway. She swung the metal door open, and Nathan followed, a new fear hanging over him. Rosalind never let her emotions rule her. She finally felt the situation was beyond her control, and panic reached the sinews of a Griffon on the brink of shifting.

Rosalind must have sensed it. She stopped and wheeled around. "How many extra injections did you bring?"

"Enough."

"Take another now. We have to go around to the UBN entrance for this Umbilical Portal or use the old connector tunnels from the Clinic energy-generator room to get to them, and I will not take you like this. I need your intelligence, not your strength."

Nathan sensed she was speaking as much to herself as to him as her voice regained its sense of command.

"With the Bunker room Umbilical shut down, security on the UBN side will make things take longer, even for me. It'll be quicker to use the old tunnel in the clinic."

"It's an hour away by the tram."

Rosalind looked at the floor. "I know. If my network functioned, I could get us in." She rubbed over the stimulator in her back and looked up. "The tunnel is our best choice."

[35.8]

Sylvia blinked and registered that she was staring at the ceiling. The column seemed smaller when it reached the ornate tile high above her. "Ow!" she said, realizing she was on the floor when the shadow of her arm moved across the slate-tiled floor. She noticed the soft powder-blue light in the room for the first time and turned her head. Her eyes bulged at the rotating energy that appeared suspended over a platform two or three steps up. Four arms arched from independent obelisks standing at each corner of the platform. She rotated her bent leg and shifted her weight. The mass underneath her didn't budge as she pulled her leg free, then froze at a new shadow that cast across the floor.

Kita reached out a hand to help her stand.

Sylvia recoiled and scrambled to her feet. Meki's mass lay between them. Fear strained her face.

"You didn't kill him."

Sylvia looked up. "But I could have." Sylvia looked down at her hands. "I almost..." The words trailed off, lost in anger, misplaced, but real.

"What do you want from me? I know you're a Watcher, and you killed—"

"What?" Kita cut her off, which just made Sylvia more angry.

"I know you're an EvP. Xenos told me what you can do." Sylvia paused, swallowing back the nausea at what she had felt in Meki's arms. "But, Meki showed me." She looked up at Kita, the blue light casting a shadow around the woman's taught frame. "The light I hold fills that empty place inside you." Sylvia unconsciously lifted her hand toward her neck but remembered the chain was inside her shirt. She forced her hand down and looked back at Kita. "You need me."

Kita laid something on a large rectangular stone block behind her and stepped to the now swirling Portal bright with color that had spun blue behind her until now.

"I'm not going to let you keep killing people. What do you want from me?" Sylvia said.

"Trust," Kita whispered.

"Yeah, well, get in line. Oh, wait, don't bother. I'm all out," Sylvia shouted, then relaxed slightly when Kita stepped back. Sylvia hadn't used any of her self-defense training from college, but she prepared to give it her best shot. The least she could do was protect Meki till she figured out what happened.

But Kita climbed the stairs, stepped into the Portal, and was gone.

CHAPTER THIRTY-SIX

SYLVIA'S SHOULDERS RELEASED THEIR tension as she touched the carved stone with its repeated nesting pattern on the rectangular block where Kita had laid the book. She held the new photograph close, checking every detail in the faces of the children. One child held the hand of the woman seated on the steps of the old white farmhouse while the other child leaned lazily on the woman's knee. It was a different picture but the same farmhouse. Sylvia blinked away tears and stared at the page in her book Kita had marked with the photograph. Parts of her past were missing, her present was falling apart, and she didn't trust herself even to hold the pieces together.

Meki stirred. Sylvia folded the photo and tucked it in her bra. She stepped over to help him.

"Don't touch me!" Meki shouted.

Sylvia withdrew her hand and backed away, then felt her ears burn with the retreat. "You touched me. This is your fault, not mine."

"I didn't know you were still a cripple."

"God! Who are you? Sylvia said, shocked at his words. She stared at her hands despite her frustration with Meki. There was something wrong with her. "I thought you said she would try to make me go with her."

"She was here?" Meki asked.

Sylvia picked up the copy of her book and waved it at him. "She left this."

"You can't govern the light. You almost killed me. You're useless to her," Meki said as he watched her turn and touch the nesting patterns on the capacitor.

Sylvia sensed something shift in Meki as he watched her.

"Maybe I can train her," Meki whispered but Sylvia heard him calming his anger with mumbled ideas of having a protégé companion, not these constant profile reviews for staffing projects. He had invested a lot of time in her already; maybe he shouldn't let it go too quickly. He stopped muttering and spoke up. "I can help you with it."

Sylvia continued to trace the stone.

"I'm sorry Sylvia, I was harsh." Meki stood and walked stiffly toward the capacitor where Sylvia now squatted, the book propped open on her knees. She traced the emblems repeated one inside the other. She turned, and the book dropped from her knees.

"I'm taking this to Rosalind," Sylvia said, picking up the book and placing it back on her knees.

"It's not necessary. She will be here soon."

"How do you know?"

"You shifted the electromagnetic field and breached the security of the Umbilical Portal." Meki pointed at the cascading wall of color he had pulled her through, then thumbed over his shoulder at the spinning blue vortex that Kita had stepped through. "Believe me, Rosalind will be here." Meki stepped toward the spinning blue triangle of light.

"What are you doing?"

"I'm going to find Kita before she causes more trouble. I wanted to take you with me, but you can't help."

Sylvia looked up. Meki saw the weight of her inability heavy in her eyes.

"Yet," Meki added, then smiled.

"Where does it go?"

"Your early home." Meki stepped toward the Portal. "Kita's mother killed your father and brought you here. From here, you were placed in a home—" Whether he was finished or not, his sentence disappeared as he stepped into the Portal's vortex.

[36.1]

Sylvia collapsed on the steps that climbed to the vortex and thought about the picture, about her family, a family she couldn't remember. Kita was taunting her.

"Sylvia, Sylvia." The sound of Nathan's voice pulled her from her thoughts.

Sylvia touched the photograph. She knew now, in a very deep place, this house had been her home, and it was on the other side of that Portal vortex.

"You don't need to yell, Nathan. She's alive." Rosalind's voice was confident but concerned.

"How do you know?"

Sylvia heard the pause in Rosalind's stride and spoke up. "I'm here, but I'm leaving." She could be gone before they came in.

"What?" Nathan said and Sylvia heard their pace pick up.

Sylvia climbed to the Portal as they came through the small doorway of the old tunnel system.

"It's not safe to travel the Portal. Tell her, Rosalind."

"It's not safe to travel the Portal," Rosalind parroted in monotone, her lack of conviction further evidenced by her focus as she closed the door firmly and appeared to be making a mental note to have security systems put on them.

"This Portal goes to my home. I have to try." Sylvia climbed the steps. She was in no mood for another fight with someone who said they knew what was best for her.

"It's the Umbilical," Rosalind offered, turning away from the tunnel, now apparently satisfied it was appropriately closed.

"You don't know what you're doing." Nathan stepped closer, Rosalind by his side.

Sylvia paused on the landing of the Portal. She explained briefly. "Meki left me because I can't hold the light, but I understand it now. Look." Sylvia turned the book, holding it from the top with her right hand, and turned out for them to see. Her left hand tapped structures along the Portal base. The single emblem of the two glyph figures facing each other across a large rectangular box was replicated here — there was no nesting pattern, only the one design consumed the box-like structure that formed the base of the Portal's vortex. She closed her eyes and blinked once. The energy appeared glowing in the tangle at her mind, and she pressed her index finger to what she now knew was the back side of a lock.

Rosalind gasped, then stiffened. "That's power." Rosalind turned to Nathan. "I know Sahaja Intuits can hold massive amounts of energy, but did you feel that?"

Sylvia pulled her finger away from the lock, then pressed it again.

The room pulsed — Sylvia felt it.

"Is that really possible?" Rosalind said, then looked from Nathan to Sylvia. "I've got new reasons to dust off my notebooks in the Archive basement." The words were whispered, but Sylvia heard them.

Sylvia swallowed at the realization that her energy was impacting the lock even from this side. "The missing relics are keys for the TEA Portal locks on the Earth side for each Umbilical." She touched the emblem at the vortex again. *The knobs, or back side of the locks, are here on this side.* "Stay where you are. I'm not sure who to trust right now." Sylvia walked to the corner of the platform and laid the book down, open, nodding to Rosalind to take it as she backed up near the Portal.

"Kita left this copy of my book. I presume it is hers. She has notes on that page. If the lock Earthside looks like this," she said, pointing to the base of the spinning vortex, "the lost relic key locks it open or closed Earthside." Sylvia now pointed at the rectangular stone across the room. "Is there a similar stone and design in the Bunker room?"

Rosalind nodded, trying not to recall the body found on the stone in the Bunker room.

Sylvia sighed, grateful for the honesty. "The nesting patterns are different from the ones in my book." She pointed at the capacitor stone. "Compare them."

Rosalind followed Sylvia's gesture and faced the capacitor stone.

Sylvia noted Rosalind's discomfort and sensed Nathan's anger when Rosalind handed him the book, her eyes indicating she had memorized the nuances of patterns in Sylvia's book. Rosalind cautiously crossed the room to the rectangular stone. Sylvia had a visual advantage from her perch near the Portal vortex, and she angled herself to create a triangle of view to see both Nathan to her left near the foot of the stairs, and Rosalind to her right, directly across from the vortex.

"They all look the same," Nathan said, closing the book with only a glance. Rosalind, however, had begun to trace the edges of the glyph on the stone, seemingly feeling each detail of the nesting pattern.

"No, they're not. That's why I wrote the damn book." Sylvia covered her face and rubbed her eyes, frustrated with her temper. "I think that's why," she conceded, frustrated at the fluctuation of knowledge, memory, and emotion that danced from the tangle in her mind.

Rosalind said nothing, still kneeling next to the stone.

"Alright," Nathan said, opening the book again. "Is her book different from the stone's patterns?" He flipped through the pages as he spoke. "Rosalind?"

"Yes," Rosalind said, touching the third nested pattern of two hieroglyph characters facing each other across a rectangular stone. For a moment, she touched the larger box on which the third nested picture was carved.

Sylvia stepped toward the steps and then paused. She needed to go toward the Portal, but part of her felt Rosalind and Nathan should know this before she left. *Just in case I don't make it.* "See the third pattern in my book, how there appears to be damage to it on the right side?" Sylvia watched Nathan trace the picture in her book, then looked to Rosalind. "It's not there on the nesting pattern of the stone."

Rosalind traced the small circle barely visible at the base of the rectangular box of the third emblem again.

Nathan looked up. "Yes, but—"

"But it's here," Sylvia said, pointing at the base of the Portal as Rosalind slowly stood. "They are not damaged. It is the knob which connects to the lock on the Portal Earthside."

"I'm still waiting for the important part," Nathan said, but Rosalind was moving toward the stairs to the vortex.

Sylvia pointed Rosalind and Nathan to the rectangular base of the Portal. "This one is on the left. She knelt and slipped Rosalind's hand against the aberrant area. The other two will be—"

"Superior and inferior," Nathan interjected.

"Top and bottom," Sylvia continued.

Nathan didn't seem to notice her anger at the interruption as he moved toward the steps.

"The last will have none," Sylvia finished as Nathan again flipped through the book pages as he climbed.

"So, they've all been damaged on different sides?"

"No, it's not damage. The slits are to allow access of the appropriate key. Inside, connected to the knob, is a lever that can only be shifted from one angle. An angle that fits exactly to one of those relic keys from the other side." Sylvia flipped her hand in a gesture to get Nathan to turn back to the page where Kita had drawn the picture of the Earthside lock relic key beside Sylvia's diagram of the GCS lock carved here on the base of the Portal.

Nathan paused a few steps from the top, his lips drawn tightly. Then he read aloud Kita's notes about the natural disasters, the chaotic weather changes, and her accusation that the energy for the Earth Sector was being intermittently turned off by the GCS. "That's ridiculous," Nathan said, holding the book near the Portal base to compare the book's picture with the GCS knob. "There's no reason for it."

Rosalind pulled her hand away from the notch on the Portal base. "That explains the tiny fuel cell I found. She wasn't stealing energy, she was measuring it. She put it there to tell her when someone tried to steal the energy."

"What?" Sylvia and Nathan both asked.

"Nothing," she said. "Just putting some pieces together. But you're right, Nathan. It doesn't make sense. Something like that would jeopardize the peace between the Tokoleh and the Earth Alliance."

"I don't know what that means," Sylvia said, "but I think it has something to do with the murder on my tour, and it explains why Kita wants me dead. She thinks I'm part of whoever is doing it." *So, why does she want me to trust her?* Something about it didn't fit, and the answers were on the other side of that spinning vortex. Sylvia moved toward the Portal.

Rosalind made no effort to stop her. Instead, she stepped back away from the base to take in the Portal vortex better.

"Oh no, you don't," Nathan said, jumping two stairs but pulling up shy of grabbing her.

Rosalind seemed to return from another world at Nathan's movement. "Nathan's right, you can't just jump through a vortex. You said you and Meki fought. Tell me about that first."

Sylvia explained, and Rosalind responded with cold calculation. "I need to check the Bunker energy-generator room and see if it's functional enough that Sylvia can reset the flow so we can reopen that Umbilical. All of Earth is at risk," she said, then steepled her hands and tapped them against her chin. "Actually, two solar systems."

"You see more of it than I do," Sylvia said. "But right now, Meki needs my help, and I think I can govern the light now." She pushed a loose strand of hair back toward her bun, almost as if she were reaching to tuck it into the tangle that glowed at the back of her mind. She knew how to use this vortex. Well, some part of her knew. She had to trust it.

"Are you trying to find Kita?" Nathan asked, as if discussion might be a viable way to convince her to stay.

"I'm trying to find myself." And with that, Sylvia stepped into the vortex.

CHAPTER THIRTY-SEVEN

K ITA FINGERED THE CHARM in her pocket. She had barely dug it from the safebox in the ground, glad for the extra daylight in Sector Three this time of year. She knew the trail from the woods to the house, even overgrown as it was, like the back of her hand. Nonetheless, sunlight at six made it easier than searching in the early dark of winter. She made it to the house before Meki arrived. She knew he would come. She tapped her ringphone and reviewed the details of Hope and Jo's report while she waited for Meki. Hope and Jo sent some significant information but still didn't know which of the 1729 Tokoleh Governors he worked for. A pull at her EvP core said he was here. She tilted her head, listening. "Your status with the Tokoleh will be terminated when they discover you are working as a Watcher," she said, standing with her arms crossed and leaning against the Formica kitchen counter in a silent, empty home, waiting for his shape to cross in front of the open window that aligned with the doorway between the kitchen and living room. He had just reached the porch.

Meki twitched as he pushed through the door. "I could say the same thing to you. You're the one they have on camera attacking her in the hallway. How do you know Sylvia?"

Kita kept her face unfazed and didn't speak, but her mind raced. *My hologram webbing must have failed. That's how Rosalind knew about me being at the GCS.*

"The Tokoleh, as an ancient council of Immortals that governs Earth and its Replica feeder planets, is in decline," Meki said as if testing Kita's position.

"Perhaps it is, but the Separatists' idea that the Immortals should be released from their obligation to the Earth Alliance and be allowed to govern without the collaboration of the other species is asinine."

Meki removed his glasses and rubbed his eyes. "You still believe the Tokoleh's ancient fairy tales about equality with other species. You realize none of the Immortals really believe in equality between the species. The Separatists just say it out loud."

"The Tokoleh-Earth Alliance peace says differently."

"So, you work for the Earth Alliance and were sent to either retrieve or kill Sylvia if she turned out to be a Sahaja Intuit."

"As were you, it appears."

Meki rubbed his chin thoughtfully. "You're an Earth Alliance assassin assigned to terminate Sylvia if she refuses to give you the coordinates and help you find the relic locks."

Kita shrugged.

Meki's smile made Kita want to grit her teeth, but she kept her poker face. "I keep my own counsel."

Meki walked to the opposite side of the kitchen and mirrored Kita's stance. She, in turn, shifted to put the island between them. She wanted him to think she felt unprepared for him.

"Assassin explains how you have access to details about Sylvia's past. Was the photo to make her think you knew her in childhood? A way to foster connection with your target?"

"You're fishing, Meki. Tell Biagio you have nothing. Make your move or leave. I have work to do." Kita watched Meki's face. There it was — brief, but she was pretty certain she saw the flinch at Biagio's name. It was a small lead, but she would take it.

[37.1]

Sylvia was unprepared for the sensation of movement she experienced when she stepped from the Portal. It was as if she only experienced the vertigo once the rotation of the Portal stopped. She rubbed her eyes and took a tentative step forward. It was two steps before she sensed solid earth under her feet. The sun peeked through the canvas of trees, but her eyes caught immediately on the farmhouse just beyond the trees. A wave of nausea made her retch. She glanced back at the cave opening nestled in the woods. The day was warm, and voices from the house were loud as she made her way to the porch.

"We both need her, for different reasons," Meki shouted.

"The reason is the same. It's the purpose that's different. She's just a tool to you."

Sylvia caught a glimpse of Meki's back as she passed the window on the porch, and suddenly, she felt the need to hide.

Meki's voice rocked the old wood beneath her feet. "Maybe, but she's an addiction to you."

"My so-called addiction is what keeps me from being you."

"You're useful now Kita, but don't press your luck," Meki said, and Sylvia could hear footsteps nearing the door.

Sylvia jumped off the porch, diving behind some overgrown shrubs near the giant oak. She held back her breath and craned her neck as Meki spoke over his shoulder, stepping onto the porch.

"Sylvia will be your worst nightmare. Everything you need, and no way to control it. She will kill you."

Meki strode across the porch toward the woods, not bothering to close the door.

Sylvia shifted to sit on her knees. Bracing her hands on a large root, she tried to breathe. Her eyes shuddered with the vision of the glyph from the base of the Portal. *These roots run back toward the cave — pure energy.*

Sylvia tried to lift her hands from the root but felt melded to it. She moaned as the energy began cycling through the network around her spine. She couldn't tell how much time passed. She trembled with the effort to pull away. The bushes near the tree shook, and Sylvia looked up to see Kita's eyes meet hers. "What's happening?" Sylvia managed with a whimper.

"Let go of the energy," Kita yelled above the wind, swirling the tree branches.

"I can't," she said, rocking back when Kita tackled her.

Kita rolled and stood as quickly as she had moved to knock Sylvia loose from the tree's energy.

"What was that? Where the hell are we?"

"This is the Third Sector, the area of Earth fed by the Museum energy-generator room and Portal. Your ability to connect to energy is stronger now that your network is open. We're about a hundred and fifty miles from where you grew up with your adopted family."

"What did Meki mean about me being an addiction?" Sylvia dusted the dirt from her pants, then used her hands on her knees to stabilize and push to a stand. She felt so weak.

Kita reached into her pocket, fidgeting with something in there as if trying to decide whether to tell Sylvia about it or not. No explanation came. Instead, she asked, "Do you recognize this house?"

"It's from the photo."

Kita made a fist in her pocket, then released it and pulled her hand free. "You're not an addiction. Get up. We have to get back."

"I'm not going with you—"

"Meki is shutting down the Umbilical that feeds the Fifth Sector," Kita interrupted.

"Can we reopen it from this side?"

"It's not that simple," Kita said, pulling a strange gun. "Now move."

"You won't shoot me. Meki said you need me."

"No, Meki and the Tokoleh need you. Not me."

Pop! The sound seemed to vibrate in Sylvia's body as strong as the sound in her ears. Her mind flashed to the dismembered body of the murdered man from this morning's news report. *Was that only this morning?* She felt the burn first in her head, then in her chest — at least till her heart stopped.

[37.2]

Sylvia awoke. She flinched at the cold that pricked her back. She blinked rapidly, orienting to the space. Her back pressed against stone, and her hands and legs were strapped. She jerked, squirming against the restraint. *Don't panic*, she thought, but now her limbs were shaking. She searched the room.

Kita paced inside bars made of light several feet away. *Did Kita create the new space made of light in the room after securing me here?* Sylvia tried to sit up and gasped at the rise of nausea when she again felt the leather straps at her wrist. *Scream*, she thought but choked it back, thinking she should use this opportunity while Kita wasn't looking.

Sylvia pulled at her wrist and feet. The leather ties were so snug they cut into her skin. She closed her eyes and tried to breathe. Her eyes twitched, and she felt the pain at the corner of her eye, near the bridge of her nose. *Focus on breathing*, she thought, unable to use her hands to apply pressure that would relieve it. She glanced at her wrist. The leather was gone; only an energy laced around her wrist.

"Stop!" Kita screamed.

Sylvia jumped, and her heart pumped as the world returned. Why did she feel so cold? Kita hadn't moved, apparently still enjoying the prism of light that danced about her, but she was glaring at Sylvia from across the room. Sylvia tried to glare back. "I can get out of these and kill you," Sylvia threatened, praying something Meki had said was right and her bluff would work.

"Yes, you can, but—"

"No buts. Let me out, and I won't kill you."

"Sylvia." Kita stared through the gaps in the prism and measured her words. "Listen to me. The leather will shift—"

Swack! Meki's clutched cane sliced through the light and met the soft skin of Kita's face, pushing her head at an awkward angle before she hit the ground.

"Meki, it's you!" *Why does he have a cane? That's my fault,* Sylvia thought but pushed the blame away for now. "How did you find me?"

Meki dropped the stick. "I knew she would bring you here."

"Okay, tell me about it later," Sylvia said, and her mood lifted at the fact that he didn't require the walking stick. "Get me out of here."

"I can't, but you can."

"No, I can't."

"Yes. You can. Someone had to teach you. Otherwise, you would have killed me with the light. You have the power, use it!"

Sylvia's arms strained at the bands that held them. *This isn't working,* Sylvia thought, letting her head fall back to the stone. A voice whispered in her mind like vapor.

"Sense the space, the calm..." The voice disappeared like smoke in a child's hand.

"What? Wait." Sylvia said out loud.

"Close your eyes. Let them shudder. Nature is a primary way to connect with energy." How did she know that voice? Sylvia pinched her eyes tight as if to force a form onto the voice in her mind.

"I'm not leaving," Meki said, thinking her words had been for him. "All Intuits can do this if functional, and you confirmed your network was open when you almost killed me before."

"I didn't mean to," Sylvia said, then stole a single glance at Kita, now on one knee as she tried to stand. Sylvia took a deep breath, realized how easily Kita could've killed her if Meki hadn't arrived, and shut her eyes. Her Guardian was here.

Meki was speaking, but Sylvia didn't hear him. Kita's bent posture flashed a memory in Sylvia's mind. A woman knelt near a forest, her head bent as she touched the ground, and the voice whispered again. *"Think about what you feel when you work your fingers through the earth."*

Sylvia closed her eyes, uncertain what these new memories would reveal. She could see everything as if they were shades of color, not objects. She twisted her head to view the leather straps.

"That's it," Meki said. "Now, breathe and pull the energy. Feel the power."

"No! Sylvia, no." Kita's shout severed the calm Sylvia had felt as the energy seeped through her wrists. She felt it moving along her spine, reaching her mind. She held it there, let it resonate with her own energy before sending it back along the path to her wrist.

Sylvia bolted upright, scarcely noticing her hands were free, till she felt the leather straps at her ankle become steel. Sylvia tasted cold energy like the taste of iron when you've bit your tongue. She expected to see blood on her legs where the steel gripped her ankles, but instead, she saw the vision of the man with the red eyes. Was he a memory, or just some animation created by her fear? Now that she had seen the woman who spoke with the soft voice in her mind, she knew there were some good things in her memory. *Why do I fear remembering?*

CHAPTER THIRTY-EIGHT

ROSALIND VIEWED THE HOLOGRAPHIC display against the wall in her office. She had barely convinced Nathan to come back here with her. Stinger landed on the phone when it rang. Rosalind lifted it and leaned against the large wooden desk. "Hello, Michael."

"How did you..."

"Stinger said he gave you the number." She pinched the phone between her ear and shoulder, rotating a small disc in her fingers. It brushed her biceps when she folded her arms across her chest.

"Can I see it?" Nathan whispered.

Rosalind handed the metallic disc to him, not looking, as Michael continued to speak.

"Your tip about Jezel's regeneration rescheduling paid off."

Rosalind looked at Nathan. She cringed at the reminder of using what she had overheard when Nathan called his office.

Nathan caught her stare and waved the disc, whispering, "Are you sure this accurately measures the energy in the rooms?"

Michael was confirming what she had suspected, so she scribbled a note to Nathan: *Yes, secondary system that lets me measure energy in all the generator rooms.*

Rosalind turned her concentration back to the call as Michael continued his report.

"I showed Jezel the desensitization chamber pictures Stinger sent. Dalen 14214, the man they had in a coma while on Orbiter C13, was in one of those damn torture devices." Michael paused.

"What is it, Michael?"

"I have a good idea who provided the warped desensitization systems they are using to mentally torment and 'reprogram' people."

"Why do I sense that whoever did it is someone that sets your teeth on edge?"

"You'd be right, but that's another issue, and I don't have any evidence on that."

"Very well. What do you have?"

"It was like you thought. Dalen 14214 is neither of the men Jezel saw in the corridor before lockdown."

"Hmm. It appears the subordinate gave the prelaunch safety check because the Overseer was busy beating someone so badly in the lockout room that they ended up in a coma."

"Good speculation. Why did you have Stinger get the man's blood?"

"Luck is when opportunity meets preparation. Let's just say I like being lucky."

"Damn straight. I'll keep you posted from my end."

Rosalind disconnected, immediately shifting back to Nathan and the energy-generator room questions. "Is Meki connected to the Tokoleh?" Rosalind walked closer to the glass wall, her head tilted in thought. "Or is someone stealing their equipment and access tools for him?" She tapped a button for the hologram screen. "Put the disc on its stand."

Nathan complied.

"The energy overflow is still at the Museum Portal."

"I told you we should have stayed there."

"I couldn't risk missing him on a hunch. I can see everything from here, and it's a good thing," Rosalind said, pointing. "We wouldn't have seen this."

Nathan stepped toward the screen. "That's the Bunker energy-generator room."

"I had Harry rebuff the system. It creates a false parameter that allows the Umbilical to stay open with a standard deviation measurement to account for the errors we haven't fixed in the system yet."

"So, you reopened the Fifth Sector Umbilical...why is it showing up like that?" Nathan looked at her as his question became rhetorical. "Someone shut it down again."

"Yes, and whoever it was had access they should not have had."

"It's Meki. He has Sylvia! He's going to use the capacitor stone to try to teach her to hold the energy."

Nathan stepped toward the door, but Rosalind spoke up. "Let's give it a minute. I want to see how the Tokoleh responds."

"We don't have time. If she's in there, it could kill her."

"Nathan. She's one person. I am responsible for thousands. If Meki is working for the Tokoleh to do this, we're all in danger."

Nathan paced.

"She's stronger than you realize, Nathan."

Nathan shifted uneasily, slung the office door open, and raced for the elevator.

"Galactic dice!" Rosalind dropped the screen and followed. "Slow down. My legs are robotic, not my heart." If he was moving that fast, he was close to burning the last telomeres between his human and Griffon DNA. Rosalind worried there would be no stopping it this time.

Nathan paused the elevator door. "Hold the railing. It will allow you to use accessory muscles to breathe."

"Thanks. Asshole," she said between breaths. "If you let your species DNA override, we can't get you back." Rosalind straightened, recuperated from the quick sprint, and poked his expanded chest with her finger. "Remember. That."

The elevator lurched, and Rosalind's free hand grabbed the railing. She had refused his advice earlier to use the rails to recover her breathing, preferring the stability of her robotic knees. She braced against them now as she caught her breath. She regained her balance and pulled up her ring screen. The hologram shimmered. She shut it down, then reopened it.

"What?" Nathan asked.

"The fluctuations are chaotic. The overflow shift isn't controlled."

"Sylvia," Nathan whispered. "It will kill her."

Rosalind recalled the dead young man only hours ago. *Maybe I shouldn't have let Harry mask its fluctuations so that I could trap the killer.*

Nathan faced Rosalind. "You did this, didn't you? You knew they would return and try with Sylvia if we restored the energy."

Rosalind looked away from the growing amber in his eyes. "The shutdown of the Umbilical allows them to steal the energy as it cycles in from the core. They are using an Intuit's network to stabilize the system to mask the energy they are stealing." Rosalind looked back at Nathan. "I needed to know what they were doing." Her voice held an unusual plea for understanding.

Nathan scrolled across the holographic screen displayed above Rosalind's ring. "I know it was a hard decision since you hold responsibility for the security of the entire Galactic Core Station, but..." He ground his teeth and refrained from blasting her with the angry words that came so quickly when he walked the line this close to his primitive Griffon form "They can't do that. It's the energy source to the Earth Sector."

"Two organizations have the authority to close off a sector."

"The UBN and the Tokoleh," Nathan whispered. "Maybe the UBN did it for maintenance."

"That goes through me, and I haven't ordered it."

"Why would the Tokoleh shut down an Umbilical? The backup systems are expensive to run and don't turn on a dime."

"The backup systems aren't set to turn on," Rosalind said, letting the screen disappear.

Nathan's arms dropped to his side. "They've been doing this for a while. That's what's affecting the atmosphere there."

"I suspect that's why Kita is here, and being there is probably why she had the rash you've been noticing more frequently from that sector."

CHAPTER THIRTY-NINE

T HE HUM OF HER robotic legs usually soothed Rosalind, but today, it
brought no comfort. Today, it reminded her she might not be enough
for what was needed. "It doesn't make sense to destroy a sector of Earth,"
Rosalind said, looking at Nathan halting at her side. He was not concerned at
this point about the Bunker room Umbilical being shut down. She, however,
had to remember her responsibility to two solar systems.

"Can you ponder these issues while you open the door?" Nathan asked
as Rosalind realized they were near the vault lock on the UBN side of the
Bunker energy-generator room. "Come on. Sylvia could be in there."

Rosalind stepped to the retinal reader and paused while it scanned her eye.
ACCESS DENIED flashed in red on the screen.

Nathan wiped the lens. "Try again."

Rosalind did, but with little enthusiasm. She understood the system. She
had been shut out. "They've overridden the access panel. We can't get in."

Nathan shuddered, and Rosalind watched as his shirt pulled tight at the
tension to maintain the structure of his human DNA over his species.

"Nathan, look at me."

Nathan pushed buttons on the flashing screen, ignoring her.

Rosalind snapped his head around to her. "Nathan!"

Starburst gold blazed in his green eyes.

Panic seized Rosalind. "I have another way in, but I can't take you in as a
Griffon."

Nathan stopped and stood still as stone. Rosalind tapped the screen. "We have forty-five minutes maximum before the shutdown is complete and my backdoor option is no longer an option."

[39.1]

The countdown had already begun for Sylvia.

Sylvia twisted her head, watching the energy that laced around her ankles and one wrist.

"Relax," Meki said. "Let me see your wrist."

"Sylvia, don't—" Kita started.

"What Kita is trying to say," Meki interrupted as he pressed her wrist snug to the table. "is that these rope bonds will become leather. When you break the leather, it becomes steel. Then finally, glass, until you can control each energy component at all four constraints."

"Don't do it, Sylvia," Kita warned from her glowing Prism-Light encasement. Sylvia blinked at the beautiful colors that held Kita like a prison.

"If you're so worried about it, come help me."

"She can't. She's trapped by her pride," Meki growled. "The prism she stands in holds enough light to make her strong enough to handle both of us, but she refuses the Prism-Light of the Tokoleh."

[39.2]

"They're not real connections," Kita said, her stance prepared this time for a blow if Meki attempted. The struggle to refuse Prism-Light was harder after using so much energy on this trip, but the knowledge she could do so gave her strength. *Meki answers to one of the 1729 Tokoleh Governors. I need to confirm if it is Biagio.* "Real connections come with an Intuit and trust. If you had ever known such a thing, you would understand, but you'd rather be dependent on Tokoleh-controlled Prism-Lights built by your precious Immortals. Does Biagio give you extra playtime in the Tokoleh prisms for all your hard work?"

Kita smiled when Meki whirled around, crossing the ten feet between them. She'd struck a nerve. Anger would make him careless. He appeared to ignore the steel click on Sylvia's arm, restoring one arm lock and starting a new rotation of restraint.

Kita watched Sylvia from her peripheral view, keeping her focus on Meki. Sylvia pulled at the new restraint, but there was no give. She tried to relax, her eyes narrowed as if trying to see the energy, but she couldn't focus. Then Kita felt it and shuddered once as Meki stumbled to one knee when Sylvia pulled hard on the energy. Meki seemed to grapple with his rage and moved back to Sylvia.

"Focus, Sylvia. See the one thought."

"I can't. I won't."

"Sorry dear, that's not an option." Meki pulled a blade from a sheath Kita hadn't noticed. The vortex light glowed bright against its dark boundaries, creating an eerie shimmer over the blade and the stone. "I need you to focus."

[39.3]

Sylvia swung wildly at Meki with the wrist she'd once again freed.

Meki caught her wrist and pushed it toward the table. Sylvia closed her eyes to breathe and find strength, but it was not enough to keep her arm free. *How can he touch me now when I feel the energy will explode from me?*

Sylvia flashed a brief look at Kita, who paced in her Prism-Light room.

"The Tokoleh do not want her maimed," Kita shouted, looking around at the light, and Sylvia marveled at Meki's words that they had the power to both hold and free her.

"A fingertip will not maim her, just focus her." Meki's words brought Sylvia's focus back to the blade in his hand while he overcame her one arm with his body weight. The steel band clanged into place around her wrist. Sylvia closed her eyes and felt the shudder that gave her the lens of energy. She could see a glow dim behind Meki. It had to be the Prism-Light encasement because she felt an equal pull on the energy in the room.

"That's it. Focus. The blade always helps with focus."

Sylvia swallowed hard. She could see the energy at the steel cuff and the glow from the vortex that silhouetted Meki as the blade came down at the joint of her index finger. The pain seared like hot coals. She tried to pull the energy to free her arms.

"Breathe through the pain, Sylvia, and hold the light," Meki said, pulling the blade's sharp edge through the first layer of Sylvia's pale skin.

Sylvia repeated Meki's chant in her mind between gasps of breath. She squeezed her eyes and gritted her teeth. The tangle in her mind tugged at a ribbon of memory — her father. She could only see his back, but she knew instinctively it was a memory of him. She heard a new voice in her mind. A tear streamed down her cheek to the table. *My father's voice.* How had she forgotten that deep, soft voice? *"You start with compassion,"* his voice said in her mind. Sylvia's eyes shuddered almost in slow motion this time, each lens removing itself like a sequence of doors to an inner chamber. "Not pain," Sylvia shouted as she arched her back from the stone. *It doesn't start with pain,* she thought in response to the signal coming into her mind from the stimulus at her finger, but she kept slipping back to the pain as she sensed the blade inch deeper toward the bone.

Crash! The sound reverberated. Sylvia focused on something wobbling like a coin in its last spin before it fell to the table. She opened her eyes just in time to see Kita swing her body in a circle, her fist extending at the end of the rotation. Meki's body flew against the back wall like a wet towel discarded.

Kita looked briefly at Sylvia. "You do have to get yourself out while I deal with him."

Sylvia's head banged back against the table with exhaustion. Then fear gripped her again. What would Kita use to force her to find this power? Sylvia lifted her head to check her hand. She made a fist; blood dropped from the laceration and smeared across the stone before seeping into it. Sylvia swallowed back the nausea, and her mouth watered near the back of her throat. The sounds behind her said Kita would be busy for a while. She must have taken the light from the Prism-Light encasement. *Why? She would have been free to go once I was broken, wouldn't she? Think about that later.* Sylvia relaxed, taking a deep breath. She focused on the steel brace to her left, then her right, and finally her feet. She knew she couldn't control it well enough to be free with any skill, but she could be fast, like ripping off a bandage.

Sylvia had two arms and a leg free. The other leg felt trapped still — she had used that foot as a lever against the stone as she jerked free of the steel before they recycled to the next rotation.

Rosalind's voice penetrated the room. "Nate, no!"

Nathan ignored her, and now he stood at the foot of the table, his hands wedged at the metal cuff almost closed around Sylvia's leg. His fingers kept it from locking, but his knuckles dug into her leg with the pressure.

"Nathan," Sylvia whispered, pulling the ribbons of energy back toward the tangle in her mind. She still didn't understand the process or how to do it well, but she knew with the energy pulled back to the tangle, it wouldn't hurt Nathan. Her head throbbed immediately, and she almost passed out.

"Nate," Rosalind shouted again, making her way to them.

Nathan shook his head. A wild brown curl fell over his left eye, the green of it beyond starburst and almost buried in amber.

"Work your leg free," Rosalind said.

Sylvia complied, ignoring the pain in her head.

Nathan lifted her from the table and returned to the vortex where they had come in.

"Fifteen minutes. Move," Rosalind said with a glance at the fight across the room.

Sylvia didn't feel afraid in Nathan's arms even when his eyes flashed at Rosalind when she wordlessly tugged his sleeve.

"I'm fine," Nathan said.

Sylvia was not. She fought with vertigo as she watched the blood from her finger stain Nathan's crisp, clean shirt. She watched the red spread across the white as if she could see it soak into each thread as her energy ebbed with it, then everything went black.

[39.4]

"She passed out," Nathan said, his voice controlled.

Rosalind released his sleeve as they stepped toward the vortex, her quickened steps telling Nathan nothing about the fight behind them except that there were competing strengths she had not seen in many years. "We'll go to the clinic vortex from the core, and I'll go on to the Bunker room once she is in cryo for recovery."

Nathan froze at the wide-eyed look that glazed Rosalind's face as she looked past his shoulder.

"Hurry," Rosalind said, pulling them into the vortex.

Rosalind's pull rotated his shoulder and he watched Kita shove a limp Meki to the floor, then leap twenty-five feet for the vortex right behind them.

CHAPTER FORTY

ROSALIND SHIFTED SO NATHAN could step from the vortex into the Clinic energy-generator room.

"She's right behind us," Nathan said.

"Put me down." Sylvia tugged at her shirt bunched up where Nathan's arms held her. "I'm fine now. Thank you."

"Nate," Rosalind commanded, afraid his battle with the Griffon would win. "We have to keep moving, can you..." But the starburst was now small in his eyes. She knew he fought to regain himself, but he wasn't lost to them yet. A sound caused Rosalind to spin.

Kita stepped from the vortex, bumping Rosalind and ducking as if anticipating a punch.

Nathan sat Sylvia down, and Rosalind moved to stand with Nathan between Kita and Sylvia.

"Sylvia needs to come with me," Kita said.

Rosalind stepped back without a fight.

"You understand more than I thought," Kita said, taking a tentative step forward. "I haven't forgot our conversation in the cell."

"Me neither." Rosalind shifted her weight to her back leg. "First, I want to know why the Tokoleh is shutting down the lifeline to the Fifth Sector."

"Sylvia is not leaving," Nathan chimed in, adjusting the cuffed sleeves that had pushed up his forearms when he had lifted Sylvia.

"I don't have time to explain it, but if you want to stop this shutdown, she has to read the relic on the Earth side to reopen the dimension and lock it open."

"You have the relic key for the Fifth Sector lock?" Rosalind questioned.

"Not with me." Kita's answer told Rosalind she could access it if Rosalind was inclined to help but indicating she wouldn't share any more.

"How do you know she can do it?" Nathan asked, mirroring Rosalind's weight shift. "A functioning Sahaja Intuit network is required. She has not had the additional tests. There are other things that could explain her MRI."

"I don't know anything about the MRI, but she is capable." Kita did not offer explanation for how she knew as she looked at Sylvia. "Let's go." Kita turned, as if expecting Sylvia to follow.

"I'm Sahaja? You knew this!" Sylvia crossed her arms and waited for Kita to realize she wasn't following. "That is why you have been trying to kill me."

Rosalind sensed Sylvia was feeling Meki's betrayal as she cupped her injured hand. It had stopped bleeding, but the dried blood crusted the whole length of her finger. Sylvia was playing a game where she was a queen who thought she was a pawn, and she didn't know the rules.

"You're a Watcher..." Sylvia paused, as if unable to finish the sentence, then whispered, "Like Meki." Sylvia reached to brace against Nathan's arm like it could help her breathe, but she withdrew before touching him. Rosalind knew that feeling of isolation and felt a new connection with this woman who knew so little about this world, yet also knew things no one else seemed to know if she could just remember.

"She's not a Watcher," Rosalind said, breaking the silence.

Nathan's eyes snapped away from Sylvia to Rosalind. She watched his eyes communicate that his human mind was working with his Griffon instincts to put the puzzle pieces together. "Meki is the Watcher," he said, pulling Sylvia's MRI up on his phone with his free hand and then pointing Sylvia to it. "He saw this but needed proof from our testing." Nathan looked up at Kita when he spoke. "Watchers who work in hospital settings are trained to look for these changes."

"Exactly," Kita said, turning toward them. "Now, let's go."

[40.1]

"But that doesn't make sense," Sylvia whispered, the betrayal still heavy in her chest. "Meki doesn't work at the hospital. He has been my publicist for years."

Kita tapped her ringphone in annoyance. The hologram screen flashed with a newspaper article and picture. The headline read "Unexplained Deaths of Three Soldiers Attributed to Hospital Oversight." Meki's eyes were clear above the mask. Kita seemed to watch all their faces. "Meki has been around longer than you realize. Maybe lifetimes. Jo, my...one of my colleagues, sent me these redacted articles. He's Immortal. It is the only explanation for his endurance when he's an EvP, but not Sahaja EvP," Kita said.

Sylvia realized none of this seemed to surprise Rosalind. *This woman is intelligent. And Kita — definitely a smart woman.*

"So, now you understand why I need her help. She is a Sahaja."

"A Sahaja Intuit, or something else?" Nathan asked.

Kita didn't answer.

"She can't help you till I complete her testing. It would be dangerous if her network isn't fully functional."

Sylvia stepped away from Nathan toward Kita. Nathan dropped his hand, and the MRI on the screen disappeared. His movement behind her pulled Rosalind to him. Sylvia knew he would fight to keep her safe.

Sylvia barely registered Rosalind's quiet hand movement.

"Sorry, Nathan." The sound of an electric current preceded his collapse to the floor.

Sylvia spun, and Kita stared. Rosalind stepped toward them. "The decision is yours, Sylvia." She replaced the taser at her side, her gaze never leaving Sylvia's face.

Sylvia glanced at Nathan, crumpled on the floor, then at Rosalind's focused stare. This woman expected — no, believed — she could help. *Why?* Sylvia thought, recognizing she didn't want to let her down. "The emblems. I recognize them because I have seen them before." She began trying to pull all the pieces together. "The pages marked at both..." Sylvia swallowed back the nausea. "...at both murders..." The death on the Orbiter had not been a random fight. She was sure of that now, though it could probably never be proven. Sylvia looked up, dropping the chain she had begun to twist at her neck, and continued. "The pages marked at both murders may represent hiding places for the lost relic keys. I thought they were just ideas, pictures from my dreams — not real." Sylvia turned from Rosalind to Kita. "I don't know how to put the keys in place." Sylvia closed her eyes to push back the tears. *How could I forget something so important, something that meant the difference between life and death for an entire planet?* Sylvia pushed her chain beneath her shirt to avoid tugging at it again. "I'm sorry. If I ever knew how to restore the keys in the locks, I don't remember."

Kita pulled the charm from her pocket and extended it to Sylvia by the chain. "You will remember."

Rosalind stepped forward, watching the chain and charm as it dangled, suspended like a moment stopped in time. "Sylvia?" she asked, reaching toward the chain then pausing.

"Yes," Sylvia answered, never looking away from the chain dangling from Kita's hand. It would fit the grooves of the chain she wore. "It was you reaching for the charm in the photo left in my room. You put the photo in my room and stole the one you gave me at the signing."

"I didn't take anything, but I did leave the photo of me at the cryo facility here when I was young. I'll explain all I know when we have more time," Kita said.

"The choice is yours, and so are the consequences," Rosalind said. "May I inspect the charm?"

Sylvia looked at Rosalind. "You're thinking about the portrait at the UBN."

Kita watched their conversation. She, too, seemed to note the discomfort in Rosalind. Whatever Rosalind's irritation, she would not be sharing. At least, that is what her face said as she pulled her features blank.

"Never mind," Rosalind said. "Kita is correct about time being imperative."

Sylvia touched the charm, and Kita released the chain. Sylvia looked up, met Kita's eyes, and gently pulled its mate from under her shirt. "I'll go."

Rosalind stepped aside and then looked at Kita. "I tased Nathan because he would have fought you, and we don't have that time. The Bunker energy-generator room Umbilical is down on our side. You have twenty-four minutes before the core will shut off from the Umbilical on the Earth side."

"I have to take her to the gardens first," Kita said. "They are in the Third Sector. Twenty-four minutes in the core is twenty-four hours there." She looked at Sylvia. "That will be enough."

"I hope Nathan is wrong about her synapses," Rosalind said.

"She just needs some practice holding the light," Kita said confidently.

"I'm not going back to that table." Sylvia froze mid-stride.

"You don't need a table." Kita took a deep breath.

Sylvia saw Kita's energy dim as if someone closed a door on a candlelit room. It was subtle, but she saw it. "What do I need?"

Kita took Sylvia's hand and stepped toward the vortex. "Me."

CHAPTER FORTY-ONE

T HE MORNING SUNLIGHT SEEMED brighter than the vortex when they stepped out. Sylvia took a moment to let her eyes adjust. The transition caused her eyes to shudder, and for a moment, everything showed as energy. *It's beautiful.*

"These are the Gardens of Aza," Kita said.

"They're...breathtaking."

"I wouldn't know," Kita mumbled.

Sylvia smiled, and Kita grimaced as they brushed through the overgrowth. Sylvia swam in the gladiolas, foxglove, and hollyhock. Color, design, and texture marked the only distinction between flowers and grass that swallowed her thighs, caressed her chest, and stroked her outstretched hands.

Kita propelled in Sylvia's wake like a rudder rusted at the stern, untouched by the water of green around her.

Sylvia closed her eyes. Fragrance arrested her senses. She breathed then tilted her head but never slowed her pace.

Kita moved beside her, confident. The line of strength in her jaw was set to void any waver of emotion, whether results brought hope or sorrow. Her face said she recognized the reality that this might not work. Sylvia moved quicker, taking in the gorgeous view. Kita fell in behind her again. Sylvia gasped, turned, and stopped, eyes closed. Kita halted, but it was too late. She stood well within Sylvia's personal space.

Sylvia opened her eyes.

[41.1]

Transfixed by Sylvia's blue eyes, Kita stared, taking in every feature. They were tired eyes but strong, bloodshot from fatigue and glassy from unshed tears. Kita reached for her but paused. The gesture caused a flash of pain in those blue eyes, and Sylvia spoke before Kita could explain.

"I'm dangerous, aren't I? People are afraid to touch me, afraid to connect because I could hurt them."

"You're not danger—"

"I don't want to hurt anyone," Sylvia blurted, then reached for both charms at her neck. "Sorry, I didn't mean to interrupt you. And that's not true. There are parts of me that would lash out." Sylvia looked up and released the necklace. "That's why you brought me here, so I could use the human network I'm familiar with to see the Immortal network I don't understand."

"Yes."

[41.2]

Kita's voice was a whisper, and Sylvia took in the transparent green eyes that held her own. They were beautiful, and she felt this uncontained sense of care for this woman she barely knew. "This place allows me to use my human senses to see my Immortal self, but I have to view it all. Even the dark places." Sylvia spoke, finding comfort, letting her eyes remain fixed on Kita's. "And you came with me to help me hold the dark places."

"I did."

"Why?"

"My reasons are my own for now, but know I...You matter to me." Kita waved her arm at the expanse of the garden. "Sparring with me here will teach you how to use this energy. It connects to the Source. Its power is something you learned to govern years ago and do not remember."

Sylvia nodded, thinking it was possible since there was so much she couldn't touch in her memory. "And doing this will help restore that memory."

"I suspect most of what has your memory trapped you will find in the connection to the Simultaneity, not the Source. You need to remember how to govern the Source energy before you touch the dark places of energy connected to the Simultaneity. The Source and the Simultaneity are neither good nor bad in themselves, but the Simultaneity's chaos lends itself to things that destroy."

"The picture is forming, but I don't fully understand."

"What is the difference between sparring and fighting?"

"The danger! One is done carefully with a friend. The other, not so careful, with an enemy."

"No," Kita said firmly. "The difference is the choice."

"The choice?"

"Yes, and the Immortal network is where you make that choice."

"So, if I use my human network and senses to take in this place, then spar with you holding that energy, I'll understand how to use my second network, the Immortal network, to control the energy?"

Kita didn't answer but stared off into the distance, and Sylvia took that as a cue to try.

Sylvia felt her chest lift with her breath, pause, fall, then lift again. "Jasmine climbs the oak behind me..." Her breath came faster as her words matched the pace of her thoughts. "Peonies form an arch over the gardenias that reach out at the base dancing between sun and shadow..." The pause seemed to hold both her breath and thought. "but, there's a gap." Tears came unexpectedly, and Sylvia tasted them with her words as she opened her eyes again to find Kita. "There's a gap between this field and the tree. I...can't feel anything there. It's so terribly empty. What is it?"

"You created it." Kita held Sylvia's eyes with her own.

"How did I create it?" Sylvia began, then breathed out a sigh of exhaustion as a ribbon of color whipped from the tangle in her mind with the vision of red eyes. "This place in some way reflects my Immortal network," Sylvia whispered as if quiet words would hold back the vision as she teased small truths from its grasp. This expansive emptiness wasn't new, but it was reopening like a wound in this beautiful place. "My past is there."

Kita nodded.

Sylvia sat down amidst the tall grass and foxglove to let the ribbon of color unwind from the tangle in the back of her mind. Anticipating the vision didn't reduce the shock of it. Red eyes glared above her, and sticky, bloody hands gripped her collar. Then she fell. There wasn't a splash because the liquid was more dense than water. It sucked at her arms, legs, and back like liquid quicksand. "No, no, no." She screamed the words, but they had no sound.

The red eyes were beyond the liquid now, and the sound was muffled. Sylvia wanted to pull free of the vision. She had gradually extended the amount of time she could tolerate the vision. *If I can just push a little further.* Her lungs burned with the need for air.

The familiar darkness settled around her as the eyes disappeared, and a lid covered her submerged body. Her heart pounded a rapid staccato that thrummed in her ears. She'd never made it this far before. The liquid shifted, or maybe she moved, but at her fingertips, she could no longer feel the liquid. She flexed her fingers, and air flooded her lungs so fast she coughed, then gasped, jerking upright.

She was back in the garden. Sweat beaded at her neck, and she leaned to support her weight on her hands and knees. She crawled till she was beyond the tall grass and collapsed.

Kita was seated two feet away, eyes closed, face serene.

"You were helping me somehow," Sylvia said, her chest still heaving with the exertion. "I think I began to pull the energy of the liquid around me in my vision."

Kita opened her eyes. "I can help some, but there are limits when we are not connected."

"Give me a minute to catch my breath, then I'll try again."

Kita unfolded from her seated position, transitioning to a squat beside Sylvia. She pushed a strand of hair from Sylvia's face. "Once you can control your energy, we can connect fully, and I can help you hold the dark places better."

"What did you do just now to help?"

"I connected to the Simultaneity that is externally here. It is a physical representation of what you carry inside." Kita stood.

Sylvia watched the strong line of Kita's jaw. It never wavered as she stepped away from her, moving toward that open, dark space Sylvia could still feel. Sylvia closed her eyes. She sensed Kita step from the field and pull the energy of the negative space like it was dark matter. It seemed to dive swiftly to her core, to the empty place, the compartment only an Escape velocity Puller has at their center.

Sylvia sighed with relief as she sensed the dark space recede — not disappear, but almost. "That's how EvPs help Intuits," Sylvia said, something in her memory turning the idea over. "You can hold the dark matter, help us bear it in exchange for the light we can give you."

"Yes. In the physical world, I can slide the mass of an object into this empty space inside me, and it becomes part of the Simultaneity, no longer part of this world. Reducing a thing's mass decreases its hold. If I make the mass of the earth around me less, then its gravity lessens, and I can escape the hold gravity typically has on my body, making me stronger or able to jump as if no gravity or at least less gravity is at play. We can do similar things to hold pain or negative emotions. For the Intuit, EvPs connect them to the Simultaneity while you link us to the Source. When I hold your pain, I place it in the Simultaneity, making it feel less heavy here and easier to carry."

Kita stepped deeper into the gap, and Sylvia's sigh steadied her resolve. She felt Kita push to take in the great emptiness that created the divide.

"Spar with me here, and you will understand better. You don't have to face everything in one day. Just recognize it is there for now."

Sylvia fisted her hands against the tremble she felt. "What if I fail?" Kita's words had awakened an intuition in her; every nerve tremored with the risk of this new responsibility. "Am I really the only one who can do this?"

"In this moment, yes. This is your place of choice."

Sylvia felt there was a mere thread of hope tethering the moments of her life. *That huge empty space Kita absorbed is more than what it seems.* The reality of her own ignorance weighted her thoughts. "Really, Kita. What if I can't do this?"

"Then, I will die. Soon after that, the people of the Fifth Sector will die, and eventually, the entire planet will be lost."

"How can you say that?"

"We don't have time to discuss the whys of everything. This is the perfect place for you to learn to govern the light, and you are who we have right now."

Sylvia thought about all Kita had done to reach her. She remembered Nathan slumped on the floor and Rosalind's effort to protect the Galactic Core Station, only to see its safety beyond her control. They each had a part. She had to learn to do this. She had to help, but she didn't trust herself. Her own mind was hidden from her. *I can only start with now*, she thought and closed her eyes to watch the silver tangle at the back of her mind as it laced out to form the networks that wrapped down her spine. She opened her eyes. "Let's do this."

Kita rotated to stand opposite Sylvia. "Focus on the energy closest to your human senses. Like the liquid at your fingertips in your vision. Pull it in through your Intuit network. I'll explain it more once we see how you naturally use the energy," Kita said, taking a formal fighting stance.

Sylvia fell into an unpracticed fighting stance she vaguely remembered from some college training. "That doesn't make me feel confident about this. What if I hurt you?"

"Have you sparred?" Kita asked, reorienting to the garden surroundings with a quick look.

"Some," Sylvia answered, following Kita's gaze. "I'm more concerned the combination of my poor understanding of Intuit ability and my even worse fighting skill will do more damage than a trained assassin." Sylvia hesitated, expecting a laugh from Kita, but it didn't come.

"That's a reasonable concern. EvPs are usually paired with Intuits in training for that reason. We can take the excess for long enough that in a training situation, someone can stop you before you kill them."

Sylvia dropped her hands from their fighting position. "So, you want me to govern the light energy here for you as practice, and you just hope I don't kill you?"

"Yes," Kita said. "Trust yourself. You've been trained even if you don't remember."

"How do you know that?" Sylvia asked, realizing her hand was twisting at the two chains she now wore like unlinked puzzle pieces.

Kita relaxed her stance. "Because I know the woman who gave you that chain."

Sylvia jerked her head up. "What? You do? Was it—"

Kita cut her off and reformed her stance. "You want answers? Spar."

Sylvia tucked the charms inside her shirt. "Okay. If I can control the light, then our fight will have only the expenditure of the natural energy of a fight, but if not, the energy will be exponential when the light energy I'm holding escapes to you. Do I have that part right?"

"Yes." Kita swallowed as she shifted her stance. "You must trust her if you want her to trust herself," Kita said to herself but Sylvia heard her.

Sylvia felt Kita's frustration at her own nervousness, and Sylvia wasn't sure how she felt about that.

"You can add energy to any blow, and it is easy for you to pull energy here in this place," Kita said as she scanned the area again then shook her body, readying for the fight.

"What are you doing?" Sylvia asked, noticing that a circle of dark gray that glowed silver at its edge begin to circle Kita's abdomen. Sylvia blinked her eyes and sensed it was energy she was seeing. She recognized the flare of energy, as if the door on that candlelit room had been opened. It glowed like the straps of energy when Meki had her strapped to the stone. The thought made her shudder, and the circle at Kita's center hummed.

"You're thinking about Meki and the betrayal you felt. You're pulling from the Simultaneity energy I'm holding for you. The energy here is powerful, and you have access to all of it. I'm holding the mass I just pulled from that dead space earlier, so I'm faster and stronger than you, but you could kill me with the choice to use one of the tools in that darkness."

"What? I can't do this. I don't want to hurt you."

"Then don't. You've had some fight training if you can spar. Think of it like that. Hold the light and try to touch me. I'm *open*, which means I've put up no barrier to the energy."

Sylvia bit her lip and tried to recall those handful of lessons from college. Carefully, she punched, and Kita dodged. Sylvia breathed deeply. She could do this. Kita was a skilled fighter. She would probably never even touch her. She took a stance and focused, then took an easy practice punch. Kita stepped into it. Energy sparked, and Kita landed twenty feet away. Startled, Sylvia stared at her hand, then ran to her. "Kita?"

Kita rolled onto her side and shook her head. "I'm fine, let's try again."

"I can't do this. I'm going to kill you."

Kita stood. "Again."

Sylvia took her stance. The repetition continued till the sun was high overhead and there was no shade from the large oak.

"Again," Kita commanded with fatigue.

"No, Kita. I'm exhausted, and you can barely stand. I've improved enough to spar consistently with control. I don't want to make a stupid mistake because we're both tired. Besides, I still need to take back the weight of what you have helped me hold of that darkness that touches the Simultaneity."

Sylvia watched Kita look at her hands as if noticing, for the first time, the slight tremble in them. She was pushing her limits.

Kita rolled her shoulders, then her neck, in a gesture that made her look more relaxed. "You've done well but still struggle with the dark places connected to the Simultaneity that allows the time stretch. Maybe you need a different setting for that. The Simultaneity allows you to stretch time, but you must hold it all."

Sylvia swallowed. It was making a little more sense. The Source was readily available to her in all that she sensed around her in the garden that was alive and thriving. The Simultaneity held equal power of death, disconnection, chaos, and entropy. She had to hold both the Source and the Simultaneity for balance to govern the energy. "Each of us must hold it alone as individuals."

"We each hold it as individuals, yes, but not necessarily alone. Come."

Sylvia blew out a breath, placed her hands on her hips, and took a long, full breath before following Kita. They walked through a path of high-growing wildflowers to a gate. It enclosed a more organized but exquisite garden of texture and beauty. Two beautifully carved chairs sat by a stone-made fire pit. The sun was still two hours from setting. Sylvia watched Kita walk to a stack of wood.

"Set the chairs side by side but facing in opposite directions," Kita said, carefully building the fire low and small.

Sylvia noticed the temperature was cooling now that the sun was going down, and they had stopped moving. Sylvia adjusted the chairs and sat down, rubbing her hand over the seat beside her leg. There were no arms on the chairs. Kita stood and walked to the chair beside her. Sylvia realized she had put the chairs too close. "Sorry."

"No, it's perfect. Sit straight and let your arm hang loose to your side, bent at the elbow so your forearm is parallel to your leg."

"Okay."

"Close your eyes. I'm going to slide my arm to the inside of yours, but you should only feel me touch you at the soft bend of your elbow. When you feel that, give the bend of my elbow the same pressure you feel from me."

"Why?" Sylvia said, then realized she could see a layer of energy with her eyes closed and she was getting better at interpreting it. Kita was close. Her energy was warm as the fire, and somehow Sylvia knew she had just smiled though her eyes were closed. "Is this seeing the Immortal network?"

"Yes, slowing things down like this lets you see the second network better, the Immortal network. In a fight, there is stimulus and response. The stimulus — for example, the force of a punch — comes in through your first network. The response —say, a block versus a counterpunch — you send out from your fifth network. That decision happens fast. You make that choice in your second network. *What* you select in that second network can be too quick to see, but..." Kita paused, smiling at Sylvia. "When you develop skill in your second network, it gives you time — time between what comes in network one..." Kita traced the number 1 on the soft inner side of Sylvia's right arm. "...and what goes out through network five." Kita traced the number 5 on the inner side of Sylvia's alternate arm.

Sylvia smiled. She could see the numbers Kita drew on her arm as colors in her mind.

Kita placed two fingers gently over Sylvia's heart. "Network two..." Kita tapped Sylvia's chest lightly twice. "...is what you decide to do between network one and five. It is the strength of who you are. Your choices." Kita laid her hand flat over Sylvia's heart. Sylvia wanted to cover Kita's hand with her own, but Kita pulled her arm back to rest parallel to Sylvia's, the inner side of their forearms almost touching. "With practice, you will be able to stretch time in that second network. Stretching time is the gift of the Immortal line."

"How do I do that?" Sylvia asked, taking a deep, relaxed breath.

"You stretch time by connecting to the Simultaneity. It is the dark half of the Immortal network."

Sylvia's eyes squeezed tighter as if it would help her prepare.

"In a minute, I'm going to have you open your eyes and see the garden as if for the first time. I'm going to close my eyes, and you're going to describe it to me. Then, you're going to connect with the Simultaneity and take another step at breaking the vision that guards your memories. Once you feel you have control of both the Source and the Simultaneity, you will pass the energy to me."

"I can do the describing part," Sylvia said, then tightened her closed eyes again. "Will it hurt when I pass the energy?"

"Maybe," Kita said hesitantly. "I can only see the emotion of what I hold for you, not the actual events. Whatever is blocking your memory can be overcome, but there is a lot of pain there, and Meki's betrayal has added a bitterness that wasn't there before."

"How do you know that?"

"I held part of this for you that day on the Orbiter when I found you in the steam room. I was in the biosuit, hiding from the Marshals."

"That's why I felt so connected and comfortable with you. You were using your connection to the Simultaneity to help me hold all the chaos." Sylvia sat forward and opened her eyes, then quickly closed them at the rush of input from the world around her. "All of my decisions run through the Immortal network, so they will be impacted by the Simultaneity connection there." Sylvia sat back in her chair, a new understanding bathing the tangle in her mind. "I have to look at my own chaos and disconnection to govern how it impacts my choice of what I put out in the world. What I pass to you."

"Yes, yes, and yes. I'm an EvP, so like the other species, I have a single, species-specific network that wraps around the human network. All species use the human network to experience and impact the world around us, and in the human network, all five species are represented."

"So, you have an EvP network that wraps your human network and enhances the EvP component of the human network."

"Yes."

"And a Griffon has a species network that wraps around the human network and enhances the Griffon component of the human network, and so on."

"Correct."

"So as an Intuit, whose strength is in pulling energy in from the world..." Sylvia tapped her chin with her free hand, careful not to move the arm she had positioned inside and parallel to Kita's. She didn't open her eyes. "I have an Intuit network that wraps around my human network and enhances the Intuit component of the human network."

"Actually, you have all five networks, which is why you have such a strong connection and impact on each species."

It was the first time Sylvia recalled anyone confirming to her what she thought she was seeing in her networks. She swallowed back the lump in her throat at what she was beginning to realize that meant. Her fingers, just inches away from the inside of Kita's elbow, wanted to close the breath of distance between them just to be connected. There was the danger. "With the power to connect with every species comes the responsibility of holding both the Source and the Simultaneity in its fullness, not just within the human network."

"Now you are understanding."

"And to do that, I have to be able to bear seeing my responsibility in the chaos, disconnection, and death that is in the Simultaneity." Sylvia's words were a statement rather than a question, but Kita answered.

"Yes, we all must, and many do not like what they see when they try to practice this step to look inside. And for you, it will have the added weight of feeling the impact on every species because you can touch them all."

"Do I have to do this part?" Sylvia asked, knowing intuitively why some people used blades and stone capacitors to get what they wanted rather than find balance. It was hard to look at the chaos and disconnection of oneself.

"You can use your network without this step but can't govern the energy."

Sylvia swallowed back her question, knowing the answer already. There were fewer and fewer people willing to take this step. It would be hard to look inside. "How do you know all this?"

Kita closed her eyes. "I will tell you, but first, let me explain this process. When you are ready, open your eyes. Let the sights, sounds, smells, and stimulus of your environment in through the first network. You should see it form from the tangle. I can't help you with network two, but when you choose what to do with the energy, it will flow into network three, then from there, four and five. I will explain in detail later, but simply put, the third network refines it. The fourth network, the Griffon network, known for its passion and instinct, converts the energy. The fifth network reconnects the energy with our world. I've tried to help with that by putting us together like this. Regardless of whether you can control the energy or not, simply touch the inside of my elbow with your index finger. That will release the energy. If you control it, I will pass it back to you by touching the inside of your elbow."

Sylvia bit her lip. "What if I don't control it?"

Kita shifted, and Sylvia sensed her sit straighter in the chair. "I'm a Sahaja EvP. I can hold a great deal of excess energy, and being in the chairs will shove us apart, breaking the connection at our fingertips if you don't control it."

Sylvia fisted her free hand.

"You can do this," Kita said, tapping Sylvia's chest again lightly with two fingers.

Sylvia felt the tears on her cheeks. She was overwhelmed at Kita's trust in her when she didn't trust herself. "How can you trust I can do this without hurting you?"

"I know what I know about your training and skill because I was there when my mother taught you."

Sylvia's eyes flew open at those words. The sights, sounds, and smells of the garden overwhelmed her before she could speak. Ribbons of color danced at the tangle in her mind, and emotions reverberated as if they were every beat of a hummingbird's wings. *Kita's mother was one of the women I can't remember?* Sylvia couldn't think. Every color danced with at least three separate hues as roses, hollyhocks, and honeysuckle projected their energy through her senses, and sounds continued to reverberate indistinguishable from her emotions. Sylvia breathed, but it was a gasp. She closed her eyes and let them shudder once, then opened them again. The brief respite seemed to align the sensations. She could now experience the garden and see the ribbons of color in waves moving from the tangle to her spine. *I'm connected to network one with the stimulation of the external world.* Sylvia tentatively let her mind reach out beyond to network two. The hum of bees at the honeysuckle faded to the darkness of the gap. Kita's ability to take it in as if placing it in another dimension made it much easier to view. She recalled the immediate tears when she touched it the first time. Now, it felt distant, separate from her, easier to view. She breathed in deep through her nose and let her mind touch the chaos that swirled with hues of black and gray.

The tangle in her mind flashed, and a memory coursed through her mind. Her first meeting with Meki to become her publicist, then his interest in her original work, not just the completed product of her book. How had she not seen it? Ribbons of thought intertwined with a new vision that took her breath away. She was trapped in the tomb, her best friend just beyond her reach as the Earth shook and debris rained down on them anew. Sylvia felt the tears. This was why she hadn't seen Meki's intent. She was grieving when they first met and hadn't cared who he was or what his motives were. Her sense of self-preservation had been singular, and writing had been the salvation from a career in archaeology she could no longer face.

In retrospect, his timing to show up new to her publishing company right after the accident seemed more than coincidental.

Something pulled at her core like a weight had been strapped to her heart and physically pulled it toward her gut. Nausea threatened, and Sylvia swallowed hard, wrapping her arm at her center as the ribbon of memory unfurled with bursts of remembrance. The memories seemed to flow along the network, reaching out to her body. They clawed at her chest, tearing it away. Meki's look of blame when she almost killed him because he couldn't let go of her. For years, he had smiled at her, cheered her on, supported her work, and then, in an instant, disdained her and discounted her friendship as worthless. *Me as worthless.* There it was, the deep emotion of what was destroyed in her by the betrayal. *I have no value.* Sylvia gasped, pulling away from the emotion even as she felt the pull of destruction in the tendrils of this place. *What if Kita is the same?*

Sylvia felt the light touch of Kita's hand just as she started to stand.

"Stay with it. I'm right here."

Kita's hand released as quickly as it had come.

Stay with it? Sylvia let the thought swirl in the chaos, then felt it settle with a gentle brush of Kita's fingers along her own. Her breathing was fast, and she took a purposeful, long, slow, deep breath, and when she let it go, she felt emotion flow with the tears. Distrust, anger, hurt. These were the emotions she felt, with the distrust starting to bleed over to her feelings toward Kita. "This is what you meant," Sylvia said, tasting tears on her tongue that fell from her lip when she spoke. "I have to touch what is here, sit with it, so I recognize how it will impact what energy I choose to send out to you."

Kita didn't answer, but Sylvia felt her. She seemed closer, though their physical proximity had not changed. More as if, in an effort to help, Kita had pulled more of this darkness into herself to shield some of the destructive emotion away from her. Without that shield, she would be overwhelmed by the emotion. *How many people face this alone?*

Sylvia took another deep breath, now ready to face network two, the Immortal network where she could stretch time. She would sit with these emotions, let them be with her, and watch how they could influence her decisions. "I understand now."

Sylvia kicked her shoes off in a blaze of insight that made her smile. The grass and earth seemed to ground her as the energy circled inside her, and time stood still. *The voice,* Sylvia thought as she recalled the female voice she had heard in her mind when Meki tried to force her to hold the energy. It was the voice of the woman who had taught her as a child. The woman Kita spoke of. The earth at her feet and the expanse above her head became one — not just the sky, but all that was beyond it was one and still. Then it was gone. Sylvia extended one finger to touch the soft skin on the inside of Kita's arm barely beyond her reach. She didn't understand completely; she knew there were more things in that dark stillness she would have to face to improve her ability, but she knew she could hold this energy right now and not hurt Kita.

Sylvia began to describe the garden's beauty with detail only one who holds its energy and who has sat with the chaos that destroys it could express. The heightened non-physical connection she had with Kita was tangible. She reached to the inside of Kita's elbow to bring the physical and Immortal world together as instructed with her touch.

[41.3]

Kita tensed with the anticipation of genuinely seeing the garden's beauty for the first time and squeezed her eyes tight at the gentle flow of energy from Sylvia's touch as she spoke. Kita touched the inside of Sylvia's arm to return the energy. An EvP's first lesson was to return the energy to the one who gifted it.

Kita sensed that Sylvia felt the energy dance on the inside of her arm where Kita touched her and where she touched Kita. It was so dynamic, moving and circling between them. Lost in the single connection between them, Sylvia no longer sought words but rather re-created a vibrant world of color, fragrance, sound, and energy with her touch. Quiet tears streamed from Kita's closed eyes.

"Am I hurting you?" Sylvia whispered as if knowing the moment could hold no more sound than that.

"No." Kita's voice was thready.

"Why are you crying?"

"I can see the garden now, feel its energy, the connection to the Source."

"You can't sense it without an Intuit."

"No, we are desensitized to it so that we can shift mass."

Sylvia wiped Kita's tears with her opposite arm, never dropping the connection they had with contact at their elbows.

Kita placed her hand over Sylvia's. "Thank you. Do you understand now why you have to govern the light?"

"I think so." Sylvia looked at Kita's bronzed, long fingers wrapped over her own pale hand still pressed to Kita's cheek. "There is always a risk you can't let go of the light when it is given."

Kita nodded. "I have to trust you to gift it and me to return it."

Sylvia swallowed hard. "Will it hurt when we disconnect?"

Kita knew Sylvia was dreading this loss of connection. "Some, but you've done really well. I can hold energy in mass, and you're only disseminating small amounts in a balanced flow to me right now. We will feel the separation, but it will be tolerable."

"That's why you said I needed you. Only a few EvPs can hold all that I can hold and be capable of returning it without being lost to it, forcing me to pull it away."

"Yes."

"That's why Meki used the table. He couldn't let go." Sylvia let her hand fall away from Kita's face but kept the energy exchange between their arms. "I almost killed him."

"Mom only taught you three responses for your Immortal network before you...well, before you disappeared."

"Before I disappeared? Responses? Do you mean choices?"

"Responses is what Mom called them. I call them choices, which is why I explained it to you that way. You've not used your network system since coming out of cryo. I think the responses Mom taught of listening, compassion, and retreat remained your three choices. That is why you didn't kill anyone. You instinctively selected one of those three as your response each time."

Sylvia looked down at the small space between their arms. Kita's index finger still lightly touched her inner arm near the elbow. "Was she my mother too?" Sylvia asked, then held up her other hand to stay Kita's response. "She isn't because there is another female voice I have heard in my memories."

"I wish I had more answers for you, but know my mother loved you like you were hers. I promise to tell you what I know once we reopen the dimension."

[41.4]

Sylvia blinked at the reminder that an entire sector, and eventually Earth itself, weighed in the balance of what they accomplished in the next few hours. Her own history could wait. She closed her eyes and let the energy in her ebb back toward the tangle. "Are you okay?" she asked as she felt the slight disconnect between them. Energy still hummed in the air like static, and their fingers kept the physical touch between them, but the energy was less. It carried only the physical touch she felt with her human senses. For a moment, Sylvia appreciated how that, too, had its own energy without the network.

"Yes. I'm okay," Kita said

Sylvia gradually opened her eyes, realizing she had been seeing with some form of second sight. "I still don't understand why you can do what you do but not hold light. You were holding as much as me just now."

"You are holding it as energy. I hold it as mass. I can explain this, too, a little better later. The short version is an EvP cannot tell when it is too much energy. They will literally keep taking it in until their physical body is consumed, like walking into a fire when you can't feel the burn."

"No wonder we used that small point of contact. You didn't trust I could govern the energy." Sylvia dropped both arms to her lap. She almost fell from her chair with the immediate vertigo, chest pain, and nausea she felt with the disconnect. She clasped her hands together in her lap to stabilize. It was very reasonable, but for some reason it hurt. The human touch had more energy than she realized.

Kita took Sylvia's face in her hands, as if knowing it would help the wave of nausea and chest pain Sylvia felt. "You can pull light energy into your network and convert it to any of the five energy types: mass, gas, heat, light, and mind. You govern it now."

Sylvia averted her eyes to avoid the transparent green of Kita's. Tears dropped to darken the wood of the chair between them. She had briefly seen the expanse in her second network. The innocence of her childhood Intuit self so cryopreserved had already begun to feel the seeping of emotions from a life lived while her network skills slumbered. A life that had known pain that wanted more responses than listening, compassion, and retreat. What would she find when she looked at that second network again after she broke through the guard on her memories? "Is it safe to trust me to help you?"

Kita gently tilted Sylvia's face to see her eyes. "I have always trusted you. You just had to trust yourself."

Sylvia's arms flew from her lap as if unchained, and she embraced Kita. She felt the flash of energy between them, warm, safe, balanced. They held each other for a moment, the past and future merging to an undefined but comfortable now.

"Well, enough of that," Kita said, standing and wiping her eyes. "We still have a dimension to reopen."

CHAPTER FORTY-TWO

O RANGE LIGHT BLAZED AGAINST a black sky beyond the cave opening, and smoke stifled the air as Sylvia stepped from the Earthside vortex in the Fifth Sector, Kita just ahead of her. Wailing assaulted her ears, reverberated on the stone walls, and followed them as they moved through the subterranean tunnel. Sylvia turned back, but only darkness and carved quartz remained where the electric blue triangle had spun within the Earthside TEA Portal, creating their entrance seconds ago.

"Isn't the lock here?" Sylvia asked, wrapping one arm around her stomach as she pointed back at the Portal. She braced her hand on the wall at the vertigo. It wasn't motion sickness, but she didn't feel right. Kita continued ahead of her, sleek and comfortable in the shadows.

"Yes, the lock is, but not the relic key. You have its location around your neck."

Sylvia paused mid-stride. "I have its location around"—she reached for the charms—"my neck." Sylvia looked up and caught Kita's eyes staring back at her from her position, braced with her back to the cave wall at the entrance.

"I want you to understand why we are doing this first, then we'll decipher where it is hidden. You may feel nauseous. It's the Simultaneity of the Portal Vortex."

"What time is it?" Sylvia asked, registering the conflict of the dark sky. The sun had just set when they left the garden, and the horizon had still glowed with the waning sunlight. It was well past that time here.

"Tomorrow," Kita answered.

"Tomorrow is not a time. It can't be tomorrow, today." Sylvia stopped moving. The weight of Kita's single word lassoed around her previous use of the word *simultaneity*, and she couldn't breathe. This wasn't jet lag. There was no lag, no time between where they had been and here, but it was tomorrow here.

Kita leaned her shoulder on the cave opening and scanned the sector.

Sylvia nudged close, breathing fast and shallow, almost at her ear. Kita reached back and pushed her against the rock behind her. "Quiet your breathing. This area is a hot spot, but I think the troops have moved on. You can lose weeks or years depending on the time difference between the places you travel."

Sylvia swallowed hard to slow her breathing. "Years?"

Kita sighed and pushed back from the wall to see Sylvia. "The Simultaneity has no time. Can I explain this later? This place is dangerous. I want you focused."

Sylvia swallowed bile at the stench of decay from the scorched earth beyond the cave entrance. The fluctuation between muted cries and the remains of exploded humanity rocked Sylvia with every distant blast and wane to stillness.

"This is the impact of the Separatists," Kita said. "This is what they've been doing for years." Kita pointed to several landmarks and explained how different they'd once looked when the place was vibrant. Sylvia tried not to notice the indistinct mounds. She knew instinctively they were collections of bodies.

"I've never seen such devastation." Sylvia's eyes darted from one tragedy to another, uncertain where to let her eyes settle.

Kita took Sylvia's hand. "Come on," she said, pulling them back away from the entrance a few feet. "Can you look at the charms together? I could feel the engraving on the back of the one I gave you, but the back of the charm is black, and I cannot determine any more than that."

Sylvia lifted both charms, fitting them together like puzzle pieces. She didn't need to remove them because she could already see the color Kita described on the back was several different hues of black, and they each were a number to her mind. "Two, zero, three, three, twelve- N." She tilted her head as her fingers rubbed again across the charm Kita had given her. Unlike the one she rubbed often from habit, this one was unfamiliar. "There are some engraved letters," she whispered, though it probably wasn't necessary since the fighting outside seemed distant. "I wonder." She traced a fingertip over the two charms together. "R-T is on your charm. And H-E-A is on mine. The engraving, when put together, says *heart*, and the numbers on my charm..." Sylvia paused, lifting her finger away till the hues of black on the back of her charm no longer resonated along the tendrils of ribbon in her tangle. "I already know these numbers. Seventy-five, forty-two, zero, one-E."

Kita was already typing the coordinates into her ringphone as she headed back toward the entrance. "You okay?" Kita asked when she scanned the sector beyond the opening and reached for Sylvia to find she was not there.

"I'm not okay, but we can't afford to sort that out right now." A noise behind her startled her into motion. She dropped the charms and jogged to Kita's side. They moved cautiously, then more quickly out onto the fire-ravaged earth.

A sudden aerial explosion shoved Sylvia to one knee. Her outstretched hand balanced on the ground, and a bolt of crystal-white energy laced around her finger, squeezing her network with a gentleness misplaced in this world. She lifted her hand and blinked, then blinked again, trying to determine what held such tender energy in this shattered place. "Kita." Sylvia's voice cracked, and she leaned away when the bile rose in the back of her throat. Her stomach spasmed with such force that her entire body lunged forward, causing her hand to land again on that soft energy. She leaned back on her heels, tears fresh in her eyes as she lifted the knitted baby shoe. Sylvia cradled the mud-soaked shoe and let the tears fall.

Kita turned and saw Sylvia knelt but refused to return. "Come on! Meki just came out of the cave." She pointed, but Sylvia didn't turn. Kita pressed. "He and his Nazri may have heard you decode the charms."

"No," Sylvia said, staggering to a stand. "I've seen enough. Get the relic key. I can lock the Umbilical open." Sylvia looked down at her hand and then closed it into a fist, wishing away the vision of the tiny shoe. She had to help restore energy to this barren place. She could feel the rage in her second network, and this time, she knew both the cost and value of the Simultaneity. She was not opposed to using it if Meki tried to stop them.

"I'll get the key," Kita said, then bolted out of sight.

Sylvia shuddered at the sensation of cold that moved along her spine, then jumped when boots stomped the ground to her left in a dead run. It had to be a soldier, what with the military headgear and Kevlar, but she had never seen one like this before, and he was after Kita. *Please get to the key before he does so I can lock open the Portal.* Sylvia's thought repeated in her mind like pure energy that could push Kita to success. Anger tinged the thread of ribbon unwinding from her tangle.

"Sylvia." Meki's voice pushed the cold at her spine, and she spun, the tangle prepared to unleash.

Meki's look was composed, and Sylvia now wondered what terrors he had created. The momentary thought caused a brief flash of her own terror with red eyes. She used the anger and pushed it away.

"Why are you killing them?" Sylvia shouted, the energy of innocence from the child's knitted bootie flowing as a ribbon of memory to wrap the anger with indignation that seemed to fan its flame.

"I'm not killing them. They are killing themselves."

"You've been tampering with the energy that feeds this sector. Killing them *is* what you're doing!" Sylvia waved her hand at the desolation.

"The people are starving," Meki said, taking a step toward her. "But their food sources started waning years before we intervened. They did nothing. Lazy and feeling entitled, they wanted the Tokoleh to supplement their lack of effort. Many of the Tokoleh officials offered plans to do so, but only one offered a plan that made sense to me. A plan to start taking energy from this dimension to utilize in other sectors where the initiative was stronger."

"You can't be judge and jury for entire populations."

"Yes, we can. We are the few Immortals who recognize the true role we must play. Humans need us to govern them. They cannot do it themselves."

"So, that's what the Separatists think is best? For Immortals to have full power?"

"Yes. Effort and innovation should be rewarded. Neglect, such as this sector showed, should be destroyed. We diverted small amounts of energy at first. The people did nothing to conserve, adjust, or aid each other. With time, the accumulation became fewer months of rain, hotter summers, and then gradually the land became barren as insects and necessary species died off."

"So, that makes this okay?" Sylvia stomped to within inches of Meki and shoved the tiny knit bootie at him.

Meki lifted the small crafted piece. An emotion flitted across his eyes and was gone. "The choices this sector of people makes are choices they make for or against themselves. What we do is an external stressor. Their actions to it are their own." He shook the bootie near her face. "'This is who they are. Why shouldn't we shut it down?"

"Kita's not like that. She's trying to help." Sylvia recalled her time in the garden connected to the Simultaneity. Meki wasn't wrong about each individual needing to take responsibility, but he wanted everyone else to do what he was unwilling to do, and that was to look inside.

"Kita is a fool. These are not her people, they're yours. Earth's very own originals."

Sylvia's lip curled in a snarl. "A new lie of yours. You said there was a mix of species in Earth's sectors."

"There is, but this sector had the most concentrated population of the original DNA. There was intermixing before the Great Splintering, but it was slow and decreased for several thousand years when Centerworld collapsed. It is called 'Shambala' in the old tongue. When it collapsed, the land splintered once again into its separate continents. Earth schools only teach of the changes two hundred million years ago because the Great Splintering was the first Singularity for humans — their win over the Neanderthal, their first taste of power. Humans do not recall it, just as a child does not remember its own birth, and the Tokoleh doesn't teach it."

"But they will if the Scholar's Council votes for transparency during their Earth Week convention."

"Yes, but it will not be a true telling. Too many of the Immortals have given up their memories of the past with regeneration. They have forgotten the first flash of human power. The first war." Meki showed his teeth. "I will not forget."

Sylvia saw someone familiar, yet someone she'd never seen before.

"Humans have proved time and time again they cannot manage power."

"So, you want to destroy the original human DNA by destroying the Fifth Sector?"

Kita's voice broke the conversation. "Not the original human DNA," she said, pacing toward them. "It's the Rainbane Reborn DNA they want to destroy."

Sylvia sensed Kita was talking for her benefit, but Kita's eyes never left Meki. "The Rainbane Reborn had all five networks. And, like the Original Rainbanes that left the galaxy during The Void, the Rainbane Reborn were born of the combining of Immortal and human DNA. However, this second pairing had a mutation. Only three bloodlines survived, and those were hunted by the Separatists. What is mostly left, now, of their existence is the occasional woman or man with a flare of diverse human talent. It is that small residual Rainbane Reborn DNA the Separatists constantly work to destroy, but they have to do it secretly because it breaches the agreement between the Tokoleh and the Earth Alliance."

Sylvia looked around as if she had been transported to a new place. *It's not the place that has changed,* she thought before looking to Kita. "Did you get the key?"

"The soldier you saw follow me was Nazri. He and Meki must have overheard you reading the charm inscription. He knew exactly where to go."

"How did he know what the HEART clue meant?"

"There is a story about a pilgrim passing through the caves and touching two unique places before he became a great leader for his country. It is said that he touched the Earth just before entering and said, 'The Earth provides enough to satisfy every man's need but not for every man's greed.' Then he entered the caves and was said to rest for a single day near a mural he called the Heart of the Caves. When asked why he slept instead of praying, he answered, 'To give pleasure to a single heart by a single act is better than a thousand heads bowing in prayer.'"

"So, the key was hidden near that mural, the HEART, and the Nazri found it."

Meki spoke. "There is controversy about which mural the pilgrim considered the Heart of the Caves." He shifted as if he wanted to go and help the Nazri find the key but paused when something in Kita's hand caught the light from the burning night around them.

Sylvia's reaction to Meki's voice now had her shoulders lifted, and her ear twisted toward her shoulder in a physical effort to stave off the grinding sensation along her network. Kita touched her arm, and Sylvia felt her jaw start to relax. She was so angry, and she felt that burning in her spine. Kita squeezed her arm gently, but the smile in Kita's words brought Sylvia to face her. Meki was still visible in her peripheral view.

"Yes, there is controversy about the HEART of the caves the pilgrim spoke of, but no question of the EARTH he touched when entering. It is marked for every pilgrim that comes, which is why when our mothers made this engraving together, as EvP and Intuit, they knew the hiding place was in the EARTH, not the HEART." Kita held up the relic key, and Meki's eye twitched.

"Our mothers," Sylvia whispered, lifting the charms at her neck as she stared at them, then at the key Kita held. If you stabbed an exquisitely cut diamond through the center of a playing card made of crystal graphite rather than paper, you might have an idea of the beauty the relic held. Sylvia's mind rearranged the words as she traced her fingers across the engraving. Her mother helped make this engraving. Her mother knew about the locks. "My mother probably told me many things."

"I'm sure she did. Right now..." Kita paused, adjusting slightly to improve her placement in relation to Meki. "I need you to go lock the Umbilical open." Kita placed the heavy relic in Sylvia's hand. Kita's eyes never left Meki as Sylvia swallowed the recognition that flashed in her mind at the now familiar hieroglyphs carved in the stone's center.

Sylvia noticed Meki's effort not to focus on it, but he could sense its power.

Sylvia backed away, walking behind Kita and giving a wide berth to her and Meki as she moved toward the cave and its dark tunnel. She could feel the vibration of the stone in her hand. The hum was like a song in color to her mind. The code was as clear as a written language. How could Kita not feel that? This was going to be easy.

A tremor shook the earth, and Sylvia fisted her hand around the relic just in time.

Meki's face was stern when Sylvia looked back. She had seen that face before when he touched that empty cavern within himself. He smiled, and the ground began to shift. He was converting its mass, displacing it to the Simultaneity just as Kita explained, but this felt different. Sylvia yelped when the ground cracked and splintered in a vicious branch that raced toward her. Kita spun to use her total momentum in a back fist, but it was too late. Sylvia's voice echoed from the earth as it opened up at her feet, and she fell.

[42.1]

Meki closed his eyes for only a moment of regret that Sylvia had to be sacrificed, but the relics could not be found. It would ruin everything.

Kita's fist connected, and Meki rolled to the ground. He released his hold on the mass he had shifted.

"No," Kita screamed as mass reformed a stone edge, closing the chasm that split the earth to the cave tunnel. "Sylvia?" Kita raced toward the wider crevice near the tunnel entrance.

[42.2]

Sylvia looked up and took a shallow breath. She had an edge gripped in her hand outstretched above her head, and her feet now managed to push her weight underneath her on a ledge that pinched between the two walls. She shoved the relic into her pocket and reached for another handhold.

"Sylvia, you have to catch the mass Meki just released, or it will cover the chasm and bury you alive. Can you hear me?"

Sylvia groaned as she felt the wave of the returning mass in the earth and rock. "What? We didn't practice catching mass. I'm not ready for this," Sylvia shouted, but the words just reverberated back to her from the rock closing around her.

"You did practice. It's what you did when I sent energy back to you. There is just more of it. Stabili—" Kita's words were cut off.

"Kita?" Sylvia shouted when the sounds above her escalated. Meki must have attacked her again.

Sylvia let the energy hit her, spooling it like thread through her networks and back to the tangle. She climbed frantically. She could see the eerie shadows of Meki and Kita larger than life on the stone cliff as they fought.

Kita shifted, and a blow knocked her shoulder, spinning her to the ground. She missed the ravine but hit the ground awkwardly in her effort. "Damn shoulder."

Sylvia heard the muttered curse. Kita had slipped that bad shoulder in its socket. Sylvia paused at how much she had learned about Kita in a short but intense time. Kita's arm was dislocated, but she scrambled to her feet and faced Meki as Sylvia saw the shadows dance again.

Sylvia was both hot and cold. She felt the sweat trickle down her spine as she began her climb against the ravine and the energy trying to bury her here. She focused on the sounds above her. Though she couldn't see them, their figures in the glowing orange of a burning world still cast shadows against the cave's stone. She could still make them out through the opening above her.

Kita landed a kick as she pretended to be off-balance with her shoulder injury. Meki's knee hyperextended, but he didn't fall.

Sylvia panted with exertion, and stone formed a shadow overhead before she pushed back against the energy, trying to escape her hold on it within her tangle. "This is worse than a spin class workout," she shouted to no one. She took a breath and found a new network along her spine. That made five now. *The final network is the EvP network.* She realigned the energy now that she could see its resonance with her mind. It was different from the energy of light. She felt a surge of panic at the remembrance of that open space, and she shifted her position to climb toward the small hole that now remained her only exit. The panic shifted the resonance, and the energy leaked out, returning to mass and closing the gap further.

"Sylvia, don't panic. Trust yourself," Kita shouted over the sounds of destruction that seemed to grow with each passing minute.

Sylvia felt warmth move along her spine and a gentle nudge of pressure near her elbow. It was only a memory, but it was all she needed. She closed her eyes and let the memory of Kita in the garden wash over her. *I can do this.*

A loud *thwack* startled Sylvia from her thought, and she looked up to see Kita's face at the opening. She was less than three feet away.

"Hurry," Kita said, then rolled onto her back. With her entire body against the ground, Kita started pulling the mass of the stone to the EvP space at her core, tugging the hole open as much as she could. Sylvia felt the assist immediately. She had been pulling the hole wider in small increments.

Sylvia noticed the hole opening quicker with the two of them, but Kita was hurt, badly.

She pulled herself free from the hole in time to see Kita shove Meki's unconscious body with her feet. Sylvia rolled onto the ground beside Kita. "Is he dead?"

"No," Kita said in a broken effort to say more.

Sylvia touched her arm and felt the energy race from her to Kita. Nausea swamped her as she jerked away. "You're dying."

"Get the relic in the lock before Meki regains consciousness. You don't have time to help me now. You can come back."

"You won't make it till I get back." Sylvia reached for Kita.

"No." Kita's voice was so firm Sylvia paused. "You don't know how much energy you need to open the lock. These people are your kin, your DNA, your family. Open the lock. There may be more like you here."

"You're family to me now," Sylvia said, touching the inside of Kita's elbow and noticing the awkward slant of the shoulder.

Kita paused at the words. "I will take what you have just given," she said, then pushed Sylvia's hand away. "If you don't open the lock, we'll all die here."

Sylvia noticed the slight improvement in Kita's strength with the little energy she had given her. She could come back after she opened the lock. Sylvia stood to make her way into the cave's tunnel.

[42.3]

Kita watched till Sylvia slipped beyond the darkness of the tunnel. She was thankful for the extra energy. It would be enough. Kita closed her eyes and used the energy to heal, not her shoulder or any other broken part, but the synapses that made her who she was — an EvP. An EvP who had learned to destroy. Healed to barely function, she began pulling the mass beneath Meki. If she focused the energy she had left, she could bury him alive before she died. "Karma's only a bitch if you are," she said as she barely lifted her head to see the earth disappearing beneath him. She was glad she had told Sylvia that the Separatists had killed her family. At least she would understand. "For my family," she said on a shallow breath before her head fell back against the ground.

CHAPTER FORTY-THREE

S YLVIA BREATHED IN THE dampness of the tunnel. The notch where the
relic fit was cool to her touch. The energy humming in her network along
her spine was warm. She lifted the relic. Its vibration whispered notes of color to
her mind. *It isn't a disease,* Sylvia thought, letting the colors flow in her mind and
through her five networks. *This complexity that makes me unique is the diversity
needed to help the team save the world I call home.* She placed the key in the lock.
She closed her eyes, and the colors were as visible as paint on a wall shifting in
her mind's eye. A kaleidoscope danced on the relic, scrambled color in a sequence
she had to hear, feel, and see to set the combination that would open the lock.
Burnt orange flashed in her mind, and something seemed to snag it, pushing it
aside with a signal of pain Sylvia couldn't release. She tried to focus again on the
combination. Only one more color was needed. The burnt orange was pulled
away because it wasn't part of the code. She somehow knew this, though it seemed
more instinctual as she watched the network weave. Sylvia synchronized the signal
from her hands, ears, closed eyes, and mind to see only the combination as she
held the relic in place.

*Terracotta. That's the last color of the combination, not burnt orange. As different
as five from six in a number sequence.* She hummed a resonance that matched
the color. The lock tugged at the relic, and Sylvia smiled as the lock spun open,
pleased with this ability to discern between the two colors for the accuracy needed.
I did it. The smile faded as ribbons of color released their connection to the lock
and flashed chaotic with visions shrouded in scarlet. Then crimson flashed at the
tangle in her mind. Sylvia stumbled. The tunnel warped like a heat mirage laid
over chaos as shrouded visions filled her mind till the world beyond the tunnel

snapped into focus, and she saw the world with Kita's eyes. Sylvia leaned forward, bracing against the wall, then bent double with nausea at the scene. She sensed Kita's ebbing energy. Visions of death and exhaustion— "Kita!"

Sylvia wasn't prepared for the flood of sensations in her mind and braced again against the wall from vertigo. Crimson traced an outline of boundaries she could see in her mind. "The Oscult," Sylvia whispered. She realized for the first time what it was, or rather, she remembered. She stood in a darkened tunnel with her eyes open, but her mind saw Kita's vision of a starlit sky, cast in the glow of a burning world, as she lay dying outside. Sylvia closed her eyes to stop the swimming in her head, and Kita's vision crystalized. Sylvia held her chest, sensing Kita's ragged breath. Then it was gone.

Sylvia lurched forward, her feet moving faster than her mind. She caught the wall for support, never losing pace as she darted for the tunnel opening. Sylvia wondered at the strange weakness she felt on her left side as she fell just feet from where Meki stood inside the cave opening, a twisted pose to his torso as he appeared to be watching Kita die. Sylvia felt her anger swell as blackness flashed along her network. She stood, and her rush caught him off guard, but he slipped from her grip, shoving her as he moved away. Sylvia hit the ground. The crimson in her mind faded, and Sylvia sensed more than heard Kita's shallow breath. *No, no, no!*

"She's dead, but you'll be glad to know she tried to kill me before she died."

"The dimension is locked open now," Sylvia shouted over her shoulder even as she half crawled, half scrambled across the rubble to where Kita lay. She saw in the shadows Meki's face, both familiar and strange, as he raced deeper into the cave. "It's not too late," Sylvia said to herself, fear building in her chest, then turning to anger. "Why are you trying to hurt everyone who ever cared for you?" she screamed as the hurt of his betrayal and the loss of Kita pushed open a new response in the Immortal line of her network. A response she would not want to look at in the light of day, but it gave her strength now.

Sylvia heard the pause in Meki's steps.

"You have only minutes to try, but if you help her, you can't stop me." Sylvia noticed his pace picked up, and the sound drove her even faster to Kita's side. She reached her just as his words echoed back. "No one cares about you but you. One day, you'll figure that out."

Sylvia swallowed hard. She heard in his threat that he would close the Umbilical again if she didn't stop him. Now, this close to Kita, she didn't care. This wonderful soul had tried to help her, had wanted to save Earth, too. Every sense she had seemed to be magnified a hundred fold. Even Kita's damp skin from the light rain seemed a sound to her, a weak thrumming, like the last vibration of a musical cord. Without her heightened sensations, she doubted she would have known it. Kita's energy was almost gone, and Sylvia felt her legs like lead as she forced herself to keep moving to climb the last pile of debris to reach her. Everything Meki had ever done for her had been for himself and his ends. She suddenly felt as if she didn't exist in the world around her, and she pulled energy into her hands from the rock rubble to connect, to know something real and keep her focus. "You can't close the Umbilical," she shouted in defiance as she shoved away from the pile, using it as momentum to propel herself toward Kita. "The relic key has the lock open," she whispered, wanting Kita to know her efforts had not been in vain, but her defiance felt swallowed by exhaustion and fear when she saw Kita. *I'm too late.* The thought shot through her network, and she screamed her defiance. "You can't close the Umbilical!"

"Oh, but I can," Meki shouted loud enough for it to echo in the cave behind her. "The Earthside locks only override the Tokoleh-side locks if all the relics are in place and open in all the sectors."

Sylvia thought Meki's words seemed to reverberate through the tunnel, but she knew it was just her heightened senses. She wanted to race inside to stop him, but Kita's ebb of energy, where Sylvia's hand pressed her neck, made Sylvia scramble to be atop her, connecting at as many points as possible. She recalled the exchange of energy in the garden.

Kita lay still, and Sylvia didn't bother to be gentle. Energy sparked through her, and Kita jerked and gasped at the rush of energy. Sylvia pulled away slightly and then pressed her cheek to the exposed area near Kita's twisted shoulder. She could do this. Sylvia felt the tear as she watched the energy lace through each of her five networks. She forgot Meki, and all there was in that moment was her love for this woman who had almost died to save people who would never know. A woman who showed her how unique and valuable her gifts were to this world.

Kita shifted, and Sylvia pulled back on the energy, reaching to touch the now visible pulse at the woman's neck. She felt her smile till she noticed Kita's dislocated shoulder as she examined for secondary issues. She gently pressed at the shoulder, feeling the weakness on her left side as she pressed energy into the muscle. Kita shrugged Sylvia's hand away from her dislocated shoulder with equal parts weakness and determination.

"You have to help me get inside."

Sylvia took in Kita's face, her hand still resting near Kita's collarbone. "You can't stand, and I'm not sure I can. My leg and left side feel funny."

"It's demyelination sickness," Kita croaked. "Using your network unevenly causes weakness." She dropped her head back to the ground after a small attempt to lift it. "It usually gets better with rest."

"That makes sense. It seemed to get better when I..." She looked at Kita. "I was more careful about balancing the energy for you. Once I knew you were still here."

Kita smiled. "Use your right side and try to stand."

"I can't leave you here. I restored some energy, but you've lost a lot of blood."

Kita rolled onto her good shoulder and tried to get on one knee. "You have to...get Meki before...he shuts down the Umbilical again."

"You heard that too?" Sylvia asked, surprised.

"You were still in my head a little, and I could hear what you could hear. Some of it."

"Okay. I'll go, but you have to stay." Sylvia struggled to stand. Her left foot couldn't sense the ground, and the spasticity made her calf draw. She put her weight on her right leg, her hand on her knee, and pushed to a stand. Her balance wavered, and her calf spasmed again as she tried a step. She reached the tunnel wall and blinked, closing one eye and then the other. She could see better with her Ensight, at least with her left. She opened her left eye and closed her right as she felt her way along the wall. Her closed right eye saw only thermal cues and energy. Her open left eye saw nothing. *I'm blind in my left eye!* Sylvia took a breath and swallowed back the bile of betrayal in her throat. Meki did this. He tried to kill her and now pushed her beyond what she could manage for his own power games. The rustle of loose stone pulled her attention, and she turned, closing her eyes to see the energy signal with both rather than the physical world with only one good eye.

Kita removed and wrapped her shirt as support for her dislocated, bleeding arm. She pulled through the loose stone of the tunnel on her knees and the strength of her right arm.

Sylvia didn't want to think about what had happened to Kita's ankles. With her eyes closed, the energy signals looked worse than the swelling and disfigurement of them when she opened her eyes. The two of them looked like the walking dead.

Sound near the Portal pushed Sylvia to focus. Meki was still there. "He must be having problems," Sylvia whispered over her shoulder.

"I think I know what it is, but we need to hurry. He will bypass it soon."

The short distance seemed eternal as Sylvia struggled to maintain her balance at a faster pace. There was nothing quiet about their approach, and Meki turned. The triangle of energy whirled behind him. He studied them. Then, as if he considered the effort and deemed them unworthy, he stepped toward the vortex. Sylvia leapt. Her left leg gave way mid-lunge, causing her to reach out at an awkward angle. Her fingers grasped for his pants. He jerked his leg, and Sylvia's finger caught in the material and snapped. His foot disappeared from her view when the fabric escaped her broken finger and tenuous grasp, then her temple banged the stone.

[43.1]

Blackness shifted to gray stone and earth. Sylvia could taste blood in her mouth as voices pulled her from unconsciousness.

"Let me tell you what I do know. Your puppet master has disappeared, and you are here holding all the evidence of an attempted coup against the Tokoleh and the Earth Alliance. You are stealing energy from the Portals to create supply and demand issues in an Earth region already unable to maintain its population?"

Sylvia recognized Rosalind's voice and swallowed with relief, regretting it as the iron taste of blood coated the back of her throat.

"I am not at liberty to discuss this sector's condition," Meki said. His words held authority, but his voice did not.

Meki is still here? A tiny spark of hope flickered — the Umbilical might still be open — but Sylvia squashed it. They would need the other relics to keep it open. An enraged voice interrupted her thoughts.

"Condition? These people are killed with blatant genocide motives because you've created a shortage of food and water by impacting the atmosphere, and you call it a condition?" Nathan's voice sent a ripple across Sylvia's exposed back, and she tugged at her shirt to pull it down.

"Sylvia's awake," Kita said.

Sylvia heard someone move toward her as Kita continued to explain what she knew of events in the local area.

"The militia come through these areas and destroy designated groups to re-duce the population," Kita continued. Sylvia thought maybe Kita was standing because her voice seemed to fall to her, but then she realized she was face down on the stone floor, and everything was up from here.

"Designated groups," Nathan said, his raw anger pushing heat into Sylvia's spine.

"It's a real permanent way to keep the demand for supply low," Kita answered.

A familiar energy touched Sylvia as a shadow bent over her. It was comfortable, and she surrendered as someone gently shifted her over to her back and helped her sit up against the wall. It was Michael. He smiled, and she nodded to indicate she was fine even as she rubbed her head where it had hit the floor. He stepped back to stand beside a handcuffed Meki, who looked worse than she remembered.

"When did you guys get here?" Sylvia said, pushing herself back a little better against the wall.

"Just in time, apparently," Rosalind said, looking at Kita.

By the looks of it, Kita almost killed him, Sylvia thought but didn't say out loud. She could barely walk and yet had nearly killed him. Maybe the energy exchange had healed Kita more than she realized. She smiled at the admiration she had for this woman. It was as if the EvP network inside her squeezed with joy when she was near. There was definitely a difference from one EvP to the next. *Am I ever going to figure all this out?*

"It appears your effort slowed him down..." Rosalind paused as she knelt and pointed at what appeared to be a burn hole through the cuff of his pants and a nasty-looking red streak up his leg where the skin was burned and raw. Rosalind stood, not careful about hitting the interesting braces around his ankles. "It was enough for Kita to...subdue him so that we can return him to UBN headquarters for questioning. He is a primary suspect in the two murders under investigation."

Subdue him. Sylvia almost laughed, but she knew it would hurt. She reevaluated Meki's less-than-healthy condition. *Murders?* Sylvia recalled Jezel and Tessa's words: *There is someone alive who knows where the lost keys are hidden.* She knew now that person was her. If she could just access her memories...but Meki knew her book held all the bits and pieces. He had been trying to cobble them together. "You had access to my original work." Sylvia pushed to her feet and felt pain in her finger, the anger and betrayal rekindled. "You placed the eye hieroglyph on the page to mark it for yourself because you knew it held clues to one of the Portal keys. You gave the Dalen the coordinates to Jezel's manor. In my original work, you saw the emblem drawn on the manor wall that matched the one Jezel drew in her book." The cascade of words snowballed and crashed into a single thought, and the full weight of his deception hit. Sylvia staggered, reaching for something to ground her. The stalagmite's cool moisture sent tendrils of blue and brown coiling in her mind. She let it pull the pained truth from her. "You knew what I was when you offered to be my publicist." Sylvia's hand fell away from the stalagmite, and the loss of connection was fitting.

"I never touched Jezel's book," Meki said.

Sylvia noted he didn't deny her other accusations. She looked to Rosalind. Meki had lied to her so often she could no longer tell.

Rosalind raised an eyebrow at Meki. "We'll look into that detail." She then looked at Sylvia. "Presently, we have evidence that places him at the site where they found the dismembered man from the signing. In addition, he has connections to the Dalen killed on the Orbiter."

"They have no such evidence," Meki said calmly.

Sylvia felt her shoulders tighten. She ground her teeth to stave off the shout of anger she wanted to unleash on him. She was sure he played a role in all of it, somehow. She was glad now she hadn't told him of the two additional books of the series she had written at home. He would not be privy to those, nor would anyone else, until she had answers. *But the book already published has clues to where the keys are hidden.* The thought made her want to cry, and she felt her back press against the wall. She could feel her legs giving way as she slid down. *Meki has seen my original work on all of those clues.* Clues she thought were from her imagination, many of which hadn't made it to the final book because she had a terrible dream of a man with red eyes and pools of blood when she reached into her imagination for more — an imagination she now knew was a place of memory. Sylvia pushed back the tears and glared at Meki. She was pleased to see his smile at her moment of weakness falter when he read the determination in her eyes.

"The Tokoleh will never put him on trial," Kita said, her anger brimming but controlled.

"The UBN will," Rosalind said, stepping over to squat in front of Sylvia. "You did well. Thank you. The Umbilical is open, and now we know what is happening."

"It doesn't matter," Sylvia said, looking to her left at Kita, who had been closer to her than she realized. Kita sat on the single step to the TEA Portal. Rosalind's words regarding the Umbilical success were a reminder of the greater problem. Meki didn't look at her from his slumped place on the far wall.

"What do you mean?" Kita released the bandage she was reworking around her ankles and dropped from the step to her knees, angled toward Sylvia. Sylvia realized Kita must have missed that when their minds had been together. It reminded her how near death she'd been.

"I'm okay, Kita," Sylvia said, almost in a whisper. Kita paused, and Sylvia smiled. "I'm going to need your help."

Nathan moved to stand behind Rosalind, and Kita adjusted the shirt sling on her shoulder.

"Help with what?" Kita asked.

"The Umbilical locks Earthside can only override the Tokoleh locks if all five are in place. I will need your help to find them before they do." Sylvia pointed at Meki, who had a look on his face she had never seen. For the first time, she realized he was concerned that they were on opposite sides.

Kita seemed to notice it, too, and she twisted to put her back against the wall and fold her arms against her chest, a duplicate image of Sylvia as they faced Meki across the room.

"Meki's trial will keep the Separatists exposed while you guys find the rest of the relics," Rosalind said with a nod to Michael, who lifted Meki to his feet with only one hand and pushed him toward the cave exit. They apparently weren't taking risks jumping him through the Portal.

Sylvia stood, feeling both invigorated and weak at the challenge. She reached her good hand to Kita, who took it and stood, gritting her teeth against what had to be painful weight-bearing on her ankles. Sylvia noted the spasm in her leg was relieved, and her vision was back. "Nathan, I think I need to talk to you about demyelination sickness."

Nathan knelt to adjust a strap on Kita's brace, then stood and reached for Sylvia's hands. She let him take them. Sylvia was confident she could balance the energy even though she couldn't slow her racing heart. The chemistry with him just pulled her close. She knew he was right about the line between patient and doctor, but she didn't trust anyone else to be her doctor at this point. He would have to decide.

"This is now broken and cut," he said, examining her finger gently.

If he remained her doctor, she'd have to keep her distance to maintain the doctor-patient relationship. Sylvia sensed Nathan's wavering decision. "Don't start something you can't finish," she said and stepped back to smile at him as she let go of his hands.

Nathan took her shoulders and squeezed them. A primitive shadow seemed to move in his mind like the Griffon had stepped from a cage for consideration. Nathan closed his eyes as if to settle it in his mind. He opened his eyes, released her shoulders, and smiled.

Sylvia smiled back. She knew his answer. There was hope in him that he could recover Elizabeth from her Griffon form. He would never be hers. She was glad Kita told her what she knew about Nathan and Elizabeth when they were fighting in the garden. Kita knew Elizabeth from some work she did to help the Earth

Alliance and admitted only knowing that Nathan was considered a good doctor. "I could use a good doctor."

"I know," he said, trying to smile, and part of Sylvia hoped that meant it was hard for him, too. "Someone will have to keep the two of you stitched together through two solar systems of travel on this wild relic hunt." Nathan nodded toward Kita, who was tightening the strap around her other ankle. "They look a little better already," he said, stepping back and giving the two women space.

Nathan must have adjusted Kita's shoulder and treated her ankles while I was unconscious, Sylvia thought. She was uncertain why Nathan hadn't checked on her, and then she remembered it probably took both Nathan and Rosalind to keep Kita from killing Meki. Sylvia felt a little twinge of guilt for even thinking about it; Kita looked more in need of medical care than herself. Her ankles were still swollen, and she leaned heavily against a stalagmite for support yet still managed to look like she could kick some ass.

Sylvia turned toward Kita. "I'm sorry..." she began, finding Kita's eyes, then bit her lip, feeling the words were feeble and not remotely close to all she felt. She continued speaking, pulling the two charm necklaces from inside her shirt. "I'm sorry Meki's people killed your family." Her fingers fumbled as she unhooked the latch to remove the necklace Kita had given her. She closed her fist around the charm to stop the tremble in her hand, but the chain seemed to swing in rhythm to the chain she still twisted back and forth around her neck. "I know we were close. I wish I could remember." Sylvia opened her hand to stare at the charm. "Are we family?" She felt the need in her voice was as eager as the hope for remembrance in Kita's eyes.

"I had a great family," Kita said. "But they have been gone a long time." She tapped her lip as if something had just occurred to her, and then, as if deciding to share her thoughts, she took the charm from Sylvia's open hand.

Sylvia smiled at the quiet energy exchange between them when it touched a memory of connection from the garden. Then she startled when Kita placed the necklace from her hand around Sylvia's neck.

"This one is actually yours," Kita said, closing the clasp and lifting the one Sylvia had worn for years to unclasp it. "We exchanged them the day you disappeared, and I have tried to find you every day since then."

"We are family, in a way," Sylvia said, squeezing Kita's hand.

The gesture caused Kita to pause in her effort to wrap the necklace around her own neck.

"Let me," Sylvia said.

Kita released the necklace. "There is family you get and family you choose," Kita whispered as Sylvia stepped closer deftly closing the familiar clasp.

Their eyes locked as Sylvia stepped back and Kita touched the charm at her neck. "You will remember. The hunt for the relics will help you find your way home."

CHAPTER FORTY-FOUR

S YLVIA SMILED AT THE brown wave of curl that wrapped perfectly around Nathan's ear. It joined the curls at the base of his neck, shifting with his movement. He raised his champagne glass to the air and looked at her. Their eyes locked, and she felt that dip in her stomach find balance. He began to speak.

"I'd like to toast the first rediscovered Sahaja of the Rainbane Reborn bloodline." Nathan smiled as glasses clinked around the table.

Sylvia bit her lip. He had told her the results privately yesterday over coffee. They were working on their new dynamic, putting their emotions away to be part of a team.

Sylvia smiled through the happy tears as she looked around at the group of people who had gathered to celebrate the results of her tests. She wasn't abnormal or losing her mind; she was finding herself. It was a very personal and profoundly moving gesture that they were all here and cared for her this much. She squeezed the hands of her mom and dad, who sat to either side of her, her pale skin against their brown skin reminding her she had four parents. These two chose her. "I'm so grateful for both of you," she said as they leaned into her and glasses clinked around the table.

"We love you."

She lifted their free hands to her chest, pulling them to her as Kita snapped a photo with her ringphone from down the table. Sylvia smiled, released their hands, and opened the screen on her own ringphone to see the picture when it pinged.

Kita rounded the table and kissed the top of her head as she scanned the photo on her screen. Sylvia relaxed at the comfort she felt when Kita was nearby. It was something she couldn't explain, but in the last month, it had grown. Sylvia grinned at the photo. Her dad had held her book up, not a champagne glass, as their three heads squeezed together. *My book. The one that isn't fiction after all.* The book now had two solar systems in a race to save the keys of the Earthside Portals from whatever the Separatists planned next. She squeezed Kita's hand on her shoulder as she looked up at her. "Thank you. You are an amazing woman and an incredible friend."

Kita grinned. "You say that now. I'll remind you of that when I add the physical training to the mental gymnastics Xenos will have you doing with your network." Kita squeezed her shoulder gently before releasing it. "I'll see you in a bit."

Sylvia acknowledged Kita's words with a nod. It was a huge responsibility, but she was ready for it, and as she scanned the table, her feeling of betrayal by Meki was pushed away by the sincere care and genuine support she had found in the people sitting here today. Jezel and Tessa leaned close to each other, talking. Jezel gave her a broad smile when their eyes met, which caused Tessa to turn toward her. Tessa gave a softer smile, but one she knew was just as grateful. Together, they mouthed a thank-you, and Tessa's arm around Jezel squeezed her close. She had promised to advocate for their direct involvement when the search for the manor Portal key began. She had signed a new copy of her book for Jezel since her original copy was now securely locked up with evidence at the UBN. Xenos and Kinley raised their glasses in salute when her eyes met theirs. She was glad they were back. Kinley had agreed to help her work through some of the hieroglyphics. She had already started searching for the other clues in her book. Four keys were still hidden. She had to overcome the hurdle that held her memories captive. Xenos gave a gentle nod in her direction. He had agreed to help her push through the barrier the vision kept creating in her memories.

She clasped the charm at her neck. It was strange to have this one on while Kita wore the one she had always thought was hers. Its role in locating the Portal key confirmed her book held secrets. She, Kita, Tessa, and Kinley had pored over the chapter that, in retrospect, guided them to put the two charms together just as she and Kita did to find the key's location. It was strange to read that guidance after the fact and discover she wore Kita's charm all these years. She squeezed the charm and let it fall, focusing on an empty chair at the table.

Rosalind's seat beside Xenos was empty, and Sylvia scanned the room, finding her in a conversation with Dr. De la Cour. The two women parted with an Immortal handshake Sylvia now recognized. Sylvia swallowed back the lump in her throat. She still needed to have the conversation with De la Cour that she both anticipated and dreaded. She stood when De la Cour nodded at her, then headed into the foyer beyond the dining area.

Sylvia squeezed her mom's hand. "I'm going to the foyer to speak with Dr. De la Cour."

"Do you want me to come with you?"

"No." She wrapped her mom's shoulders in a hug from behind her chair. "Thank you, though." She pressed her cheek to her mother's.

Pulling away from the moment had a tangible aloneness. Sylvia felt as though she stood in this large open room in a transition between her past and her future. She turned and faced the foyer where Dr. De la Cour waited.

The foyer beyond and the two suites were once part of the archives. Rosalind petitioned to make them the living area for the UBN director when she had been appointed. *I still can't believe she offered for me to live here.* As if her thought conjured the woman, Sylvia looked up at the light touch of Rosalind's hand on her arm.

"I'd like to speak tonight once everyone is gone," Rosalind said when they passed each other.

"Yes, but…" Sylvia stopped and let her pause ask Rosalind to halt. She admired Rosalind's attention to detail. Whatever she learned from De la Cour, a discussion with Rosalind would only enlighten it more. "I have a proposition."

Rosalind raised an eyebrow.

"My dad is determined to see the archived archaeological documents taken by the Tokoleh during the war. Mom is certain she can regenerate native plants in Pittsburgh from the seeds preserved in cryo." She winced. "I may have promised them that I would ask you about both things."

Rosalind rolled her eyes. "Fine," she said, and Sylvia smiled so broad her face hurt. "But you tell me everything from De la Cour."

"Absolutely," Sylvia said, then felt her palms start to sweat. *Deep breath,* she thought as she prepared to leave the dining hall for the equally expansive foyer to unravel one more thread in this tapestry of her life.

Sylvia panned the high-ceiling room of the foyer that split the two suites. It was as large as the grand foyer at the Kennedy Center in Washington, DC, and it was hard to believe it was now part of her living space. Rosalind lived here in a suite to the right of the central shared living space, refusing to rent out the opposite suite, saying it was a security risk. However, Rosalind had offered her the suite in exchange for staying here at the GCS as an independent consultant to the UBN. She now occupied the suite to the left of this central foyer. One hundred years ago, the foyer opened to a large stone veranda with stairs down to the archives. Now, a stone wall with a built-in floor-to-ceiling bookcase bordered by two large arched windows blocked the access but not the view of the archives. The large window to the left drew her attention as Dr. De la Cour stood there looking out into the archives, much as she had at her clinic the first day they met.

Sylvia set down her glass of wine. She'd not been able to eat or drink much as she anticipated this conversation. Would Dr. De la Cour's information and artifact help her unravel her own history? *Well, you'll never know till you have the conversation.* She had put it off long enough. She scanned the room, drawing courage from the small group of people gathered for her through the open archway in the formal dining hall. She ran her palms down her slacks and considered lifting her wine from its perch behind some old books on a display pedestal. She smiled. Kinley would have a fit to see her wine seated next to books. There were both perks and drawbacks to living in a space once an active part of an archive. It felt like the perfect fit for her.

"Congratulations on successfully finding the key, opening the Fifth Sector Portal, and not dying," De la Cour said, turning from the window.

"I think I'm most proud of the latter," Sylvia said, taking in the piercing blue eyes bearing a weird mix of haunted and happy. It was a look she had come to anticipate with Immortals — the haunted part, at least with the old ones. Sylvia folded her arms, holding De la Cour's eyes. "And I made it before time ran out."

"Both for the Fifth Sector and yourself," De la Cour said with a respectful nod.

"By the way, how did you know that the Portal was going to be threatened during Earth Week and that it might kill me to help stop it?" Sylvia shuddered once, and for a moment, it seemed time paused, giving her time with this new emotion of suspicion. *The feeling had been foreign until Meki's betrayal.* Her thought dipped toward her second network, and she held her chest at the pain of it. Sylvia rolled her shoulders but couldn't shake the weight of it. It was in her second network now, this response of distrust.

"When you've lived as long as I have, your ability to predict bad events becomes strikingly accurate. But I had other reasons for my speculation that the time was close for the Separatists to attack the system outright." De la Cour gave a gentle smile. "Call me Inesa."

Sylvia noted how beautiful the woman's smile was when she was relaxed. She didn't look a day over thirty-five with her red cupid-bow lips and the healthy shine in her wavy black hair, but her eyes had seen many more years.

"As to the risk for you, I fear that has always been there." De la Cour opened her hand, revealing the leather bracelet and silver bead. "Hold it up to the light," she said, pointing at the stunning chandelier in the center of the room.

Sylvia moved toward the center of the room, holding the silver bead up to the light. It was the size of a pencil eraser, but she could see something inside when the light came through it. She shifted it to change the way the light came in.

"When I took over Shiro Estate, I had things remodeled. In the process, I removed the bungalow fireplace. It was massive and way too large for the space."

Sylvia turned the bead as she listened. She knew this was what Inesa had never told anyone else, and she felt her shoulders tighten. She closed one eye. She could now tell it was a photograph inside the bead, but she had it upside down.

"There were human bones in the fireplace."

Sylvia dropped her arms and turned, locking eyes with Inesa.

"Smashed into the dirt and stone of the doorway, I found a prototype of the ringphones we now use."

Sylvia swallowed the bile burning her throat and lifted the bead to the light. She instinctively knew the picture in this bead came from that ringphone.

"The artifact you hold I had crafted to protect the photo and allow me to keep it with me till I could use it."

Sylvia could see a desk, and it looked as if the photo was taken too low. The image cut off at the shoulders. She gave a sigh. It wasn't anything grotesque. It appeared to be a man, by the build of the body, standing behind a desk leaning forward. "What does it have to do with unraveling my history?" Sylvia decided to start her scan of the picture again from the bottom since that was the focus of the photo. The desk was dark, and there was a painting on the wall at the man's back, though his body blocked much of it.

"You'll have to tell me that," Inesa said.

"It's a man. His arms appear strong, and there is a tattoo or marking..." Sylvia dropped the bead and stepped back, searching the room with an instant panic.

"What is it?" Inesa bent, lifting the bead from the floor.

Sylvia wrapped her arms around her waist and took several deep breaths. *I'm fine. I'm with my friends and family.* She pushed at the fear. She had just walked through one of the most difficult times of her life. She was here now, familiar with herself. She was a Sahaja of the Rainbane Reborn, a direct descendant with a history to uncover. She was one of the few with all five functional networks, she would use this strength to find answers. *I will not choose fear.* She relinquished her grip around her waist and locked eyes with De la Cour. "The marking on the man's right wrist...I think the photo was taken to focus on that."

"What makes you think that is important?"

Sylvia turned, straightened her shoulders, and fully faced Dr. De la Cour. "The vision that blocks my memories...it is a man with red eyes, which I know is part of some conjured portion of my imagination, but the marking on his wrist is identical to that one."

Inesa nodded but did not appear surprised.

"You knew I might recognize it."

"Yes," Inesa said, taking a seat.

Sylvia saw a kindness and pain in her eyes that asked for patience. She folded down into the chair, her mind a whirl of thoughts.

"The man named Coriolis was responsible for a program that abducted men, women, and children who had species gifts during the war. He had this mark on his wrist," Inesa said, reaching the bracelet out to her. "It may help you sort things out. Unravel more threads, as it were."

"No," Sylvia said. "Give it to Xenos. Maybe it will help him find Coriolis. I have to focus on the Portal keys." Sylvia realized she was gripping the arm of the chair. She didn't want to chase down a man who may have abducted her, maybe her whole family. It felt too personal. Just when she thought she was filling the shoes her ancestry had laid out before her for something bigger than herself, she felt small again. *I won't let that emotion win, not after what I've learned. I've got a job to do.* She relaxed her hands and gave Inesa a tight smile. "Thank you. I do think it will help, but right now, I need to focus on helping the team save the Earthside Portals."

Inesa nodded, squeezed her hand closed around the bead, and stood. "I'll give it to Xenos."

Sylvia stood, and Inesa surprised her with a hug. There was something so genuine about the woman that Sylvia let herself relax in the embrace.

The shuffling of feet and the low murmur of voices pulled Sylvia from the hug. She turned to see her family and friends gathered in the archway spilling between the two rooms. Kita held a large cake with a small forest fire blazing atop it.

Kita grinned. "The UBN plans to announce tomorrow that the Rainbane Annual Celebration will be reinstituted. I convinced Rosalind it should be on your birthday."

Sylvia felt the tears welling. "You know my real birthday?"

"I do, and now we have years to collect all the other missing pieces."

Sylvia moved to stand in front of Kita. She took a deep breath and blew across the candles. Two flickered while the others turned to smoke. Sylvia closed her eyes, reaching close to them to feel their heat. She pulled the energy in through her first network, watching the light of the candles wink out as the energy coursed along her five networks before settling safely at the silver tangle. She took the cake and set it down on the low coffee table where Rosalind now stood, cake knife in hand. Kinley arranged the small plates on the table as Rosalind began to cut the cake. Sylvia turned and wrapped Kita in a hug. She pulled that light energy from her tangle, pushing it into her fifth network, where she let it hum till she knew Kita had opened her connections to let her share it. "Thank you," she whispered in Kita's ear, watching the energy escape her hands where she had them wrapped at Kita's back. The energy was as light as the words, but Kita's back arched toward her, pulling her tight to Sylvia as if it melded them.

A strange beeping sound made both women turn.

Nathan moved through the foyer archway and headed toward the corridor for the door.

"Is everything okay, Nathan?" Sylvia asked.

"Yeah, just an alarm I have set at the lab. Probably nothing," he said, but Sylvia could see the hint of worry in his eyes.

EPILOGUE

C AJAL BRACED AGAINST THE cold wall of the lab, the plastic bag on his arm banging his leg. The door to his right smoked ever so slightly from the energy he had used to burn the lock to get in. *Stupid, stupid, stupid*. He leaned his head against the wall and listened to the couple walking just outside. *Please pass by, please pass by,* he thought, realizing he was holding his breath and letting it out slowly. It shouldn't be noticeable that he had used energy to burn the lock until someone tried the door, but he had needed to get inside fast before the people in the hallway could see him. He quickly passed the laboratory tables to the back room, where he more carefully picked the lock the way Wesley had shown him years ago. The memory of his missing brother made his heart ache as he inched down the stairs. Cajal shuffled the containers in his hands as he walked toward the climatized habitat. "I'm back," he whispered, unlocking the bar that allowed entry and exit to the habitat. "I brought Italian food." He smiled as the beast stretched its front legs, working the talons, and yawned with his thick tongue draped over the giant canine fang. Cajal reached to scratch the beast beneath its heavy mane.

I am glad you are back, Light Wielder. The beast spoke to Cajal's mind through the Griffon network.

Cajal smiled. He liked the name Tient had given him. "I'm worried," Cajal said, placing the to-go box of meatballs between the beast's talons before sitting down with his back to the beast's side. "I almost got caught in the hallway and had to burn the lock to get in. They are going to know when they come into the lab tomorrow."

It is time we tell them anyway. You have been with me a whole moon cycle now.

Cajal rolled the spaghetti on his fork. "Yeah. Actually, a little over a month if you count the first week. I'm glad I didn't listen to the doctor on the Orbiter." Cajal absently rubbed Tient's talon between bites.

Me too. Any luck locating your brother in the hospital today?

No. Cajal answered only with a thought.

The laboratory and research department connection to the hospital made it easy for him to slip into the hospital each day and check for Wesley. But even after a month, he had not seen or heard from him. Now, he would have to leave this nice place he had found with Tient and go back to the school where he had first waited for Wesley. "I don't want to leave," Cajal said, pulling his knees up and setting the food down.

I think we can convince Dr. Renner of your value to him here, Tient said, pushing the thought to Cajal. *There is a program at the school that will let you work here.*

"You really think so?" Cajal asked, the small hope lifting his words.

I know a lot about the school, remember?

Cajal squeezed his massive head. "I remember," he said. "Your secret is safe with me, Asher Tient Sharma."

Tient nodded his massive head but allowed his thoughts to coalesce as Cajal picked his box of food back up from the floor. *Asher Tient Sharma. I remember my name and my humanity. Thank you.* Tient rested his head on his talons and closed his eyes. *Dr. Renner and I will need you, Light Wielder, when we rally the Griffons. We will surely need you before the battle to save Earth is over.*

ACKNOWLEDGEMENTS

WHEN YOU COMPLETE A task like writing a book, you look back and see the footprints of so many incredible people that you are certain you will forget someone when you start to mention names. So, to begin, if you know me, then you know I treasure the people in my life, whether I see you once a year or every weekend. I value those relationships that stand the test of time. Those in this category know who you are – you have impacted my life, and I am grateful for each of you.

Editors: It takes a team and I've had an amazing one!

Thank you, Betsy Mitchell. When an excited writer sent you a manuscript that demonstrated she was eager to jump off the high dive when she had simply escaped the bubble-blowing class, you kindly cheered her on and gave her structured guidance and support. Your consistent feedback allowed me to build the skill that led to your gracious referral to Patrick Lobrutto.

Thank you, Patrick Lobrutto, for your well-balanced approach to editing that fostered my growth as an author while supporting the voice of my storytelling. I am grateful for the application of your years of expertise in science-fiction and fantasy writing.

Thank you, Heather Flournoy, for your expertise, diligence, and efficiency. I could not have brought this book to the polished final product without you. I am eternally grateful for your "make it happen" mindset.

Beta Readers: Thank you for your infinite patience and constructive critiques. It is an immeasurable joy and advantage to have such prolific, gifted, and well-rounded readers in my corner.

Writing Colleagues: I could write a book just to scratch the surface of my gratitude to the old and new writing friends I have made along my writing journey. At each phase, there were friends sharing laughs and miseries as we spurred each other along this unique, creative craft we call writing. There is a place in my heart where I hold each of you dear. Thank you for every laugh, hug, and cheer.

Family: Listing my gratitude for my family would take several pages, so I will simply say there is an evolving love story in my heart for each of you. I love you and value the special things that make you so unique in this world. Your support has allowed me to succeed - even greater still - your love has allowed me to fail. That is the hard step that is necessary for every success.

Readers: Thank you for picking up this book and taking this journey with me. I am eager to foster the reader-author relationship with you as we tackle the ups and downs of this life together, one book at a time.

www.ingramcontent.com/pod-product-compliance
Lightning Source LLC
Chambersburg PA
CBHW060808030726
47503CB00002B/385